ALL SOULS NEAR & NIGH

SOULBOUND II

HAILEY TURNER

©2019 Hailey Turner
All Rights Reserved

Cover design by AngstyG.
Professional Beta Reading by Leslie Copeland: lcopelandwrites@gmail.com
Edited by One Love Editing
Proofing by Lori Parks: lp.nerdproblems@gmail.com

Don't miss out on sneak peeks, exciting news, and more!
Sign up for Hailey Turner's newsletter
to stay up to date on her upcoming books.

WELCOME TO THE WORLDS OF HAILEY TURNER

Urban Fantasy
Soulbound

Science Fiction Romance
Metahuman Files

Steampunk-inspired Epic Fantasy
Infernal War Saga

To May Archer
Salt bae for life.
May the snark and cat love be with you always.

DISCLAIMER

This book contains a brief scene of on-page sexual assault.

Special Agent Patrick Collins winced as he clattered down the stairs of the Brooklyn Bridge-City Hall/Chambers Street subway entrance, the motion jarring his still-healing nose. The medical tape slapped over the bridge of it itched his skin, but he refrained from scratching at the annoyance.

The passage down into the subway was packed with people from a delayed rush hour commute on a Wednesday night. Despite the crowd, everyone got out of his way when Patrick said, "Federal agent, coming through."

Patrick's Supernatural Operations Agency badge hung from his neck, and his semiautomatic HK USP 9mm tactical pistol was holstered on his right hip. The gods-made dagger he never went anywhere without was securely strapped to his right thigh. Patrick had opted to leave his jacket with the agency lettering across the back in his car. August in New York City was too fucking hot to wear anything but short sleeves.

Patrick had been upstate dealing with an incursion of Redcaps for the past week. He'd been looking forward to going home once he landed at LaGuardia. One call from Special Agent in Charge

Henry Ng before he even deplaned and he'd been assigned an emergency case with the NYPD's Preternatural Crimes Bureau. It was a familiar song and dance he was too tired to perform but didn't have a choice.

He raked a hand through his dark red hair as he made it to the fare gates and kept moving past the officer on guard duty. No one tried to stop him.

At least this case is local.

Since June, Patrick had called New York City home. The transfer from the national office to a field office had taken some getting used to. The majority of the cases he handled now came out of New York state, though he still got sent out on national ones if the need was great enough. Media focus aside, Patrick was enjoying how less chaotic his job was lately.

Nothing about a dead body ruining a rush hour subway commute was enjoyable though.

Detective Specialist Dwayne Guthrie waved Patrick over once he made it to the subway platform. "About damn time, Collins."

"Would've been here sooner, but traffic was terrible," Patrick said.

"Maybe you should look into getting some lights and sirens put into your car. Or convince the mayor he needs a better outreach program for troubled youth so shit like this doesn't happen and we all get a night off for once. The dumbasses who sneak into the tunnels to tag turf keep getting eaten and it's annoying."

Patrick jerked his thumb over his shoulder. "There were signs up by the gates. No feeding the trolls."

Dwayne rolled his eyes. "Do you think any of the fools selling shit on the corner actually read? And what happened to your face?"

Patrick made an aborted motion to touch his face, his healing nose and bruised green eyes throbbing a little. "Went face-first into a tree. I took a potion before I got on the plane. I'll be fine."

A witch's brew was better than painkillers some days. The accelerated healing it could produce meant the swelling had gone down enough that Patrick could see out of both eyes, and the cartilage in his nose would mend straight in a couple of days rather than weeks. His head was still sore, not to mention the rest of his body, but ignoring the discomfort was second nature at this point.

Patrick gazed around the crowded center platform of the station. Several uniformed police officers were keeping the area near them clear, but no trains were running on their side of the platform. Patrick tugged at the collar of his T-shirt, feeling sweat trickle down his spine. Summer in the city was a swamp-like hell of high heat and high humidity, especially down in the subway.

"Where's the body?" Patrick asked.

"In the Old City Hall subway station," Dwayne replied.

"You've confirmed it's not a suicide?"

Dwayne nodded as he headed toward the end of the platform where a set of gated stairs were located, guarded by an officer. "You'll see why. A train operator spotted the body when his train looped around. Victim wasn't found on the tracks, but the MTA is holding the 6 line until we're done processing the area for evidence. We've been waiting on you."

"Bet the commuters aren't happy about that."

"Not my problem."

Patrick followed Dwayne off the platform and onto the subway tracks. The tunnel itself was dark, so Patrick called up a couple of witchlights to guide their way. Pale blue sparks erupted from his fingertips as he pushed magic out of his damaged soul, the illumination bouncing ahead of them. Casting the spell was harder than usual, but he chalked that up to the location.

Patrick grimaced at the feel of the wards that lined the tunnel walls. Subways were built through swaths of the veil, which meant their construction had been done by both mundane and magical means. The magic protecting the subway system was old, extensive, and powerful, with the anchor points of the wards radiating out from Grand Central Terminal. The wards made casting magic difficult, but an innocuous spell to conjure light was doable.

Minutes later, Patrick's witchlights merged with the brightness put out by portable floodlights, and he let his magic fade away. He and Dwayne came out of the dark tunnel into a station that made it feel as if they were stepping back in time. The vaulted ceiling with its leaded glass skylights and chandeliers were part of a bygone era that seemed out of place in today's modern world.

The body on the platform ruined the retro atmosphere.

Patrick lowered his personal shields, trying to get a read on the area, but his magic recognized no discernable threat. Members of the PCB's Crime Scene Unit were diligently working on collecting evidence while PCB officers kept watch. Patrick spotted Dwayne's partner, Detective Specialist Allison Ramirez, almost immediately. She waved them over, frowning at Patrick once they got closer.

"I know the chief requested federal help for this, but I didn't think we'd get to work with you again so soon," Allison said. "You look like you went a couple of rounds in the boxing ring and lost."

Patrick shrugged. "Actually, I won. What do we got?"

This was only the second time Patrick had been assigned to take over a case from the PCB. June had been a clusterfuck of epic proportions, but he'd come away from it having earned a little of Bureau Chief Giovanni Casale's respect. The people under his command were less antagonistic when dealing with Patrick this time around, which he appreciated. Usually local police didn't much like it when federal agencies took over their cases.

Allison gestured at the body. "Victim's state in death is similar to the murders in June, but they don't seem related. No heavenly signs sliced on his eyes. Body was chewed on for dinner though. Considering the amount of demonic cases the PCB has wedged in its pipeline, I'm inclined to add this one to the list."

"The wards down here should've prevented any demonic incursion. Any magic user on the MTA's payroll should know what to look for when it comes to damage while checking the lines."

"Maybe they missed something."

"It's possible. Sometimes the damage doesn't show right away and you get holes later on. The London Underground had a basilisk incursion about thirty years ago. Things ate their way through a weakened section at a switch point. Made a meal out of the morning commute."

"I read about that. Not a fun way to start your morning."

New York City had seen an increase in demon activity ever since the veil had torn over Central Park. Patrick had closed the hole between worlds at the end of that fight, but demons and monsters had still slipped through. It was possible the subway wards had taken some unnoticed damage.

Since June, the homicide rate had gone up in the city, faith in the SOA's ability to handle the problem was in the gutters, and Patrick was still the House Committee on Supernatural Oversight's favorite whipping boy at the moment.

Thinking about politics made Patrick want to drink.

The kid lying dead on the subway platform was never going to learn the joys of the legal drinking age. He was your typical troublemaker because it was usually troublemakers who decided to ruin public property. Cans of spray paint were scattered over the platform, each one tagged with an evidence number. Strangely enough, there wasn't any graffiti on the walls.

"Maybe it's a dump job," Patrick said.

"Hard to dump a body in the subway, especially in this spot. Access isn't easy on tracks with trains running, even for MTA workers," Dwayne pointed out.

Patrick approached the body and the woman crouched down taking notes on a clipboard. He was mindful of the numbered evidence tags in the area and made sure not to knock any over. "We have a time of death yet?"

"Sometime this morning, but it has to be verified back at the lab," the woman said. Her jacket had Medical Examiner written across the back, and her brown hair was twisted into a messy bun at the base of her neck. The identification dangling around her neck had her photo ID and the name Catherine Margolin printed on it beneath the medical examiner's logo.

"No chance of getting a more accurate time frame?"

Catherine shook her head, looking up at him. "Wards in the tunnel are messing with my equipment. Think you can stop the interference?"

Patrick pulled out a pair of black nitrile gloves from her work case. "No. Anchored protective wards on this scale aren't something you mess with. Besides, I don't really have an affinity for defensive magic."

"Then you're stuck waiting until I get back to the morgue for a more precise answer."

Magic users made up a quarter of the world's population, but everyone born with magic had a different affinity. Patrick excelled in offensive spells, and the damage done to his soul as a child meant he was better at recognizing threats from all the hells than most other magic users. That unwanted talent had come in handy throughout his nine years in the Mage Corps under the US Department of the Preternatural, and the past three with the SOA, usually at the expense of his health.

Crouching down, Patrick frowned at the corpse. "Trains were running during his time of death and all day today. The body would've been seen before now. It has to be a dump job."

Catherine waved her pen in the general vicinity of the crime scene. "Killed here or somewhere else, no one saw the victim until the train operator spotted the body. You'd be surprised at the things people don't see."

"No, I wouldn't. You already got your pictures?"

"Lots. Feel free to poke around. The PCB is starting to bag up evidence. We were waiting on you before we bagged the body."

The victim was missing the left arm up to the elbow, and the left leg was barely hanging on at the knee. The right arm lay mangled about a meter away, as if tossed there. The tears weren't clean, nor did they have the pulverized look to them that would've indicated being run over by a train before being laid out on the platform.

His head looked strangely misshapen until Patrick realized it wasn't damage, but most likely the body caught in the middle of a shift. He prodded at the stiff, cold lips, managing to get a look at the too-sharp, large teeth in the corpse's mouth.

"Werecreature," Patrick said.

Catherine nodded, still taking down notes. "Yeah. We're going to need to bring a hazmat crew down here to clean up the crime scene. Judging by his eye color, he's not god pack, so we can rule out that strain of the werevirus."

"Can't rule out dealing with the god pack."

Patrick wished he could.

The two strains of the werevirus had segregated the werecreature community into packs that were able to hide their status and god packs who couldn't. Those infected with the god strain of the werevirus were visual scapegoats for society, and the New York City god pack was hostile to anyone who didn't share their disease.

In the past, god packs used to have a connection to their animal-god patrons, but those were a rarity these days. The only god pack alpha Patrick knew of with a patron was a man the Fates had thrown at him without either of their consents.

Jonothon de Vere was an ex-pat Englishman, exiled from the London god pack and refused acceptance by the New York City god pack when he emigrated three years ago. The attraction between them upon first meeting two months ago had been purely physical. What Patrick felt for Jono now went deeper, though he wasn't sure if he could trust his own emotions in that area.

At the end of the fight in June, Patrick had unwittingly bound their souls together through the magic buried in the gods-given dagger he carried. The soulbond enabled Patrick to once again tap ley lines and nexuses by virtue of his newfound ability to channel his magic through Jono's soul. He'd spent three years since the Thirty-Day War carrying a soul wound that prevented him from accessing such an integral part of his magic. Having that ability back was life altering. That it came at the expense of Jono's autonomy meant Patrick had yet to do anything with his returned strength.

The soulbond was illegal, despite the accidental creation of it. Messing with a person's soul was a capital crime in the United States. Patrick couldn't ask for help in breaking the soulbond without being arrested, so he and Jono had agreed to keep it a secret, the same way they'd kept their newly formed pack a secret from the New York City god pack.

It was a good thing Patrick knew how to keep his mouth shut.

But like any good federal agent, he was adept at speaking for the dead and getting justice for the crimes committed against them.

The skin around the teenager's throat was mottled with bruises that lined a strip of burn scars too uniform to be anything but intentional. Werecreatures were severely allergic to silver, and aconite poisoning could be lethal. Patrick traced his gloved fingers over the burn area, measuring the space with his fingers.

It was just wide enough for the shape of a collar, which spoke of enslavement of some kind.

"He put up a fight," Catherine said.

"Against who is the question," Patrick said.

"Werecreatures have enhanced strength. Whatever killed him would've had to have been stronger."

"A silver bullet to the heart is just as lethal as a fight for dominance. He's got bruises, and werecreatures can heal those in seconds."

"Then he was killed before the bruises could disappear and before he could fully shift." Catherine pointed at the arm lying some distance from them. "His hands have defensive wounds. He didn't die easy."

"Nothing about his state in death suggests that. I'm going to need to know the werevirus strain he was infected with to figure out what pack he came from."

"I can type him once we get the body to the morgue and get you that confirmation tonight."

"Appreciate it."

"If you want to talk to the dead, we can call in the necromancer."

"I doubt a judge would sign off on a Resurrection Order for a murdered werecreature."

Necromancy was illegal in most countries. Calling back a soul gone to rest in order to raise the dead was anathema in most cultures. There were exceptions. Sometimes the government allowed a necromancer to work with strict government supervision, usually at the federal level or with a Preternatural Crimes Bureau in a major metropolitan area. Getting a Resurrection Order out of the courts was damned difficult most days.

All they had was a body and no motive. Setting aside society's inherent biases toward werecreatures, no judge would rubber stamp an order with that little evidence in hand.

Patrick lifted up some of the stiff jean fabric out of the way to get a better look at the cavity ripped into the left thigh. The femur bone was intact, but the femoral artery had damage to it reminiscent of bite marks. The only creatures Patrick knew of who liked blood as much as flesh were vampires.

"He had to have bled out somewhere else before getting dumped here," Patrick said thoughtfully. That was a headache he really didn't want to deal with.

Patrick's experience with vampires and their Night Courts was unique in a way he could've done without. He hadn't crossed paths with any of the Night Courts that claimed the five boroughs as their territory since transferring here. Looked like that was going to change.

In the grand scheme of things, vampires were still better than dealing with his father and twin sister. Their toxic family reunion back in June could've gone worse, but only if Patrick had put a gun to his own head and pulled the trigger.

Patrick straightened up, wincing as his bruised muscles pulled from the motion. The witch's brew could only heal so much. "Anything else I should know about?"

"Ramirez has the evidence I pulled out of the vic's pocket," Catherine said. She put her notepad into its metal carrying case and tucked it under one arm as she stood. "You might want to take a look at it."

"Allison?" Patrick called out as he stripped off his nitrile gloves and deposited them in the biohazard bin. "What was the guy carrying?"

Allison pointed at where evidence bags were laid out on the platform, hastily marked with a Sharpie pen. "Over there."

When Patrick got close enough to see, it wasn't what he was expecting. The first bag carried a handful of white pills, some broken and a few others whole. The intact pills each had a tiny red-black dot staining the center of each one, and Patrick frowned, poking at them through the plastic.

"Is this what I think it is?"

Allison nodded as she came over. "If you're thinking shine, then most likely. The drugs still need to be tested and verified."

Patrick rubbed at his mouth, staring hard at the pills in the evidence bag. Shine was a drug that had been around for hundreds of years through various iterations. Its origin stemmed from vampires, though historians couldn't agree on which Night Court first created and introduced it to their human servants.

These days the demand for shine meant most of it was lab synthesized. Its popularity came and went, but it looked like the city was having another love affair with the drug. The pills showing up this summer were cause for alarm though. Patrick had read a memo the SOA had sent out about them back in May.

The stuff hitting the streets right now was the real deal. Made with true vampire blood and all its supernatural properties, shine was a potent drug that offered a euphoric, sexual high to those who took it. Highly addictive, it allowed mundane humans the ability to see a person's aura, the bright shine of a person's soul that only magic users could sometimes see. Mundane human eyes weren't meant to process a sight like that, and they craved darkness—any kind of blindness really—while high.

Vampires had no souls and were more than willing to comfort an addict in the throes of addiction and withdrawal. The drug running through an addict's veins didn't affect them, merely gave the blood a different flavor.

Shine was how some Night Courts enslaved their human servants. Addiction could happen on the first hit, and the list of industrial chemicals that made up the drug could literally rot a person's brain. Bartering sex and blood to stave off some of the harsher effects of the drug wasn't a great trade-off. Most people in their right mind didn't want to be owned by a vampire, but addicts never made rational decisions.

Some mundane humans liked dancing with the darker aspects of the preternatural world. Magic users who took shine never handled the drug well and almost always ended up on a bad trip. They could already see a person's aura; shine stripped away their safeguards and could tip their magic dangerously out of control. Patrick, despite using cigarettes and alcohol as a crutch to get through his adult life, had never gone down the black hole of hard drugs.

As for werecreatures? Patrick knew the god pack had treaties with the Night Courts here marking off territory. The only way to get shine was through street gang dealers or directly from the source. Werecreatures shouldn't be working for vampires or buying from them, except he had a dead kid that said otherwise, amongst other things.

Patrick dropped the evidence bag onto the platform and reached for the second one that held a small figurine. Made out of white plastic, the skeleton reaper was shrouded in a hooded robe, carrying a scythe in one hand and a globe in the other. Despite the wards down here, Patrick could sense traces of black magic emanating from the figurine.

"This is an artifact," Patrick said, weighing it in his hand. Artifacts, portable objects capable of holding magic that nonmagic users could wield, felt heavier than they looked.

"Not surprised, considering what it is. Any idol of Santa Muerte is usually handled by a witch in this city. Our evidence bags are lightly warded, so anyone transporting it should be safe enough," Dwayne said as he approached.

Patrick was familiar with the religion that had sprung out of Mexico over the last few decades or so and spread through North and South America. It made him uneasy, but not for reasons most people would assume. Worship was a powerful tool for any god or goddess in the modern age, but he didn't much care for those who presided over the dead.

Patrick carefully set the sealed figurine down on the platform. "I doubt the kid worshipped Santa Muerte. Possibility of him being either a dealer or a junkie isn't something we can discount. The toxicology report is going to take weeks to confirm."

"The drugs could've been planted," Dwayne said, staring at the body. "Kid is African American. There's no love lost between black and Mexican gangs. Werecreature aside, he wouldn't be part of *any* Mexican gang unless he was killed out of retaliation or for an initiation. If that's the case, I don't know why he ended up down here and not in his own turf as a warning."

"Something to look into," Patrick said as he got to his feet.

"You may want to talk to someone in Narcotics and the Gang

Unit. They have a better handle on the shine problem than we do, even if they haven't tracked it to the source yet," Allison said.

Dwayne snorted. "Good luck with that. The DEA has been trying for years. Everyone knows the Omacatl Cartel has a monopoly on shine in the five boroughs, and every gang member the DEA has managed to arrest hasn't confessed to any alliance with vampires. Been that way for decades. I doubt it'll change anytime soon."

"Killing a werecreature goes against the treaties the Night Courts have with the god pack here though," Patrick pointed out. "That's an angle we need to figure out."

"We're always looking for hard evidence to pin on the blood-sucking bastards. Maybe we'll get lucky with this case." Dwayne cocked an eyebrow at him. "You can be our lucky charm."

Patrick made a face. "Like last time? No, thanks. I'll let you handle the transport of the body and evidence to your morgue. The sooner we get the autopsy report, the sooner we'll have some answers."

"Not handling it at the federal level?" Allison asked.

"I *am* the federal level, but I think everyone will feel a lot better if it all stays within the PCB."

He might hate politics, but Patrick could play the game when required. The SOA didn't have a stellar reputation at the moment, especially here. The PCB, on the other hand, was viewed far more favorably in the public eye right now. Patrick would prefer to work with the PCB rather than work out of the SOA field office, which would cut down on communication issues. His individual efforts with the PCB back in June had gone over a lot better than the SOA as a whole in media polls.

Besides, Patrick didn't have an assigned partner, and he'd learned over the years that relying on local help tended to smooth things over.

"You heading back to the PCB with us?" Dwayne wanted to know.

Patrick shook his head. "I'm going to run down the werecreature angle."

"I don't envy you talking to the god pack alphas at all."

Patrick shrugged and said nothing. Estelle Walker and Youssef Khan were the god pack alphas of New York City, but they weren't who Patrick was going to talk to.

2

Jonothon de Vere's mobile buzzed on the metal desktop where he'd set it while doing up next week's schedule for the bar. The text notification was from Patrick, and he ignored the open spreadsheet on the MacBook Pro in favor of his mobile. Unlocking it, Jono read the message.

On my way.

Jono breathed out a quiet sigh of relief. He set the mobile back down and picked up his mug of tea, taking a sip. He'd brought the box of PG Tips from home, along with the small electric teakettle that no one else ever used. Tempest was a bar that catered to the werecreature community and served up craft brew and cocktails. While Jono would normally be behind the counter helping out the two bartenders on shift, Wednesdays were usually slow, and he'd opted to retreat to the employees-only room in the back to do some paperwork.

It was tedious, but part of his job as bar manager for Tempest. On the flip side, it kept him away from other people. With Patrick having been gone a week for an SOA case, Jono hadn't been the friendliest of blokes lately. He knew his surliness had everything to do with his only pack member being gone and the soulbond tying them together drawn tight with distance.

The heaviness deep inside his soul had eased over the last few hours, coinciding with Patrick's return. Now, Jono was counting down the minutes instead of the hours until he saw the mage again.

Jono took another sip of his tea before getting back to work, the heat of the drink not bothering him. He managed to wrangle the schedule for next week into some semblance of order when a familiar heartbeat cut through the muffled noise of the bar beyond the closed door. Jono turned his head and was half out of his chair when the door pushed open without a knock.

"Bloody hell, mate," Jono swore, reaching for Patrick. "What happened?"

Patrick kicked the door shut behind him, which was fine with Jono because it gave him something sturdy to shove the other man up against. Gently, though, because Jono didn't know what other injuries Patrick sported besides the ones on his face. Jono framed Patrick's face with his hands, staring at the slightly swollen nose with a strip of medical tape arching over the freckled bridge and faded bruises around bloodshot, tired green eyes.

"I took a potion. I'm fine," Patrick said, blinking at him.

Jono rolled his eyes before sliding his right hand down to Patrick's throat, discreetly scent-marking him. The stench of travel, of too many bodies packed too closely together, clung to him. Beneath that was a hint of forest and blood, neither of which stopped Jono from worrying. Beneath all *that* was the familiar, bitter scent that was Patrick's alone and had come to mean home to Jono.

"*Fine* doesn't look like you took several punches to the face."

Patrick's mouth quirked at the corners. "Gonna kiss it better?"

"Cheeky. Could've just asked rather than go out looking for a fight."

"Hazard of the job."

"Bollocks."

Jono shook his head before leaning down to gently press his mouth to Patrick's. Those familiar plush lips immediately parted, letting Jono in. The quiet sigh he drank down told him more than words how tired Patrick must be. The mage wasn't one to show weakness, even amongst friends, but Jono had started to learn the little quirks and half-hidden actions that spoke of Patrick's true feelings.

Patrick was still a hard read on the best of days, soulbond or not, but Jono was figuring him out.

"Gonna ward the office," Patrick said once Jono broke the kiss. His hands had fallen to Jono's waist, fingers plucking at the gray short-sleeved button-down he wore.

Jono frowned but didn't protest the action. Neither did he move, content to stay where he was, hands sliding beneath the black T-shirt Patrick wore. He pressed his palms against warm skin, reveling in the closeness after a week alone and liking the way Patrick arched into his touch.

"You're not going to move, are you?" Patrick grumbled.

Jono pressed a kiss to the top of Patrick's head. "You've been gone. Allow me this."

Patrick leaned forward, resting his forehead against Jono's shoulder. Out of the corner of his eye, Jono saw him raise a hand and conjure up a mageglobe.

The small, pale blue sphere of raw magic pulsed once. The silence ward that Patrick cast filled the back room with a wash of static, the white noise a barrier even Jono's enhanced hearing couldn't break through. The bar, and all its myriad of noises, went silent around them. Patrick flexed his fingers and the mageglobe floated away to hover near his shoulder.

They stood like that for a moment in the quiet, leaning into each other, the soulbond a distant hum to Jono's senses. Jono reluctantly let Patrick go after a minute or two, knowing they could no longer put off the conversation.

He took a step back in the small space and crossed his arms over his chest, never taking his eyes off Patrick. "What's going on?"

Patrick carefully knuckled his right eye. Jono reached out and tugged his hand away before he could make the bruises there worse. "I've been assigned another case with the PCB."

"Okay," Jono said slowly, not letting Patrick's hand go. "Is this going to be like the last mess?"

"Who knows? But I think it might be worse in a way."

"Your idea of worse is bloody frightening, anyone ever tell you that?"

"It's been mentioned once or twice."

Jono sighed and ran his free hand through his black hair. "What's going on, Pat?"

"They found a body in the subway tonight. Blood still needs to be typed, but the kid was partially shifted."

"Kid?" Jono asked sharply.

"Teenager," Patrick amended. "Late teens. I'm wondering if you've heard of anyone who has gone missing in the werecreature community lately?"

Jono frowned. "Not that I'm aware of."

Until this summer, Jono had been an independent-ranked werewolf, with no pack to claim as his own over the years, either back in London or here in New York. Carrying the god strain of the werevirus meant he should have been absorbed into a god pack, but he had never been accepted by any. He knew now part of that reason was because of the Fates and Patrick, and the rest because of the animal-god patron who clawed at his soul.

Fenrir was a presence in Jono's life that had come on slowly and subtly, a voice in the back of his mind that had kept him company off and on through the lonely years of running without a pack. But he had Patrick now, even if no one but his closest friends knew he'd finally formed a pack after living so long without one.

He and Patrick had told no one about the soulbond.

"Do you know anyone who could tell me about the independent werecreatures that pass through here? Anyone who *isn't* Estelle or Youssef?" Patrick asked.

Jono scratched at the edge of his jaw, fingernails scraping over the shadow of a beard on his face. "Might do."

"Great. Got a number for me?"

"You already have Sage's number, but you'll want to chat with her in person about something like this."

Patrick seemed surprised at that announcement. "Sage?"

"Yeah, mate. She was an independent before Emma took her on."

While Jono didn't have a pack, he'd grown close to those in the Tempest pack. Led by Emma Zhang, she and her partner in all the ways that mattered, Leon Hernandez, were best friends with Marek Taylor, a powerful seer who owned one of the premier social media tech companies in use these days.

Marek was the one who'd pulled Jono out of London three years ago for reasons that didn't become apparent until Patrick arrived in New York this past summer. Marek had been dating Sage Beacot well before Jono ever came to the States. Sage was the lone weretiger in a pack of werewolves, though no one ever treated her differently after Emma claimed Sage for her pack.

The four of them were his friends—family, really—but Jono and Sage had similar backgrounds in how they'd lived within the werecreature community. They'd bonded over that early on after he first arrived to manage the bar. Jono might have been instructed to not act as an official god pack alpha in any way while living in New York City, but that hadn't stopped Sage from coming to him for advice.

"Sage keeps tabs on the independents better than the god pack does. She does pro bono work for them through her law firm when the need arises," Jono said.

Patrick grimaced. "I fucking hate dealing with fae lawyers."

"Lucky it's not the fae we'll be seeing. Right, then. Let's be off. The sooner you chat with her, the sooner we can go home."

The Chelsea flat they called home had felt far too empty over the past week. Jono was keen on dragging Patrick to bed for a full night's rest.

"Yeah, all right."

Patrick waved his hand through the mageglobe and it vanished, along with the silence ward. Sound rushed back into Jono's ears with a *pop*. Enhanced senses meant he could see, hear, and smell better than a mundane human, but control had been hard earned over the years.

Patrick left the back room and headed out of the bar. Jono took a minute to chat with his closers before joining him outside. The temperature difference between the air-conditioned bar and muggy night air didn't bother him. Patrick was waiting for him on the sidewalk, mobile pressed to his ear. Jono kicked up his hearing a couple of notches to listen to the conversation on both sides of the line.

"…you're sure about the werevirus type?" Patrick was saying. He raised an eyebrow at Jono, jerked his head to the left, and started walking. Jono matched him stride for stride.

"Werejackal," a tired-sounding female voice said through the speaker. Her voice echoed with a bit of static in Jono's ears. "I'm starting the autopsy, and that was the first test I ran."

"Send me your preliminary report when you're finished. I don't care what time it is, I'll take it."

"It'll go to you and the chief."

"Thanks, Catherine." Patrick ended the call and shoved his mobile into his pocket. Jono wanted to kiss the scowl off his face. "You heard that?"

Jono nodded. "I heard."

"So. Dead werejackal. You know one of those?"

"Not personally, but Sage might."

"Then let's hope she's home."

Jono held out his hand for the car keys. "I'll drive."

THE TEMPEST PACK home was located in an Art Deco building on Fifth Avenue in the Upper East Side. Marek had bought it when he became a billionaire overnight after PreterWorld, the social media company he founded and owned, went public. Marek shared the apartments within with Emma and Leon, Sage, and a couple other pack members. When Jono had first emigrated to New York City, Marek had put him up in a tiny studio walkup, but he'd spent a lot of his time here. These days, it was almost like a second home.

Jono parked the Mustang in front of the car park entrance since they weren't staying long. The government plates it carried would keep the car from getting towed. Jono wrapped his arm around Patrick's shoulders as they headed for the building's entrance, holding him close. Patrick didn't try to pull away, and Jono let out a quiet breath at the way the soulbond had finally stopped tugging at his awareness now that the mage was within reach.

Jono let them through the warded front door, and they took the lift inside up to the topmost flat that Marek and Sage called home. When it opened onto the small foyer, they were greeted by Emma. She was a petite Chinese American woman with thick black hair currently tied back in a long braid. She wore a cotton camisole and sleep shorts, feet bare as she waved at them. Jono had a feeling she'd put clothes on for Patrick's sensibilities.

"Hey," Emma said. "We're all here. You hungry?"

"No," Patrick replied.

"When was the last time you ate?" Jono wanted to know. Patrick hesitated, which was all the answer Jono needed. "Could do with some grub, Em."

"With a pack of bottomless stomachs, that's always available," Emma said as she waved them inside. She didn't ask about the fading bruises on Patrick's face, but her slight frown told Jono she was worried.

Emma and Leon owned the flat below Marek's. Not everyone who belonged to the Tempest pack resided in the building. None of them carried the god strain of the werevirus in their veins and preferred staying under the radar as much as they could. With Marek being a seer, sometimes staying anonymous was difficult, and distance was the only cure.

Marek and Sage were sat on the sofa in the family area of the open-plan flat. Leon was already in the kitchen down the way to make up a couple of plates. The first time Patrick had ever visited here, Emma had conducted hospitality with him, a ceremony of welcome to a person's hearth and home.

Hospitality greetings were binding welcomes that protected a home from threats while a magic user was present. Tied to the threshold wrapped around the building, it was another layer of magical protection. Emma had deemed the traditional greeting unnecessary for Patrick after June, and he'd been welcomed with open arms ever since.

"Your texts said you wanted to talk, but you didn't say about what," Sage said once they'd sat down on the other sofa.

Jono eyed Patrick. "You didn't tell her?"

"It's not something I'm willing to leave an electronic trail on with an unsecured phone on her end," Patrick retorted.

"That doesn't sound good," Leon said from the kitchen.

Patrick leaned forward and rested his elbows on his knees, hands clasped loosely together between them. Jono studied his profile, taking in the tight line of his jaw as he clenched his teeth before blowing out a heavy breath.

"I got called in for another case with the PCB," Patrick began. "You see the news tonight about a body in the subway?"

"I've been working on a demurrer ever since I got home. I haven't seen any news," Sage said.

"The three of us have been remotely overseeing back-end work on PreterWorld being handled out of our Silicon Valley office,"

Marek added, waving a hand to encompass himself, Emma, and Leon.

Patrick met Sage's gaze with a calmness that had Jono wondering how many bodies it took for someone to become inured to death. "A train operator saw a body in the Old City Hall subway station. He notified his bosses at the MTA, and they called in the PCB due to the wards. The SOA assigned me to the case. The victim was a teenager, partially shifted in the head, and the medical examiner's office confirmed he was a werejackal."

Sage never looked away from Patrick, never blinked. Her left hand slowly curled into a fist, knuckles turning white. "New York City has one werejackal pack in Brooklyn. As far as I know, they aren't missing any members, and none of theirs have been exiled."

"So he was independent?"

Sage's lips pressed into a hard line, and Jono could smell the anger and distress pouring off her. "About six months ago, an independent werejackal went before the god pack asking for permission to approach local packs for possible placement. He only approached a few before word got around he wasn't a good fit."

"How so?"

"Too ready to fight. Too keen on power. Pack alphas would have been challenged by him the moment they accepted him into their pack." Sage leaned forward, her gaze piercing. "He was still a teenager."

Patrick nodded grimly. "Yeah, so is our victim."

"Most of the other independents didn't want anything to do with him. I was an independent like them for years before Emma offered me a place in her pack. They know to come to me when they feel they can't go to the god pack." Sage glanced over at Emma before her eyes flicked Jono's way. "I've been hearing rumors over the last couple of months, but hearsay is just that without proof."

Jono stiffened at her words, sitting up straighter. "I haven't heard anything."

Emma held up a hand as Leon finally came back over to them carrying two plates piled high with leftover pasta. Werecreatures burned through a lot of calories, and Emma made it a point to always have a full refrigerator.

"Can you ward the apartment for silence?" Emma asked Patrick.

In response, Patrick uncurled his hands, a mageglobe sparking into existence between his fingers. The same hint of static from the bar flowed across Jono's ears, silence following in its wake.

"Silence ward is up," Patrick said.

"What have you been keeping from me?" Jono wanted to know.

He was god pack, even if he had never held any territory. By virtue of the god strain of the werevirus running through his veins and the animal-god patron that had claws sunk deep in his soul, Jono had an obligation to the packs around him, even if he couldn't act on his rank. He'd discreetly dispensed advice to those Emma sent his way, helping to quietly mediate lesser disputes that Estelle and Youssef never cared to handle with packs he could trust wouldn't turn around and narc on him.

"You had a rough time of it in June," Emma said, calmly meeting his gaze. "Anyone who asked, I said you needed some space."

Jono clenched his hands into fists. *"Em."*

"You were *tortured*, Jono. That's not something you just shake off after a shift and a night's rest. You had both the PCB and the SOA breathing down your neck wanting answers and interviews. You'd just made a pack with Patrick and you both needed time to adjust. I handled what I could with the packs."

Jono didn't much care to think about what he'd gone through at Ethan's hand. Waking up from nightmares with Patrick by his side was loads better than waking up alone. "If there was a problem, you should've told me."

Emma gave him a frustrated look. "What more could you have done?"

Jono opened his mouth—then closed it. He clenched his teeth, feeling the pressure in the hinge of his jaw. She was right, and he hated it. New York City wasn't his territory. He wasn't judge, jury, and executioner for the packs that called the five boroughs home. That was all Estelle and Youssef and the self-serving arseholes enforcing their orders.

Deep down, Jono knew he could do better.

Patrick pointed at the plate of cooling food in front of him on the coffee table. "Eat."

Patrick had practically inhaled his food and was already more than halfway finished. Jono picked up the plate because it would be rude not to.

"What's going on with the independents?" Patrick asked.

Sage shifted on the sofa and tucked one foot underneath her. "Pack law commands any independent werecreature who comes to the city must go before the god pack to get permission to stay. Not everyone is granted that permission, and not all those who receive it stay. I've been hearing rumors that some independent werecreatures have gone missing."

"You sure they didn't just leave to go try their luck somewhere else?"

"Independents stick together. Doesn't make us a pack, but it's a safety thing. We usually tell someone what we're doing," Jono said.

"I got a few who say their friends never came home, or didn't show up for work. Their calls are going unanswered, and no one has seen them or scented them in any pack territory," Sage added.

Patrick viciously stabbed at a meatball. "Until now."

"Yes."

Patrick eyed the meatball on his fork before sighing heavily and setting his plate on the coffee table, apparently no longer hungry. "The victim had shine in his pocket. That information stays between us."

The sound of ripping fabric had Jono looking over at where

Emma sat on the armchair, peeling claws out of the expensive furniture. She didn't seem to notice the damage she'd done.

"*What?*" she growled.

Jono's anger matched hers, a vicious, ugly emotion he had to throttle back. No love was lost between vampires and werecreatures, and Jono had a hatred for them that went deeper than most. His infection by the werevirus was due to a dodgy blood transfusion at a hospital after an auto accident when he was seventeen. The Edgware Night Court had done a tidy little side business in blood procurement through the hospital, and safety standards hadn't been kept up.

He'd come to terms with his lot in life years ago, but Jono's opinion on vampires had remained the same—he bloody well *hated* them. Dealing with Lucien and his transient Night Court in June had only cemented that feeling.

"The treaties the god pack has with the Night Courts here mean we have pass-through rights in each other's territories, but we don't *stay*. It was a bloodbath in the middle of the last century during the Civil Rights era before City Hall worked out the treaties," Leon said.

In a major metropolitan city, territory was measured by blocks, sometimes by a single address. The density of New York City meant all sorts of various monsters and creatures claimed territory that ran right up against each other. As with street gangs, sometimes fights broke out. Humanity hated when the preternatural world went to war, which was why laws targeting territory rights were so draconian.

Not that any of the groups affected by those laws ever strictly obeyed them.

"Well, the kid was either dealing or using, and either answer isn't going to play well in the press or with the groups in question. If he was a mundane human, it would've been a nonissue," Patrick said.

"He's dead. I don't consider that a nonissue," Jono said flatly.

Patrick shrugged. "Drugs, as shitty as they are, aren't a drop everything and eradicate now sort of problem. It's a losing fight against supply and demand issues that will never go away. People die from overdoses every day. That's not news. What *is* news is a dead werecreature in a place he shouldn't be with possible evidence of contact with vampires."

"He could've got shine from anywhere," Sage said, playing devil's advocate.

"Kid had burn marks around his neck that looked like they came from silver. The wound was the right size and shape for a collar. In my experience, that speaks of time spent in captivity."

Jono got to his feet to prowl around the living area, unable to sit still any longer. He could feel Patrick's eyes on him but was still too angry to speak.

"If I had my way," Patrick said into the tense silence, "I'd dump whatever vampire killed the kid in the middle of a desert a couple of minutes before sunrise and wait for the party to start."

"You sound confident the perpetrator is one of the undead," Sage said.

"In my experience, nothing human dumps a werecreature in the middle of a hidden subway station wrapped in protective wards."

"But you don't have proof."

"I'll find some."

Jono rested his hands on the back of the sofa Marek and Sage were sat on. He looked over their heads at Patrick, meeting his determined gaze head-on. He knew the lengths Patrick would go to to close out a case—they were both living with the fallout of his stubbornness, after all.

"Estelle and Youssef should be told what's going on."

Jono *growled*, the sound ugly and mean. "*Fuck* that."

Sage shrugged, turning to glare at him. "I said they *should*, not that we need to be the ones to do so. From a pack law standpoint, that's what has to happen."

"I'll deal with them at some point but not tonight," Patrick said.

"Too bad you can't deal with Jono instead," Emma said, chin tilted up in a defiant angle.

Jono dug his fingers into the cushions, mindful of his strength. Emma could destroy her own furniture all she liked, but Jono would feel terrible at making a mess of her home. "You know why, Em."

"Yeah, well, they're shitty alphas. You'd be better."

Patrick arched an eyebrow at Jono but kept quiet. Jono's mouth twisted and he let out a harsh breath. "A two-person pack won't stand a chance in a challenge, mage or not. You know that."

"My pack is not the only one who would follow you," Emma said in a quiet, firm voice. "*You* know *that*."

Jono closed his eyes, feeling the echo of Fenrir's presence deep in his soul. No one other than Patrick knew of the immortal's favor bestowed on him. He'd carried that secret with him out of London and abided by the rules Estelle and Youssef had laid down for him around Marek's insistence. Moments like this made Jono wonder what would happen if he gave voice to a truth few believed in.

Fenrir's voice rumbled through his mind, the sound like teeth gnashing against bone. *War.*

Jono opened his eyes, shaking off the voice of a god. "Not the time, Em."

Emma stared him down before pointedly showing her throat in a submissive manner, a gesture she offered to no one else but Estelle and Youssef, and that only grudgingly. "When it arrives, you know where to find me."

Jono dipped his head in acknowledgment. "We'll let Pat sort out the god pack and keep you lot updated."

"If you need someone to identify the dead, call me," Sage said.

"I might take you up on that if the god pack pisses me off too much," Patrick told her as he stood, the mageglobe hovering beside him still. "Thanks for dinner."

"You're always welcome here," Leon told him, the sincerity in his voice a far cry from the initial antagonism that had colored their first few interactions.

The monthly pack dinner Patrick had been invited to in July had gone a long way toward getting the Tempest pack to be comfortable around him. Jono knew Patrick was still a bit stand-offish, but that was to be expected from someone who lived with the secrets he carried. With Marek, Emma, Leon, and Sage, he was more himself.

Emma got up to hug them goodbye and walk them to the lift. She barely came up to Patrick's chin in her bare feet, but size didn't mean anything in the preternatural world.

"I don't like this," she said bluntly, not bothering to lower her voice since the silence ward was still up. "If it's the Night Courts, we have a problem that Estelle and Youssef most likely won't do anything about."

Jono glanced at Patrick, catching the other man's gaze. "We'll get it sorted, Em."

She nodded, her brown eyes flicking between the two of them. "I mean it, Jono. We'd follow you."

"Cheers, love."

The mageglobe faded away and Jono assumed Patrick had removed the silence ward. Emma stepped back, letting the lift doors shut. Jono didn't know what to say in the face of that pledge of loyalty. On the one hand, her faith in him was humbling. On the other hand, fracturing the packs in New York City would turn the werecreature community into a hellish, bloody mess.

Patrick didn't seem in a conversational mood, and they made their way back to the car in silence. They were halfway to the Mustang when a scent rocked Jono to a halt, hand snapping out to grab for Patrick and hold him back. A burning ozone smell filled his nose, sharp and cutting.

A scent he only ever smelled around immortals.

"Smells like an immortal took a walkabout," Jono said.

"Motherfucker," Patrick spat out.

Protective wards were embedded in the Mustang. Jono had been there when Patrick had laid them down despite not having the greatest affinity for that kind of magic. The wards were minor, set to shield the vehicle if someone with magic tried to access it, and warn him of the attempt. Patrick should've been aware of the tampering. The fact that he apparently wasn't made Jono hyper-aware they were out in the open on the street.

"Stay here," Patrick said.

Jono snorted. "Not bloody likely."

Patrick opened his mouth to argue before abruptly shaking his head. "Sorry. Habit."

The bitter scent emanating from Patrick grew stronger as his personal shields expanded around them both. Jono couldn't see the movement of magic, but he could feel it, the way power skittered across his skin.

They approached the car together and Jono stayed right by Patrick's side as he circled the Mustang. The ward runes flared up brightly at each corner and the doors before turning invisible again.

Patrick frowned. "The wards weren't broken."

Jono pulled the keys out of his pocket and hit the fob to unlock the door. "Someone still got inside. Can I open the door?"

"Should be safe. I have you shielded."

Jono nodded and hauled the passenger-side door open, lips curling into a snarl. "Someone left you a gift."

Jono didn't recognize the black plastic doll sitting in the cup holder in the center console, but Patrick did judging by the amount of swearing that left his mouth. Jono stepped aside so Patrick could lean in and grab the figurine, magic sparking around his hand in a protective layer. Pale blue light flickered and folded around the doll, encasing it in a protective mageglobe.

"What is it?" Jono asked.

Patrick glared at the skeleton-shaped reaper in his hand. "A

Santa Muerte idol. It matches the one we found in the subway tonight."

"You didn't mention that to the others."

"It's not something they needed to know."

Jono stared at Patrick. "That's not how pack works, mate."

Patrick sat down in the passenger seat and wouldn't look at him. "I'm telling you."

Jono should feel grateful about that, considering how he knew Patrick played things close to the chest—only he didn't. "What immortal are we dealing with this time?"

"I don't know yet."

Jono sighed deeply before shutting the car door and going around to the driver's side. He got behind the wheel and started the engine, sitting there for a moment before saying, "Where to?"

He desperately wanted Patrick to say *home*. The answer he got was unsurprising.

"The PCB."

Jono pulled into the street and headed for the corner. As he braked to a halt, movement flashed across the rearview mirror. His eyes cut to the reflection in the mirror, but nothing appeared.

"What is it?" Patrick asked.

"Thought I saw something."

Patrick twisted around in his seat to peer out the rear window. "What did it look like?"

"Not sure, but it was running on four legs."

A werecreature would be the obvious answer because the god pack wasn't above spying on the people they were supposed to protect. Emma's pack was no exception, and only the bought magic sunk into the threshold around their home or Patrick prevented werecreatures from listening in some days.

Somehow, Jono had a feeling what he thought he'd seen wasn't a werecreature.

3

PATRICK PUSHED THROUGH THE FRONT DOORS TO THE Preternatural Crimes Bureau with the Santa Muerte idol in hand and Jono at his back. He unearthed his badge from his back pocket and presented it to the desk sergeant on duty. The woman buzzed them through the security doors without comment.

Rather than head up to the fifth floor where Bureau Chief Giovanni Casale's office was, they took the elevator down into the basement where the crime lab and morgue were located. The basement also housed the evidence lockup, which was always manned by a magic user.

The officer working third shift greeted them with a friendly enough smile. The badge pinned to her shirt showed her last name and was etched with a small pentacle beneath the letters, denoting her rank as a witch.

Submitting the Santa Muerte idol into evidence and tagging it with the correct case number took a few minutes and only one form. Patrick left the idol in the evidence lockup, contained inside a warded wooden box with Latin prayers carved on all sides.

"I need to see if Casale is in," Patrick said, knuckling one eye as they waited for the elevator.

Jono nodded. "Want me to wait at the car?"

Patrick's first instinct was to say *yes*, but Jono had been with him for the second idol's appearance and he had insight to the werecreature community Patrick didn't have. Aside from that, Patrick just plain missed him after a week apart.

"No. Stay with me."

Jono's hand brushed the back of his as they stepped into the elevator, a silent signal of support that Patrick was still getting used to.

The bull pen was busy despite the late hour when they walked by it. Some of the offices on the floor were dark, but Casale's had light streaming from beneath the closed door. His assistant, Paula, had left hours ago, so Patrick knocked on the door. The office was warded for silence, but the wards would let Casale know someone was outside waiting.

The door opened seconds later and Patrick came face-to-face with the PCB's bureau chief. He hadn't seen Giovanni Casale in weeks. Considering the backlog of cases cropping up since summer solstice, it wasn't surprising.

"I'm back," Patrick said in lieu of hello.

Casale opened the office door wider, gesturing for them to enter. "I wish you weren't."

"One of these days you'll miss me."

"When I'm dead, maybe."

Patrick couldn't help the bark of laughter that escaped his mouth. He respected Casale despite knowing the NYPD didn't much care for when a federal agency came in to take over a case. But Casale would've been the one to reach out to the SOA asking for assistance in the first place. Henry had offered up Patrick out of the field office's Rapid Response Division and Casale hadn't said no.

"Did you receive the preliminary officer report on the subway homicide?" Patrick asked as Jono shut the door behind him.

"I was advised about the case when it hit dispatch. It's why I sent the request to the SOA in the first place and stayed late," Casale replied. "Heard you'd gone to talk to the god pack tonight. Thought that would've been Estelle and Youssef, not Jonothon."

"They were busy," Jono said with a careless shrug. He didn't move to take a seat, and Patrick stayed by his side.

Casale gave Jono a pointed look as he went behind his desk to start shutting down his computer. "You don't speak for the packs."

"I trust Jono more than I trust Estelle and Youssef. Besides, he's an independent and so is our vic," Patrick said.

"You sure about that?"

"Yes."

Casale frowned. "This case is going to get messy."

"Tell me about it. Is Catherine fast-tracking the autopsy?"

"Yes. I've signed off on the overtime. Body like that in a warded subway tunnel? You can bet people will be questioning the protection. I had a call with the president of the MTA about an hour ago. They're initiating a survey on the wards in that area tonight. They're hoping to beat morning rush hour."

"Good. Let me know what they find out."

"So long as you're more of a party player than last time. Try not to get knocked out and go off grid for twenty-four hours or more this time."

"I'll do my best," Patrick said, not promising anything.

Casale nodded. "All I can ask for."

Their working relationship in June had ended on a high note, despite the mess that happened. Casale's good name hadn't been dragged too deep through the mud since the SOA took the brunt of the public's anger. Patrick didn't have his finger on the pulse of NYPD internal politics, but he figured since Casale was still around and leading the PCB it was a sign of tacit approval from the brass at One Police Plaza.

Casale shifted his attention to Jono. "Unless you're here under Marek's order, this case doesn't concern you no matter what Patrick thinks."

Jono's mouth ticked downward a bit. "You know I'm an independent and a better source than the god pack alphas."

"But you aren't the New York City god pack alpha, despite your background. I can't discuss the case with you."

"I'd rather work with Jono than Estelle and Youssef," Patrick said.

"I won't tell you how to run your cases, but I need to abide by the law for mine. City ordinance requires me to go through whoever is in charge of the god pack here, and that's not Jonothon."

"Okay."

Patrick's answer was less agreement and more *I'll do what I want*. Casale seemed to pick up on that, judging by how he rolled his eyes.

"Why are you here, Collins?"

"You know how we found a Santa Muerte idol in the subway? Someone got through the wards on my car to leave me a second one as a present."

Casale's eyes blinked wide before narrowing. "They did *what*?"

"I don't know who did it. There's no trace signature on the damn thing, but whoever managed it has to be powerful."

The lie came easily to his lips, as they always did. Patrick wasn't about to talk about immortals, no matter how entrenched Casale was in the preternatural world. The old gods weren't believed in much outside what followers they could scrape together these days.

"Do you think it's Ethan Greene and the Dominion Sect again? Revenge, maybe, for what happened in June?"

Patrick fought back a flinch. Casale's words hit a little too close to home, something the older man could never know. Patrick's familial ties to Ethan was a secret very few knew. As far as the public was concerned, Patrick was dead, murdered by his father when he was eight years old, along with his mother and twin sister, Hannah. In reality, he'd lived under a false identity for over twenty years, protected and used by the Greek goddess of the Underworld, and bound by a soul debt he couldn't escape.

"Who knows?" Patrick said, forcing himself to sound unworried. "I'm leaning toward vampires."

"Think your criminal informant might be able to shed some light on the issue?"

Lucien was still around, but Patrick hadn't seen him since summer solstice. He hadn't disclosed his CI source to anyone after the fact, despite pressure to do so. "I don't know. Not sure what they're up to."

Casale looked like he didn't believe Patrick, but was too much of a professional to call him out on his bullshit answer. Casale pulled his suit jacket off the coat rack in the corner and shrugged it on. "We'll discuss the case later when we have more at hand than a dead body. Keep me in the loop, Collins."

That was something Patrick couldn't outright promise to do, but he liked Casale. He knew from experience that working with local law enforcement was better than working against them. No one was helped in the end by different departments and agencies refusing to share leads.

Patrick and Jono preceded Casale out of the office and to the elevator. The three of them didn't speak on the way down to the ground floor and went their separate ways. Patrick was relieved to discover the Mustang was untouched this time around when they made it back to the warded parking garage.

"Home?" Jono asked as he unlocked the car doors with a push of a button.

"Yeah."

WHEN PATRICK WAS A BOY, before his mother and twin sister were murdered by his father, he called Salem, Massachusetts, home. He had vague memories of that house and his mother's family who would visit, bringing treats and charms to entertain Hannah and him.

After—after the blood and the scars and a life granted in exchange for a promise he wasn't sure he could keep—Patrick grew up in an Academy for magic users, a ward of the state with a brand-new identity. Ten years of tutelage earned him a contract with the Mage Corps and a roster spot in the Citadel, the premier military school for magic users.

None of those places had a bed he enjoyed sleeping in. When he finally deployed, he slept where he could: cots, bunks, foxholes, and always with a weapon close at hand.

Patrick never had a home, not since Salem, but the apartment he shared with Jono was slowly becoming one. Learning to live with someone else in his personal space so intimately was a process, one where compromise was key.

Despite the low-grade headache building at the back of his skull from stress and nicotine cravings, Patrick wasn't going to light up a cigarette. Quitting smoking because Jono asked was something Patrick was committed to. At times like this, he desperately wished he could have just one more smoke break. Jono made a pretty good distraction though.

That fact was proven when they finally made it home, the threshold around the apartment a comforting barrier between them and the rest of the world. Patrick kicked the door shut behind them and locked it. Jono dropped Patrick's luggage by the door before taking his hand and pulling him toward the bedroom.

Patrick followed willingly, feeling the long day—hell, the entire week—in his muscles. As much as he wouldn't mind a night full of welcome-home sex, the siren song of sleep called to him.

"Don't think I'm up for much right now," Patrick said.

He started undoing the straps that kept his gods-given dagger strapped to his right thigh while Jono worked at unholstering his sidearm.

"Happy to have you home, is all," Jono murmured, leaning down to press a warm, openmouthed kiss to the pulse of Patrick's throat. "You need to shower?"

Patrick didn't particularly want to, but considering the day he'd had, it was probably the better option. "Yeah. I'll be out in ten minutes."

Washing off the grittiness of travel went a long ways to making him feel better. The warm water helped loosen his muscles and eased some of the lingering bruising he still carried. The scars on his chest from nearly being sacrificed as a child by Ethan were pale against his skin, the dog tags he still wore falling on top of them. He couldn't feel the metal in certain spots, the damage too deep.

Persephone had healed him after Patrick unwittingly agreed to her terms years ago. She'd let the wound scar, a reminder of his mistake in saying *yes*. Patrick had kept them covered up as much as possible until Jono came into his life.

Patrick finished getting clean and got out of the shower, drying off before pulling on a pair of boxers. Summer was in full swing, but the apartment was cool due to the air-conditioning Jono had running most of the day in anticipation of Patrick coming home.

Jono was in their bed when Patrick exited the master bathroom. Unlike Patrick, Jono slept in the nude, and was already under the duvet, the covers pushed down to his waist. He was on his phone but put it aside once Patrick turned off the lights and crawled into bed. Jono dragged him close without a word, the heat he gave off a counter to the coolness in the bedroom.

In the dark, Jono's voice was a deep rumble between them. "Think it could be the same group of immortals from before?"

Patrick grimaced and slung an arm over Jono's torso. "Doubtful, but I won't rule it out. Hermes has a tendency to pop up like a fucking cockroach."

"Do vampires have a god?"

Patrick stiffened, his reaction impossible to hide, not when he was pressed so close to Jono. He swallowed thickly, the sound loud between them. "Yes, but it's not her."

"You're sure?"

Patrick closed his eyes, a flash image of fire burning across the back of his eyelids—Ashanti disintegrating right in front of him. The mother of all vampires had died in the Thirty-Day War three years ago, sacrificing herself to deliver Patrick's dagger to him and help break the Dominion Sect's spell. Growing up, Ashanti had been an unholy mentor to him from time to time. Her absence in the world was a reality Patrick hated living with.

"Yes," he repeated with more conviction.

"Then I suppose the only place to go for answers is the god pack," Jono said, sounding vaguely irritated at that fact. "I doubt they'll be very forthcoming."

"If they obstruct the case in any way, I'll be within my rights to charge them over that."

"As much as I'd love to see them get a bit of comeuppance, it'd be a right mess within the werecreature community if you did. People might be unwilling to chat with you about whoever's gone missing."

"They'd talk to you."

Jono's hand stilled where his fingers were stroking soft circles over Patrick's hip beneath the covers. "Not sure they would."

"Maybe the packs aligned with the god pack won't, but I bet the independents would. You were one of them."

"Still am outside these walls."

Patrick moved his head to press a kiss against Jono's warm skin. "I never understood why you independents wouldn't just form your own packs with each other."

"Mixed viral strains. There's a reason people stick with their own kind. You see it even in mundane society with discrimination and cultural mores. It takes a lot of effort to try to make something like that work. Most werecreatures can't be arsed to try, not when forming a new pack in established areas means you get sod all in the territory department."

"You tried."

"You're a hard bloke to say no to, Pat." Jono pressed a kiss to the top of Patrick's head. "Now go to sleep."

Patrick closed his eyes, relaxing in slow degrees against Jono. Sleeping on the road was no longer normal for him. He'd gotten used to sleeping with another body in the bed, the sound of someone breathing close by a white noise he'd missed in his hotel room.

Waking up together after being apart had its own appeal, one he'd missed while upstate.

Sunrise in summer came before 0700, and after a night of no dreams or nightmares, Patrick woke to warm lips pressing soft kisses down his spine. Cracking open one eye, Patrick flexed his fingers against the sheets. He'd rolled onto his stomach sometime during the night, arms shoved beneath the pillow. He had a vague sense memory of Jono pressed close throughout the night, but that was overtaken by the present teasing touches.

"You turned off my alarm," Patrick mumbled. His internal sense of time told him it should've gone off five minutes ago.

Jono licked at the dip of his lower spine, the warm drag of Jono's tongue making Patrick twitch. He'd gone to bed in boxers, but those were missing now. The fact that Jono was able to strip him without Patrick waking up just proved his subconscious had firmly put Jono in the non-threat box.

"You get up too bloody early most days, but it works in my favor sometimes," Jono said, his breath ghosting over the curve of Patrick's bare ass. "Figured I could welcome you home now since I didn't get the chance last night."

Patrick helpfully spread his legs, hissing at the way his already interested cock moved against the bedsheet. Warm fingers gripped his ass and spread him open. Patrick turned his face into the pillow at the first lick of Jono's tongue over his hole, the scrape of Jono's five-o'clock shadow against sensitive skin making him gasp.

This was—hands down—Patrick's favorite way to wake up these days. He had Jono to thank for teaching him how good sex could be when he wasn't rushing to get off. Patrick bit his lip as Jono licked at his hole again, hot breath tickling his skin. Heat zinged up his spine at the wet touch, and he moaned when the tip of Jono's tongue pushed inside him.

He curled his hands into fists beneath the pillow as he pushed back against Jono's mouth, heat suffusing his face. Getting eaten out was intimate in a way he'd rarely experienced before Jono came into his life. Patrick had to admit he'd been missing out.

"Gods," he moaned, hips jerking as Jono sucked at the rim of his hole. "I want you in me."

Jono flicked his tongue over his hole before sliding a slick finger inside him, causing Patrick to inhale sharply.

"Like this?" Jono teased.

Patrick would've answered, except Jono curled his finger at just the right angle to rub against his prostate and Patrick couldn't remember how to speak for a couple of seconds.

Jono chuckled, the sound muffled against Patrick's ass. "I'll take that as a yes."

Patrick sucked in air and turned his face to the side again, blinking open his eyes. "I have to work today."

"So you do." Another hot, wet kiss to his hole made Patrick's mouth part on a near-silent gasp. "Bloody shame I can't spend all day working you over."

Patrick bit his lip at that drawled confession, wishing he could spend the day in bed letting Jono come in him and on him, sinking into a scent his too-human nose couldn't parse. Other werecreatures could, and Patrick had never once been embarrassed at the way Jono laid claim to him.

Patrick slid a hand free from beneath the pillow to reach behind him for Jono. He blindly tangled his fingers in wavy black hair, getting a good grip and tugging. "I spent a week without you. Don't make me wait."

Jono bit lightly at Patrick's upturned ass before pushing a second finger inside him. The hot burn of the stretch, sudden and nerve-piercing, had Patrick moaning and tightening his hold on Jono's hair.

"Say please."

Patrick opened his mouth, but the word didn't immediately come to his lips. It took a few seconds for him to push back against a lifetime of stubbornness where begging was concerned. Jono was proving to be an exception to all his rules these days.

"Please," Patrick finally forced out, shuddering on the exhale.

Jono licked his way inside again, tongue curling over his fingers in a distracting way that had Patrick panting wetly against the pillow. Jono teased his prostate for a few more seconds with light touches that made Patrick's cock throb. Then he pulled his fingers free and grabbed Patrick's ass, touch warm like it always was.

Patrick let go of Jono's hair in order to get his elbows underneath him as Jono pulled apart his ass cheeks to press an open-mouthed, sucking kiss right over his hole. Patrick moaned, giving in to the full-body shiver that made his toes curl.

Jono slid his hands along Patrick's body to fit them over his hips. With a firm tug, he pulled Patrick closer. He would've got up on his hands and knees, except Jono pressed a hand between his shoulder blades and pushed him back down onto the bed. Patrick instinctively pushed back against the strength holding him down before relaxing, reaching out with one hand to snag the pillow again.

He turned his head, the angle making his neck go tight, but seeing the smirk on Jono's gorgeous face was worth it. When Jono leaned over Patrick to kiss him, he didn't turn away, not caring where the other man's mouth had just been. Jono's cock slid into the crease of his ass, rubbing against him as they kissed. The thickness was something Patrick wanted in him, sooner rather than later.

"Hate when you're gone," Jono said after he broke the kiss. He bit down gently on Patrick's shoulder before reaching for the bottle of lube again.

"Soulbond," Patrick muttered.

Patrick dug his fingers into the pillow as Jono poured lube over his cock where it was nestled between Patrick's ass cheeks, getting them both messy. That thick length slid against his body, the fat head teasing over his hole and catching on the rim.

"*You*," Jono retorted before nipping at Patrick's shoulder.

Patrick wanted to argue—partly because he still had trouble believing someone could care for him like that in such an intimate way—but all the words fled his mind as Jono finally pushed into him. His mouth opened on a silent groan, lungs locking up as that thick cock split him open. Lying on the bed how he was, with his hips tilted up, knees spread wide, and Jono practically lying on top of him to keep him there, all Patrick could do was take it.

Jono worked his way inside with slow, agonizing pushes, each inch gained causing Patrick to draw in a shuddering breath. Jono's cock was long and thick, filling Patrick up in the best way possible. By the time Jono's hips were flush against his ass, Patrick was half out of his mind with need.

"You're such a fucking *tease*," he gasped out, entire body tight as he clenched around Jono's cock.

Jono laughed, and Patrick could feel the vibrations through his rib cage. "Want to enjoy you. Is that too much to ask?"

"Fuck yeah it is."

"Too bad you have to work. I had plans for you that would've taken all day," Jono murmured as he flexed his hips and pulled back, the long drag of his cock leaving Patrick's body making him whimper.

"Yeah?" he said, licking his lips.

"I wanted to take my time with you. Wanted to make you come over and over until it hurt. Then I'd take my turn."

Patrick squeezed his eyes shut and breathed into the damp fabric of his pillow as Jono thrust back in at just the right angle to rub against his prostate. "*Fuck*. You're gonna kill me in bed one of these days."

Jono's chuckle was warm in his ears. "Be a fun way to go."

"For *you*."

"Nothing wrong with that, love."

For all his magic, Patrick was human, and Jono's preternatural strength meant he could never let go entirely in bed. Some nights he wanted more than what Patrick could give, and stretching out the pleasure helped to temper that need.

"Maybe next time," Patrick muttered, digging his knees into the mattress so he could push back against Jono's next thrust.

"Yeah?" Jono asked, fingers digging into Patrick's hip bones as he straightened up. The movement had him grinding against Patrick's prostate. "You want that?"

Patrick flushed at the thought, but he wasn't going to deny he wanted that. He knew Jono could smell his desire and wasn't ashamed of that fact. Jono rewarded Patrick for that nonverbal agreement by snapping his hips forward, driving his cock in deep and hard. Patrick nearly swallowed his tongue on the second thrust, groaning at the way Jono made sure to catch his prostate.

He reached between his legs to stroke his cock in time with Jono's thrusts, the pace picking up. Patrick closed his eyes, sinking into the sensations of his body climbing toward orgasm. The tightness in his balls warred with the fire in his nerves as Jono fucked him, sweat sliding over his skin.

After a week with nothing but his right hand to help him get off, Patrick didn't last—he *couldn't*, not with the way Jono so easily took him apart. The thick heat of the hard cock inside him was impossible to ignore; Jono's warm hands like a vise around his hips. Patrick came, tipping over the edge with a muffled cry as he turned his face into the pillow, shuddering through his orgasm. Hot cum spurted over his fingers, body tightening around Jono's cock.

Jono didn't stop thrusting, but his movements slowed until Patrick was a limp mess on the bed, muscles shaky with exertion. Jono leaned over him and kissed the back of his sweaty neck, licking at his skin. Patrick managed to flop a hand onto Jono's head, lazily tugging at his hair.

"Want you to come in me," Patrick said on a satisfied sigh.

Jono obliged, taking Patrick apart in the best way possible. Every thrust burned with a teeth-tingling sensation of *too much* that Patrick ignored in favor of giving Jono what he wanted. And Jono took, driving in deep and hard until Patrick wanted to scream. When Jono finally came, Patrick had to bite his lip, hands twisting at the sheets as Jono's cock throbbed in his body, coming deep inside him.

Jono stayed buried deep for a few more seconds before he slowly pulled out. Patrick groaned, body clenching around the emptiness. Jono lay down beside him as Patrick straightened out his legs, resting his hand possessively over Patrick's ass.

"Have fun at the office today," Jono said, sounding smug.

Patrick reached out and pinched one of Jono's nipples. "Fuck you."

Jono's laughter echoed in Patrick's ears long after he left the apartment for work.

4

"WHAT DO YOU *MEAN* YOU AREN'T COMING BY TO IDENTIFY THE body?" Patrick growled. He paused in pouring the creamer into his thermos of coffee as Estelle's irritated sigh echoed in the kitchen through the speakerphone.

"We've had no word of anyone under our protection dying outside any sanctioned challenges," Estelle told him coolly.

Patrick glared down at his phone where it sat on the kitchen counter. "What part of *murder* don't you understand?"

"Today isn't a good time, and neither is the weekend. We can set up an appointment with the medical examiner's office on Monday. The body will keep until then."

Patrick ended the call, not in the mood to argue, and opened up the kitchen cabinet to grab a bottle of Jameson. Today might have been Friday, but in his line of work, the week never ended.

"Jono," Patrick said, not bothering to raise his voice as he poured a finger's worth of whiskey into his thermos. "I'm gonna need you to come with me to the PCB."

Patrick had spent all day yesterday at the SOA opening the new case when he wasn't taking meetings with SAIC Henry Ng. He'd decided to reach out to Estelle and Youssef after he'd read Catherine's preliminary autopsy report.

One Andre Scott, werejackal, had died from blunt force trauma to the torso and head, propounded by a sustained allergic reaction to silver. Results on the toxicology report would take weeks, but Patrick wouldn't be surprised if shine and aconite were found in his blood. The cause of Andre's allergic reaction hadn't been located, but Catherine's notes had detailed out her suspicions of a collar. The bruising and burn scars had formed the right shape around the teen's neck.

Aside from all that, Andre had teeth marks that matched the general shape of vampire fangs in the flesh surrounding his veins and arteries.

Fucking vampires.

"She's in a mood," Jono said as he came out of the bedroom, voice gravelly and making Patrick think of sex instead of work. The sight of Jono padding naked into the kitchen didn't help any.

"Like hell I'm waiting until Monday. I'll pay you what the SOA would for an expert witness fee out of pocket for you to identify the body."

Strong arms wrapped around his waist, and a chin settled on top of his head. Patrick scowled into his coffee but couldn't help slumping back against Jono.

"You don't got to pay me for this. But you'll need someone who's actually seen the bloke to confirm it's him before I handle any paperwork."

"Hope Sage isn't needed in court today."

"She'd technically need the god pack alphas' approval to help."

"Lucky for us, you fit that bill."

Jono sighed heavily but didn't protest Patrick's pointed comment. "I'll get dressed. Put the whiskey away and get a nicotine patch. You're stroppy."

"The fuck I'm stroppy," Patrick muttered, taking a sip of his Irish coffee.

He still got the nicotine patch.

Jono called Sage on the way out of the apartment, catching her when she was already in the office at 0730 in the morning. Patrick half listened to the quick conversation as they clattered down the stairs to the street, sipping at his coffee and scratching absently at the nicotine patch on his arm.

Jono swatted his hand away from messing with it. "Ta, love. We'll pick you up on our way to the PCB."

"Oh, good. She's available," Patrick said as Jono ended the call.

"She says her boss isn't happy she's being called away from the office."

Patrick shrugged. "Sage could've said no."

"You knew she wouldn't."

"I was counting on that."

Maybe it was a little underhanded playing into pack politics like that, but Patrick had a dead werejackal lying on a slab back at the morgue and a recalcitrant pair of god pack alphas annoying the shit out of him. He'd use what avenues he had to move this case along, and if that meant leaning hard into Jono's status? Then he would do it, and the guilt could go fuck itself.

Patrick felt bad about not letting Jono get some rest that morning. He'd taken a closing shift last night, which meant taking last call at 0345 and locking the doors at Tempest at 0400. Cleanup had taken another hour, and Jono had caught an Uber cross-town to get home rather than take public transit. Jono had arrived in time to lie down with Patrick for thirty minutes before his alarm had gone off.

Late-night bar hours and the weird hours cases took meant sometimes they didn't see each other awake for more than a few minutes at a time. Despite their schedules, they still knew the other was close by through the soulbond—at least, when Patrick was in town. Distance was never easy to navigate, and Patrick was half-tempted to bring Jono along the next time he went away on a case. He doubted Emma and Leon would mind, but he didn't want to mess with Jono's job too much.

Friday morning traffic from uptown, the tunnels, and the bridges meant it took a while to get downtown. Gentry & Thyme, the law firm Sage worked at as a senior associate, was located in Lower Manhattan. The firm had been founded by a group of Seelie fae in 1850, years before the five boroughs were consolidated into a single city.

Patrick hated dealing with the fae. Most were lawyers, plying their trade in words with the courts and whoever was stupid enough to sign a contract with them. You always had to watch your words with the fae, and Patrick had no desire to find himself owing a debt to the descendants of the Tuatha Dé Danann. He owed too much already.

Sage was waiting for them outside her work building when Patrick finally pulled up to the curb behind a yellow taxi discharging its passenger. Jono opened the door and got out to push the seat forward so he could climb into the back.

She tossed her Birkin bag onto the floorboard and took the front seat. Birkin bags were his best friend's favorite style of purse, which was the only reason Patrick knew what they were called and what they looked like. And like Special Agent Nadine Mulroney, a mage out of the Preternatural Intelligence Agency, Sage was a coffee thief.

"That's mine," Patrick said as he pulled into the street.

"Guess what? You're sharing now," Sage replied curtly before gulping down a mouthful of hot, whiskey-laced coffee. "I have a ten-o'clock meeting I can't miss, so I need to be back at the office before then."

Patrick glanced at her and decided his coffee was a lost cause. "You look tired."

"Long night dealing with a client's case. I didn't leave the office."

"I know what that's like."

The turquoise pendant artifact hanging from a slender platinum chain around her neck sifted through Patrick's magic as an afterthought. The recognition of the artifact's fae magic was a normal feeling to him these days. The fae magic embedded in the stone masked Sage's true nature. As a mage, Patrick could pick out magic better than most, but even he couldn't sense Sage was a werecreature through that spell.

The drive to the PCB didn't take long, and Patrick parked in the adjacent warded garage when they arrived.

"So Estelle and Youssef didn't want to come?" Sage said on the walk to the elevators.

"They'd make time Monday. I need the kid IDed today," Patrick said. "If that means I keep them out of the loop longer, so much the better."

Sage side-eyed him but said nothing. There wasn't much she *could* say. Patrick knew she hated the god pack alphas just as much as he did.

The sergeant on desk duty buzzed them through the security door once they made it into the PCB, and they took the elevator down to the basement. The morgue was located in the lower levels and had protective wards etched into every wall. The intake assistant at the receiving desk jumped to his feet when they arrived, wiping crumbs from his breakfast pastry off his mouth.

"How can I help you?" he asked.

"Body from the homicide in the subway Wednesday night. We're here to ID it," Patrick said.

"Dr. Margolin isn't in, but Geoffrey Davis is in workroom three talking with the chief. I can take you to them."

"Great."

The intake assistant led them down a sparse hallway to a warded door. He unlocked it with a scan card to the sensor pad and a press of his hand to a pentagram carved in the metal of the door itself.

The dead had to be handled differently than the living, especially those that died by way of magic or worse. The morgue was a place of death despite its white hospital-grade sterile walls, floors, and brightly lit workrooms, one of which they found themselves entering. The room smelled strongly of bleach and ammonia, with a deeper scent of formaldehyde and rot. The preservation process didn't matter; death would always find a way to stick around.

Casale and Geoffrey, the medical examiner on duty, were standing on either side of a metal slab that had been rolled out of a refrigeration wall unit used to store the dead. Casale looked up at their arrival, his brown eyes narrowing as he took in Jono and Sage. Geoffrey was a tall, almost too-thin man who kept his brown hair buzzed short and was currently wearing scrubs.

The body lying between them had his chest stitched up in the quintessential Y-incision from an autopsy. Patrick eyed the runes painted on the dead teenager's chest. The runes were standard procedure in murder investigations to keep the dead from being raised. Nothing ruined a case more than having a body reanimated through necromancy and the zombie walk out the front door.

"Different company than I thought you'd bring, Collins," Casale said.

"Jono's god pack and I need the victim identified," Patrick replied.

Casale's gaze flickered to Sage, but he didn't say anything about her status. "All right. I take it Estelle and Youssef weren't available?"

"Something like that." Patrick eyed the teenager lying on the slab for a few seconds before looking at Geoffrey. "You got the form we need for identification?"

"Yeah, right over here," Geoffrey said.

He walked over to a nearby worktable and picked up a folder sitting on top of a metal field case that doubled as a clipboard, and a pen. He carried both back to where everyone was gathered around the body, clicking the pen into use.

"Andre Scott," Jono said after a moment. "Independent were-jackal. No one has seen him in weeks."

Geoffrey furiously wrote down the information before handing the form and pen over to Jono to sign in the statement's signature line. Jono scrawled his name in the small box.

"What's going to happen to him?" Jono asked.

"Well, since he's an independent with no pack, we'll try to get in touch with his family. If we can't reach them, or if we can and they refuse to claim the body, we'll wait the requisite time period for the god pack to accept the body. Doubtful that they will, so he'll most likely be sent out for cremation and interred in one of the city's burial plots for the unclaimed," Geoffrey said, taking the form back.

"What do you mean it's doubtful the god pack will claim the body?" Sage asked, careful to keep her tone curious instead of accusatory.

Geoffrey shrugged, not paying any attention to them as he finished filling out the rest of the form. "They haven't for years when we get unclaimed werecreatures showing up in the morgue. We've had a few that have come through this summer, and the god pack refused to claim them."

Jono clenched his jaw. Patrick wasn't surprised when he spoke up in defense of the dead.

"If they don't claim Andre, call me," Jono said. "I will."

Geoffrey raised his head and blinked at Jono. "Sure. You want the burial information now or later?"

"Now, please. I can take a look at the paperwork for my client," Sage said.

"It's in a different office. I'm not supposed to leave anyone alone with the body, but if the chief is here, I don't think it should be a problem."

Casale waved him off. "Go. It's fine."

Geoffrey left, giving them a short window of privacy Patrick pounced on. "How many other werecreatures have turned up dead this summer, Casale?"

"Only a couple. I didn't think anything of it because the god pack delivered the bodies. We were told the deceased died during a pack challenge and wouldn't be claimed. It's not considered murder when it's a pack challenge, and the number of dead wasn't egregious," Casale said.

Patrick glanced at Jono, who grimly shook his head. "No way to know for certain without asking Estelle and Youssef. But I haven't heard any rumors about pack challenges going down and those spread like wildfire."

As much as Patrick didn't want to deal with the god pack alphas, that was beginning to look like a task that needed doing. If more than one independent werecreature was missing, they needed to know. Whether or not Estelle and Youssef would come clean about that was a different story entirely.

Geoffrey came back into the workroom and passed the burial information packet to Sage, who tucked it away in her purse.

Casale gestured for them to follow him outside. "Store the body, Geoffrey. Thanks for your help."

The four of them left the workroom for the hallway. Casale led them toward the elevator bank.

"Vampires and werecreatures don't mix, Collins," Casale said.

"I know," Patrick replied. "I'm working on it."

"You say that and it's enough to give me nightmares for a week."

"Not my fault."

"My therapy bill says otherwise. Keep me updated."

Patrick shrugged. "I'll do my best."

The case was his now, and as a federal agent, Patrick was in charge. But he wasn't going to step on Casale's toes unless he absolutely needed to.

Casale took one elevator up, and they took another. Patrick walked Jono and Sage out of the PCB, squinting at the sunlight.

He'd left his sunglasses in the car, but Jono had remembered his own pair to hide his distinctive wolf-bright eyes in public.

"I'll take a taxi back to the office," Sage said, already lifting her arm to flag one down.

"I could drive you," Jono said.

"I need to work. You need to sleep."

"Think we could both do with a bit of a kip." Jono winked at Patrick. "You up for working from home? I sleep better with you around, Pat."

They both slept better with the other around. Whether it was the soulbond or not, Patrick had yet to figure it out.

"I go home with you now, we both aren't getting any work or sleep done," Patrick said.

"What a bloody shame."

A taxi pulled up to the curb and Jono opened the door for Sage, helping her into the back seat. The taxi sped off, taking her with it, and Patrick tilted his head at the adjacent parking garage. "I'll walk you back to the car. You can drive it home."

Jono smiled at him. "Lead on."

They were nearly to the pedestrian entrance to the garage when a spark of recognition burned through Patrick's magic. He rocked to a halt as that familiar warning hit low in his gut.

"Bloody hell," Jono swore under his breath.

Patrick's hand strayed to the handgun holstered to his hip out of habit before he shook that reaction off. Shooting Lucien's partner would start a fight he really didn't want to join.

"You could have called before showing up where I don't want you," Patrick said, raising his voice to be heard over the rumble of cars on the street as they went to meet Carmen halfway. "For that matter, how did you know where to find me?"

"Now where's the fun in telling you all my secrets?" Carmen responded in a sultry voice as she sauntered down the sidewalk.

Carmen smiled widely at them as she approached, her brown eyes narrowed against the sunlight. Her long black curls hung loose down her back, and the diamond necklace she wore sparkled, drawing the eye to her ample cleavage. The white linen, off-the-shoulder jumpsuit she wore left little to the imagination. Her hips swayed from side to side as the punch of sexual energy hit against Patrick's personal shields. The glamour that kept her skin human never flickered, but Patrick's eyes traced the air above her skull where her horns would be anyway.

Carmen was a succubus, and while sex kept her alive, she lived for Lucien. She was his proxy when he wasn't around, and just as annoying as her master.

"I'm busy, Carmen. I don't have time for your games."

"You are never too busy for us." She came to a stop before both of them, her gaze locked on Patrick's face. "Come along, *bastardo*. You know better than to keep my master waiting."

Patrick was mindful of the fact they were still in public and didn't hesitate to conjure up a tiny mageglobe that nestled against his palm, mostly hidden from sight. He cast a silence ward through it, restricting the static to their area only. A bubble of quiet settled over them, his ears ringing from it.

"No, really," Patrick demanded once it was safe to talk. "How did you find me?"

"How's that dead body you found the other night?"

"The fuck do you mean by that? Is Lucien fucking with the werecreature community here?"

"He best not be," Jono said in a flat voice full of leashed anger.

Carmen waved off his words. "We aren't the ones dealing shine."

Patrick snorted. "*This* time. It still doesn't stop you from taking in the addicts."

"When food shows up willing and free on our doorstep, we aren't going to tell it *no*," Carmen said derisively.

Carmen's hand was a blur when she reached for him, but Jono was faster. He grabbed her hand in a way that made it look like they were romantically involved if one ignored the way they both sought to use their strength against the other to break bone.

"You *don't* touch him," Jono bit out, the threat in his voice easy for Patrick to make out.

Carmen smirked. "You might have claimed him, but he owes us. I'm sure you understand the price of a debt."

"I understand Patrick isn't going anywhere with you alone."

Carmen raked her talons over the underside of Jono's wrist as she wrenched her hand free, drawing blood. "We thought as much. Lucien is waiting, Patrick. Now be a good puppet and do as you are told."

"*Fuck* you," Patrick ground out.

"If you like," she practically purred, licking Jono's blood off her fingers. "I doubt your wolf would approve."

Jono looked like he was contemplating murder, and Patrick really didn't need to deal with that fallout. Relieved that he wouldn't be facing Lucien alone, Patrick still resigned himself to preventing what amounted to World War III between Lucien and Jono.

"Where does he want to meet?"

"Ginnungagap."

Patrick made a face. "Fine."

He could've gone the rest of his life without going back to that void masquerading as a warehouse, but Lucien always did like to make things difficult.

"Naheed will drive us," Carmen told him.

"We're not getting into a car with you," Jono retorted. "We'll meet you there."

Jono grabbed Patrick by the arm before he could protest and hauled him back to the pedestrian entrance of the parking garage. He could feel Carmen's attention like knives between his shoulder blades, and he resisted the urge to look over his shoulder. He made a fist, snuffing out the mageglobe, and the silence ward died away. Sound rushed back with a *pop* that made him tug at an earlobe.

One look at Jono's face as they waited for the elevator told Patrick he was *pissed*.

"You don't—" Patrick began but was instantly cut off.

"Don't bloody tell me I don't have to go," Jono growled. "I'm *going*. We're a pack, and like fuck am I letting you face that psychopath alone."

"I've done it before."

The elevator doors pinged open and Jono crowded Patrick into the space. He hit the button for the third floor before settling one hand over Patrick's waist, fingers biting into skin. The other gripped his chin, forcing his head up with a firm push. Patrick stared into Jono's face, barely able to see his wolf-bright eyes through the dark lenses of the sunglasses he wore.

"Stop it," Jono told him in a low voice. "We're in this together, whatever it is this time around. We're a pack. You don't get to sod off and pretend otherwise. I won't let you."

Patrick swallowed in the face of Jono's frustrated anger, not knowing what to say to that. He didn't have an SOA-assigned partner, and learning to keep Jono in the loop about things was still a work in progress.

"Sorry," Patrick finally said.

Jono let out a heavy sigh before brushing his lips against Patrick's in a soft, close-mouthed kiss. "If that fucking bastard touches you, I'll murder him."

"He's already dead."

"Then I'll murder him *twice*."

Patrick wondered what it said about him that Jono promising murder to defend his honor made him want to drop to his knees and suck Jono's cock as a thank-you.

PATRICK WAS unsurprised to discover that Lucien had been busy in the weeks since summer solstice.

The warehouse was fenced off for construction purposes, and while there wasn't any parking on the street, the alleyway between it and the neighboring building worked well enough. A sleek red Aston Martin that Patrick parked behind looked completely out of place.

The otherworldly threshold wrapped around the warehouse felt the same. The side door had been replaced with a heavy oak door lined with runes at the edges. The old brass nameplate hadn't been thrown away, but nailed back into place in the center of the new door. Someone had cleaned off the green patina that had covered the letters naming the place.

Ginnungagap would never be a home, but it was a hole one could hide in, as Lucien was doing now.

Patrick pushed open the heavy door, wincing as the metaphysical threshold came down hard over his soul. His shoulders slumped against the invisible weight of Ginnungagap, and even a quiet, mental promise of *I mean you no harm* wasn't enough to completely appease what lived inside these walls. Some of the pressure on his magic eased, but not all of it. Like last time, the sound of the city was muffled inside, the dead zone Ginnungagap created blocking out most of the world.

Patrick shook his head, taking in the space. Where once it had been full of trash and debris accumulated over years, now all the garbage was gone, walls had been refurbished, and the area had been built out into the skeleton of what would become a club someday soon. Patrick could see it in the private booths being finished, the long bar covered with a dust tarp, and the measured-off space for a dance floor.

"Bit different," Jono said, taking it all in. "Still stinks of the undead."

"Then leave. I didn't ask you to come."

Lucien's voice came from above in the brand-new second level that would probably be used for VIP guests. Patrick thinned out his shields, the familiar spark of recognition one he wished he could forget, but there was no forgetting Lucien.

In the middle of the day, most vampires who weren't Lucien would be in a death coma right now. Vampires didn't sleep, and they didn't rest, but the stasis their undead bodies went into for repair purposes every day meant they needed to be somewhere safe, guarded by those they owned and trusted. Patrick didn't know where Lucien's Night Court went to ground, but he knew they weren't here.

Lucien was the last child Ashanti ever turned, a direct descendent of the mother of all vampires. He could walk in daylight without burning up and dying, a rare gift few of her children had acquired. He was a living reminder of Patrick's mistakes, here only because of a promise Lucien had made to Ashanti. That he'd stayed in New York after summer solstice, putting down roots in an up-and-coming business, told Patrick the master vampire wasn't ready to move on yet. Which, in the long run, wouldn't bode well for anyone.

Really, fuck his life.

"Guess it was too much to hope you'd head back to Europe like Zeus and Hera did," Patrick said once Lucien came into view on the stairs.

Carmen trailed after him, her glamour tossed aside in favor of her true form. The horns that marked her kind curled away from her forehead and back over her skull. The sexual energy she exuded made Patrick hastily solidify his shields. He didn't want to be lust-addled when dealing with Lucien.

Behind Carmen walked a human servant Patrick was familiar with. Naheed was thin and tanned, showing off a lot of skin in her cutoff shorts and tank top. The Afghani woman hadn't been a practicing Muslim since Lucien spirited her away from her remote village in Afghanistan when she was a toddler.

While no longer religious, Naheed belonged to Lucien and guarded Carmen during daylight hours. The necklace of scars around her neck from vampire fangs showed her as a willing human servant. For all her delicate appearance, Lucien wasn't one to keep those who wouldn't or couldn't fight. Lucien only took in the best the preternatural and mundane worlds had to offer into his Night Court, which was a nice way of saying he only accepted those with sociopathic, psychotic tendencies.

The Browning holstered on Naheed's hip wasn't just for show. Naheed, Patrick knew from personal experience, was an excellent shot.

Patrick eyed Lucien as the vampire approached, taking in his black jeans and white T-shirt, and the combat boots that had seen better days. Messy dark brown hair was styled away from black eyes full of the same hate he'd carried even before Ashanti had died. Lucien dressed like a punk and acted like a bastard. That would never change.

It was the promised violence in Lucien's expression that probably had Jono stepping in front of Patrick. That didn't stop Lucien from getting in his face.

"My business is with Patrick, not you," Lucien said, lips curling to reveal the jagged mess of fangs in his mouth.

"You'll do business with both of us," Jono snapped.

"Is that so?"

Patrick stepped forward to stand by Jono. "Jono isn't promising you anything, Lucien. I'm here. What do you want?"

Carmen stood off to Lucien's right, observing them, while Naheed wandered away to poke around the construction tools left in the work area. Patrick wondered if Lucien had sent the construction workers on a break or told everyone not to come to work today in order to have this meeting.

"I want New York City," Lucien said, finally looking away from Jono to pin Patrick with a hard glare. "And you're going to help me get it."

Patrick grimaced, not really surprised at the demand. Territory in any major metropolitan city came at a price. Lucien's Night

Court never stayed in one place for longer than a decade or two, if that, before moving on. Most vampires tended to claim territory for centuries, tied to the history of the cities they called home.

Lucien was like his mother—a wanderer.

While he didn't have a city to lay claim to like other vampires, Lucien had built an empire based on black-market arms dealing, drugs, and illegal magic across dozens of countries. What Lucien lacked in territory he more than made up for in money and power. Patrick doubted he was willing to give all that up without a damn good reason.

"Why now?" he asked.

Lucien smirked, though it didn't reach his eyes. "Why not?"

"Bullshit. You don't do anything without a reason, Lucien."

"There are five Night Courts here, one for each borough," Jono pointed out. "What do you expect us to do? Carve up a new one for you? Why not just take Jersey?"

"Don't be ridiculous," Carmen said with a disdainful sniff. "It's *Jersey.*"

Half a summer spent living in here and Patrick was well aware of the visceral disdain the city had for New Jersey, and vice versa. Rivalries aside, he still wasn't getting any answers.

"You want territory? Buy a fucking skyscraper. Stake your claim here in Ginnungagap for all I care. You don't need my help to gain territory. You never have," Patrick said.

Lucien moved before Patrick was even aware of the vampire coming at him, that preternatural speed impossible for the human eye to track. Patrick was shoved back hard enough by Jono he almost fell, and only just managed to keep his footing. He jerked his head up at the loud snarl that ripped through the air, staring in disbelief at where Jono had Lucien by the throat and the vampire had a 9mm Sig Saur shoved against Jono's chest, right over his heart.

"Don't you fucking dare pull that trigger," Patrick growled.

He could see Jono's fingers had shifted, claws digging into

Lucien's pale skin deep enough to make him bleed thick, fat drops of sluggish red-black blood. Lucien didn't seem to care, since his other hand was busy trying to shove a knife through Jono's wrist, the gun never wavering.

"You don't get it, wolf," Lucien said. "Patrick owes the gods, but he owes me as well."

"The way I hear it, *you* owe *him*," Jono said in a low, vicious voice. "Something about a promise, yeah? Don't fucking murder him, right? Isn't that what you promised Ashanti?"

"Keep my mother's name out of your mouth, or it will be the last name you *ever* speak."

"Patrick doesn't owe you anything. You can fuck right off with your demands."

"Jono, let him go," Patrick ordered. "*Both* of you cut this shit out."

Lucien's eyes slid his way, dismissing the threat Jono presented in the way only a nearly thousand-year-old master vampire could. "I'm going to take over the Manhattan Night Court, and you're going to help me."

If he didn't have a dead werecreature lying in the morgue, probably killed by vampires, Patrick would've told Lucien to go fuck himself. Instead, he swallowed his misgivings and ran full tilt into another bargain he knew would ruin his life.

"Yeah. Fine. I'll do it just to fucking spite you. Now back the hell off, Lucien."

Lucien thumbed the safety on his gun and raised an eyebrow expectantly at Jono. It was a tense few seconds before they both removed their hands from each other in a quick motion. They each took several steps back, blood spattering on the floor from the claw marks in Lucien's throat and the rapidly closing cut in Jono's right wrist.

"What the ever bloody fuck?" Jono demanded, stalking over to Patrick. "You don't need to help this arsehole."

"His word is binding, and it has been witnessed," Lucien said, the smirk on his face telling Patrick this was exactly what he'd wanted to happen.

"For this territory fight *only*," Patrick stressed. "That's what you asked for, and that's all you're getting."

The weight in his soul got heavier, Ginnungagap's presence all around them making it impossible to breathe for a second or two. Then it was gone, but the promise he'd given voice to remained a bitter, living thing he would have to see through to the end.

"You," Jono said, leaning down to growl the words directly into Patrick's ear, "are utter *shit* at taking care of yourself."

"You're fine, Jono. You didn't promise anything."

"We're a fucking pack, Patrick. What you promise commits *both* of us. So yeah, mate. It's my problem now, too."

"Not for this. You are not tied to this."

He spoke the words like a promise, refusing to drag Jono into this mess through an oath that couldn't be broken. One of them needed to be free and clear. Patrick turned his head to the side, unable to meet Jono's gaze, hating that he'd put them both in this position. As with everything else in his life when the shit hit the fan, Patrick barreled forward because he had to.

"Why the Manhattan Night Court, Lucien? Why not any of the others?" he asked.

"Because it is led by a rat who should know better than to bite the hand that fed it for three hundred years," Lucien said scornfully.

It took Patrick a couple of seconds to work through what Lucien meant. When he understood the implications, he wished he hadn't promised a damn thing. Only one of the master vampires who called the five boroughs home was old enough for that age to fit.

"You're going after Tremaine."

The master vampire who had laid claim to New York City before it even *was* a city. A vampire who had apparently been born by Lucien's fangs and blood, two degrees removed from Ashanti.

One who had left Lucien who knew when and how, because Patrick knew the only way to leave Lucien's Night Court was to die a true death.

Patrick wondered what had happened to make Tremaine run, and why Lucien had let that leash stretch out for so long.

"Tremaine knows we are here and that we are not leaving. He allied himself with the Omacatl Cartel years ago and is seeking to point the police away from that cartel's drug dealing and get them to focus on our businesses, both legal and not," Carmen said.

"Are they the ones dealing shine?" Jono asked angrily.

"Yes, along with other drugs. Not to mention a thriving human-trafficking and prostitution ring."

"So you're what? Going for a hostile takeover? Kill off the bastard and claim everything he owns?"

Lucien pulled out a lighter and a crumpled pack of cigarettes from his back pocket. He lit one up, the smell of nicotine making Patrick's nose twitch. "I have no interest in keeping what businesses Tremaine thinks he owns. My Anahuac Cartel will fill the void Tremaine's death will create."

"Going the scorched-earth route, I take it? Mundane humans don't like it when the preternatural world has turf wars on their doorstep," Patrick said.

"Then you better hope the fighting never leaves the tunnels." Lucien blew smoke at Patrick, the cloud making him crave a cigarette. "There is a meeting between the five master vampires tomorrow night at Tremaine's Crimson Diamond club. They didn't invite me. We will be rectifying that oversight."

Before Patrick could answer, the threshold wrapped around Ginnungagap heaved in warning, making his stomach swoop in an uncomfortable way. Lucien moved before Patrick could get his bearings, becoming a streak of motion he was hard-pressed to track.

Naheed spun around, gun now in hand and aimed at the side entrance to the alleyway. Carmen stayed where she was to act as backup if needed. Patrick swore and ran after Lucien, his ears ringing from the sound of the door slamming open. He conjured up a mageglobe, filling it with a barrage spell as Jono took point, exiting Ginnungagap seconds before Patrick.

Jono skidded to a stop once outside and Patrick nearly ran into him. Magic burning between his fingers, Patrick got eyes on their vehicles and swore.

"Motherfucking *shit*," he said, taking in the claw marks that now adorned both cars.

No normal animal could shred metal. Paint, yes, but whatever creature had raked their claws over doors, hoods, and trunks had ripped into the body of the cars themselves, cutting through Patrick's defensive wards without him sensing it. Metal was butterflied open, the paint peeled around the damage. Sitting on top of each car was a tiny Santa Muerte idol, the white figurines spattered in red.

Patrick really hoped the red color was paint, but he knew he was never that lucky.

In the sunlight, Lucien looked washed-out and strange, pale skin starting to flush from heat that didn't burn him as he circled the Aston Martin and the Mustang, black eyes memorizing the damage. Patrick shifted the magic in his mageglobe, silently recasting it into a look-away ward. He lobbed the mageglobe toward the mouth of the alley to keep any curious bystanders at bay.

"Smells like immortals," Jono said, nostrils flaring.

Patrick stared at the Santa Muerte idol sitting on top of his car and wished he could burn it. Fire could cleanse almost anything, but it couldn't cleanse the debts he owed.

Lucien circled back around and came to a stop in front of Patrick, his black eyes boring into Patrick's green. "You have death hunting you."

"Yeah," Patrick said, stomach twisting. "That's nothing new."

Seriously, fuck his life.

5

Jono wanted to slam open their apartment door but knew if he did so, the knob would go through the wall and there was a very real chance the door might come off its hinges. Still, he thought about it.

"You're in a mood," Patrick said from right behind him.

"Yeah, mate. I'm in a fucking mood," Jono snapped as he stalked into the kitchen.

The front door shut with a quiet click. While he couldn't feel the threshold snap into place, Jono could sense the aftereffects of it sealing the apartment. The hint of electric ozone that had lingered on the Mustang during the drive home and on themselves abruptly faded away.

Jono shook his head as he opened up the refrigerator and took out a bottle of stout. He popped the screw cap off with ease and tossed the bent bit of metal in the bin. He took a long drink of the Guinness, swallowing half the beer, careful to not break the bottle.

Patrick followed him into the kitchen, incapable of running away from a fight or an argument. That stubbornness was what drew Jono to the other man, amongst other traits, but sometimes he wished Patrick would *think* before acting.

"I owed him," Patrick said after a moment. "You don't."

Jono slammed the beer bottle down on the counter hard enough to crack it. Jono had to force his fingers off it rather than drive them through the glass.

"You owe *enough.*"

Patrick's expressive mouth thinned out, eyes narrowing, despite the shadow of bruises still lingering on the delicate skin in that area. "This isn't your problem. Lucien isn't—"

"Did I not," Jono interrupted icily, trying to choke back his anger and absolutely failing, "tell you earlier we're a fucking *pack?*"

"Yeah, I get that."

"No, I don't think you bloody do!"

"I didn't want you to owe Lucien anything, Jono. How is that a bad thing?"

"The only thing I'll ever owe that blood-sucking bastard is an early grave. His, specifically."

Patrick rolled his eyes. "That attitude is exactly why I didn't want you making any deals with him."

"You're being a right fucking arsehole about this, you know that?"

"Congratulations," Patrick bit out. "You've met me."

Jono threw his arms into the air. "You didn't even fight his demands. You just accepted without asking, without making better terms. I *know* you, Pat. I know the word games you play, and you didn't bother playing them with Lucien."

"Because I *owe* him."

"Why?" Jono took a step forward. "What do you think you did to merit being at Lucien's mercy for even a second?"

"I killed his mother."

The words dropped between them like an anvil, heavy and bitter and full of a self-loathing Jono was all too familiar with when it came to Patrick. Jono stared at him, seeing the way his hands were clenched into fists and the way he was holding his breath, air locked in his lungs.

"Come again?" Jono said, his anger dying beneath the twist of old *grief* he could smell coming off Patrick.

Patrick refused to look Jono in the eye. "Ashanti is dead. She's dead because of *me*, Jono."

"Why?"

"She was the mother of all vampires and a goddess in her own right. Ashanti was the immortal who delivered the dagger to me at the end of the Thirty-Day War, but it brought her within the bounds of Ethan's sacrificial spell. She died because of it, and I couldn't save her. I know there's no comfort to be found in missing the dead, only damaged judgment, but that doesn't change the fact it's my fault she's gone."

Jono could smell the truth in his words, but that still didn't explain why it smelled like Patrick was in mourning over a *vampire*. Shaking his head, Jono closed the distance between them and curled a hand over Patrick's chin, tipping his head up. Patrick reluctantly met his gaze, a grimace tugging at his mouth.

"You don't mourn the monsters of the world," Jono said quietly. "What was she to you?"

He thought Patrick would lie to him, maybe ignore the question and shift the conversation to something less personal. Jono had stumbled into more than one of Patrick's walls since moving in together, and he'd respected the memories that built them. But Jono couldn't do that here, not when Patrick's familiarity of working alone had fucked them both over in a way Jono refused to accept.

"A teacher," Patrick finally said, lips barely moving, but Jono heard him anyway.

The riot of emotions Jono got half a lungful of before Patrick locked his personal shields down tight made his fingers loosen on Patrick's chin. Jono let his anger die away completely, unwilling to hold on to it in the face of Patrick's old trauma.

"She must've been brilliant," Jono said, not quite believing he was singing a vampire's praises.

Patrick stepped back, out of reach. "The best. And it's my fault she no longer walks the world. That's why I promised Lucien my help. Ashanti would still be alive if it weren't for me and my family."

Jono sighed. "Should've rung Sage and told her to skip that meeting and do the bargaining for you."

"I can bargain just fine." Jono could not believe those words had come out of Patrick's mouth and stared at him. Patrick rolled his eyes. "Don't give me that look."

"I'm trying to decide if I've ever met a bloke as thick as you when it comes to asking for help."

"Jono—"

"No, hear me out. I'm still bloody pissed you made that deal. You didn't ask me what I thought and I was standing *right there*. That's not how pack works, and if we want to make it work, you need to stop acting like you're in this alone. Because you aren't. Not anymore."

Patrick's jaw worked for a moment before he took a deep breath and let it out on a heavy exhale. "I'm not used to having a partner."

Jono reached out and grabbed Patrick's hand, giving it a gentle squeeze. "I know. I'm not asking you to change your habits with all your cases, just the ones that involve me."

Before Patrick could answer, Jono's mobile rang, the *Psycho* ring tone echoing from his back pocket. He fished it out, scowling down at Youssef's name on the screen.

"Ignore it?"

"They'll just keep ringing." Jono swiped his thumb over the green icon to answer. "Yeah?"

"We need to discuss you overstepping your place, Jonothon," Youssef said coldly. "The morgue informed us you signed off on the body when we called to schedule a viewing appointment. You had no right to work with the PCB."

Jono kept his heartbeat steady from long practice, making sure no one on the other side of the line could get a read on him. "Is that so?"

"You are to submit yourself to our authority immediately. Any delay would not be advisable. You know where to find us."

Youssef ended the call, and Jono pulled his mobile away from his ear with a scowl. "The god pack alphas want to see me."

"About what?" Patrick asked.

"Andre. Seems they called the morgue and got told their services were no longer needed."

Patrick frowned, eyes narrowing thoughtfully. "If they think they can threaten you about the case, I should be there to tell them to mind their own fucking business."

"Doubt they'd agree to let you through the door."

"I have a badge for a reason. Let's go."

While it was like pulling teeth to get Patrick to acknowledge they were a pack in a crisis and not go off on his own, he apparently had no problem remembering in order to piss off the god pack. Jono would be annoyed about that later, after they'd dealt with the current problem. At the moment, he was glad for the solidarity.

Back out the flat they went, returning to the car, the damage from unknown claw marks hidden from sight by Patrick's magic. Jono got behind the wheel since he knew where the god pack lived and Patrick didn't. The drive there was filled with leftover tension from their argument. Jono didn't know how to break it before they got within hearing range of the god pack's territory in the Upper Manhattan neighborhood of Hamilton Heights.

Jono hadn't been back this way since after the mess in Central Park, when the god pack had demanded answers from him while Patrick was in DC, packing up his life there. Jono hadn't been forthcoming at all at the time; neither Estelle nor Youssef had appreciated his silence.

"Looks almost like suburbia," Patrick said as Jono drove down a street filled on either side with spacious apartment buildings or brownstones. "Do they enjoy their perfect credit scores out here?"

Jono snorted. "God packs have shit credit. Why do you think they live off tithes?"

"So no white picket fence, is what you're saying?"

"No."

Jono circled a block with a familiar stretch of brownstones and spent five minutes looking for a parking spot until Patrick reminded him about the government plates. He parked in the red zone in front of a fire hydrant and locked the door when they got out.

"They own the homes on this block," Jono said as they walked up the street. "House deeds are passed down through the pack alphas. It's the same way it's done in London. Most people won't rent to god pack werecreatures, so god packs had to carve out their own territory in legal ways."

"Let's go say hello," Patrick said.

The muggy midday heat beat down on their shoulders as Jono led the way to the brownstone Estelle and Youssef called home. In the center of the block, the outside façade was indistinguishable from its neighbors, but the brownstone wasn't a home. What mundane humans couldn't scent was the dread that seemed to permeate the area, carried there by the packs who came looking for help and only left with despair.

Patrick side-eyed him as they approached the stoop. "You're showing teeth."

Jono didn't bother to acknowledge that statement, just let his teeth shift against bone, the sharp fangs pricking at the inside of his cheeks. He didn't care for how Estelle and Youssef led their god pack. Neither did he appreciate their lack of focus on the packs whose privacy they were supposed to oversee and protect.

But what he'd told Emma was true—he couldn't fight the god pack alone. Emma could say she wanted to follow him all she liked, but Jono knew it wasn't the right time for a challenge.

Fenrir would let him know when it was time to go to war.

Jono and Patrick climbed the steps together, reaching the porch right as the front door opened. Jono eyed the man standing in their way, refusing to show his throat. Nicholas Kavanaugh, the god pack's dire, was several centimeters shorter than Jono and carried maybe a stone less of muscle than him. What Nicholas lacked in height and weight, he more than made up for in the underhanded ways he enforced pack law on behalf of Estelle and Youssef.

Nicholas was one bloke Jono wouldn't mind seeing out of a job and buried in some out of the way unmarked grave.

"The alphas requested to speak with you alone, Jonothon," Nicholas said, glaring at Patrick.

"Yeah, I heard." Patrick crossed his arms over his chest. "About a case they definitely have no jurisdiction over. I'm just here to remind them who has a badge and who doesn't. So you can either let us in or tell them to get their asses down here."

"You aren't welcome."

Patrick didn't move in the face of a threshold denying him entrance, staying on the porch situated in the outside world. "Then call your masters so we can get this over with."

"They asked for Jonothon." Nicholas shoved the door all the way open and stepped aside just enough to make room for one other person to walk by. "So he can get inside."

"Nah, mate," Jono drawled. "You heard Patrick. It's his case."

"And the deceased was a werecreature you had no right to claim," Estelle said as she stepped into view with Youssef by her side.

Unlike Jono, Estelle was a born god pack werewolf who refused to hide. Her bright amber wolf eyes were set in a heart-shaped face, wavy brown hair twisted up off her neck and shoulders. At thirty-five, she'd been leading the New York City god pack for six years—piss poorly, if Jono was ever asked.

Youssef was her husband of five years, and while he wasn't a born god pack werewolf, he shared his wife's ruthless way of laying down pack law. At forty years old, Youssef had become accustomed to a sense of deference from the packs under his control. Jono didn't bother showing his throat in greeting to either of them. He never had, not even when Marek had first brought him to New York City.

Jono was allowed to stay in New York City by dint of godly interference under the guise of a promise so long as he didn't form a pack with anyone under their protection. He'd broken that promise in a way, but no one needed to know that just yet.

Patrick rolled his eyes. "It's not your case. Quit acting like it is."

"You had no right to ask Jonothon to identify the dead," Youssef said.

"You weren't doing your job," Patrick shot back derisively. "I don't have that luxury."

"How *dare* you," Estelle growled.

She took a step forward, her hand a blur of motion as she crossed the threshold to reach for Patrick. Jono lashed out without thinking, grabbing Estelle by the wrist and shoving her backward. She didn't seem prepared, which was surprising, and stumbled back into Nicholas' waiting arms with a snarl. Youssef looked just as pissed, his bright amber eyes locked on Patrick.

"Don't touch him," Jono said in a low, vicious voice that was more growl than English syllables.

"That indiscretion could be taken as a challenge," Youssef said, his voice colder than the nights got in August these days.

"That wasn't a fucking challenge, and you know it. He just saved your ass from an assault charge," Patrick snapped.

"The identification of werecreatures has always fallen to the god pack. You didn't follow protocol, Patrick," Estelle said, shaking off Nicholas' support in order to stand up straight again.

"That's Special Agent Collins to all of you. We aren't on a first-name basis, so fucking remember that."

"You couldn't be bothered to identify the dead, so the SOA came to me," Jono said, staring at Youssef without blinking. "Patrick asked me to identify the bloke, so I did."

"That's not your right," Youssef spat out.

"It should be yours, but you lot didn't seem arsed to do your job at the time."

"You think just because you have an SOA mage backing you that we'll ignore your act of rebellion?" Estelle demanded as she crossed the threshold once more, this time going toe-to-toe with Jono instead of Patrick. He could smell her anger, thicker than the heat bearing down on them. "You agreed to a set of rules in order to stay here, and those rules are *binding*. You break them, you can leave New York City for good."

Patrick shook his head. "Jono isn't going anywhere. You even *try* to kick him out of this city and I'll open up a federal investigation into your pack's management of the people under your care. All those tithes you collect? Won't be worth jack shit in the face of the United States government and its deep pockets."

Estelle ignored Patrick and refused to look away from Jono's eyes. "You made a promise, Jonothon. You better abide by it."

Jono's mouth curled, fangs cutting into his lips. "I promised not to make a pack with anyone under your protection within your territory. I haven't done that, Estelle. You, on the other hand, took an oath to protect the packs who tithe to you and those who cross through your territory searching for safe passage. Ignoring a dead independent werecreature with vampire markings on his body isn't doing your fucking job, is it?"

It was the truth, in the literal sense of the word, because Patrick wasn't under the god pack's protection. While Jono knew they wouldn't be able to smell anything but the truth on him, what he got off Nicholas, of all people, was a single, barely skipped heartbeat that had Jono breaking eye contact with Estelle to zero in on their dire.

Dires were essential to a god pack. They enforced their alphas' orders, the traditional role held by their most loyal pack member. Dires would steal, fight, and die for the god pack alphas they served. In Jono's experience, Nicholas was no different.

Except he was a shit liar when it mattered, because that little tell echoed loudly in Jono's ears.

"Independents come and go. They tithe to us on an as needed basis," Estelle said.

"They still show their throats to you, asking for rights to enter your territory. They still ask for protection when it matters," Jono replied, never taking his eyes off Nicholas. "I never did."

"Is that a *threat?*" Youssef asked in a low, harsh voice.

Jono shrugged, rocking back on his heels in a bored way that would never come across as backing down. He forced his teeth back to human shape, swallowing the tang of blood that had bloomed across his tongue. "It's a fact, Youssef. Best remember that."

A tiny, pale blue mageglobe formed between Jono and Estelle, forcing her to take a step back. Patrick's magic didn't cross the threshold. That didn't stop everyone but Jono from eyeing it warily.

"Leave Jono alone about this, and stay out of my fucking cases," Patrick ordered them.

"Having a federal mage on your side won't save your position here," Estelle warned, her mouth curling up in an expression Jono had seen in the past, right before she tore out a werecreature's throat.

Jono smiled, feeling Fenrir waking up deep in his soul, the immortal's growl thrumming through his mind where no one else could hear. "I'm not the one who needs saving, love."

It wasn't a challenge, not in any official capacity, but the underlying threat was there, and Jono refused to take it back. Let Estelle and Youssef and their god pack snarl about the promise they thought he was breaking; he'd throw their own mistakes back in their faces.

Jono wasn't the one turning his back on the werecreatures who needed help.

Patrick drew down his magic, the mageglobe disappearing in a soft spray of sparks. Jono turned his back on the god pack alphas, a deliberate show of disrespect that made Youssef growl. Jono made it to the sidewalk before Patrick even bothered to leave the porch, casually taking the steps one at a time on the way down.

They walked back to the car, the silence between them one of necessity since who knew how many ears and eyes were attuned to their position.

It was when they turned the corner that Jono's instincts reared up with a vengeance. Patrick went still behind him, reaching for his dagger rather than calling forth his magic. The electric scent of ozone after a lightning strike filled the air around them, thicker than the last time they'd been in this situation.

"Gods fucking damn it," Patrick snarled as he stalked toward the Mustang.

Jono followed after Patrick and drew in a lungful of air that tasted like lightning on his tongue, reminding him of the beach in the Hamptons when Patrick had faced off against Hades. The electric scent of a god overrode the smell of the dog piss, garbage, and exhaust that permeated every Manhattan street Jono had ever walked down.

Patrick yanked open the car door, glaring at the black Santa Muerte figurine lying on the passenger side seat. "Not a fucking word, Jono."

All the questions swirling through his mind remained on the tip of his tongue for later. Jono watched Patrick encase the figurine in his magic to contain it.

Something moved out of the corner of his eye and Jono jerked his head around. The only things in the street were cars, but he thought—just for a moment—he saw the flash of a four-legged animal in the rearview mirror of a passing car. Jono took in the street, seeing no werecreatures in their shifted form prowling the area. Nothing seemed out of place, except something had gotten through Patrick's wards *again* without either of them noticing.

"Come on, let's go," Patrick said, dropping down into the passenger seat. He still held the Santa Muerte figurine in one hand, magic flickering at his fingertips to keep whatever was buried in it contained.

Jono wanted to chuck it out of the car into the gutter where it belonged.

"Where to?" Jono asked as he walked around to get in the driver's seat. He couldn't shake the feeling that someone was watching them.

"PCB. I need to stop by the evidence lockup."

Jono started the engine and pulled into the street. Only when they were far enough out of the god pack's territory, where too-interested ears couldn't hear him, did he speak. "Overall, that could've gone better."

Patrick snorted. "Which part? The nice little chat we had or the gifts some asshole keeps leaving us?"

"Both."

"Next time, you should just rip out their throats."

Jono rolled his eyes. "I'm not challenging them."

"Yet," Patrick said succinctly.

Jono thought about arguing, but he hadn't approved of the way Estelle and Youssef governed the werecreature community for years. Emma's quiet, pointed words about her preference of a leader had ratcheted up in the past couple of weeks, and this new case Patrick was handling was making Jono question his reasons to abide by a promise that only hobbled him.

Jono braked for the amber light and leaned across the console to kiss Patrick. "Let's keep that between us, yeah?"

"You know me," Patrick muttered, chasing after Jono's mouth when he tried to pull away. "I'm all about secrets."

"Wish you weren't," Jono said, stealing one more kiss before the light turned green to shut him up.

He didn't want to hear what Patrick would say to that; didn't want to smell the lies Patrick still couldn't give up.

Some things, Jono knew, you just had to live with.

6

"I'M REALLY NOT HAPPY ABOUT THIS," EMMA SAID OVER THE MOBILE.

Jono dodged around a group of women wearing club dresses for a Saturday night out on the town, ignoring the interested glances thrown his way. Aside from them not being his type, he doubted they'd be at all interested if he took off his sunglasses and revealed his eyes.

"Not your place to decide, Em. Just keep everyone home tonight or working full shifts at the bar in case anything goes wrong. Alibis are good, yeah? I don't want the god pack to accuse you of breaking any rules."

Neither of them were supposed to be anywhere close to vampire territory in this manner. Passing through was fine—that was the only way to live in a major metropolitan city—but Jono didn't want Emma to suffer the consequences of breaking a treaty when it was all on Jono.

"Everyone is where they should be except for Sage. Her mediation was today and it's running late, but she's with a senior partner of her firm. Estelle and Youssef won't argue with the fae over her whereabouts."

Jono snorted, ignoring the sounds of taxis honking to his left on Broadway. "Because they'd lose."

"We're safe," Emma told him. "You're the one in the crossfire."

Jono kept his eyes on Patrick, watching as the mage sidestepped a couple of posh-looking blokes as they continued down the street. "I'll be fine. We both will."

"Keep an eye on Patrick. Don't let him do anything stupid."

"Ask for a miracle, why don't you."

Emma laughed in his ear, but there was little humor in her voice. "Call me when it's over."

"Can do. Ta, love."

Jono ended the call and pocketed his mobile, lengthening his stride to catch up with Patrick. Despite the muggy heat that lingered over the city an hour past sunset, Patrick had a baseball cap on to cover his distinctive dark ginger hair, and he wore his leather jacket with the defensive charms set into the material.

"Everyone good?" Patrick asked.

Jono nodded. "Yeah."

"Carmen texted. ETA five minutes."

"Brilliant."

Honestly, Jono could've thought up a dozen better ways to spend a Saturday night in SoHo than invading a master vampire's territory. But he hadn't been asked, so here they were.

The Crimson Diamond was one of those swanky luxury clubs Jono used to always feel out of place in as a young lad back in London. Located in an old industrial, cast-iron building, with an interior converted into something more modern, the Crimson Diamond could hold its own against all that the rest of Manhattan's clubs had to offer. The windows had been sealed shut and darkened over time. Jono couldn't see any signage save for red neon bent in the shape of a diamond above a single door.

A lone doorman stood outside in a dark suit, but there was no velvet rope to showcase the popularity of the club. No one loitered outside because the Crimson Diamond was an invite-only sort of place, where membership and the perks that came with it was tiered, but even the lowest level cost several hundred thousand dollars. No one could just walk in off the street and expect to be granted entrance—but that was exactly what they were going to do.

Patrick came to a stop a meter away from the entrance and ignored the doorman in favor of his mobile. Jono eyed the bruiser standing watch, discreetly taking in his scent with a quiet sniff. Human, but there was an underlying chemical note to the man's scent that made Jono almost gag. When the man turned his head away after a long minute of staring, Jono's keen eyesight caught a glimpse of the jagged scars half-hidden by the suit's collar.

Bite marks.

Jono ran his tongue over the back of his teeth, tilting his head toward the building. He couldn't hear a bloody thing coming through those walls, just a silence that spoke of secrets wanting to be kept. No one spent loads of money on a high-level silence ward without reason.

"Thirty seconds," Patrick finally said, putting away his mobile.

Jono counted down the time in his head, and right when he hit zero, a black Escalade turned left at the corner of Grand Street. It braked to a stop in front of the club, two of the four doors opening before the wheels even stopped moving. Jono arched an eyebrow behind his sunglasses at the vampires and their chosen outfits.

He'd figured Lucien would've gone for the toff look, all designer suit and expensive accessories. Instead, the master vampire had opted for his usual attire of black jeans, studded motorcycle boots this time around, and a gray T-shirt beneath a battered leather jacket. The cigarette clamped between his lips was half-burned, the smell of nicotine making Jono's lip curl.

Einar got out of the front passenger side, the tall, blond vampire dressed as casually as his master. Both vampires were that washed-out pale of the undead one couldn't help but notice. Einar moved off to the side as Lucien helped Carmen out of the car. Feet clad in a pair of red stilettos slid into view; Jono winced at their absurd height.

The vibrant, red leather corset dress she wore barely covered her bum, the strapless sweetheart neckline molded to her breasts. A choker of diamonds and rubies fit snug around her throat, matching the earrings she wore. The small fortune was easy to see since her thick, curly black hair was tied back in a fishtail braid that cascaded down her back. Carmen looked human, and Jono wondered how long she would carry her glamour before shedding it.

Patrick cocked his head to the side, gaze raking up and down her body. "That's an interesting place to hide a knife."

Carmen smirked at him as she curved her hand around Lucien's elbow. "Surprisingly comfortable."

"If you say so."

Lucien stared at Patrick with those eerie black eyes that Jono fantasized about clawing out of his skull. "Keep your promise and don't fuck this up."

Patrick gave him a one fingered salute. "Just get us inside so you can kill him."

"There's no fun in killing unless you make it hurt first. The rat won't die tonight."

The doorman, realizing their intent, took a step forward. "This is a private club—"

Einar had him pinned against the door before Jono finished blinking, the vampire easily holding the man off the ground by his neck.

"Open the door," Einar growled.

The doorman didn't answer, too busy trying to breathe around Einar's strong fingers. The frantic kicks the vampire received didn't seem to bother him.

"No murder where people can see," Patrick snapped.

Lucien didn't seem to care about bloodshed, but Jono was all for a bit of finesse if it got them inside without anyone ringing the police.

"Is the door warded?" Jono asked as he headed for it.

Patrick's eyes cut his way before focusing on the entrance, gaze going distant as he looked for something only he could see. "Yes. Check the guy's pocket for a key. Undoing the wards will take more time than we have available."

Einar had choked the poor bloke into near unconsciousness in less than a minute, so it was easy to pat him down and find the key. Einar tossed it to Jono, the key larger than modern ones, heavy with the weight of iron. It seemed normal enough until he slid it into the lock. The ward flared up over the key itself, magic spreading into the lock and door handle. The tumblers clicked loudly in Jono's ears as the door unlocked.

Einar dropped the doorman to the ground as Jono pushed open the door. Jono took off his sunglasses and hooked them over the collar of his button-down. Sound popped back into his ears as he crossed the threshold with Patrick on his heels.

The reception area floor was made of black and gold marble, with a small mahogany hostess stand perched in front of a floor-to-ceiling backdrop wall made out of fresh flowers charmed to always bloom. In the center of the flowers, above the hostesses' heads, was a red neon sign: *No Holy Items.*

Patrick snorted. "Very hipster."

The sweet floral scent wasn't enough to overpower the under-lying smell of blood and chemicals. Jono's nose twitched as he and Patrick moved to the side, ignoring the hostesses who didn't seem pleased by their arrival.

He couldn't really ignore the two male vampires standing guard on either side of the door they'd just stepped through.

"This is a *private* club," the blonde hostess said. "You need to leave."

Jono put himself between Patrick and the vampire guard who moved to touch what he really shouldn't. He slammed one hand against the vampire's chest and *shoved*, putting all his strength behind the hit. Bone crunched beneath his hand as the vampire was thrown backward into the far wall. He hit with enough force to dent it before sliding down to the floor.

The vampire didn't get up. Since his heart didn't beat, Jono couldn't tell if he was unconscious or truly dead.

"You know I could've stopped him, right?" Patrick said, raising a hand and wiggling his fingers. Pale blue sparks danced around his fingertips as a pointed reminder of his magic.

Jono shrugged. "Best be quicker next time. Point goes to me."

Patrick arched an eyebrow. "So we're keeping score now? Are we rating by bodily harm or murder?"

Jono had killed his fair share of vampires back in London during territory fights but hadn't crossed a single line here in the States. He had a feeling tonight was about to change that.

"The rat has poor taste," Carmen said with a sniff. "Inferior children and terrible decorating ideas."

"He never did learn," Lucien replied.

Jono glanced over his shoulder and watched as Carmen turned her head away from the vampire Einar had taken care of with brutal efficiency. The vampire was missing the front of its throat, and Einar's left hand was bloody, with bits of flesh sticking to his fingers that he casually shook off.

"Guess we're going by murder," Patrick muttered, a small mageglobe now nestled in the palm of his left hand.

Jono watched as Carmen's glamour sloughed off like water, her true form slipping into reality. The twisted horns of her kind spiraled away from her forehead and curved back over her skull. Brown eyes with the dark red pupils that marked her as a succubus took in the club. Desire rolled off her in waves that Jono could smell, but which didn't have any effect on him. He'd never quite figured out if it was his strain of the werevirus or his patron that enabled him to withstand manipulation like this.

Patrick grimaced, and between one breath and the next, Jono

lost his scent as he tightened down his personal shields. Jono looked worriedly at him, and Patrick shrugged.

"I don't want to fight with a hard-on," he muttered.

Jono snorted. "Would rather we weren't here fighting at all."

Lucien slung his arm over Carmen's shoulders and veered to the left, the hostesses no longer interested in keeping them out. Arousal thickened the air around them, focus turned toward carnal wants rather than what their employer dictated they do. Succubi were distracting that way.

On either side of the floral wall, the marble floor turned into several steps that met dark red, wall-to-wall carpeting on the main floor. Lucien and Carmen led the way, with Einar prowling behind them. Jono and Patrick took up the rear, and he let his eyes wander over the crowd in the club.

The building had been hollowed out for at least three floors, with a short mezzanine one might find in a theater jutting out from the rear of the building. Crystal chandeliers hung from the ceiling, but Jono easily picked out more modern light fixtures tucked away in hidden recesses. The walls were made of wood panels interspersed with iron molding instead of wood, the better to anchor wards and spells with. Jono tracked the iron over every wall, noting how it all disappeared into the next floor when it didn't twist over the ceiling edges.

As cages went, the Crimson Diamond was a good one.

Men and women dressed in expensive suits and dresses mingled in small groups around tall glass bar tables or lounged on chaises. Not everyone was human, but those that were either worked at the club as human servants in the literal sense, or were there as showpieces. The showpieces, as far as Jono could tell, were food, and high out of their minds on shine.

When they weren't sprawled across the laps of the wealthy or cradled in their arms, shine-addicted humans undulated seductively through the crowd. They begged for relief from the brightness of the souls they could temporarily see in the only way they'd get with their chosen drug—through sex and darkness.

Couples or groups drifted in and out of a pair of elevators that most likely led up to the higher floors in the building. Jono didn't need to think very hard on what they'd find up there because the vampires enjoying their spoils on the main floor weren't shy about the way they fed on the addicts.

Lighting was low-lit, giving the club an intimate feel, and the music was more background noise than anything else. The dance floor the gathering areas encircled and which the mezzanine over-looked was surprisingly empty. Past it, along the far wall that didn't lead to the loo, were two sets of double doors guarded by more vampires, the employees-only signs discreetly labeled.

Jono swallowed against the scent of everything around him, the chemical aftertaste needing something stronger than saliva to wash away. He wondered at how no one seemed to notice them as their small group walked on by, until he remembered the mage-globe in Patrick's hand.

Magic wasn't making them invisible, just unnoticeable. People looked right through their group as they made their way to the grand staircase that led up to the mezzanine against the side wall. The staircase was blocked by multiple vampires who didn't seem quite keen on being in such close proximity with each other. Considering the meeting they were about to interrupt, it stood to reason these vampires belonged to different Night Courts.

Jono saw Patrick clench his fist, snuffing out the mageglobe, and with it, his magic. The vampires in front of them became immediately aware of their presence, heads snapping around to stare at them in shock.

Lucien let go of Carmen and strode forward with all the swagger of an apex predator.

"Move, or I will kill you," Lucien ordered.

Jono saw the hesitation in one or two of the vampires, the older ones who maybe knew who Lucien was. The younger, brasher vampires bared their fangs in a challenge they were destined to lose.

Jono had heard stories of Lucien through the years, hushed rumors of the mad vampire who held no treaties with any human, who claimed no territory in any country. Yet he had evaded any and all law enforcement with ease to build a criminal empire the envy of anyone who lived on the wrong side of the law. A vampire whose Night Court was smaller than all others in the world today, but whose reputation was enough to make any master vampire think twice about moving against him.

Lucien proved why in mere seconds.

With a speed even Jono was hard-pressed to track, Lucien tore into the vampires blocking his way with hands and teeth. The brutal fight was a blur of torn limbs and dark blood, with Lucien a whirlwind at the center no one could stop. The handful of vampires who hadn't dared step up to the fight weren't spared either, and the last one to try to flee ended up with Lucien's hand buried in his chest.

The vampire's mouth worked soundlessly, his hands coming up to clutch at his chest. Lucien put a foot against the vampire's legs and shoved him forward, the motion wrenching his own hand free. He came away with a black heart that didn't beat clutched tight in bloody fingers.

The commotion hadn't gone unnoticed. Casual conversation had stopped, the music almost too loud in Jono's ears. Lucien stepped over the bodies and headed up the stairs, biting into the heart as he went, all eyes in the room on him.

"Is this the way you greet your master, Tremaine?" Lucien said, not bothering to raise his voice. Everyone with enhanced hearing and who was paying attention would hear him.

Jono was acutely aware of the silence that followed Lucien's question.

Einar extended his arm to Carmen and guided her through the mess of bodies on the floor. If the vampires' Night Courts claimed them, got them somewhere safe, then some of the undead might be salvageable after a day's sleep and enough blood from willing human servants.

Jono doubted the one whose heart Lucien was eating was ever coming back.

He caught Patrick's eye and tipped his head at the stairs. "We going up?"

"Yeah," Patrick replied.

Jono's boots squelched in the blood saturating the red carpet as he stepped over the bodies. It didn't escape his notice that Patrick kept his hat pulled down low, face averted from the curious eyes of the club guests who'd been offered unexpected entertainment for the night. It probably wouldn't bode well for people to recognize him here. The SOA didn't really need the headlines that would generate, not after what happened during summer solstice.

The pair of them climbed the opera theater-like stairs to the mezzanine. When they reached the top, Jono realized immediately they had a problem aside from the gathering of master vampires. Perched in a seat between the ranks of vampire guards affiliated with the Manhattan, Brooklyn, Queens, the Bronx, and Staten Island Night Courts who shifted around their masters was Sage.

"Bloody hell," Jono muttered under his breath.

Sage kept her eyes locked with his from where she sat but said nothing, refusing to acknowledge them. Patrick's face was devoid of all emotion, the blank mask of a special agent in the midst of a job. He said nothing, keeping quiet in a way Jono didn't really like. Jono wondered if Patrick holding back in the face of Lucien's reign of terror was how their promise was going to set the tone for the evening.

Fuck that.

Jono clenched his hands into fists as Carmen let go of Einar and sauntered forward, hips swaying with every step she took. Between one breath and the next, Jono could smell when her power hit, the sexual desire a wave that brought more than one vampire to their knees from want. Incubi and succubi fed off sex, and they weren't particular about how they got it. Human, vampire, werecreature, demons—if it was dead or alive, they would fuck it to feed.

Making anyone want them was a potent power that had hobbled more than one army over the centuries.

Carmen carved a path through the vampire guards, pulling orgasms out of many of them in the span of seconds. They went down, and the rest who tried to fight off Carmen's sexual power by fighting her were stopped by Lucien's vicious smile and the threat he gave voice to.

"Touch her, and I will raze your Night Courts to the ground," Lucien promised.

Jono was grudgingly impressed at the way Lucien could command a room. Every single vampire made the decision to survive instead of die a second, more permanent death. They let Carmen pass without protest, the ranks shifting into huddled groups that coalesced around five of the seven chairs that formed a circle in the center of the mezzanine. Seated in those five chairs were the master vampires of New York City.

Maria, of the Bronx Night Court, had ruled her territory for over a century, and was the youngest of the five at somewhere around three hundred years of age. She'd died old for her time but looked in her late thirties now, with brown skin faded to a paler tan and black hair styled in a pixie cut. The amount of gold jewelry she wore wouldn't have looked out of place in a music video. The tiara she wore, made from the fangs of those who tried to take her throne and failed, certainly would.

Devon, of the Staten Island Night Court, reminded Jono of every posh Wall Street wanker who thought they were better than everyone else. Power suit and Rolex couldn't take away from the death cast to the master vampire's face. Sharp featured, with slicked-back gray hair and brown eyes, he was five hundred years old and had called New York City home for two centuries

Rajesh, of the Queens Night Court, still wore the dastaar of the Sikh religion he'd followed when he was alive six hundred years ago. Considering the master vampire's reputation for viciousness, and the body parts that always got strewn in the streets when a territory fight happened, it was doubtful he followed those teachings any longer. His brown eyes remained locked on Lucien even as one of his vampires, a tiny blonde thing, leaned close to whisper in his ear.

Jamere, of the Brooklyn Night Court, wouldn't have been out of place at a local high school or university in the jeans, T-shirt, and heavy gold jewelry he wore. He'd died before he was twenty some four hundred years or so ago. No one was too sure which Caribbean island he once called home, but he eventually carved out territory in New York City in the mid-1800s after the Civil War ended. He guarded his borders zealously to this day.

Then there was Tremaine, of the Manhattan Night Court, the entire reason they were here. Tall, broad-shouldered, with white-blond hair and icy blue eyes, Jono had never crossed paths with the master vampire before, though he knew Estelle and Youssef had. Tremaine's gaze was riveted by Lucien's arrival, pale face stripped of emotion. Jono couldn't get a read on the master vampire who held more clout than the others, and he didn't like that.

"This is not your territory," Tremaine finally said, rising to his feet in a fluid motion, that force of presence all master vampires had filling the mezzanine.

"My Anahuac Cartel says otherwise," Lucien replied as he came to stand by Carmen, not bothering to respond to that show of power.

"You are not *invited*."

The statement was an order, a command to the threshold wrapped around the club. Public domains were near impossible for thresholds to thrive in, but Jono supposed an exclusive club could count as a home if one was desperate enough. Tremaine's words rang through the air, louder than the music pouring through speakers—but they did nothing.

Jono was reminded of how Patrick had broken the sacrificial circle he'd been tied to in June. Blood always slipped through magic in the most inconvenient of ways.

Lucien smiled, black eyes like holes in his head. "*You* were made by *me*. Your bought magic knows that."

Tremaine's lips peeled away from his jagged fangs in a snarl, but he made no move against Lucien. No one spoke until the fae lawyer seated by Sage stood to address the crowd.

The Seelie fae was beautiful, in a way that caught everyone's attention. Silver hair that fell to his shoulders parted around delicately pointed ears, and unearthly violet eyes gazed at the fractious crowd without fear. Impeccably attired in a tailored dove gray three-piece suit with a silver and black striped tie, the fae lawyer wore a crown of hawthorn flowers on his head and carried a sleek, gold-tipped wooden cane.

"May I remind you of the oaths you took to do no harm to each other during this mediation?" the fae said, his voice light in tone, though firm, with a thread of power running through his words that made Jono want to flinch.

Fae and their words were always such dangerous weapons.

"Tremaine's sire gave no such oath," Maria said pointedly, not looking at Lucien as she spoke.

"I give oaths to no one," Lucien bit out. "I *take*."

Tremaine stepped forward, braver than his brethren, or just utterly thick. Jono couldn't quite tell. "You come into my territory—"

"*Your* territory?" Carmen drawled derisively, cutting him off.

"Manhattan is mine." Tremaine's gaze cut their way, and Jono found himself on the receiving end of a murderous glare. "Nothing you do, no one you bring with you, will change that."

"Is that right?" Patrick asked, his right hand resting close to the dagger strapped to his thigh. "Because I'm pretty fucking sure my agency can put a dent into the shit you're selling on the street."

Tremaine dismissed Patrick's words with a mocking wave of his hand. "You have no warrant. If you did, you would have presented it before entering. Whatever you might see here, whatever you think you'll find? None of it will be admissible to the courts."

"It's funny how you still believe a piece of paper gives you all these rights," Lucien said as he sidestepped Tremaine to walk a circle around the low table all the chairs sat in front of. No one moved to stop him. "I gave you your second life, Tremaine. I can take it away just as easily."

"Is there a problem?"

The voice came from behind Jono, and he had to force himself not to react. If he'd been in wolf form, his hackles would've raised. Jono kept his heartbeat steady as he turned around to face a man whose arrival he hadn't heard or initially smelled in any degree. Judging by the flash of wariness in Patrick's eyes, Jono wasn't the only one who had missed the approach.

There was a reason for that.

The newcomer standing on the top step had long black hair shaved at the sides and tied back in a low ponytail at the nape of his neck. The white linen suit he wore stood out against his brown skin. He wore a gold signet-style ring with a large obsidian face that matched the obsidian studs he wore in each ear. His eyes were so dark a brown they looked black, like Lucien's, but his teeth were human-looking when he smiled.

For all the man's human appearance, Jono could smell the electric ozone scent no amount of magic could completely hide from him these days. He didn't know if it was due to the soulbond tying him to Patrick and the soul debt the mage carried, or an ability Fenrir had gifted him for this fight against the Dominion Sect.

In the end, it didn't matter. The nameless immortal was a threat Jono couldn't ignore.

"The entertainment has arrived, Tremaine," the god announced, gesturing toward the main floor below. His voice carried the heavy Spanish accent of someone where English was their second or even third language. Unlike the Greek gods Jono had stood before, this one didn't bother to strip away his accent to blend in. "Shall we begin?"

"The drugfest orgy isn't the star attraction?" Patrick asked no one in particular.

Movement out of the corner of his eyes made Jono turn his head. Sage stood and headed for the railing, sliding between the ranks of vampires without fear. The dress she wore was a muted charcoal, making her turquoise pendant stand out where it hung around her neck, the magic embedded in that artifact hiding what she truly was. The fae she'd accompanied watched her leave with an unreadable look on his face, but he made no move to stop her.

Then Jono's preternatural hearing caught what had drawn Sage's attention—the sound of a hoarse voice begging *no*.

Jono moved without thinking, leaving Patrick's side in favor of getting eyes on what was happening below. Standing between him and the railing were vampires belonging to the Queens Night Court, and they didn't seem inclined to move.

"I will go through you," Jono promised darkly, voice coming out in a growl.

"Should've stayed home, wolf. Do your alphas know you're in vampire territory, breaking the treaty?" a vampire sneered.

Jono kept moving, the shift fighting against his bones as he closed the distance between them. "Not my god pack. Not my treaty. You can fuck right off."

The statement was one Jono refused to regret, even though he knew it would get back to Estelle and Youssef. They'd make his life hell for it, but he was utterly done with their shit.

The fae tapped the floor with his cane a single time. Despite the carpet beneath their feet, the sound it made upon contact was like shattering glass that made Jono's ears hurt.

"The mediation is not over. This is still neutral ground. There will be no blood shed while I preside," the fae announced.

His words fell on everyone like a weight. Jono wasn't sure how high up in rank the fae must be, but it had to be pretty fucking high to get the vampires to reluctantly step aside at a single commanding look from Rajesh. Either that, or the threat of breaking a promise made to a possible fae lord was too expensive a mistake to make.

"I didn't promise a fucking thing to anyone," Jono said to the mismatched group at large as he stalked forward.

"And you complain about *me* rushing into things," Patrick said from behind him.

Jono didn't respond, having finally reached the railing where Sage stood. He gripped the railing in both hands and peered down below at the sudden commotion disrupting the vibe of the club. He took a breath, the scent of sex and drugs fading beneath the sudden spike of adrenaline and anticipation. Underneath all that was the sharp, stinging scent of *terror*.

Below on the marble dance floor, golden lines of magic flowed quickly across the area, forming not just a large circle, but an intricate, ancient design. Pictures appeared within the concentric circles of the casting, symbols and animals flaring into existence in four quadrants around a warrior's face in the center. What would have been radial lines in a modern casting looking like sunbeam carvings on this one.

The fiery light finally settled into smooth lines that burned against the marble, a containment circle that two vampires tossed a crying, bloody teenager into.

A teenager who wore a collar around his neck.

Jono didn't know he'd broken the railing until the metal cut into his hands, making him bleed.

The teenager sprawled onto the floor before quickly getting to his knees. The outermost circle rose high into the air, creating a transparent barrier he couldn't break through, no matter how hard the teenager clawed at the magic.

The music gave way to a bright, peppy voice announcing, "Last call to place your bets on tonight's special entertainment. Minimum buy-in is fifty grand. Will your champion win again in this fight to the death, or will your prayers be answered?"

In the circle that was a cage, across from where the teen huddled on his knees in torn and bloody clothes, dark gray fog drifted upward. From its depths erupted a black jaguar that Jono knew was no werecreature, not with that scent of a god cutting through the air.

"Is it true?" Sage asked, getting the words out through clenched teeth. "That you made no promises?"

"Not to Lucien," Jono hedged, because he'd made promises to Patrick in many ways. They were bound together, but the promises Patrick made on his own didn't bind Jono no matter the pack they had. He could see now why Patrick had stressed that fact back in Ginnungagap.

"You're learning."

"Learning what?"

"How to speak without losing pieces of yourself." Sage looked at him, the rage in her eyes burning straight through to his own. "I can't interfere."

She was here at the behest of the Night Courts, in the capacity of the fae firm that employed her. Jono understood that. He also understood what Sage was asking him without saying a single bloody word.

Jono was a god pack alpha, and he'd be damned if he wouldn't act like one.

Jono didn't hesitate when he threw himself over the railing, the snarl escaping his mouth that of a wolf born of fury, Fenrir howling through his mind and soul.

7

J‌ONO LANDED ON BOTH FEET BETWEEN THE TEENAGER AND THE jaguar, legs folding beneath him to absorb the force of impact. He stayed crouched in the center of the circle, one hand pressed against the floor. His fingers spread over the open mouth of the drawn face, the heat of magic burning against his skin.

Around him the crowd became more vocal. Jono would've ignored them all in favor of the threat right in front of him—except he saw a face he only remembered in his nightmares.

Jono had done his best to bury the memory of what Ethan Greene had put him through, but there had been others in that house somewhere in Manhattan. People he remembered in flashes and could never forget. The crowd was a blur of faces, but one stood out because the high, mocking sound of her laughter as she drank wine while he bled was embedded deep in Jono's mind.

He saw her in the crowd before she slipped away, head ducked to hide her face, but she wasn't quick enough, and he had a feeling she knew it.

She disappeared, and Jono let her because he had other things to worry about. His gaze snapped back to the jaguar, watching as it lashed its tail and bared its teeth in a snarl that cut into words.

"Do you wish to die?"

The voice of a god was never easy to hear, but Jono had spent nearly half his life listening to one. While some in the crowd clutched their heads in pain, Jono merely tipped his to the side, letting the words wash over him.

"That's a dumb fucking question, mate," Jono ground out before letting go of the bits that made up the human part of him these days.

The shift hit like a lorry, vicious in the way the wolf clawed its way out of his skin. For a single instant, Jono suffered through the agony that came with the shift from human to werewolf, fiery pain lighting up his brain and central nervous system to a point where it drowned out the world. Then it switched off, the werevirus blocking the pain so suddenly it left him momentarily light-headed.

It was long enough for his body to twist itself into something new.

Bones broke, a distant crunch Jono could feel as pressure but not pain. The world wavered at the edges, his eyesight shifting, still seeing in color but muted, picking up motion his human eyes couldn't. His body grew, the clothes and shoes he'd worn to the club shredding as mass redistributed itself into the heavy bulk of his werewolf form.

Muscles grew and reattached as his center of gravity changed to incorporate moving on four legs instead of two. The itch of fur rolled over his skin in a wave, nose flaring as scents he couldn't pick up even as a human with enhanced senses hit his brain with information Jono could easily make sense of after all these years.

The shift took less than a minute, but in that time, the jaguar wasn't waiting for Jono to complete it. The godlike creature launched itself not at Jono but at the teenager cowering behind him. The teen smelled rank from blood, urine, and fear mixed in with the scent of foreign magic keeping the teen from shifting.

Jono tossed his monstrous head upward midshift, jaws opening wide to snap at the jaguar, catching a hindfoot between his teeth as they sharpened into fangs. Jono wrenched his head to the side and slammed the jaguar to the ground, biting down on the hindfoot with all the strength in his newly formed jaw.

Hot blood filled his mouth in a gush before he had to let go or risk losing an eye to sharp black claws. The jaguar roared, twisting out of reach with an unearthly speed that had Jono's teeth snapping at air. He crouched lower, tracking the way the jaguar retreated to the outer circle to regroup.

Power flowed through Jono's mind, claws digging into his thoughts as Fenrir used his eyes to see the mortal world. The double vision they shared brought with it the shining bright aura of a god spilling out of the jaguar, save for a dark spot that incorporated his left hind paw.

It is mortal, Fenrir said. *A construct. Kill it.*

The aura said otherwise, but Jono wasn't one to question his patron. A head-on attack would put the teenage werecreature at risk of dying, so Jono stayed where he was despite Fenrir's warning growl that echoed in his soul.

Piss off, Jono shot back. *Let me concentrate.*

His paws didn't burn from the magic in the containment circle, not how his hand had while human. Fenrir's power was pushing through his soul, sinking into his bones, filling his mind with a wrath that Jono found difficult to shake off.

Let me feast.

On the people in the club, in the streets beyond the iron-barred walls, on any immortal who fell beneath his teeth and claws—it was all Jono could think of in the early days of his infection. Fenrir was made for the end of the world, but that moment was not now, and Jono had learned to stand strong against an animal-god patron who would use him until nothing of himself remained if he let it happen.

No.

Vicious in his denial, Jono held tight to a new anchor that kept him tethered to his humanity—the soulbond. It pulled at him, a wound in his soul that would never close, would never let him go. It helped him keep his thoughts, keep his sanity, in order to fight as clearheaded as he could. But Jono needed more space than the containment circle gave him, and Patrick seemed to sense that through the soulbond. It was the only explanation for the dagger that landed between him and the jaguar, channeling the power of gods.

The matte-black blade sank centimeters into the marble, directly into the mouth of the center face that glowed. White fire erupted from the blade, carried by words in languages that Jono couldn't read which drifted over the blade.

"I said *I* wouldn't fight," Jono heard Patrick say from the mezzanine. "I never said they wouldn't interfere. There's a fucking difference, Lucien."

They being the gods of every heaven that had crafted the dagger which broke apart the containment circle in a burst of magic that nearly blinded Jono, even with Fenrir's protection. The force of the blast upended people, vampires, and furniture. It shattered the chandelier directly above the fight area, raining crystal down on them. Jono shook it off as magic rebounded against the iron embedded in the walls and ceiling, crackling through everything electronic.

The Crimson Diamond was plunged into darkness, but Jono had no trouble seeing. Fenrir's sight lit up the area for him in grays and shadows that turned night into a washed-out twilight. The jaguar had been flung back, out of the circle. With magic no longer a barrier, the teenaged werecreature Jono had sought to protect barreled toward the exit at a speed no human could match.

Jono howled a warning, but he couldn't speak in this form, not unless he channeled Fenrir, and that was a card he had no intention of showing.

Not yet.

Jono pursued the teenager, but he wasn't the only one. The jaguar was quick on its feet, despite only having three working ones at the moment. But what it lacked in its body, it more than made up for in its pack.

Jaguars in the wild were solitary. Here, driven by a god whose name Jono didn't know, half a dozen more swarmed out of fog that appeared from nowhere.

"They're crossing over from the veil!" Patrick yelled.

Jono heard him through the screams and cries of the crowd, everyone's night of debauchery ruined for the better in his personal opinion. Jono's night?

Just getting started.

He barreled through the crowd, using his size and speed to clear a pathway to the entrance the werecreature had already vanished through, the jaguars between them. His paws crunched the door lying broken on the ground as he launched himself through the open doorway.

Passing over the threshold brought with it the sounds of the city at night—honking horns, distant music, the chatter of people inside buildings and the screams of those on the street who didn't expect a pack of jaguars and a god pack alpha werewolf on the hunt.

Jono knew Patrick wouldn't be able to keep up with him, not at the speed Jono was running, four feet pounding against the pavement as he raced down Broadway, following the scent of a panicked teenager. But he knew Patrick would follow.

The jaguars swarmed ahead of him, wreaking havoc in the streets as they dodged into traffic, the pavement too narrow to contain them. They bounded on top of moving cars, and Jono had no choice but to follow them. He launched himself on top of the nearest taxi, denting the boot from his significant weight, trying to get eyes on his prey.

The car next to his juddered to a halt as Sage in her weretiger form slammed on top of the bonnet with a roar that shattered a windscreen or two. Jono shared a single look with her before they both raced forward again, a single goal in mind—rip the bloody jaguars to shreds before they killed an independent werecreature, or anyone else.

Jono's fury fueled him in the chase down Broadway, cars, people, and buildings flashing by. Some of the screams sounded like people in pain, but Jono couldn't stop and see if they were all right. All his focus was on the flash of blood-stained T-shirt he saw flit around the corner up ahead, followed by the jaguars.

Traffic was fucked, and Jono veered off the street for the pavement again now that it seemed the way was clear enough. Sage stayed right with him, her weretiger form smaller than his wolf but no less menacing. Muscles bunched and extended beneath her black and orange striped fur as they took the corner into the Canal Street Subway Station together. Their claws shattered the pavement when they dug in to move their bodies into the turn.

Jono saw people lying on the stairs, blood hot in his nose, as he and Sage took flying leaps to the lower landing in order to clear the wounded. They careened down to the lower level, closing the distance between them and the jaguar pack.

Screams echoed in the underground ticketing area as the jaguars leaped over the fare gates. Jono and Sage followed in their wake, but the fare gates didn't survive their way through. Both Jono and Sage were too large to easily fit through the entry made for humans—so they made room. Jono slammed through the nearest one, taking the brunt of the hit on his shoulders, head tucked low.

Metal screeched as the fare gates broke from the force of their passage, throwing off electric sparks from the damage as Jono and Sage crashed through to the other side. Jono fought for traction when his front paws hit the floor, claws digging in deep as he followed the scent of the teenager deeper into the subway.

Saturday night wasn't rush hour, but there were still plenty of people in their way. Sage roared a warning that reverberated through the subway corridors. Jono hoped it was enough to make people get out of their fucking way as they raced to the lower level.

They closed the distance between them and their prey, Fenrir's howl urging Jono on. Wards flared up along the subway walls, old magic making his nose prickle, but nothing impeded their way.

Jono put on a burst of speed and leaped forward, landing on the back of a jaguar right before it went down the final set of stairs to the platform. Jono dug his claws in deep and sank his teeth into the back of the animal's neck as they tumbled uncontrollably down the stairs. Cement steps jarred his body on the way down, but Jono's teeth finally found bone, and he wrenched his head to the side in a killing motion.

Vertebrae snapped, blood flooding his mouth as Jono broke the jaguar's neck. The body went slack in his jaws and Jono let it go, already lashing out at the jaguar going for his jugular. Jono jerked backward, sinking into his wolf instincts and letting Fenrir guide him. He lashed out with his left paw, claws slicing over the jaguar's shoulder before following with his teeth.

Jono clamped his jaws around as much of the jaguar's skull as he could before rolling, dragging the beast with him. He kicked up with his hind paws, got claws in that soft belly, and raked them down the jaguar's body with all the force he could muster.

Blood and organs from the jaguar poured over his body as the beast shuddered in its death throes. Jono let go of the corpse, tasting blood, feeling it stick in his fur as he rolled to all four feet, the jaguar's organs sliding off him to the platform. His ears filled with the screeching sound of an approaching train. Jono swung his head around, seeing that Sage had taken down two of the other jaguars and was cornering another. The last one made a run for the teenager standing too close to the platform edge with no hope of an easy escape.

Jono howled a warning, but it was too late. The jaguar leaped toward the teenager, who had nowhere to go but onto the tracks right as the subway train entered the station. Jono moved without thinking, launching himself off the platform with a leap fueled by desperation. The train horn blasted a piercing warning note even as the train operator hit the brakes, the screech of metal melding with people's screams from those still running for the exits on the platforms.

This level of the Canal Street Subway Station was built with four tracks between the two platforms, steel pylons interspersed between them. No other trains were coming through, and Jono hoped his luck would hold.

He slammed into the jaguar in midair and knocked the beast away from the sprawled teenager on the tracks. Jono twisted hard, his bulk making it difficult to land where he needed to—within reach of his dazed target. He carefully clamped his teeth around the teenager's left shoulder, got as good a grip as he could, and leaped between two steel pylons for the closest set of empty tracks right as the train screeched past where they'd been lying.

The tip of Jono's tail whipped against the side of the subway train, a chunk of fur getting torn off, before his front paws hit the ground.

Fuck, Jono thought with a giddy mental laugh, the roaring sound in his ears that of his heart beating and not Fenrir or the train that had finally come to an emergency stop.

Sage roared, the sound worried, and Jono snarled back a wordless answer, keeping one paw on the teenager's chest to keep him from trying to escape. Hands grabbed at his fur, tearing at it as the teen struggled to get free of Jono's weight, ignoring the bloody gouges in his shoulder.

"Let me go!" the teen gasped out, wide brown eyes so full of terror Jono didn't think he even knew he'd been saved.

Jono hesitated before he started to shift, needing to lean his weight on the teenager throughout the process because he kept trying to wriggle free. Jono's body broke itself down into human skin, blood spattering on the dirty tracks around them and the teenager. Jono gripped the teenager with human hands, using his strength to keep the youth in check.

The collar around the teen's throat was made of silver, etched deep with wards that Jono couldn't read. They glowed an ugly orange-red, and Jono made sure not to touch it. He leaned over the teen, blocking out as much of the world as he could.

"Oi! You're safe!" Jono said loudly, trying to be heard over the panicked breaths the teen couldn't control. "You're safe."

Kneeling naked on the subway tracks and covered in blood from the fight was probably not the best place to have a conversation. Jono glanced up, seeing the opposite platform was now empty. He knew the set of tracks they were on weren't active at this hour, only during the weekday rush hour. The tracks by the opposite platform were definitely running trains though, and Jono didn't want to risk fighting with the teen while another train barreled down on them again.

Jono tightened his grip on the teenager, hauling them both to their feet. He wrapped his arms around the teen, wincing as bare feet slammed into his legs from frantic kicks.

"I'm not going to hurt you—*fuck!*" Jono growled. "Would you get your sodding teeth out of my arm?"

The teenager didn't seem to hear him, clawing desperately at Jono's arms with blunt human fingers, keening around the flesh he was biting into. Jono had to let go with his other arm and grab at the teenager's dirty brown hair, yanking his head up with a firm tug. The bite wound on his arm would heal in moments.

"Calm the fuck down," Jono ordered, grimacing at the burn from silver against his chest as the collar rubbed against his skin.

Jono kept talking as he half carried, half dragged the teenager down the tracks, fighting him the entire way. The train hadn't reached the end of the platform, and there was space to walk around the front. The train operator lowered her side window and stuck her head out, face pale despite the frantic anger in her voice.

"What the hell is going on?" she exclaimed.

"Federal agent!" Patrick's shout carried loudly through the air. "I want everyone off the subway train."

The train operator ducked back inside, slamming her window closed as Jono reached the front of the train, bare feet crunching over dirt and metal. He froze when he got eyes on the mess in the tracks that had once been a jaguar.

The train should've torn the body to bits, shredding flesh beneath its heavy steel wheels. Instead, what lay scattered in front of the train was broken bits of obsidian glinting between the rails. Resting on a wooden tie was a red Santa Muerte idol with a black scythe and golden globe carried in each hand, larger than the sort they'd discovered in the Mustang. Its black painted eyes seemed to stare right at them.

The teenager went rigid in his arms, breath coming so fast he couldn't possibly get enough air in his lungs. Jono was afraid he'd pass out. "Patrick. I need you over here."

Footsteps pounded their way and Patrick skidded into view on the platform, dagger in one hand and mageglobe in the other. He'd lost his baseball cap somewhere in his mad dash here, face a little flushed from his run.

Green eyes widened before narrowing, mouth twisting. "Motherfucker. *Don't* move."

"Too right I'm not."

Jono waited as Patrick shielded the evidence lying on the tracks, still fighting to keep hold of the teenager. The wards that stretched through the kilometers of subway tunnels appeared up on the platform walls and along the tracks.

"Wards don't like what ran through here," Patrick said.

"Can't imagine why."

"Okay." Patrick shook sparks off his fingers. "You're in the clear."

Jono crossed the tracks and leaped back up onto the platform, carrying the teenager with him. Patrick conjured up a second mageglobe and tossed it into the air between them. The washed-out blue sphere of magic pulsed twice before a ribbon of magic snaked away from it.

"You can let him go now," Patrick said once the binding ward had wrapped itself securely around the teenager's body.

Jono adjusted his grip, glad to get away from the silver collar pressing against his chest. He guided the teenager down to the platform and crouched down next to him. The burn the collar had left behind on Jono's skin was tender and hot, stretching in an uncomfortable way as he steadied the teenager. Patrick grimaced at the sight of it before shrugging out of his leather jacket and handing it to Jono.

"Here. Your extra set of clothes are back at the car, but this is the best cover I can give you right now," Patrick said.

"Should give it to—" Jono cut himself off, remembering at the last second not to use Sage's name in public. He turned his head and stared down the platform at where Sage crouched, wrapped in one of Patrick's shields to keep her safe from the police who were bound to show up soon.

"The weretiger isn't changing until we're somewhere private," Patrick said, going for gender-neutral terms to preserve Sage's identity. "Keep his head still. I'm taking off the collar."

Jono moved to kneel behind the teenager, reaching around to grip his chin in one hand and hold his skull with the other. Patrick knelt beside them, dagger in hand as he tried to get the teenager to look at him.

"Hey," he said gently. "I'm Special Agent Patrick Collins with the SOA. I'm here to help, okay? So is Jono. He's kind of like my criminal informant, only not."

Jono snorted. "Is that what I am now? What happened to your actual CI?"

"They left the club."

"Tremaine still alive?"

"For now."

Jono had more questions he wanted to ask, but the warning look Patrick shot him told him now wasn't the time. Jono focused on keeping the teenager still as Patrick pressed the point of the dagger against the silver collar.

No latch was visible, but the seam where it had been welded shut around the teen's neck sat over his spine. Patrick ignored that area, instead cutting through a particular ward that reacted with a crackle of red energy that died beneath the magic the dagger wielded.

The silver didn't melt. Instead, it broke apart beneath the steady pressure of the dagger as it easily cut through the metal. The white glow of magic burned along the matte-black blade in response to the containment and binding spells in the collar. With a crackling hiss, the collar separated beneath the cut, and Jono was surprised to see no burn scars on the teen's flesh as Patrick worked the collar off with steady hands. Once it was completely removed, Jono took a breath, expecting the scent of a werecreature.

What he got was a lungful of air filled with hints of smoke.

Patrick blinked rapidly for a couple of seconds at the teen before abruptly turning his head to the side. He squeezed his eyes shut, as if he were suddenly blinded.

"Fucking *hell*," Patrick said.

"What?" Jono asked, body going tense, adrenaline pumping through his veins.

"Kid's not a werecreature. He's a gods be damned *dragon*."

And wasn't *that* a kick in the fucking teeth?

8

"I HAVE THE PRESIDENT OF THE MTA BLOWING UP MY LINE, A DOZEN wounded people being treated at hospitals, numerous vehicles ruined by werecreatures, the Manhattan Night Court demanding I arrest you for trespassing, and the press camped outside waiting for a statement. What the *hell* am I supposed to tell them?" Casale demanded.

Patrick never looked away from where Wade Espinoza sat in Interview Room 1, staring right back at them through the two-way glass window as if he could see them when he shouldn't be able to. He was a little difficult for Patrick to make out clearly because his aura was goddamn *blinding*.

"He can hear you," Patrick said.

"Then ward the fucking room, Collins."

Patrick didn't think he'd appreciate being told that wouldn't work this time around.

Casale's anger was impossible for anyone to miss. The bull pen beyond the small observation room they were in had been tense ever since Casale stormed through it twenty minutes ago. The mess in the subway had taken hours to clean up, not to mention the time Patrick had spent at the hospital for Wade to get treated. Bringing him back here to the PCB hadn't been his first choice, but protocol dictated it for the case.

Patrick scratched at the side of his neck, careful not to drop the file with Wade's limited juvenile arrest records and family records tucked under his arm. "He thinks he's a werecreature."

Casale glared at Patrick, a vein throbbing in his forehead. "Are you going to stand there and tell me he isn't?"

In response, Patrick passed the file over to Casale, still staring at where Wade sat in the interview room. The teenager was nervously chewing on a thumbnail, wearing a pair of hospital scrubs and slippers. He'd been treated at New York-Presbyterian, Lower Manhattan for his ailments which had amounted to being underweight, underfed, dehydrated, and exhausted. Wade had been adamant he was a werecreature, but a standard blood-typing test hadn't produced any signs of the werevirus.

Dragons didn't exist because of an infection.

Once Patrick had removed the collar in the subway, Wade had started healing from his immediate physical injuries the same way a werecreature would. Except that was no werecreature sitting in the other room. Wade's status didn't seem to matter to Jono, who was treating the teenager like his responsibility.

Jono had ransacked the vending machine for all his wallet was worth when they'd arrived at the PCB. The pile of empty wrappers from his haul lay in the center of the interview table, Wade having eaten his way through every last one. The three soda cans Jono had bought him were empty, crunched down to little aluminum balls by Wade. Currently, Jono was standing guard outside the door to Interview Room 1 in a set of purloined hospital scrubs.

They'd taken Sage with them to the hospital in the back of a different ambulance because the bus had been large enough to accommodate her bulk. She'd shifted back to human form in the emergency room department's werecreature unit under Jono's watchful eye, been given scrubs by a nurse since the change had shredded her dress at the club, and left the premises the second Emma had arrived to whisk her home. Patrick had signed off on her leaving without being interviewed because it was his case and he knew where to find her.

"I called SOA Director Setsuna Abuku to give her an update while at the hospital," Patrick said, though he hadn't mentioned Wade's status to her. "We aren't telling the press anything. I need time to work out a way to serve an arrest warrant on Tremaine. The SOA has its in-house lawyers working on that front right now."

"You went into the Crimson Diamond without a search warrant to begin with."

"I went with my CI."

"That doesn't make this situation *better*."

Casale was right. It didn't. But that was the least of Patrick's problems at the moment. "The Manhattan Night Court is trafficking independent werecreatures for death fights as entertainment. Their club members get to bet big money on who wins and who dies."

"Yeah? That's *inadmissible* now, Collins."

"We have Wade."

"The kid won't talk. He hasn't even asked for a lawyer yet."

"He's eighteen years old. Legally an adult. We can question him."

"The *kid*," Casale stressed, "isn't fucking talking. Clammed up on you and every detective I've sent in there."

"Haven't tried Jono yet."

"You just said he wasn't a werecreature, so what good will it be to send in a god pack alpha?"

"What good indeed?" a new voice asked.

Recognition belatedly burned through Patrick's magic, making the hair on the back of his neck stand up, as if he'd been shocked by a live wire.

Patrick was getting real fucking tired of gods creeping up on him.

He turned around, hand straying toward his dagger rather than his gun. The god standing in the doorway to the observation room was around Patrick's height, but stockier, his skin a medium brown that came naturally and not from baking in the sun trying to get a tan. He wore khaki cargo pants and a navy blue polo shirt underneath an unzipped black windbreaker with the image of a gold badge screened over the left side of his chest.

His real badge hung from a chain around his neck, glinting in the fluorescent light. The chain was tangled with a leather strip used as a choker to carry a string of miniature conch shells. A gun was holstered on his hip, and Patrick spotted a knife tucked into the man's left combat boot. Short black hair was slicked away from his face, and his brown eyes seemed to look right through Patrick straight down to his tainted soul.

The immortal had the same look as the god back at the Crimson Diamond who had crashed the party worse than Lucien. The similarities made Patrick want another goddamn exit out of the room. These immortals were not familiar to him *at all*.

"And you are?" Casale asked with all the suspicion of a cop who didn't want to cede any more jurisdiction.

The immortal stepped inside, flashing a quick smile that showed off even white teeth. "DEA Special Agent Juan Delgado. I'm part of the Organized Crime Drug Enforcement Task Force."

"That's a mouthful, and not in the good way," Patrick said, trying to move closer to Casale without making what he was doing obvious.

"I'm working on the shine case the OCDETF has against Tremaine. I got word some hotshot federal agent might have ruined about two years' worth of hard work for us."

"Yeah, that'd be me. What of it?"

Juan—it was like calling oneself Mr. Smith with that name— stared him down for a long moment before smiling in that polite way federal agents did that was just plain mean. Patrick would know; he'd flashed that same smile plenty of times before.

"This is the DEA's case."

Patrick jerked his thumb over his shoulder at the two-way glass window separating them from Wade. "Kid says otherwise."

Tapping on the window had them all turning around to find Wade standing right there instead of sitting at the table. His wavy brown hair was in desperate need of a cut, and it flopped across his forehead, making him look even younger than he was. Wary brown eyes in a too-thin face easily tracked their positions through the two-way window.

Patrick had to look away. Wade's true self shining out of the teenager's aura made his eyes water. Wade apparently lacked that thing called control, which made him stick out like the *Welcome To Vegas* sign in the middle of the desert.

"I'm not a kid," Wade said, voice coming through the speaker system in the room from the mic pickups on the other side of the glass.

"Could've fooled me," Casale said. He eyed Juan with the distrust of a state official used to getting overridden and not liking it one goddamn bit. "We already called in the SOA for this."

Juan shrugged. "My two years' worth of evidence says the case is mine."

"Nope," Patrick replied.

Casale shook his head. "I'll leave you two to argue this out while I get on a conference call with the commissioner. It's one in the morning and he's not happy. *I'm* not fucking happy."

Casale left and didn't bother closing the door behind him. Before Patrick could focus on the immortal, Jono stepped through the doorway with a grim look on his face.

"Patrick," Jono growled.

"That is your murder voice," Patrick said, eyeing him. "No murder allowed on the premises where cops can see."

"Aw, that's a shame," a gratingly familiar voice drawled. "Don't shoot the messenger, Pattycakes."

Patrick reached for his tactical handgun anyway because greeting Hermes over the barrel of his pistol was pure fucking tradition at this point in his life.

"Why aren't you in Greece?" Patrick demanded as Hermes squeezed past Jono to enter the observation room, dragging the door shut behind him.

"Because Zeus and Hera are having their usual fight over where he puts his dick and I want no part of it," Hermes retorted. "I don't consider that a vacation."

Patrick could grudgingly agree about that, but he'd never admit it. "What the hell are you wearing?"

Hermes ran a hand over the same sort of DEA windbreaker the other immortal wore. "A uniform, what does it look like?"

"And you talk about me murdering a bloke," Jono said. "Put your gun away before someone sees, Pat."

"I saw it," Wade piped up from the other side of the glass.

"You don't count," Patrick said.

Wade very pointedly waved his middle finger at them. If the teenager was bringing attitude, then he was probably feeling better. Patrick opted to ignore him for the moment. He'd cast a silence ward except he knew from experience that it wouldn't stop a dragon from eavesdropping.

Hermes reached out and tapped the muzzle of Patrick's pistol. "You know these don't kill us."

"I am well fucking aware of that fact, but filling your chest full of bullets would make me feel better."

"We didn't come here to fight," Juan said.

"Of course you didn't," Patrick said, rolling his eyes. "Your kind usually makes me do the dirty work for you."

The immortal spread his hands and shrugged. "I have asked nothing of you."

"*Yet.*"

That wide mouth quirked at the corners. "Yet."

Patrick shoved his pistol back into its holster. "Who are you? And why are you dressed up as a federal agent?"

"You may call me Quetzalcoatl. As for the uniform, being a DEA agent is actually my job."

Patrick pinched the bridge of his nose, wincing when he forgot it was still tender from getting broken during his case last week. He'd never had any interaction with the Aztec pantheon before now, but it looked like that was about to change.

"Are you here for Wade?"

The question made sense in his head. Patrick was standing between an immortal feathered serpent and a dragon, both in human form, so it stood to reason they were linked somehow.

Quetzalcoatl's gaze darted over Patrick's shoulder at where Wade was probably still standing and eavesdropping. "I am not here for the fledgling."

Or not.

"Then why are you here?"

"I am hunting my brother."

"Your brother?" Jono asked, scowling. "Tall bloke, long hair, thick accent, has a shit slave business involving my kind? That brother?"

"And he likes cats," Hermes said with a smirk. "*Big* cats."

"Not a winning argument, mate."

Patrick ran both hands through his hair and linked them behind his skull so he didn't punch someone. "Which brother is he?"

Quetzalcoatl crossed his arms over his chest. "Tezcatlipoca."

The jaguars made sense now. Patrick remembered those animals had always been favored by that immortal. As a kid, Patrick had learned about the stories of gods how they were told in this day and age—written down as myths. But many of those myths were alive, having walked the Earth for thousands of years. Their power had waned through the millennia as their followers faded into history, driven by the rise of a more entrenched religion and the rediscovery of magic in the face of science.

If Patrick never had to deal with an angel of any choir, he'd consider himself lucky.

The day a god heard their name said for the last time was the day their immortality became a living grave. Gods needed to be remembered and worshipped in order to have power. He had a feeling Tezcatlipoca was gunning for a return of epic proportions.

"Is it too much to hope he's the one leaving us creepy-ass gifts?" Patrick asked.

"I know what you speak of, but no, those are not his doing."

Patrick scowled, letting his arms drop back down to his sides. "Then we're done here. And by the way? The case is mine."

Quetzalcoatl opened his mouth to argue, but Patrick made a slashing motion with his hand. The space between them was suddenly filled by Jono. He shouldn't have looked intimidating in his borrowed hospital scrubs, but he did.

"Piss off," Jono growled.

"Persephone owns a soul debt that says I can't," Hermes said with a smirk.

Jono eyed the messenger god with the contemplation of a predator figuring out which limb to tear off first. Hermes seemed amused, but Patrick thought he saw a surprising flash of wariness in those gold-brown eyes of his when the immortal looked at Jono.

In a fight between Hermes and Fenrir, Patrick's money was on the wolf.

"We're not done," Quetzalcoatl said, staring at Patrick.

"It's after oh-one-hundred in the morning. Yeah we fucking are," Patrick retorted.

"Tezcatlipoca is in love with death," Hermes told him. "We need you to break them up."

Patrick thought about the Santa Muerte idols the case had accrued in less than a week. They paled in number to the ones worshipped by cartel members and civilian devotees throughout

Mexico and in Mexican American communities. The warning was impossible to ignore.

If there was one thing death and the Aztec gods held sacred, it was human sacrifice.

"You gods need to get with the modern times when it comes to dating. Dead bodies don't make good gifts."

"My brother's partnership with death is not one this world will survive," Quetzalcoatl warned.

Patrick shook his head. "You think way too highly of your kind."

"I have been trying to stop the spread of his new empire for years. The Omacatl Cartel should not have grown as large as it did."

"Your opposing viewpoints mean nothing in the face of addicts looking for their next high. And for the record? I'm still not giving up the case. You don't like it, talk to my director."

Quetzalcoatl didn't seem pleased with Patrick's attitude or declaration, but Patrick didn't care. He had enough problems on his plate as it was; he refused to give up the case he'd been assigned just because a god said so. Lucien wanted to kill Tremaine, who was doing business with a god that had no qualms about killing werecreatures for profit and love.

One debt at a time, he told himself.

Patrick made to walk out the observation room when Hermes grabbed him by the arm, fingers pressing down hard enough to bruise. Those gold-brown eyes slid his way, head tipped in his direction.

"Tezcatlipoca and his Omacatl Cartel do business with your father. Ask yourself why the Dominion Sect would want a goddess of death at their disposal, hm?" Hermes said.

Patrick wrenched his arm out of Hermes' grip, getting free only because the immortal allowed it. "*Fuck* you."

If the two immortals wanted to play at being law enforcement, then he'd let them. Patrick would deal with the real DEA agents when they came around. Right now? He was done with their shit for tonight.

I need a fucking drink, Patrick thought as he yanked open the door and left the observation room.

He nearly ran face-first into Casale.

"You don't look happy," Casale said.

"The case is mine, which means it's still yours," Patrick bit out. "I'm leaving and taking Wade with me."

"You never told me what he was. If he's a danger, he shouldn't leave the premises."

Patrick waved aside his worry as the others filed out of the observation room. "It'll be fine. I've dealt with his kind before."

"What is he, Collins?"

"Sorry, that's classified."

"You know I hate that excuse."

"It's the truth. Can't change anything about that."

"I'm a werecreature," Wade said when Patrick opened the door to Interview Room 1.

"Keep telling yourself that. You're coming with me."

Wade's brown eyes looked past Patrick at where Jono stood behind him, the taller man's body heat impossible to miss.

"It's fine, mate," Jono said.

Wade seemed reluctant to go with them but even more reluctant to stay. One hand lifted to his throat, touching the spot where the warded collar had been, keeping his true self locked away. He was about Patrick's height, but way too thin, which made him look younger than his eighteen years of age. They needed to get some food in him.

"I can keep you safe," Patrick told him, trying not to squint. "I *will* keep you safe."

If Ethan, the Dominion Sect, and fucking gods aligned with the hells wanted a fledgling dragon, they'd have to go through Patrick first.

"Let's go," Jono said.

Quetzalcoatl and Hermes didn't try to stop them, but Patrick knew he hadn't seen the last of the gods. Casale looked like he wanted to argue, but the SOA had the case, and no one in the PCB was a mage. Patrick was the best person to keep Wade contained and safe.

He couldn't do anything about the teenager's thieving ways though. Hoarding was ingrained down to a dragon's soul after all.

"Whoever's badge you have in your pocket, I'd like it back now," Patrick said once Wade had stepped out of Interview Room 1.

Wade blinked, giving him a wide-eyed, innocent look Patrick didn't believe for a second. "What badge?"

Patrick held out his hand. "I'm too tired to play games. Badge. Now. And anything else you have in your pockets."

Wade side-eyed Casale and the immortals before reluctantly pulling out two RN hospital IDs, a detective's badge, and someone's watch.

Casale frowned at the hoard a scowling Wade set into Patrick's hands. "What the hell?"

Patrick passed the items over. "Can you see that these get back to their rightful owners? Let's skip the pressing-charges part."

"You know, his file said petty theft, but this is ridiculous."

Patrick gestured for Wade to walk ahead of him so he could try to keep an eye on the teen's hands as they walked through the bull pen. "See you tomorrow."

No one tried to stop them on their way out, though both Jono and Wade earned themselves a couple of curious looks. Patrick was sure everyone at the PCB had seen stranger things walking through the corridors, so the three ignored the glances as they left the building.

"Don't even think about making a run for it," Patrick warned Wade. "You try, and I'm sending Jono after you."

Wade honestly looked too tired to get very far, but Patrick knew looks could be deceiving. Patrick and Jono flanked the teen on the walk back to the car, both of them remaining on high alert.

Jono hustled Wade into the back seat once they reached the Mustang. For once, they had no gift waiting for them in the car. Patrick didn't know if that was because of the situation tonight or the fact the car was parked in the warded parking garage at the PCB.

Patrick tossed the keys to Jono. "You drive. I have to make a phone call."

Jono nodded and got behind the wheel. Patrick let Jono worry about getting them home while he worried about how to get in touch with his former commanding officer, three-star Army General Noah Reed. General Reed still oversaw the US Department of the Preternatural, the military branch the Mage Corps was attached to, and was based out of the Pentagon.

It had been three years since Patrick put on his uniform for the last time as an active-duty combat mage, but Reed had always insisted he would be available if Patrick ever needed him. The general had worked hard to shield Patrick in the aftermath of the Thirty-Day War, and Patrick had long held suspicions that Reed knew he was indebted to the gods.

Dragons, Patrick had learned while serving in the Mage Corps, hoarded information like no one else.

When Patrick had left the Hellraisers, his old team had continued on without him, gaining new members after burying those who had died on the front lines. Patrick still kept in touch with the survivors, but even a mage didn't have the personal phone number of a three-star general.

But he knew someone who did.

Patrick called SOA Director Setsuna Abuku, his boss and the woman who'd distantly raised him for ten years after helping secure a new identity for him as a child. Despite being in her fifties, Setsuna wasn't a stranger to late-night emergency phone calls, and she'd already fielded one from him tonight.

"Yes?" Setsuna said, sounding wide-awake despite the hour. "What is it now?"

"Line and location are not secure. I need to speak with General Reed. It's an emergency. Can you reach out and have him call me?"

"You haven't requested communication with him in years. Why now?"

When Patrick had called Setsuna earlier to update her on the case, he'd left out what Wade was until he figured out what to do. He really only had one option, and that meant reaching out to those who could get him what he needed. He might not trust Setsuna, but they weren't above using each other to get the job done.

"I found someone of interest to him. Just have him call me."

Patrick ended the call, gripping his phone as he stared straight ahead. Jono braked for a red light and looked at him. "Thought the SOA was a civilian agency?"

"It is, but everyone that high up in the alphabet soup agencies are in each other's pockets, including the military."

"And Setsuna can demand an audience with a general just like that?"

Patrick leaned his head against the window, eyes darting along the street for any new threat. "He was my CO at the top when I was in the Mage Corps."

"Ah."

"You were military?" Wade asked from the back seat. "Are you kidnapping me into the military? Let me outta this car, man."

Patrick scowled at the heavy hit against the back of his seat. "You put your foot through any piece of my car and you'll regret it."

"How? Gonna sell me off to the government? Fuck you!"

"No one is selling anyone to anything," Jono said loudly as the light turned green and he hit the gas pedal. "Calm the fuck down, Wade."

Patrick's phone rang loudly from an unknown number, the person's identity blocked. He answered it anyway. "Special Agent Patrick Collins. Line and location are not secure."

"I suggest you rectify that, Collins," General Noah Reed rumbled from the other side of the line, sounding more than a little irritated.

The raspy voice in his ear made Patrick think he could almost smell the cigarette smoke the general used to cover the scent of fire that always lingered around him. Patrick unconsciously straightened his shoulders.

"Sorry, sir. Habitual statement. I'm in a car with a god pack alpha werewolf and a fledgling."

A heavy silence filled the line for a moment before Reed's voice came back. "A fledgling?"

"I'm a *werecreature*," Wade snapped. "I just can't shift, is all."

Patrick rolled his eyes. "Yes, sir. It's been an interesting night."

"You always did have shitty luck when it mattered, Collins. Report."

Strange how the brusque order made him feel calmer in the face of his current clusterfuck of a case. Patrick rapidly explained what had gone down at the Crimson Diamond, only leaving out Lucien's name from the verbal report, knowing that Reed wouldn't demand he give up the identity of his criminal informant.

"You need to see the fledgling, sir," Patrick said when he finished. "The kid doesn't have any control, and I don't think he's ever shifted mass before."

"I'm not a *kid*," Wade spat out.

"Shut it," Jono growled as he took a left turn.

"He can't shift mass in New York City, sir. He's liable to bring down a building or level an entire city block," Patrick added.

Wade shifting mass into his dragon form—something the teenager had apparently never done before and wouldn't know how to control—was a disaster waiting to happen. Patrick had ruined enough of Manhattan real estate already this summer. He really didn't need to wreck any more of the city.

"Where is his family?" Reed asked.

"Mother is dead. Father left a few months after he was born, according to his records. He ran away from his foster care group home in San Diego when he was fourteen and was eventually listed as a missing child."

"Hey!" Wade said angrily. "Are you spying on me?"

"Federal agent," Patrick snapped over his shoulder.

"He has a temper," Reed mused, sounding *fond*.

If Wade ended up being a fire dragon, Patrick didn't know what he would do. Maybe take that vacation to Maui after all and make a detour to the Big Island to throw Wade into a volcano. Pele might take him in.

Or eat him.

New plan, Patrick reluctantly thought before saying, "I'm well aware of that fact, sir. I'm taking him home, but I can't *keep* him there."

Because dragons were immune to nearly all magic to a deep degree, even if they weren't immune to most modern weaponry. Bullets they could withstand, but missiles and grenades were a different story entirely. As for magic? Patrick could lay down however many thresholds he liked on the apartment, wrap however many defensive shields he could around it—Wade would walk through it all as if it didn't exist.

The collar Wade had worn in that fight ring shouldn't have kept him contained in his skin as it had, but Patrick had a feeling Tezcatlipoca was the one who had created it. Dragons could shrug off human magic as easily as they breathed, but the primordial power gifted to immortals was something else entirely.

"*Fledgling*," Reed said, his voice grating through the speaker in a way that had Patrick yanking the phone off his ear. The power in that suddenly inhuman voice filled the car, pressing down on him with a weight that made it difficult to breathe.

The car swerved a few times before Jono got it back under control, swearing all the while. Wade whimpered loudly from the back seat, caving beneath the power of an elder who belonged to his species.

"You will obey Special Agent Patrick Collins until you and I meet. Do you understand?"

Patrick thought his ears were going to rupture as the general's order echoed through the Mustang. He resisted the urge to clamp his hands over his ears because he knew it would be a useless gesture.

"Okay," Wade said in a panicked, squeaked-out voice. "Okay!"

"He will stay with you, Collins," Reed said, the power from before gone from his voice. He sounded human now, the echo of a roar ringing in Patrick's ears no longer actually present.

Patrick swallowed, trying to get moisture back in his mouth. He put the phone back up to his ear. "Yes, sir."

"I'll have my aide clear my schedule at the first available date. Off the record," Reed stressed in a hard voice. "Keep the fledgling contained, Collins. Keep him safe."

Patrick looked over his shoulder at where Wade was curled up in the back seat, a miserable ball of teenaged angst. "Yes, sir. I will."

Because dragons, for all their long-lived lives in this world, had seen their numbers dwindle over the millennia as humans spread across the Earth. Hunted down to endangered numbers, they'd learned to adapt, learned to take on the form of the dominant species and blend in. Shifting mass took power, but dragons in all their terrible glory were impossible to hide.

Patrick knew a thing or two about impossible tasks.

"Good."

The line went dead and Patrick dropped his phone in his lap, running a hand over his face. "Fuck."

"*He* was the one giving you orders in the field?" Jono asked a minute later, breaking the tense silence.

"General Reed is a three-star general. He issues the orders. Other people passed them down to us."

"I can see why you'd jump for that one when he barks how high."

Patrick snorted, swallowing back the punch-drunk laughter that wanted to crawl up his throat. "Just get us home."

In response, Jono pressed down harder on the gas pedal. It wasn't too much longer until they finally made it to their apartment in Chelsea. At this hour, Jono didn't even bother circling for parking; he just took the first available spot in a red zone.

Patrick shoved the car door open and got out. He turned, intending to reach down and move the seat forward so Wade could get out, when someone across the street caught his eye. The man in question wore casual clothing, though it was difficult to see his face from where Patrick stood. The streetlights down the block weren't close enough to cast decent enough illumination at this hour, but the man's strange yellow eyes caught and held Patrick's over the distance between them.

Time seemed to slow in that moment, and Patrick's heart beat faster in his chest as the man—*god*, a voice argued in the back of his lizard hindbrain—stared at him in a way that had Patrick feeling as if he was being peeled apart from the inside out.

"Pat?"

Jono's voice broke the tableau, and Patrick blinked, staring at Jono over the roof of the car instead of the shadow of a god. "Get inside."

Patrick appreciated the way Jono didn't question him. Wade got out of the car, and Jono locked it with a push of a button. He grabbed Wade by the arm and hauled the protesting teen down the street to the apartment building. Patrick followed, half running to keep up.

Even when they got upstairs to their apartment, the threshold humming in Patrick's ears, he didn't feel safe.

"What happened out there?" Jono wanted to know.

"I saw something," Patrick said as he twisted the lock on the door and added a few extra wards.

Patrick didn't know what had followed them home, and he

wasn't sure if the threshold wrapped around their apartment would be enough to keep a god out.

If it *was* a god.

Jono cupped Patrick's face in his hand and leaned down to kiss him. "Let's get Wade sorted, yeah?"

Patrick nodded, willing to let Jono take the lead on the sulky problem that had taken over their couch.

9

JONO ROLLED OVER WHEN SUNLIGHT HIT HIS FACE, BLEARILY RUBBING at his eyes. Beside him, Patrick was lying on his side, dead to the world, mouth slack and drooling into the pillow. His dark ginger hair was a mess, flattened on one side from sleep. The chain his dog tags hung from had twisted together during the night. Jono reached out to gently untangle them, letting the flat metal tags rest against Patrick's body.

He didn't wake, scarred chest rising and falling slowly as he breathed. Jono settled his fingers against the scar tissue over Patrick's heart, feeling it beat steadily underneath his touch. That Patrick didn't wake up pleased Jono to no end. It said more than words about how much Patrick trusted him, and Jono knew how difficult it was to earn that.

Leaning forward, Jono pressed a light kiss to Patrick's forehead before carefully crawling out of bed, trying not to disturb him. Mindful of their guest, Jono grabbed a pair of pants and trousers from the dresser and pulled them on. He slept in the nude, and Patrick had never once complained about Jono wandering around the flat naked, but he had a feeling Wade would protest.

Jono had woken twice during the night to the teenager wandering around the flat, listening as Wade approached the door and retreated every time. He didn't know what sort of compulsion had been buried in the general's order, but it seemed strong enough to get Wade to stay.

Jono took over the master bathroom long enough to take a piss and brush his teeth. When he made it to the living room, he saw Wade asleep on the sofa, half sliding off it, left arm and leg dangling over the side as he snored. The blanket Patrick had offered him was kicked to the floor, but Wade didn't look cold.

Jono checked the time on his mobile, seeing that it was nearly 1100. Last night had been hectic and long, and they all needed the sleep it seemed like. He padded into the kitchen to get the coffee started for Patrick and put the kettle on the hob for his own tea. He opened the fridge and studied its contents, wondering if he had enough to do a proper fry-up. They hadn't had a chance to go to the grocer, and they needed to.

He leaned down to open the crisper, looking for the last package of bacon they hadn't yet eaten their way through. A loud thump from the living room and Wade's startled yelp after he rolled off the sofa had Jono laughing softly.

"I'm making breakfast. You hungry?" Jono called out.

He didn't expect an answer but was going to make enough food to feed them all anyway. He sorted out the eggs, bacon, cheese, and bread on the counter before digging up a skillet. Jono turned his head when Wade slunk into the kitchen, warily pointing at the coffee that was half-finished brewing.

"Coffee?" Wade asked.

Jono pointed at the cabinet where they kept the mugs. "Creamer and milk are on the bottom shelf the fridge. Sugar is in the jar over there."

Patrick didn't cook, which meant the kitchen was organized to Jono's satisfaction and no one else's. He didn't mind cooking—it saved him money rather than ordering takeaway all the time—but Jono enjoyed it more when he could cook for other people.

Wade picked out the biggest coffee mug they had and proceeded to fill it up. He left enough room for some creamer and about ten heaping teaspoons of sugar. Jono said nothing about the preparations, knowing that Wade's metabolism had to be like his own—brutally fast, and capable of burning through thousands of calories in a single day. The teen needed to put on some weight after the ordeal he'd survived. He was far too scrawny underneath the scrubs he still wore.

"You won't fit any of my clothes, but you can borrow some of Patrick's until we buy you some," Jono said as he started laying out bacon in the hot skillet.

"I don't got any money," Wade said, scowling. "And I ain't selling you anything else."

The implications made Jono tamp down on the fury burning hot in his chest. "We aren't here to take anything from you, Wade. We just want to keep you safe."

Wade didn't look like he believed what Jono was saying. Considering what they'd freed him from, Jono couldn't blame him.

"Can't keep me safe from the cartel. They own me. They'll try to take me back."

Jono tapped a finger near the corner of his right eye. "God pack, mate. And Pat is a mage. Trust me when I say no one is getting through us to get to you."

He didn't mention the gods running amok through both their lives, or the master vampire they currently were indebted to. All Wade needed to know was that Jono meant what he said.

"Tloque Nahuaque will kill you," Wade said with that strange flatness to his voice Jono had heard before in Patrick's. It spoke of deep-seated trauma, and when he looked at Wade, the teenager was staring into the distance without really seeing anything. "No one survives when they cross his path."

"Who?"

Wade seemed to shake himself out of some horrible memory, coming back to the present. "He owns the cartel. He owns me."

"No one owns you."

Wade let out a hollow laugh, the sound something no one his age should ever know how to make. "The Omacatl Cartel has owned me since they picked me up before I even hitchhiked my way out of San Diego. You can't help me. You'll die if you try."

"We'll see," Jono said with a shrug. "We don't die easily."

"The god pack here didn't do anything. I don't get why you think you can."

Jono paused in flipping a piece of bacon over, giving Wade a narrow-eyed look. "What?"

Wade hunched his shoulders, taking a long sip of his coffee. An apple from the fruit bowl on the counter had found its way into the pocket of his scrub pants, weighing them down on one side.

"I came here earlier this year with a shipment of other people. Sometimes…sometimes I get to go out on my own. If I win enough fights." Wade absently touched his throat where the collar had been, blinking rapidly. "I always come back. I have to."

"Not anymore you don't, and no one is going to blame you for that."

Wade scowled, refusing to meet Jono's eyes. "I'm a werecreature, or that's what Tloque Nahuaque told me."

"Gods lie."

"Yeah, well, I didn't know any better. They kept me collared. All the time. Made it so I couldn't shift, but I was stronger than mundane humans. I didn't have any reason not to believe what they told me."

Jono tilted his head a little. "Do you still believe them now?"

Wade shrugged jerkily. "Dunno. But when I first came to New York I thought, you know, maybe the god pack could help me? But they didn't. They just called the vampires to come get me when I asked for help. And you guys called some general and now I'm *stuck* here, but I bet you'll give me up just like they did."

"Kid, you're not a werecreature. You never were," Patrick said from behind Wade. "And I have no intention of giving you up to anyone."

Jono only half listened to what Patrick was saying, his brain still caught on Wade's statement that he'd gone to the New York City god pack—and Estelle and Youssef had returned him to Tremaine. The taste in the back of his throat was some horrible combination of bile and fury that Jono nearly choked on.

Patrick stared at him with narrowed eyes and opened his mouth to speak, but the sound of Jono's mobile ringing cut him off. Marek's name flashed across the screen and Jono accepted the call.

"The god pack has called for an alphas' meeting," Marek said before Jono could even get a greeting out. "They demanded Sage specifically appear for a ruling. Emma and Leon left with her about thirty minutes ago. The rest of us were ordered to stay home."

The stress in Marek's voice bled over the line, the sort of tension Jono could hear that reminded him of when his friend couldn't see a bloody thing back in June.

"Please tell me you can see what's going to happen," Jono said.

Marek barked out a strangled, panicked laugh. "*No. I can't.* So what fucking gods are messing with Patrick now?"

Jono grimaced. "New ones, and maybe some old."

"You couldn't have fucking let me know?"

"We only found out last night. You could've told *us* that Sage was stepping into vampire territory."

"I didn't know," Marek bit out. "It's her firm that was retained, and she takes the cases she's given. Client confidentiality sucks ass."

Patrick reached around Wade to turn off the hob, the bacon in the pan destined to go uneaten. He looked at Jono, raising one eyebrow in silent question, but Jono ignored him for the moment.

"Sage broke the treaty, but she isn't the only one."

"What the fuck does *that* mean?"

The sharp beep in Jono's ear signaled he had another call coming in. When he pulled his mobile away from his ear to look at the screen, he saw Estelle's name flashing across the screen. The world went dark around the edges before he got his rage under control.

"I need to go. Estelle is on the other line," Jono said.

"Jono—"

"Don't worry about Sage, yeah?" Maybe he was giving Marek false assurances, but Jono wasn't going to let the New York City god pack judge her and find her wanting. He ended the call with Marek before switching over to the incoming call. "Estelle."

It was impossible to keep the growl out of his voice, anger sharper than the teeth in his mouth, the shape of them like a wolf's fangs.

"An alphas' meeting has been called concerning your actions last night," Estelle told him.

"*My* actions?" Jono ground out, staring at Wade and remembering what the teenager had told him. "Best look in a mirror, Estelle."

"I wasn't the one who entered the Manhattan Night Court's territory without *permission*, Jonothon. That's on you and those who went with you. Your actions will be dealt with after we address the Tempest pack's failure to adhere to pack law."

"We'll be there."

"*You* are being summoned. This doesn't concern the mage."

Jono ended the call without responding. The black at the edge of his vision was bleeding into red, Fenrir clawing at his soul.

Let me out, Fenrir howled, the words ripping through Jono's mind. *Let me feast.*

Cool hands touched his face, tilting his head down. Jono blinked, staring into too-human green eyes that caught and held his attention in a way no one else could.

"You with me?" Patrick asked.

Jono breathed in sharply through his nose. "Never left."

"Bullshit. You weren't listening to me when I was talking just now." Patrick never blinked, never looked away. "You good?"

"Yeah, mate. I'm good."

"Okay. I'm going with you."

"No." When Patrick opened his mouth to argue, Jono covered it with his hand, Patrick's breath warm against his skin. "Marek is at his flat with the rest of the Tempest pack. Take Wade and go there. Keep Marek and Emma's pack safe. I don't trust what Estelle and Youssef might do whilst I'm in the god pack's territory."

Patrick dropped his hands down to his side, and Jono removed his own from Patrick's mouth.

"I'm not a huge advocate of murder without an alibi, but if anyone deserves a grave, it's those two," Patrick said after a tense pause. "I'll keep an eye on Marek. Maybe this time he'll even listen to me when I tell him to stay put."

Jono didn't know what he was going to do when he got to the god pack home, but he knew enough about himself that murder wasn't off the table.

He leaned down to press a hard kiss to Patrick's mouth before retreating to the bedroom to get dressed in proper clothes. Dark wash jeans, a grey T-shirt, and his second-favorite boots. Jono's fingers were steady when he laced them up, Fenrir's fury sparking along his nerves even as his heartbeat remained eerily calm.

"Take the car," Patrick said when Jono came back out. "I'll call us an Uber."

"You sure?" Jono asked.

Patrick waved him off, half-finished with putting away the food so it wouldn't spoil. "Go."

<hr>

If asked, Jono would say he remembered the drive Uptown, but in truth, it felt as if he closed his eyes in a slow blink and found himself standing on the porch from yesterday when he opened them again. He didn't have Patrick by his side this time, but he had Fenrir riding his soul, and Jono had to tamp down the desire to *kill* as he reached for the doorknob.

Guide me, he snarled at the god. *Like you promised me you would.*

Fenrir's answer was a howl in his thoughts that bit like teeth—sharp and fierce and dangerous like a feral animal.

Jono's hand crunched the metal doorknob, his strength tearing the door off its hinges when he slammed it open. The threshold couldn't keep him out because Estelle and Youssef had already requested his presence. Jono stepped inside, the sound of dozens of heartbeats drumming in his ears through the floor from below.

The single werewolf left to man the front door eyed Jono with wide amber eyes. She scrambled out of Jono's way, giving ground in a show of submission no one in her god pack would appreciate if they'd witnessed it. Jono ignored her and walked deeper into the home.

The god pack's central building had gone through many renovations over the decades. One of the biggest was a deep underground stadium that stretched beneath half the houses on the block. It was where pack challenges and trials were handled, in a dirt ring that had seen too much blood over the centuries. Jono knew Estelle and Youssef had never once cleansed the place, the same way their predecessors hadn't.

It smelled like death down there, and had since the god pack first claimed this territory generations ago.

The underground stadium, with its grave-like scent, was a place only pack alphas ever saw. It was a place Jono had visited exactly twice since coming to New York. Once to plead his case to remain in the god pack territory here, and once to witness a failed challenge from within the god pack itself in the face of Estelle and Youssef's leadership.

Jono remembered that execution. He would never call it a fight, fair or otherwise. He always thought Estelle had manipulated the discontent seeping through her god pack like rot to put on a show just for him.

A warning, if one liked.

One Jono hadn't taken to heart at fucking all.

The stairs leading below ground were lit by light bulbs now, though the old torch and candle brackets were still bolted into the stone walls that gave the stadium its shape. The winding staircase reminded Jono of the steps in the parapets of Notre Dame from a school trip he'd taken years ago as a young lad.

Unlike that sacred cathedral built on holy ground and cleansed daily by way of prayer, the staircase here and the underground stadium it led to was currently filled with the scent of unease, grief, and desperate anger. Beneath all that was the old, coppery tang of blood. The disparate scents stung Jono's nose, twining through his lungs even as he listened hard to the heartbeats he could hear, picking out the ones that mattered.

Emma, Leon, and Sage.

All three were here, all three were alive, and Jono aimed to keep them that way.

Jono strode forward, his footsteps ringing loudly against the old flagstones that led to the dirt circle. The surrounding tiers of seats were also carved from stone, encircling the dirt ring. Space was tight, with alphas from every pack who called the five boroughs home crowded shoulder to shoulder in the audience.

Members of the god pack took up the first row of stone seats, their rank earning them ringside positions to what was happening. Sage stood alone in the dirt ring before the god pack alphas and their dire, while Emma and Leon were on their knees between two god pack werewolves. Despite the shifted claws digging into their shoulders to keep them there, Emma and Leon both had their heads raised high.

Sage's head snapped to the side, her agonized brown eyes meeting his as Jono stepped forward, leaving stone behind for bloodstained dirt. His fury had settled beneath his skin like hot pinpricks, the buzz in his nerves the precursor to a shift Jono knew he couldn't give in to yet.

"What the bloody *fuck* is going on?" Jono demanded, his voice echoing in the sudden silence like thunder.

The bright fluorescent lights overhead put everything into high relief, making it easy to see the tear tracks lining Sage's cheeks. She was dressed for a day in the office, but the way she held herself —arms curled around her body, shoulders hunched—made her look nothing like the talented attorney Jono knew her to be.

The way she smelled—scentless and packless—made Jono want to howl a challenge.

"You're late," Youssef said. "If you had—"

"I wasn't asking *you*," Jono cut in, eyes moving from Sage to where Emma and Leon kneeled in the dirt. The tension in the stadium ratcheted up at the total disrespect Jono showed the god pack alphas, but no one moved.

Emma though—she only *smiled*, showing teeth even if she didn't show her throat.

"Jono," she said, ignoring the way the claws of the werewolf holding her dug deeper into her shoulder. Blood trickled down her arm some more, painting her skin with tacky red streaks.

"You have no right to speak here, Jonothon," Estelle said icily. "Know your *place*."

"Believe me, I do," Jono said as he closed the distance between himself and Sage, coming to a stop by her side.

Sage looked at him through the tears in her eyes, the absence of the pack scent she'd carried since the day Emma had claimed her gone from her body. The claim had been removed by the power of a pair of god pack alphas who thought they had the right to tear apart the people they were supposed to protect.

Their misguided attempt at control stopped today.

What Jono had learned in all his years as an independent-ranked werewolf was a truth he'd ached to share. Home wasn't a place. It was people.

Pack.

Something Jono was finally willing to claim in public whether Estelle and Youssef liked it or not. Because he knew what was happening here, knew what those two were perpetrating against the people who had become his family these past three years.

He refused to allow the god pack alphas to hurt them any longer.

"Why?" Jono asked harshly, gaze cutting to Estelle.

"Because Sage went where she had no right to go, as did you," Estelle said flatly. "The Night Courts are off-limits. They have been for decades, and your actions have put us all at risk."

"My firm requested I go," Sage said in a quiet voice leached of all emotion. "I argued today that the Tempest pack had no say in my decision, that they couldn't know for client confidentiality reasons. My actions were my own. They'll be allowed to remain in New York City."

Jono had no doubt Sage had argued successfully for Emma's pack to remain whole and within its current territory because that was just the kind of person she was. Dedicated, loyal, and willing to do whatever she had to in order to keep her pack safe.

He understood why she had been there last night. The fae lord may have been in charge of that mockery of a mediation, but Sage was there as his protection. The Crimson Diamond was encased in iron, and that metal was a critical weapon against the fae, Seelie and Unseelie alike. His power would have been severely limited, but Sage could have still shifted and fought to keep the fae lord safe.

Jono had always wondered how the fae could live in modern cities, but maybe they were like the gods in a way—worn down by the progression of time but incapable of dying off completely. Still, they could've requested someone else in the firm.

"The pack laws we set down are to be obeyed *first*," Youssef said.

"Bollocks," Jono growled. "If that were the case, you'd actually get off your arse and save the people you're selling off to Tremaine."

The sound of shocked, indrawn breaths rippled through the audience. Everyone knew better than to speak their mind here, but Jono could see the troubled looks on some faces that were quickly hidden. Estelle glared at him, her heartbeat a steady *thump* in his ears, truth the only thing he could smell on her. Jono wondered what sort of artifact she carried to give off that artificial scent, or if she was just that talented at lying.

"I take my duty of care seriously. How *dare* you accuse us of such a thing," Estelle snapped, lifting her chin.

"I dare because it's the truth," Jono snarled, taking a step forward.

Youssef's lips curled over his teeth in an ugly twist. "Sage has been removed from the Tempest pack and is exiled from our territory. It is our duty to keep the peace—"

"Peace?" Jono said around a harsh, disbelieving laugh. "Selling off those who come to you begging for help is not how you keep the fucking *peace*, Youssef."

"You are to be exiled with Sage for breaking pack law," Estelle told him, steamrolling over his accusations. "You will leave New York City and—"

"No." The word came out guttural and hard, a challenge in Jono's tone that everyone could hear. "You will not exile me, Estelle. You *can't* exile me, because I don't follow your laws."

Estelle's bright amber eyes narrowed to slits. "Is that a challenge?"

The word hung heavy in the air, people holding their breath for whatever came next. Jono could feel Fenrir beneath his skin, in his soul, and he knew he couldn't give the god what he wanted. Not today. Jono needed more support than what Patrick could give him, and they wouldn't win a fight for territory with only themselves to stand for the challenge. Fenrir was more the nuclear option Jono was hesitant to initiate, no matter how the god clawed at his soul.

"It's a warning," Jono said into the silence.

"You made a promise in order to stay here. You break it, then you break your oath. No one trusts an oath breaker," Youssef sneered.

Jono shrugged, forcing the motion to look casual instead of stiff. "You said I couldn't make a pack with anyone under your protection. Patrick isn't under your protection. Neither is Sage now, and I've claimed them both."

Out of the corner of his eye, Jono saw Sage jerk as she choked out a startled gasp, while behind them Emma sighed in relief.

"You will do no such thing," Estelle said coldly.

Jono knew Estelle had to argue about this, to stand her ground and hope to win the fight. If she didn't make an effort, it was a slippery slide down into the packs under her control questioning her status and power. Estelle and Youssef were all about power.

In response to her demand, Jono turned to face Sage and extended a hand to her in a silent question. For all that he'd laid verbal claim on her for his pack, scent-marking was something else entirely, and he wouldn't force that on her if she didn't want it. Sage stared at him for a fraught moment before tilting her head to the side, showing her throat in a submissive manner. Jono didn't hesitate to drag his hand and wrist over the side of her neck, pressing his scent into her skin.

He didn't think it would affect him the way it did. Patrick was different because of the soulbond and humanness, but Sage was the first werecreature Jono ever claimed as *his*. He wasn't expecting the way awareness shot through him, like a punch to the gut. The way her scent—dry desert sunlight buttressed by a forest after the first hard rain—seeped into him when he breathed her in.

Something in his soul broke open in a way it never had before but which felt *right*. Jono's awareness sank into it, and he knew he would always recognize Sage as *his* after this moment.

Pack.

The snarled roar from behind him was enough to break Jono free of the lull he'd fallen into. He shoved Sage aside and spun around, barely catching a glimpse of Nicholas in wolf form lunging at him. Jono didn't bother to shift, choosing instead to let Fenrir guide his actions. He leaned hard into the god's presence in his soul, and the world seemed to slow.

Jono could see the ripple of muscles across Nicholas' body as the werewolf came at him, mouth open in a vicious snarl, claws reaching for him. Jono ran toward the threat, pitching himself between those outstretched limbs. He sank his hands into the brown fur on Nicholas' chest and throat, using the other man's forward momentum to throw Nicholas over his shoulder.

With a throat-tearing roar, Jono slammed Nicholas' wolf form to the dirt floor, taking a stinging, glancing blow over his chest. He went nose to nose with the other man, wolf-bright blue eyes staring into amber.

"*Change,*" he snarled, the word coming out guttural and harsh, sounding more like a wolf than a human ever should.

God pack alphas were capable of calling the packs to them, though it was rarely used these days due to advancements in technology. But the ability to reach people, to command and control them—to strip them of their pack identity as Estelle had done with Sage—existed in their very DNA. The werevirus ran through everyone's veins, and that black magic was a magnet for power that Jono sank into with Fenrir's backing.

The command in his voice would not go unheeded.

In seconds, the fur beneath Jono's hands changed to bare skin, and the claws digging into his body became fingers. Jono followed the shift until his fingers tightened around Nicholas' throat, squeezing hard enough to cut off the other man's air.

"Yield," Jono ground out, never looking away from Nicholas' eyes.

He yanked Nicholas' fingers out of the rapidly closing wound over his ribs. The pain was a distant sensation easily ignored, cocooned as he was in Fenrir's power. It took effort for Jono to not give in to the desire to break Nicholas' neck, but he knew killing the other man now would be a disaster.

He wanted Estelle and Youssef to pay for their actions. Death was too quick a punishment for them. Jono would rather they lose their status bit by bit, werecreature by werecreature.

Starting with their dire.

Nicholas was red in the face and unable to break Jono's grip. Moments away from passing out, Jono felt the flex in the other man's neck that spoke of submission, of showing throat to someone who was more powerful. Nicholas gave in and acknowledged in that moment that Jono outranked him in all the ways that mattered.

Jono smiled, revealing fangs instead of teeth. "There's a lad."

Jono unwrapped his fingers one by one, showing mercy Nicholas didn't deserve. The harsh gasp that Nicholas let out was the only sound in the underground stadium, an echoing, bitter surrender Jono would always remember.

Jono raised his head and looked around him at the audience and the more than two dozen werecreatures who had involuntarily changed form at Jono's command into the beasts whose DNA they carried. He made note of every single person who had heeded his call, breathing in their scents in a tangle of knowledge that tugged at his soul.

Then he got to his feet and turned to face Estelle and Youssef. The god pack alphas stood across the dirt ring from him, neither having moved in the face of their dire's attempt to get Jono to show throat. The arrogance was gone from their faces, and in its place was a shocked wariness they couldn't hide quick enough.

Jono held their gazes for a long moment before pointedly turning his back on the pair, outright dismissing them. He caught sight of Emma and Leon as he moved, the two still on their knees but no longer being held down. Jono didn't want to leave them, but he knew he couldn't stay.

"Come on, love," Jono said as he held out an arm toward Sage. "Let's go."

Sage swallowed thickly before ducking her head and closing the distance between them. "Your territory?"

She always thought of the details. Jono appreciated her tenacity, but he wasn't going to stick around to have another row about where they stood amongst the rest of the packs. Jono wrapped his arm around her shoulders and guided Sage toward the stairs, aware of all the eyes on him.

"They know my territory" was all Jono said.

The flat he shared with Patrick was an island of safety in a sea of threats Jono refused to back down from. If the New York City god pack wanted to take it from him, they were more than welcome to try.

Jono would murder them all and leave them to rot.

"WHAT. *HAPPENED?*" WERE THE FIRST WORDS OUT OF MAREK'S mouth when they arrived at his flat.

Jono shook off the faint buzz of the silence ward as they crossed the threshold. Sage didn't leave Jono's side, staring hollow-eyed at Marek. "The god pack alphas exiled me for going into vampire territory."

Marek's expression could only be described as *gutted* as he stumbled their way. The sound that left his mouth would've been more appropriate on a dying man's lips. Jono hastily held up a hand and nudged Sage forward. "She's not exiled anymore. I claimed her for my pack."

"You—*what?*" Marek got out in a strangled voice even as he pulled Sage into his arms and hugged her for all he was worth.

"Who ruined your shirt?" Patrick asked from his spot on the sofa. The question was innocuous enough, but the scowl on his face belied his desire for revenge. Jono really shouldn't have found Patrick's tendency toward violence hot, but he did.

"Nicholas. I put him down and made him show throat," Jono said. "Where's Wade?"

"In the kitchen eating snacks and stealing knives."

"I am not!" came Wade's muffled shout from the walk-in pantry near the refrigerator.

Patrick rolled his eyes as he got to his feet. "Kid isn't allowed to keep a hoard of knives, is all I'm saying."

Jono gripped the hem of his ruined T-shirt and tugged it off. Cool hands touched his rib cage where the wound Nicholas had given him no longer existed. Patrick carefully scraped off some of the dried blood, safe from infection of the werevirus by virtue of his magic.

"I should've gone with you," Patrick said as he flattened his hand over Jono's side.

Jono placed his own hand over Patrick's and shook his head. "I needed to do this."

"What? Announce our pack in the most dramatic way possible?"

"I couldn't let them exile Sage."

"I know. Fucking bleeding heart syndrome." Patrick tugged Jono down for a quick, hard kiss, taking the sting out of his words. "What about Emma and Leon?"

"We had to leave them behind."

"They aren't exiled," Sage said. Jono glanced over at her, seeing that she hadn't escaped Marek's arms yet. "I argued they had the right to remain. Estelle couldn't exile them within the bounds of pack law. She tried, but I managed one win at least."

"You're still staying here, with me," Marek insisted.

Sage met Jono's gaze and didn't say anything. Jono realized with sudden clarity that if he told her she couldn't live here anymore, then Sage would move out without argument—because he was her alpha. What's more, he was god pack, and what laws he made going forward would affect her more than Patrick.

As a magic user, Patrick wasn't privy to the ebbs and flows of scent and the way werecreatures formed packs. He could walk away, but Sage didn't have that option.

Jono ran a hand over his face. "This is your home, Sage. I'd never tell you to leave it."

"I know," she said quietly. "Because you're better than they are."

"Not a high bar to clear."

"Shut up and take the compliment, Jono," Marek told him. "If you're hungry, there might be some leftovers in the fridge if Wade hasn't eaten his way through them."

"I didn't shift," Jono said.

Marek blinked at him. "You got Nicholas to show throat without shifting?"

"Not only that, Jono forced Nicholas to change back to human. His call caused other alphas to shift into their animal form as well," Sage said.

"Are you serious?"

"I never meant to force the others, just Nicholas," Jono said. He hoped none of those in the audience would face retribution by Estelle and Youssef. He'd feel awful if they did.

Sage shrugged, finally pulling away from Marek. "That just means they're yours."

Jono shook his head. "You can't know that."

"You don't give yourself enough credit." Sage walked over to him and came to a stop beside Patrick. "I grew up with bad alphas on the Rez, remember? I lived under Estelle and Youssef's rule for years. I'm not the only one who has wished for someone better to lead me and my pack."

"You grew up on a reservation?" Patrick asked.

"I'm Diné, but I wasn't born a weretiger. The alpha in my area of the Rez was an alcoholic and couldn't keep his pack under control. I got bitten when I was nine years old, and the federal government removed me from my family not long after that. I was put into foster care and eventually adopted by a witch."

"I'd say removing you should've been illegal, but I know how the federal government likes to fuck over the tribes. I'm sorry that happened to you."

Sage smiled tightly. "Can't change the past."

Patrick made a face. "Yeah. Tell me about it."

A crash from the pantry had everyone looking toward the kitchen. Wade's shout was muffled, as if he was in the middle of chewing food. "I'm okay!"

Marek looked at Jono. "If you're going to keep feeding Wade for the foreseeable future, I'll talk to Emma about having her increase your pay. He's like a bottomless pit."

"You don't know if he's staying?" Jono asked.

Marek shook his head. "Gods, remember? The Norns can't see an end to this fight right now."

"That means the Dominion Sect is definitely involved," Patrick said. Jono couldn't get a read on him since it seemed Patrick had locked down his shields.

Jono took Patrick by the arm and ushered everyone toward the sofas in the living area. "More than you know. I saw someone familiar last night at the club."

Patrick stopped midstep, and Jono had to push him forward. "What do you mean?"

When Patrick would've stayed standing, Jono dragged him down beside him on the nearest sofa. "There was a woman in the crowd who I remember from the night Ethan had me."

He spoke the words carefully, but Jono couldn't quite tamp down the spike of terror that came with that memory. Sage's nostrils flared, and she moved to get up from her spot beside Marek to come to him, but Jono waved at her.

"Stay sat," Jono said. "I'm fine."

He wasn't, not really, but he was learning to be. Patrick's knowing gaze spoke volumes in that regard, but he was kind enough not to give voice to them.

"Who was it?" Patrick asked.

"I don't know her, but I would recognize her face anywhere."

Patrick rubbed at his temple. "There are ways we can go about identifying her. The SOA has magic users in its roster with an affinity for mind magic. They'd be able to channel the memory to a sketch artist for a portrait drawing. But that's going to draw a lot of attention if we do."

"Would it get you in trouble with your agency?"

"Setsuna could try to keep the request sealed, but I'm not sure how long that order would last. Congressional oversight is still making her job difficult right now."

"Then we wait."

"Jono—"

"Ethan is the enemy, and I'll know the people who were with him if I see or smell them again. We don't need to put your position at risk."

He knew Patrick's past better than the other two. While Emma, Leon, Marek, and Sage knew Ethan was Patrick's father, they didn't know the horrible details of how the Greene family was torn apart, nor what Patrick had gone through to survive. Public records on his mother's murder case were sanitized, and only a handful of people knew Patrick had been forced to cut ties with his mother's family at a very young age when his name was changed to keep him safe.

Patrick pressed his mouth into a thin line before finally shaking his head in capitulation. "Fine."

The pantry door closing had Jono looking over to see Wade walking out of the kitchen area with his arms full of crisps and crackers, stuffing his face with a strawberry Pop-Tart.

"All the food choices and you go with junk food?" Jono asked.

"Marek said I could have whatever I wanted," Wade said, sounding sulky as crumbs sprayed from his lips.

"If you're hungry, eat some actual food."

Wade clutched one of the Doritos bags so hard he ripped a hole in it. "*Whatever* I *wanted*."

"Let him eat. It's fine. He's making room for our next grocery run anyway," Marek said.

Jono eyed Wade and the way even Patrick's T-shirt hung loose on his skinny frame. He'd much prefer to cook Wade a better meal, but calories were calories at this point. He'd let Wade demolish the snacks and then make a proper lunch for him later.

"How long do these alpha meetings usually last?" Patrick wanted to know.

"Depends on what needs to be discussed," Sage said as she toed off her high heels and curled up against Marek on the sofa. "Considering how we left, the meeting might take longer."

"I fucking hope not. I hate waiting."

They ended up waiting two hours for Emma and Leon to make it home. In that time, Jono cooked Wade the fry-up they'd missed that morning, made a pot of coffee that Patrick drank by himself, and made a second pot he banned Patrick from drinking. He also spoke to Sage's managing partner regarding her absence from the office—apparently being her alpha now meant he was qualified to excuse her from work—and hid Marek's mobile to keep him from calling the god pack alphas and threatening them with a lawsuit.

"I can keep them busy in the courts if I want to," Marek snapped when Jono refused to give back his mobile.

"Trust me, mate. Now is not the time," Jono said.

"I don't know, I'd be all for suing that bitch," Emma said tiredly as she entered the apartment.

Jono hadn't heard their arrival, belatedly realizing the silence ward Patrick had put up earlier was still active. He pushed himself to his feet at their arrival, taking in their bloodied clothes but healed bodies.

"You all right?" Jono asked.

Emma smiled in a way that spoke of remembered pain. They must have shifted at some point to heal their wounds, but their clothes were still mostly intact. "We're fine. Still a pack. Still tithing Estelle and Youssef."

"For now," Leon muttered.

Sage stood and took a hesitant step toward her former alpha, expression twisting. "Emma..."

Emma closed the distance between them and pulled Sage into a hard hug. "I'm so sorry I couldn't keep you safe."

Sage shook her head, her knuckles going white with how hard she held on to Emma. "Don't. You have nothing to apologize for."

"You know you always have a home here, no matter what Estelle and Youssef said. This is my territory, and it's your home. Your name is on the title next to Marek's." Emma looked over Sage's shoulder at Jono, never blinking. "Thank you for claiming her, Jono."

"Couldn't let that bollocks stand," Jono said.

Emma carefully put Sage at arm's length, giving the other woman a tired smile and a gentle shake. "You are *always* welcome here, Sage. Remember that. Goes for all of you."

"Don't think Estelle and Youssef will appreciate me being in your territory, Em."

"Yeah, they said as much," Leon said as he sank down into an armchair and stretched out his legs. "We expect you to be at your shift when this whole case Patrick has going on blows over. I'm not dealing with the bar after overseeing people debug code all day and sitting in meetings."

"Slave driver," Patrick said, before wincing. "Shit. Sorry, Wade."

Wade froze, one hand buried in the Cheez-Its box he'd purloined from the pantry, the other clutching Marek's mobile that Jono had hidden in the hall closet. His pockets were bulging suspiciously. "Um."

"Is that my phone?" Marek demanded.

"Uh." Wade glanced at Jono. "No?"

"Try again," Jono said.

"Empty your pockets," Patrick told Wade.

Scowling, Wade proceeded to empty his pockets of a candy bar, two sets of car keys, a steak knife that had Patrick rolling his eyes, Jono's credit card of all things, and a small bottle of vodka.

"You're under the drinking age," Patrick said, leaning forward to move the vodka farther down the coffee table.

"Fuck you," Wade muttered. "I'm an adult. I deserve a drink."

"Therapy first."

"Who's gonna pay for it? You?"

"Yes." Patrick handed Jono back his credit card before tossing Marek his mobile. "Sorry. He literally can't help it."

"He's stealing our stuff and you're saying he can't help it?" Emma asked, not sounding impressed with that explanation.

"He's a dragon. They hoard things."

Jono let the others go through the stages of disbelief as he pulled out his wallet and slipped his credit card back into its slot. "Didn't even feel you nick it. You're good."

"If they didn't have me fighting, they'd put me to work on the streets pickpocketing," Wade said, sinking into the corner of the couch, his box of Cheez-Its forgotten. He kept his gaze downcast, not looking at anyone.

"Just you?"

Wade shrugged. "There were others."

Out of the corner of his eye, Jono saw Emma open her mouth, but he held up a hand to quiet her. "Are they still alive?"

Wade picked at his borrowed jeans where the fabric stretched over his knee. "Dunno. They were the other night. Doesn't mean much though. Tloque Nahuaque kills on a whim."

His voice was back to the flat monotone that made Jono want to gnash his teeth. "Were they werecreatures?"

Wade rubbed at his throat where the collar once sat. "Yeah. Most were."

"Who the fuck is Tloque Nahuaque?" Leon asked. "Another god?"

"Tezcatlipoca," Patrick said.

Leon stared at him. "Those names aren't remotely close to being the same thing. You sure they aren't two different assholes?"

Jono snorted. "There's two of the wankers, but the other one is Quetzalcoatl."

"Tloque Nahuaque is kind of like a title for Tezcatlipoca," Patrick said. "He's got a few."

"In English please?" Leon asked. "I might speak Spanish, but that's not close to any words I know."

"Lord of the Near and the Nigh."

"He's Aztec, with ties to the Dominion Sect," Jono added.

"He lives off of sacrifices. It's why we always fought to the death," Wade said dully.

Leon shoved himself to his feet. "That's it. I'm breaking out the tequila. If we're going to talk about hell gods, I need something stronger than water."

While Leon went to rummage around the wet bar for his drink of choice, Emma claimed his seat and tucked her feet beneath her on the cushion. She looked tired, and Jono knew she probably needed to get some rest after the meeting.

"They sold werecreatures to the vampires, Jono," Emma said.

"I know," he said.

"So what are we going to do about it? And don't tell me not to get involved. I'm being forced to pay retribution to the Manhattan Night Court to pay for the damages at the club last night because Estelle refuses to dip into the tithes. I'd rather Tremaine gets what is coming to him before I have to make a payment."

Patrick looked at Jono, raising an eyebrow. "Guess I'm paying that asshole another visit."

"I think you mean we," Jono told him.

"One of us needs to keep an eye on Wade. I volunteer you."

"You're off your bloody head if you think I'm letting you go into the Manhattan Night Court alone, Pat."

"I'm a mage, remember?"

"You're a disaster waiting to happen. You need me."

Jono didn't voice why. He knew Patrick would pick up on what he wasn't saying. They hadn't talked much about the soulbond and what it meant in regards to Patrick's magic, but maybe they needed to have that conversation. This situation was exactly why

Patrick needed Jono by his side to access the full strength of his magic again through Jono's soul.

"I'll take Lucien."

Jono couldn't help the growl that came out of his throat. "The fuck you will."

"I'll go," Sage interjected. "I'm…"

She trailed off and Jono turned to look at her. "You're what?"

Sage glanced at Patrick. "I was going to say I'd be your beta if Jono is the only alpha. Unless both you and Patrick are taking up alpha roles, in which case you won't need a beta?"

"Not a werecreature," Patrick pointed out.

"I'm not god pack."

"Do you want to be?" Jono asked her. "I know I didn't really give you a choice in the ring."

He would never keep Sage if she didn't want to stay. If she wanted him to remove his claim to her, he would. But the way she lifted her chin and glared at him told Jono that wasn't going to happen.

"No. My home is *here*, through you now. I'm not giving that up. I know god packs are far more prominent in the public eye, and I can learn to live with that level of scrutiny. Besides, working with my firm and representing Marek hasn't exactly enabled me to keep my private life completely private, even with the artifact I wear."

"Great. Then it's settled. I'll take Sage and you watch Wade," Patrick said.

Jono glared at him. "No."

"*Yes.* I can get a warrant based off of Wade's testimony that will get me through the front door. I'll take Sage as backup and reach out to Lucien, see if he can't spare a bloodsucker or two."

"You'll take Lucien but you won't take me? That's a load of bollocks."

Patrick sighed in frustration. "I promised Lucien I would help him take over the Manhattan Night Court. I can't keep him out of the loop about this."

"He'd as soon stab you in the back as help you."

"I realize that but I'm *going*, Jono. I have to. Tremaine has hostages and I can't leave them there."

"That one has a god, maybe two, backing him, neither of which you've ever faced before. Sage won't be enough as backup."

"Way to show your faith in your brand-new pack member," Patrick said with a hard snort.

Jono scowled. "*Our* pack. And I know Sage can handle herself, but the two of you alone against a Night Court and gods are shit odds."

"I've been dealing with gods for nearly three-quarters of my life. I have a better chance than you at getting out alive, and I won't be leaving Sage behind. I won't be leaving anyone we find in there behind."

Jono wanted to argue—he had a god riding his soul, after all—but he wasn't a combat mage. He hadn't spent almost a decade on the front lines of the fight against the hells. He hadn't sold his soul to survive.

Patrick, Jono knew, was the sort of bloke who would break off bits of himself first before letting someone else even get a scratch.

"I don't trust Tremaine or Lucien," Jono said into the tense quiet that had settled over the room.

Patrick grimaced. "Makes two of us. That's why I need you to stay behind to keep Wade safe but also because one of us needs to be on the outside. If things go wrong, I know you'll find me. I trust *you*, Jono."

His logic was sound, Jono just didn't care for it. He'd rather be by Patrick's side, in the thick of things. What he wanted wasn't what he could allow himself to have. Not as the alpha of a pack that was more than just two people now. That realization was sobering, and Jono rubbed hard at his eyes. Part of being an alpha was knowing when to delegate. Jono had learned that through watching the packs he'd orbited over the years. He just never realized how hard it was to do.

"I'll find you," Jono promised, meaning it with everything he had.

Patrick smiled, the expression lopsided, but his shields had thinned out enough that Jono could smell the relief emanating from him. "I know you will."

11

It took twenty-four hours to pry the facts out of Wade and submit them to the court for a warrant. Patrick ran the legal paperwork through the SOA rather than the PCB because the case had federal jurisdiction. Aside from that, the DEA had already reached out to the SOA about interference and the two legal sides were squabbling. At the end of the day, the United States District Court for the Southern District of New York didn't fuck around when it came to prosecuting vampires and the warrant was issued.

The conflicts of interest were something Patrick was pretending didn't exist.

The case the SOA was building against Tremaine was in the extremely early stages, but all evidence was being filed under seal. Patrick needed to protect Wade's identity, but he also didn't want to give Tremaine a heads-up. He didn't know what kind of inroads the master vampire might have made within the legal community, but Patrick hoped they didn't go too deep.

Getting the legal paperwork done meant Patrick couldn't approach the Crimson Diamond until Tuesday night. He'd declined backup from the SOA and argued with SAIC Henry Ng over that decision. Normally, Patrick would never turn down investigative help for a search warrant, but he was going into a Night Court who held allegiances to a couple of immortals. That changed the playing field immensely, and not for the better.

Patrick refused to put the lives of people who didn't know what they were heading into on the line like that. Vampires were one thing. Gods were something else entirely. It took a direct phone call from Setsuna to gloss over the friction between himself and Henry, but in the end, Patrick got his way. He was going in armed with his dagger, HK USP 9mm tactical pistol, and his magic, with Sage as support and one of Lucien's vampires. That would have to be enough.

All his precautions weren't enough to stop Jono from worrying.

"I still think this is a shit idea," Jono said from the front passenger seat of the Mustang.

"I can think of ten off the top of my head that were worse," Patrick replied as he turned off Madison Avenue. In the backseat, Wade snorted. The familiar crunch of snacks being eaten followed the sound.

Jono sighed. "No wonder why your old captain wanted to murder you half the time."

"He did not. It was more like a quarter of the time."

"Murder is still murder, Pat."

"That's debatable. What isn't is your job tonight."

"I'll keep an eye on the kid. Just make sure Sage keeps her eyes on you."

"Not a kid," Wade muttered from the back seat.

Patrick ignored him. "You can tell her yourself if you want when we get to her place."

"I already did when I rang her earlier," Jono said.

Patrick made a face as he braked to a stop in front of the old Art Deco building Marek and the others called home, putting on his hazard lights. Lights shone through most of the windows, signaling the Tempest pack had holed up together for the night on

Emma's orders. Jono and Wade would be staying with them until Patrick returned because if shit went down, Jono would need a car and Wade would need to be protected. Emma's pack was more than willing to fight for him, no matter what Estelle and Youssef had ordered.

That way led problems, but everyone had agreed they'd deal with it only when directly confronted by the god pack. Emma was adamant she wouldn't be banning Sage from her home even if that technically meant she was letting Sage into the Tempest pack's territory. Since Jono hadn't stayed long enough to hash out territory passage, they were all operating under the general understanding that they could pass through without any issues.

Patrick knew that wouldn't last for long, but so long as it lasted beyond this case, they'd be fine.

The front door opened right as Jono got out of the Mustang. Sage came out wearing dark skinny jeans and a fitted black T-shirt. Rather than sneakers, she had on ballet flats, which Patrick figured would be easier to lose if she had to shift to her weretiger form. Her necklace with its turquoise artifact hung from her neck, the only bit of color in her entire outfit.

Marek followed her out of the building while Emma and Leon chose to lounge by the front door. Patrick hit the button to roll down the window. "You're staying put, Marek."

Marek rolled his eyes. "I know. I just came down to tell you that I have a bad feeling about tonight."

"Did you have a vision?"

Marek rested his arm on the roof of the car and stared at Patrick through the open window. Behind him, Wade was being ushered up the stairs by Jono and let in by Leon.

"Not so much a vision as a gut feeling," Marek said slowly. "The Norns still can't see the future, so whatever is going on, you're smack in the middle of it."

"That's not new."

"Yeah, well, you have my fiancée watching your back, so don't do anything stupid."

Patrick turned to look at Sage's left hand but didn't see a ring. "*That* is new. Congratulations."

"Marriage is one of the oldest forms of contracts. It's another layer of protection the god pack will have a difficult time breaking," Sage explained. "And it's not new. We've been talking about it for a while now. Sunday changed everything."

"I'm shutting down Tiffany's for Sage to pick out a ring the second this case is over. Don't ruin my plans, Patrick," Marek said.

"Now you're just asking for shit to go down," Patrick said. "Go feed Wade. He needs another meal."

"We ordered pizza," Emma said from the doorway.

Marek pushed away from the car, and Jono took his place, leaning down to tug Patrick into a quick kiss. "Keep your mobile on you."

"Here's hoping I won't need to call in the cavalry," Patrick said.

"I'd be the first one there." Jono let out a heavy breath. "Next time you want to piss off a nutter, I'm going with you."

"I'm kind of hoping there won't be a next time."

"You're helping Lucien take over the Manhattan Night Court. There will be a next time."

Patrick switched off the hazard lights and lowered the emergency brake. "Don't remind me."

"Stay alive," Jono said in lieu of goodbye.

"Admit it. You've been talking to Gerard."

Jono smirked at the mention of Gerard Breckenridge, Patrick's old team captain of the Hellraisers. "What's it you Yanks always say? I plead the Fifth."

Jono smacked the top of the roof before stepping up onto the sidewalk. Patrick took his foot off the brake and hit the gas, driving down the block to take a left on Fifth Avenue.

"Where are we meeting Einar?" Sage asked.

"At the club," Patrick replied.

After what happened Monday with the god pack, Patrick had called Lucien to give him a heads-up on what Patrick had planned. Getting agency approval to go forward first meant Lucien couldn't really tell Patrick no. Patrick's contract with the SOA superseded his promise to Lucien. It didn't quite cancel things out and never would, but it was a roadblock Lucien had to work around.

Sage had been the one to come up with that tiny bit of wiggle room. Patrick could honestly say having a lawyer in his corner was actually working out well for once.

Too bad she couldn't get the DEA off his back.

His phone rang, a number with a Washington, DC, area code flashing across the screen. Patrick answered it, thinking it was from the legal department at the SOA. He was wrong.

"Special Agent Patrick Collins. Line and location are not secure," he said, answering the phone and resorting to driving one-handed as he did so.

"I hear your agency has filed documents under seal and got a warrant," Quetzalcoatl said in greeting.

"How the hell did you find that out?" Patrick demanded.

"That doesn't matter. I told you the case was mine. Do not enter Tremaine's territory."

"I have it on good authority Tremaine is killing werecreatures. I'm not leaving them there to die."

"He's sacrificing them. There's a difference."

Patrick hunched his shoulders, feeling the scar tissue stretch and pull on his chest. "Trust me, I know."

"You don't know what is waiting for you in that club, Patrick. You cannot face death alone."

"If you're talking about your brother, I'll take my chances."

"He is protecting death because he thinks he loves her. We have destroyed the world for less."

"World is still turning, Quetz."

"My *name* is Quetzalcoatl."

"I haven't forgotten," Patrick said with a shrug the immortal couldn't see. "Seems a lot of other people have."

Immortality was a lonely existence, one Patrick would never want. The gods played at being mortal because they had no other choice in a world no longer big enough for all of them. Dwindling prayers and worship could grant them only so much power in the face of a handful of dominant religions that had no use for their stories.

Patrick wondered how the Dominion Sect planned to contain death herself. He'd say it was impossible, but he'd seen what had been done to his twin sister with his own eyes. Hannah carried a stolen godhead when she shouldn't have been able to, what was left of her kept alive by prayers, the power residing in her soul siphoned off by Ethan and his followers.

"Do not serve the warrant," Quetzalcoatl told him in a low voice filled with power that made Patrick's teeth ache.

He shook it off. "You aren't the god who owns my soul debt, and Hermes gave me a message, remember? If you want death separated from your brother, I'm going to have to piss off some gods first. Dragging Tezcatlipoca's distributor into the light seems a good place to start. If doing so allows me to save some werecreatures, so much the better."

Patrick ended the call before Quetzalcoatl could respond. Sage looked at him out of the corner of her eye. "Is that wise?"

"Pissing off gods?" Patrick lifted his hips to shove his phone back into his pocket. "Probably not, but I do it all the time. It's bad for my health, but you do what you gotta do to get the job done."

Sage blinked at him slowly before saying, "You make a good alpha."

"I'm not an alpha anything."

"You're co-leading this pack. That technically makes you one."

"I don't know anything about leading a pack. Just ask Jono."

"He does well in a pinch."

Patrick braked for a red light, scratching idly at the nicotine patch on the underside of his arm. Jono wasn't there to smack his hand away. "Are you saying that because he claimed you or because you mean it?"

Sage didn't answer for two more blocks. When she finally spoke, her voice was thoughtful. "Jono has never liked how Estelle and Youssef have overseen the packs in New York City. I thought, in the beginning, it was because he was angry they wouldn't take him in when he first moved here. I know now it's because he's a better man than they are. He cares."

"Like a goddamn mother hen," Patrick muttered.

Sage nodded. "Yes. You need that in an alpha. What's more, you need that in a god pack. We don't have it here. Not yet."

The *not yet* should've worried Patrick, but he was familiar with the way war crept up on people. It didn't always announce itself with a bullet. If he'd been in Estelle and Youssef's place, he'd have banned Jono from his territory the second the Brit touched down on American soil. They'd let the seeds of a rebellion fester in their territory for years and only had themselves to blame when it bloomed.

"I don't know what Jono has planned, but I'll back him," Patrick said slowly.

"That is what pack does," Sage told him with a faint smile. "That is what a team does, if you will."

"You aren't my Hellraisers."

"Maybe not, but we'll be enough." Considering what they were heading into, Patrick hoped she meant every last word. Sage cleared her throat. "So how are we doing this? You have a plan that's more than serving the warrant?"

"Yeah. Don't die."

"That's your plan?"

"It's a good plan." Sage stared at him with an unimpressed look on her face. "What? It is."

"Unbelievable."

The drive into SoHo took about twenty minutes, give or take an aggressive taxi cab or two. Patrick pulled up in front of the

Crimson Diamond and unbuckled his seat belt. Before he even got his hand on the door handle, a stupidly young vampire he didn't know dropped down next to his Mustang on the street, showing off jagged fangs.

Patrick hit the window button to lower it half an inch. "Don't get blood on my car."

"I'm a messy eater," the vampire hissed.

"I wasn't talking to you."

The hand that reached around the vampire's throat and sank sharp nails that could have doubled for talons into pale white skin was a blur until it wasn't. The fingers sank in to the second knuckle before ripping free, bringing half the vampire's throat with it. Thick, dark blood splattered against the glass, and Patrick hastily raised the window.

"I *said* don't get blood on my car," he yelled.

The vampire clutched at his ruined throat, mouth working soundlessly in shock now that his airway was pretty much gone. Then he was thrown farther down the street with enough force to break a few bones. Patrick could only hope he got hit by a taxi.

Patrick shoved the car door open and got out, glaring at Einar. "You're paying for the detailing on my car."

"The damage to your car is not our problem." Einar stared down his nose at Patrick, mouth curling in distaste. "You're late."

"Bullshit. We agreed to meet up an hour after sunset. We're right on time."

Sage got out of the car and headed for the sidewalk. Patrick locked the car with a push of a button and followed after her. Einar beat him to the guarded entrance of the club, a blur of motion in the dark Patrick's eyes couldn't track.

This time, the door was being manned by half a dozen vampires instead of a single human servant. The show of force told Patrick more than anything else they'd struck a nerve the other night when Lucien had waltzed in like he owned the place.

Sage stuck by his side as they approached the door. He pulled the search warrant out of the pocket of his leather jacket and opened it so the Manhattan Night Court vampires could see the SOA seal and judge's signature. He hooked his thumb around the chain his badge hung from and lifted it off his chest so the vampires couldn't miss it.

"Special Agent Patrick Collins of the Supernatural Operations Agency here with a nice official search warrant. Step aside," Patrick said.

The vampires didn't move, but the door did open behind them.

"Good evening, Special Agent Collins," a deep voice said from the entranceway. "I'm Alistair Shepard, counsel for Tremaine. I'd like to see your warrant."

The attorney in question was older than Patrick by at least a decade, if not more. Hair going gray at the temples, Rolex on left wrist, and a suit that not even Patrick's hazard pay could afford, Alistair Shepard was a tall, broad-shouldered man with sharp brown eyes and a disdainful smile.

Patrick shrugged and passed over the warrant. Alistair made a show of reading through the legalese before handing it back.

"Your warrant was achieved under false parameters. My client harbors no werecreatures here," Alistair said.

Patrick kept his shields locked down tight, hoping none of the vampires could sense his unease. That statement didn't bode well to any captive's survival.

"So you say, but perhaps his business partner does," Sage said calmly, tucking a lock of hair behind her ear. "Tremaine wouldn't be the first vampire to allow storage of other people's property within his territory."

"Tremaine is a master vampire who needs no business partner."

Patrick waved aside Alistair's statement. "I have the right to search the premises, so how about you get out of my way?"

Alistair's cold eyes flicked to where Einar stood, a silent, looming threat currently flipping a switchblade around the fingers of his left hand. "The federal government may pass. That one has no right to enter."

Einar smiled, icy blue eyes never blinking in his pale, pale face. "Tremaine is owned by Lucien. I am here as proxy for our master. A piece of paper can't bar our master's blood rights."

"There's precedent law for that," Sage added.

"Tremaine has been his own master for centuries. The person you represent has no place here," Alistair argued.

"Nice thing about being a federal agent with a warrant is that I get a say on who gets access to search. Einar is coming with me," Patrick said. "Now get the fuck out of my way."

Alistair stared them down for a couple more seconds before finally stepping aside. The vampires guarding the door didn't look happy, but no one tried to gut them on the way inside. Strangely enough, Alistair didn't follow them into the club. Patrick chalked that up to deniability.

The hostess stand was empty, but the neon *No Holy Items* sign burned bright in the flower wall. Past the heaviness of the threshold, Patrick became aware that the club was *too* silent.

"It's empty," Sage confirmed when he glanced at her.

The little voice in the back of Patrick's mind was yelling *trap, trap, trap* over and over. The warning was one he didn't have the luxury of listening to, not if there was a chance any of the people Estelle and Youssef had given up were still alive.

Recognition cut through Patrick's shields and magic with enough power behind the warning to make his stomach roil.

"It is customary to bring an offering when you meet with me," an accented voice called from deeper in the club.

Patrick's hand strayed toward the hilt of his dagger, fingers brushing over the cool metal. He didn't draw it, but knowing it was there settled his nerves a little. Gesturing for the others to follow, Patrick led them into the heart of the club, eyes skimming over the mostly empty space and all the corners the enemy could hide.

The mezzanine was empty; the dance floor was not. A golden circle had been drawn on the floor with magic, the same one from Saturday night, with its ancient designs that wouldn't look out of place on a stone temple. No barriers were raised, but that could change in an instant. Placed in the center of the circle was a seat that was more throne, less chair, and claimed by a god.

Tezcatlipoca seemed to favor linen suits that wouldn't look out of place in the South Side of Miami. The immortal was shirtless beneath his pristine white suit jacket, but his upper torso was hidden by a shining chest piece made out of burnished gold plate that hung from his neck and shoulders. Tezcatlipoca's long, straight black hair fell loose to his waist, though his head was hidden beneath a gold headdress adorned with obsidian and jade. Colored heron feathers a meter long extended from the headdress in a fan that haloed his head.

A black line edged in yellow was painted across his cheekbones and nose, the color rising almost to his eyes. What was most striking, if not downright chilling, about his appearance wasn't the headdress but his right foot. While Tezcatlipoca's bare left foot was flesh and bone, the right was carved from polished obsidian, shiny as a mirror.

Surrounding the Aztec god were humans that weren't servants, some with magic, some without. Patrick picked out the gang members carrying guns and those with magic burning at their fingertips. Interspaced between them were Manhattan Night Court vampires, their stillness and lack of breath eerie in the dim light of the club.

Seated to Tezcatlipoca's left was a black jaguar, the kind that had chased Wade into the subway Saturday night. Standing to Tezcatlipoca's right was Tremaine, who looked far too pleased with himself.

"Think he left one master for another?" Patrick mused.

"The rat has never been capable of fending for himself. Lucien has only been thinking about how best to gift a true death to

Tremaine since he fled the Ottoman Empire's old borders and left his brothers and sisters to die beneath the teeth of religion," Einar said.

The smug look on Tremaine's face devolved into one of fury Patrick could see from halfway across the club.

"Aw, I think you hit a nerve. Quick, do it again."

They moved as far as the golden circle before coming to a stop, the tips of Patrick's boots mere millimeters from the magic burning on the dance floor. They weren't safe anywhere in the Crimson Diamond, but he wasn't about to mess with a god's power.

"You are trespassing," Tremaine hissed out.

"It's not your territory," Einar shot back.

Tezcatlipoca stroked a hand over the jaguar's head. "You are mistaken if you believe your master owns anything here."

"Oh, Lucien owns a fuck ton of shit I'm sure your cartel would love to have," Patrick replied. "But he doesn't like sharing. Tremaine, though, pretty sure you can keep him."

"Speak my name with such disrespect again and you won't leave this club alive," Tremaine promised.

"As threats go, I give it a solid two. Lucien still has you beat."

Tezcatlipoca studied Patrick with a hooded gaze. "Your insolence does you no favors."

Patrick spread his hands and shrugged. "I'm here at the behest of my government for crimes committed by the Omacatl Cartel. Tremaine is a party to those crimes by knowingly giving you a space to run your fight rings and sell your drugs."

"Mortal laws do not apply to me."

"But they apply to your subordinates," Sage spoke up. "Of which Tremaine is one of them. And a warrant isn't granted without proof."

"Your proof won't be alive for much longer," Tremaine promised.

Patrick chose to have faith in Jono because not believing the other man would survive and keep Wade safe wasn't an option. "You'd be surprised what people do when cornered."

Tezcatlipoca smiled, the expression inhuman. "I look forward to seeing how you react."

The immortal raised a hand, and Tremaine obeyed like the well-strung puppet he was. The master vampire turned to one of his subordinates and said, "Bring her."

Patrick tensed at that order. Beside him, Sage went rigid. Einar cocked his head to the side, listening hard to something Patrick couldn't hear.

Tezcatlipoca stood, the jaguar pacing beside him as he walked toward where Patrick stood. Every step of his obsidian foot against marble rang sharply in the air. Patrick didn't hesitate to unsheathe his dagger, heavenly fire crawling over the matte black blade as he held it tightly.

"I heard you were gifted the power of gods. It will not help you tonight," Tezcatlipoca said.

Patrick raised the dagger between them, the sharp tip pointed at Tezcatlipoca's heart. "It helps enough."

"Such misplaced faith you carry."

Sage drew in a sharp breath, and Patrick knew he wasn't going to like what came next. Sage, with her enhanced hearing, probably heard every single sound before they got close enough to reach Patrick's ears. She stood her ground despite the expression on her face that spoke of wanting to take people apart from the skin on down. The bleak, furious look in her eyes caught Tezcatlipoca's attention.

"Daughter, you do yourself a disservice by aligning yourself with this one," Tezcatlipoca said.

"You are not of my people," Sage spat out. "Don't call me *daughter*."

Beneath her snarled words was the distant sound of screaming —thin and thready, full of agonizing pain.

It didn't sound human.

Sage closed her eyes, swallowing hard. Patrick stepped closer to her, not letting his dagger drop. Screams encroached on the silence as proof of everything Estelle and Youssef had perpetuated against their own people came into the light, dragged between two vampires.

Sage made a wounded noise and covered her mouth with her hand. Patrick forced himself to look—to see what had been done to the captive—because he needed to know how much blood to ask for in return.

The werelion looked like they had been skinned alive, one bite at a time. Most of their fur was gone, with stakes of pure silver coated in aconite pierced through each paw so they couldn't run. The vampires dropped the werelion on the floor next to Tremaine. The werelion lay there listlessly, swollen tongue lolling out of a mouth full of too many broken teeth. Patrick saw more bone in her tail than muscle. Ribs glistened through pus and blood and rotten flesh with every strained breath the werelion took.

"Do you recognize them?" Patrick asked Sage.

It took Sage a moment to regain her composure, her hands balling into fists before she spoke. "Kennedy."

Tremaine grabbed one torn ear and lifted Kennedy's head off the ground. He shook her, hard enough to almost snap her neck, before letting go. The sound her jaw made against the floor made Patrick grind his teeth together.

"Something tells me you've missed her." Tremaine's smile was nothing but sharp fangs. "You can have her back, but one of you must stay."

"We didn't come here to negotiate," Patrick said.

Tezcatlipoca raised an eyebrow, his tone mocking when he said, "Didn't you?"

Patrick had little doubt their offer was a load of bullshit. Kennedy was living proof of their crimes, and they wouldn't let her go without believing they could eliminate the evidence—*all* the evidence.

And that was something Patrick could never allow.

He readjusted his grip on the dagger and turned to offer it to Sage. She stared at him, gaze going bleak, somehow knowing exactly what it meant. "No."

"Yes," Patrick told her quietly. "I need you to trust me."

He was used to playing games the gods dictated, but Sage wasn't. Her weretiger form wouldn't be enough to keep her safe once she left his side. His dagger might be. At the end of the day, Sage was his responsibility, pack or otherwise.

Her expression twisted, but for all her background as lawyer, Sage didn't argue. When she took the dagger from him, Patrick was reminded of that instant when he was a child, giving up everything to Persephone's coaxing offer. Except he knew exactly what he was giving up here, and Patrick hoped with everything he had it was a temporary separation, one that wouldn't last years or a lifetime.

Death, he knew, didn't always come quick.

Then he turned to face Tezcatlipoca again. Patrick's mouth curled at the corners, the sort of vicious, feral expression that wouldn't be out of place on a battlefield. He was reminded of a lesson learned the hard way while serving in the Mage Corps—rules of engagement were for people who were never desperate.

And Patrick was as desperate as they came.

"What are your terms?"

12

EINAR BROKE THE TENSE SILENCE WITH AN ANNOYED SNORT. "YOUR self-preservation skills are lacking."

"My self-preservation skills are fucking amazing, don't lie." At the moment, they were telling Patrick to *run*, and he was ignoring them. "Unlike Tremaine here."

"I will take great pleasure in ripping out your tongue," Tremaine promised.

Cold sweat trickled down Patrick's spine, but it wasn't because of Tremaine's threat. Tezcatlipoca had yet to look away, and the god's regard was far too dangerous for any sort of comfort.

"Promises, promises," Patrick said, forcing his voice and heartbeat to remain even. "I still haven't heard what you want."

"The Dominion Sect has promised me a great number of worshippers if we deliver you alive. I have seen what their promises mean where it concerns my cousins. I have little incentive to bargain with them," Tezcatlipoca said.

One of the cartel members stiffened at that announcement, his eyes narrowing. Patrick could see black concentric circles inked into the man's palms, magic crackling at his fingertips. It reminded him of how Zachary Myers, Ethan's right-hand acolyte, focused his magic. All magic users needed a focus of some sort, and permanently inked ones never seemed to go out of style.

Patrick wondered what ties the stranger had to the inner circles of the Dominion Sect, and just how many gods aligned with the hells Ethan was reaching out to, and why.

"That so? I'm not a big fan of family reunions. The last one was a major buzzkill."

Patrick could think of a hundred reasons why Ethan would want him—none of them good, all of them involving a grave of some sort. Ethan had Macaria's godhead, even if it wasn't in his soul. Godhood came with a price, and Patrick wasn't willing to pay it so his father could gain immortality.

Except there was a barely breathing werelion sprawled on the floor that Patrick needed to get to safety. Choosing between Ethan and Tezcatlipoca wasn't really a choice, but he wasn't leaving Kennedy behind. It would cost him, but this wouldn't be the first time Patrick traded himself for a hostage.

I am never telling Gerard about this.

"Your life for hers," Tremaine said, gesturing carelessly at Kennedy's prone form.

"My life for theirs and hers," Patrick countered, jerking his thumb in Sage and Einar's direction.

Tezcatlipoca smiled, eyes bright with malice above the face paint. "You are in no position to bargain."

"If you ignore the fact that I'm what you need as leverage against the Dominion Sect, then sure. You don't really think they'll follow through on whatever they promised you, do you? If you walk away from a broken promise, they'll find you. The same way they found Ra and Hades and Zeus. And you'll owe them, whether you like it or not."

Tezcatlipoca shrugged, the heron feathers on his headdress rippling from the motion. "Mortals cannot own me."

"With arrogance like that, you'll only end up like Macaria. But if you have me, you've got a loophole." Patrick spread his hands, taking a step forward. "I won't even fight you. I've already given up my dagger. Just let them leave alive and you've got me. I'll stay—"

"For as long as he can," Sage cut in tightly.

As loopholes went, it wasn't much to work with, but Patrick let her words fall between them, accepting her support. He knew better than most that gods were sometimes arrogant to a fault. Whether or not he'd be able to survive that arrogance was something else entirely.

"No magic," Tremaine said. "No guns. No weapons."

"Done," Patrick promised, the weight of his acceptance like a vise around his lungs. *I really need to stop selling off bits of my life like this.*

Tezcatlipoca waved a hand at Patrick. "So witnessed. You will take shine to seal the deal."

Patrick wanted to agree but choked on the words. Sage drew in a sharp breath, opening her mouth to argue. Einar wrapped his hand around her face to cover her mouth and block her words.

"This is not your bargain to make," Einar told her.

"If you do not agree, the bargain is void, and *this* one"— Tremaine kicked Kennedy in the ribs, and Einar had to put Sage in a chokehold to keep her from going after the master vampire— "will not live to see the dawn."

Tremaine stared at Patrick, a twisted sense of superiority gleaming in his eyes that was a poor imitation of Lucien's, and always would be. Lucien might pour what he was into his children's making, but they were just shadows compared to him.

Patrick licked his lips, knowing that taking shine was a risk he couldn't walk away from. "Okay."

Sage made a sound that was more snarl than words. She elbowed Einar hard enough to draw a grunt from the vampire, and he let her go. She shoved him away and glared at Patrick. He expected her to yell, to protest, but Sage did none of those things.

All she said was "You asked me to trust you, and I do. So don't make me be the one to tell Jono he has to bury you."

Then she lifted her chin high and strode past Tezcatlipoca for where Kennedy lay on the floor. The magic beneath Sage's feet didn't bar her, and Patrick fought against the instinct to yank her out of the circle. Tremaine stepped between Sage and Kennedy, staring disdainfully down his nose at her.

"The terms of the bargain were met. Give me Kennedy," Sage demanded.

"The mage takes shine, and then you may have your prize," Tremaine said.

Sage stared him down with a ferocity that made several cartel members look askance at her, wariness in their eyes.

One of the lesser vampires came forward and poured several pills into Tremaine's outstretched hand. Patrick dug out his car keys and unholstered his sidearm, passing both to Einar. "Tell Lucien he'll still get what he wants."

"You dead?" Einar asked.

Patrick rolled his eyes. "Real fucking funny."

The warrant had got them in, got them tortured proof, but they still needed to know the extent of Tremaine's territory. Getting that information meant Patrick just had to survive an evening of drugged interrogation in order to get the lay of the land so to speak. Human laws wouldn't be enough to tear down Tremaine's Night Court, which was why Patrick hadn't once mentioned arresting the bloodsucker. That was a laughable way forward with a god standing in his way.

Einar stayed outside the circle as Patrick joined Sage in the center. Tremaine had an ugly, triumphant look on his face that Patrick itched to punch right off, but he kept his hands to himself. Behind the safety of his shields, Patrick dug deep into his scarred soul for that shining, resilient link that bound him to Jono. He refused to reach for Jono's soul and use it to draw external magic from the ley lines and nexus buried deep beneath the earth. That power wouldn't help him here, not bound by the promise he'd made.

But he could make sure the soulbond stayed wide open between them.

Find me, Patrick thought as he reached for one of the white pills with its pinprick of red-black in the center that Tremaine held out to him. *You have to find me.*

He needed to believe that Jono would before it was too late.

Patrick swallowed shine, and the chemical, rancid taste filled his mouth sickeningly quick. He gagged, the drug tasting how dead bodies smelled. Shine wasn't a drug he was familiar with. He didn't know how much time he had before the high kicked in, but Patrick still knew chasing it would fuck him up. It wasn't meant to be taken by magic users. At the end of the day, they weren't the food vampires craved.

"Go," Patrick told Sage.

She knelt down and dragged Kennedy's broken, battered body over her shoulders in a fireman's carry. The sound Kennedy made was that of a wounded, dying animal, and Sage's jaw tightened. Patrick's dagger and sheath dangled from one of her hands, a hint of white, heavenly fire sparking along the edge where the hilt pressed against the leather. Patrick only hoped the borrowed magic in its making would keep her safe as an extension of keeping him alive.

As Sage straightened up, dark fog twisted into existence at the four quadrant points of the circle. The fog rapidly solidified into jaguars, the same kind of constructs that had chased them through the subway on Saturday night.

"Alive has many connotations," Tezcatlipoca said, sounding viciously amused. "I suggest you run, daughter."

"Next time, you let me do all the talking from the start," Sage told Patrick.

Patrick appreciated her optimism. He'd appreciate it even more if they all survived this mess.

Sage darted out of the circle in a blur of speed, jaguars giving chase between one breath and the next. Einar was a streak Patrick could barely follow, the vampire tossing what looked like a flashbang at the jaguars but which turned out to be something better.

The barrier ward that exploded between them crashed against Patrick's shields. Embedded in the grenade was Nadine's magic, part of the weaponry she'd left Lucien back in June as payment for his help. The feel of her magic was like a breath of fresh air through the haziness growing in his mind. It didn't stop the jaguars, but it did stop the bullets from the cartel members. Patrick blinked rapidly, the brightness from the barrier ward not diminishing.

A too-cold hand wrapped around his throat, sharp nails cutting into his skin. His head was jerked around and Patrick found himself staring into Tremaine's cold blue eyes, body outlined in soul light that never filled him.

"I'm curious how you know Lucien," Tremaine said, his thumb digging into the underside of Patrick's jaw.

The correct answer would always come down to Ashanti, but Patrick didn't owe the vampire the truth. "I dialed a wrong number once. Meant to call a phone-sex hotline. Got a mass-murdering fuck-face instead."

Tremaine let Patrick go long enough to backhand him across the face with enough force to knock him to the ground. Pain spiked through his head from the blow, the magic making up the circles stinging his skin. Patrick blinked, shoving himself to a sitting position despite how much his head ached now.

"Starting the interrogation early?" Patrick asked as he stared down Tremaine.

The audience of humans and vampires were becoming a mix of incandescent fire and dark holes in his vision. Magic users of all kinds had the ability to see people's auras, that extension of the human soul. All it took was a little magic to slip their vision sideways in order to see that brightness. They could handle it for a short period of time before they needed to revert back to normal eyesight to prevent damage.

Mundane humans couldn't see a person's soul at all, not on their own. Shine made it so that no one could escape the burning brightness of auras, and the only reprieve was the emptiness that vampires carried because the undead had no souls.

Patrick closed his eyes, but that didn't help; he could still see the afterimage of shining souls on the back of his eyelids.

A cold hand grabbed him by the collar of his jacket, the charms embedded in the leather enough to make Tremaine hiss, but not enough to make the vampire let him go. The thing about vampires was they could live long enough to survive the consequences of their actions, and tonight was no different. Patrick swallowed against the taste of the dead on his tongue as Tremaine hauled him to his feet. An unfamiliar high scratched at his mind, making the tips of his fingers tingle with a sensation Patrick rarely experienced outside of sex.

"The interrogation hasn't begun," Tremaine said, pulling Patrick uncomfortably close.

Patrick forced his eyes open, the master vampire limned in light that burned. The body he was pressed against had no warmth, no heartbeat, nothing of substance that Patrick should want—but he did.

The pull of forced desire was an unwanted curl of heat in his gut that made bile crawl up his throat. Patrick's shields wavered against his bones, and it took every bit of his rapidly fading concentration to keep them up.

"You won't win this fight," Patrick promised. "Lucien looks forward to a change of ownership and bringing you to heel."

Tremaine laughed, harsh and low. "He will take nothing from me. I learned the bitter lessons of laying waste to my world from him, and I learned them well."

"Not well enough."

"Lucien turned his back on Tremaine, and I showed him a new

way forward. Do you know what you mortals used to sacrifice to me?" Tezcatlipoca asked as he pressed himself up against Patrick's back, the gold chest plate digging into his spine. One heavy hand reached around to press over Patrick's heart, fingers digging into the scar tissue there through his shirt. "Your life. Your heart. Your very soul."

Trapped between heat and cold, with unwanted hands sliding over his body without his permission, all Patrick could think about was how much he wanted to say no—but how some part of him kept thinking *yes*.

The push of Tremaine's mind against his own didn't help. Persuasion was a power all vampires had, though the degree to which they could manipulate a person was different. Patrick squeezed his eyes shut, falling deep into half-remembered SERE training to help keep his focus for as long as he could. He retreated behind his personal shields, though he knew they were a stop-gap only.

"Get your hands off me," he ground out.

He needed to say it, not just think it, but *no* wasn't always respected. Tremaine laughed, his hand sliding down Patrick's chest to cup his cock through his jeans.

"You'll see how we worship now," Tremaine said.

The cruel promise in his voice was a nightmare Patrick wanted no part of. His fingers twitched with the need to call his magic, but he knew if he did, it would count as breaking his word and only make the high worse. Shine was eating away at his sight, at his concentration, chipping away at his resolve with every minute that passed. The drug was hitting hard and fast, buoyed by the black magic that lived inside the stagnant blood that sat in vampire veins.

Magic which Patrick's body did not like at fucking all.

Tremaine let go of Patrick's clothed cock after a hard squeeze, only to grab him by the upper arm and drag him toward the heavy double doors past the dance floor that led to the back of the club.

Two vampires darted ahead to hold the doors open. Patrick couldn't quite keep his footing, and he stumbled, both from the brightness and the speed at which Tremaine hauled him forward.

They bypassed storage rooms and a break room, heading for a heavily warded door at the end of the short hallway. Tremaine opened it, the door swinging wide on its hinges. Inside was a heavily barricaded and reinforced steel vault that wouldn't look out of place in a bank. Vampires didn't use coffins to sleep these days, despite what the stories said. Instead, they used what could pass as bomb shelters.

Even in his altered state, Patrick knew this would lead to the heart of the Manhattan Night Court.

"We had a bargain with the Dominion Sect," someone said from behind them.

Patrick laughed, shaking his head at the sheer stupidity of some people and how they thought they could outsmart a god. The back room grew brighter in sections, washing out the halogen glare from above. The vampires who blurred through the room to open the vault door and stand guard were bits of dark respite in Patrick's vision he didn't trust.

"Kill him," Tezcatlipoca said with the casual disdain of a god who expected to be obeyed.

Loyalty was either bought or earned; that had been true for millennia. Tonight was no different. Patrick sluggishly craned his head around, watching from a drugged distance as the warlock with the concentric circles tattooed on his hands had his throat torn out by a vampire eager to obey. Magic sputtered and died around the warlock as blood splattered across the floor. Patrick blinked, the body seemingly falling in slow degrees to the ground.

"Killing their mouthpiece won't stop you from owing them," Patrick slurred.

Tezcatlipoca's aura burned like the sun when the god stepped into view. Patrick had to cover his eyes with one hand, but that didn't stop them from watering.

"I promised them nothing."

Maybe Patrick could believe that if the immortal hadn't tried so hard to keep him when his soul was owned by Persephone.

"Didn't you?" Patrick asked, lips numb, but smiling all the same.

Hands slammed into his back and he went tumbling down the stairs into a darkness that felt too alive to be anything but trouble. He scraped his chin raw on the way down before he managed to tuck his head and get an arm around his skull to protect it. Patrick bruised the hell out of his knees and elbows as he careened down the stairs, finally crashing to a stop on a cold landing. He sprawled there, ears ringing, body aching in a way that momentarily disrupted the encroaching sexual need building up beneath the terror.

Patrick forced his eyes open at the sound of footsteps on the stairs, trying to blink back the burning brightness that wouldn't fade. A shadow loomed above him, the cool darkness saving his sight.

"You wasted your life on an animal. Lucien would be so disappointed," Tremaine said as he hauled Patrick to his feet.

"Can't waste what doesn't belong to me," Patrick muttered.

Tremaine dragged Patrick down another set of stairs. Shine dulled his reflexes and he stumbled against the wall on the way down. The lurch in his stomach was less vertigo and more the collapsing of one of his shields, his magic fracturing beneath his desperate, fading control.

Patrick grasped at the edges of the soulbond. *Find me.*

It was a false sort of comfort that stayed with him on the painful journey down below the club. The cement stairwell got colder as they descended. Patrick lost count of the steps before he reached the bottom, arriving into a cold, featureless tunnel that would never be inviting.

The place stank of iron, blood, and the musty, moldering smell of the long dead. He swallowed dryly, breathing through his mouth for a few seconds as Tremaine pressed up against his back.

"You shouldn't have allied yourself with Lucien."

Patrick dragged his fingernails down the stone wall. One caught on a crack and tore over the nailbed. "I know I can't trust him, but you still think you can pull one over on Ethan. Between the two of us, I'm not the stupid one."

Fingers tangled in his hair and Patrick was slammed face-first against the wall. His teeth clacked hard together, catching his tongue. Blood filled his mouth, and a familiar spike of pain in his nose told him he might have broken it again.

Shine made him not care, when he knew he needed to. But bridging that divide was something his brain just wouldn't do.

"If this is how you like to feed, I don't know why people take this shit," Patrick said, face throbbing from the impact.

"Because it makes your kind beg."

"I only get on my knees for one person, and you aren't him."

A cold tongue licked at the blood trickling from between Patrick's lips. Patrick recoiled hard, body pressed up against the wall with nowhere to go. But even as he moved away, his cock twitched in his jeans, desire warring against the panicked refusal quietly dying in his mind.

"You'll worship a different way for her," Tremaine promised. "I'll make sure of it."

Patrick's brain tripped over *her*, and his confusion loosened up his focus. His consciousness drifted, shine making his skin itch with the desire to just let go. They were halfway down the tunnel before he remembered to carve out a different bit of pain to rival the chemical-induced desire crawling through his body.

He bit down on his bottom lip hard enough to cut it, breathing harshly as the new pain hit. Patrick chewed into his own skin to give himself something else to focus on rather than the shine and shadows in his eyes. It was a last-gasp effort that wouldn't hold up for long, but it let Patrick keep his feet underneath him when he wanted to let his body rest.

There was no rest to be found underground, in the fringes of the veil.

Patrick tried to keep track of their passage through the sprawling maze of tunnels, but he kept getting distracted. They passed rooms that would never see daylight, many of which had shadows moving in them, holes in his sight that held no souls.

He thought the earth trembled at the end of the final tunnel but chalked it up to a possible hallucination. Wavering on his feet, Patrick watched as a pair of vampires approached a steel door not unlike the one guarding the underground entrance back at the club. The only difference was this one had wards scrawled over its surface, some of which were broken and forcibly tied to newer ones.

Even to Patrick's damaged vision, he could see the areas where the wards were joined together weren't stable. Before he could try to make any sense of the magic, the vault-like door swung open, revealing a low-lit area beyond the rat-maze they'd just traversed.

Cool, musty air hit Patrick's nose as Tremaine hauled him forward into a long-abandoned subway station. Old, rusted train tracks stretched down a forgotten tunnel into the dark. The wards that buttressed the entire subway system were missing completely down here, or broken so badly as to be remade into something sickeningly new. Patrick was too out of it to really appreciate how *wrong* it all was, but he knew the broken wards weren't something he should forget.

What magic Patrick could see lining the tunnel entrance flickered with a gray, malevolent light that warred with the red-orange glow coming from hundreds of candles. Tiny votives, obnoxious candelabras, glass vases with pictures of the Virgin Mary painted on them—any kind of candle a person could buy or make surrounded an intricate shrine built on the old train platform.

In the center, seated within a large gold-leafed frame, was a life-sized skeleton clad in white robes, the cowl pulled up over long, brittle black hair that pooled in its lap. In one bony hand the skeleton held a long scythe; in the other, a golden globe. Dozens of gold necklaces were draped around its neck and shoulders, glinting on the white cloth in the candlelight. Marigolds filled the space near its legs and feet, the orange petals like bits of flame.

In the flickering candlelight, the skull of Santa Muerte seemed to grin.

Patrick dropped his gaze, eyes watering, and saw more bones than those found in a small graveyard between them and the shrine. Which meant it wasn't only a shrine, but an altar.

"My lady appreciates the offerings I bring her more than you will ever know," Tezcatlipoca said into his ear.

"Fuck you," Patrick ground out, heart pounding in his chest.

The god's laughter echoed eerily in the station, the twisted wards lining the subway entrance flaring up at the sound. "You'll beg for it soon enough. Our sacrifices always do before Tremaine sucks the marrow from their bones."

Patrick jerked away from the god's presence but didn't get far since Tremaine still had hold of him. The master vampire casually tossed him into the arms of the worshippers who had followed them down into the dark—Night Court vampires and Omacatl Cartel members whose religion revolved around death.

Even in Patrick's drugged-up state, he still tried to fight them, but his body wasn't cooperating. Shine burned through his veins, filling his eyes with the brightness of souls, need clawing painfully at his skin. The drug made him want things he never would outside the chemical changes in his brain.

He wanted the unholy darkness to snuff out the light, wanted hands on him that he'd sooner break if he could only stay focused. But the ability to think rationally was fracturing beneath the ache in his body that shine drew out of him.

Patrick was dragged to the altar laid out before the shrine. He tripped over bones, breaking some, sending others tumbling away from his feet. Two humans gripped his arms, the brightness of their souls almost overpowering his sight, especially the one to his left. The vampire ahead of them blotted out the candlelight, leading the way to the empty space at Santa Muerte's feet. Marigold blossoms lined the area like funeral wreaths.

"No," Patrick said, the word sticking to his teeth as he was forced down to the platform floor.

It smelled like blood, like flowers, and Patrick knew he would always associate this particular fear with the cloying floral scent tinged in iron filling his nose.

Two cartel members held him down at the wrists and shoulders, the bruising weight of their grip keeping him in place. His legs were wrenched apart with a strength he couldn't break. Lying on his back, Patrick watched as Tremaine approached, bright sparks burning around that human-shaped darkness like some mirage or hallucination. He would never be any oasis Patrick would pray for.

"Is this how you killed the werecreatures you didn't force to fight?" Patrick asked over the pounding drum beat of his heart.

"This is how we pray now that our mother has forsaken us," Tremaine said, kneeling between Patrick's legs.

Patrick choked out a bitter laugh, hands clenching weakly into fists. Tremaine didn't know—couldn't have known—that Ashanti was dead, but her absence had still been felt. In the void of her death, her children had gone searching for acceptance somewhere else.

Tremaine's power of persuasion coiled in his mind, digging at the breaks in resistance shine had already created. "You want this."

Some part of Patrick did, but the rest of him still fought. Cold hands rucked up his shirt, tearing at the button on his jeans. Patrick heaved against the hands pinning him down, trying to get away even as he ached to be touched by the darkness that promised a false respite. In the burning light that filled his eyes, the scythe swung down, held by a bony hand that wielded it with unearthly precision.

"I bring you a sacrifice, my love," Tezcatlipoca said from the train tracks.

The tip of the blade came to rest right over Patrick's heart, tearing his shirt and scratching at his scars. He blinked, staring in horror as the skull moved, teeth parting around a voice that sounded like the echo of prayers in a cold mausoleum.

"*Worship me,*" Santa Muerte said as Tremaine yanked Patrick's jeans down around his thighs.

Through blood and sacrifice, eased by false desire—a lamb to the slaughter in a makeshift temple.

If Patrick worshipped anyone, it wasn't death.

The hands gripping his left arm and shoulder shifted, the burning brightness of the man's soul blocking out the shadows all around him. Patrick blinked, tasting blood as Tremaine's cold fingers slipped beneath his underwear, sharp nails scraping against his cock.

In the center of that blinding light, all Patrick saw was a pair of ageless yellow eyes burning brighter than the sun.

The stranger was not a god Patrick knew.

Time stilled like it had on the street the other night, the god's presence a counterpoint to the prayer Tremaine sought to make with Patrick's body and soul.

"My cousin searches for you," the god said right before he pushed Patrick through the platform and into the cold tangle of the veil, letting him fall away from the grasping hands of death.

13

JONO KNEW SOMETHING WAS WRONG EVEN BEFORE THE OLD GREEK coin still embedded in Marek's window exploded with magic. Power rushed through the apartment's walls with a *whoosh* that made Jono's ears pop. Wade jumped off the sofa in surprise, the bag of chips falling away from his hands.

"What the *fuck?*" Wade said, eyes wide and voice gone high-pitched with fear.

"Marek!" Jono yelled as he raced for the door.

Footsteps pounding down the upstairs hall told him Marek had left his office at a run. "I still can't see a damn thing!"

"Then stay here behind the ward. Goes double for you, Wade."

Jono yanked the front door open, glad to see the magic wasn't stopping him from leaving—but someone else was. Jono drew himself up short, nearly crashing into Hermes where the messenger god stood in the foyer.

"Huh. I forgot about that coin," Hermes said.

"Get out of my fucking way," Jono growled.

Hermes' gaze flicked up and down Jono before he shrugged. "I got you a ride. Let's go."

The tugging in Jono's soul seemed to get worse the second he crossed the threshold. He didn't need to be a magic user to know what that meant.

Patrick was in trouble.

Jono shouldered past Hermes and headed for the stairs instead of the elevator, careening down them to the ground floor. Hermes met him at the bottom landing, having moved through the veil as only a god could.

The tugging in Jono's soul got sharper. A creeping, vicious unease poured adrenaline through his veins.

"What happened?" Jono snarled as he slammed through the entrance of the building, the door rattling on its hinges.

An SUV was parked on the street out front. Quetzalcoatl stood near a familiar motorcycle with two passengers that was parked alongside it. Both engines were running hot.

"I warned him not to go to the club," Quetzalcoatl said, sounding irritated.

"It's not your case," Jono reminded him savagely. He would've said more, except his mobile started ringing and he yanked it out of his back pocket. Sage's name flashed over the screen and he answered immediately. "Sage?"

"Patrick traded himself for Kennedy and us," Sage said, sounding breathless and furious and *scared*. Beyond her voice, Jono could hear the sound of honking horns, squealing brakes, and the snarl of beasts he remembered from the subway. "He gave me his dagger and said he wouldn't use his magic. He—"

She cut off, her voice overridden by the sound of metal crashing against metal. Jono balled his empty hand into a fist, blunt fingernails cutting into his skin as his heart skipped a beat. He could still hear Sage breathing, so he knew she was alive, that it wasn't the Mustang that had been hit.

"Your brother is hunting them," Hermes said, raising an eyebrow at Quetzalcoatl. "Will you deal with that problem, or shall

I? The dagger can't be lost to the hells. That is power we can't let them have."

"You are quicker," Quetzalcoatl said.

Jono was furious that all the immortals seemed to care about was the fucking dagger Patrick carried and not the man himself. Hermes took a single step backward and disappeared. Sage's surprised shout came through the line, and Jono had to remember not to break his mobile.

"Hermes is here," she panted.

"Einar, return to Ginnungagap," Lucien ordered, not bothering to raise his voice. As with werecreatures, vampires had enhanced hearing, and Jono had no doubt the other vampire was listening in.

"Ring Emma," Jono said to Sage as he stalked past Quetzalcoatl for the driver's seat. "Have her meet you at Ginnungagap to help with Kennedy."

Quetzalcoatl gave Jono a bemused look as the car door slammed in his face. The immortal disappeared on the pavement like Hermes, only to reappear in the front passenger seat in the blink of an eye.

"You should know Santa Muerte is awake," Quetzalcoatl said as he reached up to the roof and flipped a switch. "The Omacatl Cartel has worshipped her into existence over the course of decades, along with every soul who prays to her on these two continents."

The red and blue lights secured to the dash and hidden in the SUV's front grill switched on, flashing in the dark. Jono ignored the immortal in favor of undoing the emergency brake and slamming his foot down on the gas pedal.

The pull at Jono's soul got tighter. He didn't have magic, couldn't manipulate his soul the way a mage could, but what tied him to Patrick was still a connection he could feel.

One he could follow.

"You got sirens in this thing?" Jono snapped.

Quetzalcoatl wordlessly switched them on, the high-pitched sound nearly bursting Jono's eardrums until he dialed down his hearing. Following what pulled at his soul was far harder than following a neatly plotted GPS map. At least the sirens cleared them a way quicker than a borrowed car from Emma's pack would have.

Driving while following the soulbond meant Jono didn't pay any attention to typical street laws, and neither did Lucien, who kept right on his tail. Speeding down Fifth Avenue with his heart in his throat and Fenrir waking up meant he didn't have time for conversation.

Quetzalcoatl didn't care.

"He shouldn't have given up the dagger," the immortal said.

"Piss off," Jono growled. "You lot gave Patrick the bloody thing. He can do what he likes with it."

"He should have kept the dagger. At least he'd have a chance against my brother if he had."

Jono sped through an intersection on a red light, nearly clipping a car coming from the other direction that was oblivious to the sirens.

"He's got me."

"You aren't with him right now."

Jono crunched the steering wheel beneath his grip, but the thing still turned, so it was fine. The soulbond coaxed him forward to where he hoped Patrick was. He scanned the street ahead and the cars that needed to get out of his fucking way.

"I'll always be with him."

Even when he wasn't, but Jono decided then and there that the next time Patrick got the brilliant idea to go haring off on his own, Jono would laugh in his face and tell him *no fucking way*.

"You—"

"Shut," Jono bit out. "Your. Gob."

The words came out in a growl that was more wolf than human, Fenrir howling through his mind. Jono ignored both gods in favor of his soulbond and the approaching high-rise buildings of Midtown Manhattan.

The Crimson Diamond was in SoHo, and that was the general direction he was being pulled toward. Fifth Avenue got interrupted by Washington Square Park, and New York University was a congestion of traffic and people even on a weeknight. He took a left on Washington Square North, then another left at the corner, gunning down MacDougal Street.

Jono's heart pounded in his chest, the rush of blood in his ears like waves crashing on the beach at Marek's Hamptons home. He took a hard left on Bleecker Street, tires squealing as he sped around the corner.

"Watch where you're driving," Quetzalcoatl snapped. "This is a loaner."

"If we crash, you won't die."

"You aren't immortal, no matter your ties to Fenrir."

Jono bared his teeth, fangs cutting into his lips. "I'm not dying tonight, mate."

The ones who took Patrick captive were a different story entirely.

Jono thought the soulbond would lead him to the Crimson Diamond, but he was drawn to Grand Street by way of Wooster Street, wishing everyone would just get out of his way. The tugging got stronger, spreading through his soul as he closed the distance stretched between himself and Patrick.

SoHo was a bit of a posh area, with no alleys to speak of. Grand Street was one way, and when Jono's soul felt like it was about to rip out of his body, he slammed his foot on the brake. The seat belt dug into his chest, and he ripped it out of the buckle, breaking it. Jono yanked up the emergency brake and nearly tore the door off its hinges in his bid to escape the SUV.

He moved as if he were swimming through honey, the world slow and hazy around them. The flashing lights of the government vehicle were slow to spin and change their colors. The traffic behind the SUV was moving forward so slowly they seemed almost at a standstill. Lucien and Carmen had braked to a stop and were struggling to reach him.

Then Jono caught Patrick's scent—bitter in a way that was different and wrong.

"Patrick!" he yelled, frantic with worry.

The thickness in the air faded, allowing him passage. Jono threw himself toward the god standing between him and where Patrick was sprawled on the pavement. The god wore dusty jeans and a worn, tan leather jacket over a T-shirt. His straight black hair was parted in the middle and plaited in two thick braids that hung over his shoulders. Beneath the jacket was a breastplate made out of white bone beads, tied together by black leather strips.

The features of his face reminded Jono of Sage, but the god's eyes were an eerie yellow that shined with a brightness that reminded Jono of his own. The mustache framing his mouth was neatly trimmed, with none of the stupid curls some men styled facial hair in these days.

Quetzalcoatl snorted. "Áłtsé Hashké. Up to your usual tricks again?"

The god shrugged in a careless manner, glancing at where Patrick lay. "This one treated my children with far more care than I expected, so I saved him. The cousins will owe me."

"Who are you?" Jono demanded, wanting desperately to get to Patrick but not knowing which immortal stood in his way. Not that it mattered. He'd go through the god if he had to, no matter the cost to himself.

Those yellow eyes blinked at him before the god smiled. "Your kind call me and mine Coyote, though I am not the only one who wears that name. Your tongues are useless when it comes to the language of the People."

Jono had no idea which Coyote he was speaking with, but he didn't care. "I want Patrick."

Áłtsé Hashké looked at him, then *through* him, and Jono felt as if he was being peeled apart in layers. Only Fenrir's snarl pushed the sensation away.

"A fitting choice, Fenrir," Áłtsé Hashké said as he stepped aside.

"*That* is interesting to know," Lucien said from behind Jono.

Jono ignored the vampire in favor of Patrick, breath catching in his throat as he saw the state the other man was in. Torn shirt and ripped jeans tangled around his thighs, drawing attention to the hard outline of his cock beneath his underwear. The smell of other people was pressed into his skin, mingling with the chemical undertone to his bitter scent. He had both hands covering his eyes, blood smeared around his mouth from a split lip that was still bleeding.

Jono forced himself to move, hands shaking with a rage that wanted to tear whoever had touched Patrick apart in a slow, painful rendering. He dropped to his knees, hands hovering over Patrick's chest, not sure where to touch.

If he even should.

Because the signs were pointing to an act having been committed Jono didn't want to think about.

"Pat," Jono said in a low, rough voice. "It's me."

Patrick drew in a shaky breath, but he didn't move his hands. "Jono?"

Jono pressed one hand against the pavement to steady himself, the force of his touch cracking the cement at the waver in Patrick's voice. "Yeah, love. I'm here."

"They made him take shine. They would not let my children leave without him doing so," Áłtsé Hashké said.

Jono didn't realize he was growling until Patrick curled onto his side, one hand reaching toward Jono, the other still covering his eyes. "I'm gonna be sick."

He took that as permission given. Jono reached for Patrick, helping him sit up so he wouldn't choke while he vomited. Jono grabbed Patrick's jeans and pulled them over his hips, holding them up when he realized the button was gone and the zipper was broken.

"It's a sexual high. It's meant to make humans pliant while vampires feed. It isn't that way for magic users," Carmen said.

"What do you mean?" Jono said through clenched teeth.

"If you gave someone the wrong blood type during a transfusion, they'd react badly to it. The same can be said of magic. Pure shine is made with vampire blood, and that carries traces of black magic in it. The same ability that enables magic users to reject the werevirus means they react differently to vampires."

"Get to the fucking point."

Carmen arched an eyebrow at him, the dark red pupils of her eyes burning in her unblinking gaze. "The high is intense and painful. It will strip him of control over his magic. The drug will burn out of his system in a few hours, but the symptoms will remain for longer. I can raise his sexual desire so the drug leaves his system faster."

Jono had to force himself not to tighten his hold on Patrick. The younger man had enough bruises from tonight. "No."

"Then I'll deal with him," Lucien said.

"Get fucked, mate."

"Patrick is a mage. Are you willing to risk his magic going rogue?"

Jono pulled Patrick into his arms and cradled the other man close as he stood. "You even *think* about pushing desire at him or try to control him, and I'll give Fenrir the freedom he so desperately wants."

Lucien's mouth curled. "As fun as that would be, Patrick still owes me answers. I'll expect a report tomorrow if your building is still standing."

Lucien and Carmen put their helmets back on and returned to their motorcycle. On the street, the traffic around them had barely moved. Jono didn't know which god was behind the distortion, and he didn't know how long it would last. Part of him was glad that no one else would get to see Patrick in this state.

Quetzalcoatl looked at Áłtsé Hashké. "I will see them home."

"Your brother shall not be forgiven his transgressions against the Diné," Áłtsé Hashké replied.

"Your grudges are notable, but misplaced. I will deal with Tezcatlipoca, not you."

Áłtsé Hashké just smiled, the gleam in his yellow eyes a promise Jono didn't trust. Quetzalcoatl gestured at Jono to follow him back to the SUV. As he walked, the thick pressure in the air began to fade. When he looked over his shoulder, not trusting the god at his back, Áłtsé Hashké was gone.

Quetzalcoatl opened the rear passenger door and Jono got into the vehicle without letting Patrick go. He held Patrick on his lap, keeping his hands away from the obvious erection the other man was sporting. Patrick kept his hands over his eyes, panting raggedly. Jono pressed a kiss to the top of his sweaty head, breathing in the scent of wrongness seeping out of him.

"I want," Patrick rasped out, the words slurring between them.

Jono squeezed his eyes shut, clenching his jaw so tightly he cracked a tooth. Whatever Patrick wanted tonight, Jono couldn't give it to him—and it would absolutely *gut* Jono to stand firm. When he opened his eyes again, he had to blink away spots.

"I'll drop you off and reach out to the SOA to stem some of the damage from tonight on the case front," Quetzalcoatl said as the SUV lurched forward, the world back to how it was supposed to be.

"Sure, Pretzel," Patrick muttered.

Jono ignored the immortal, all his focus on the man in his arms. Patrick still wouldn't uncover his eyes, and Jono didn't try to pull his hands away. He knew what shine did, how it messed with a person's eyesight. He worried, though, about how Patrick would react to things he couldn't see.

Shifting on the seat, Jono pulled out his mobile and speed-dialed Emma. She picked up on the first ring. "Jono?"

"In a bit of a cock-up. I've got Patrick and we're heading home. Steer clear of the flat until I ring you. Can Wade stay with you tonight?"

"Yes, of course. Is Patrick all right?"

Jono wished desperately that Emma and her pack didn't tithe the god pack and have to abide by their law. Estelle and Youssef didn't deserve their loyalty. "No, but I have him."

Jono ended the call without saying another word, unsure of what he could say without taking away Patrick's choice.

Quetzalcoatl used his lights to get them home in record time, though he spared Jono's ears by not turning on the siren. The immortal said nothing when he parked in front of the apartment building, silently watching Jono get out with Patrick in his arms. Jono used his elbow to close the SUV door, and Quetzalcoatl drove away without a word.

Jono was glad to see him go.

It was late, and no one was outside to see him carry Patrick up every flight of stairs to their top-floor flat. By the time they reached the landing, Patrick was squirming in his arms, the scent of arousal thick in Jono's nose. Worse than that was the pain and the lingering scent of the undead. Jono desperately wanted to give Patrick a shower, but he didn't feel comfortable stripping Patrick out of his clothes right now.

Maybe later, when Patrick was more lucid and knew who was touching him. As things stood, Jono paused long enough to touch the wards set into the doorframe and activate the silence ward Patrick had tied to both of them when they first moved in. It flared up warm and white beneath Jono's palm before fading into familiar static that wrapped itself around the flat.

His eyesight made it easy to traverse the dark flat. Jono carried Patrick to the guest bathroom rather than the one in their bedroom because it was closer. He carefully lowered Patrick's legs to the ground, keeping him upright with an arm around his waist.

Jono ignored the way Patrick rubbed against him, trying to get off, his face buried against Jono's chest. If that's what he needed right now, Jono wouldn't fight him on it.

"You're too bright," Patrick muttered.

Jono maneuvered Patrick in the small space, keeping the door open. He got Patrick settled on the floor, back leaning up against the tub, and Jono crouched in front of him. When he touched Patrick's leg, the other man jerked as if he'd been hit, and Jono nearly bit through his tongue in his rage.

"It's me, Pat," he said, hand hovering over Patrick's thigh.

In response, Patrick's entire body jerked again and a small burst of magic sent Jono sprawling backward into the hallway. The raw force of it rattled everything not bolted down in the bathroom. Jono blinked up at the ceiling, his ears ringing. Even through that sound he could hear Patrick's frantic voice.

"Shit, I'm sorry," Patrick slurred. "I'm sorry. My shields are a mess."

Jono propped himself up on one elbow. *He's holding back.*

If Patrick didn't have some bit of control left, he'd be punching holes through the walls with his magic. A mage carried more power in their soul than regular magic users. If they lost control, there was a risk of their magic going haywire. But Patrick had more training than most, and shields set by a goddess into his very bones. Jono knew how stubborn the other man could be.

That didn't mean this would be easy.

Jono scrambled to his feet and stepped back into the bathroom. Patrick was leaning over the toilet while seated on the floor, heaving up stomach acid, eyes squeezed shut as he tried to stay upright.

"Sorry," Patrick gasped out again, spitting into the toilet. "Sorry. I can't—"

His voice broke off as he got sick again. Jono knelt and smoothed his hand over Patrick's forehead to brush back his hair and make sure he didn't hit his head. When he stopped getting sick, Jono grabbed a wad of toilet paper and wiped his face clean before dropping the soiled bit into the toilet and flushing the sick away.

"You don't have anything to apologize for."

"Need to stop thinking."

Jono knew that while Patrick used a mageglobe to help him focus, most of his spellwork was cast in silence, the commands coming through as thoughts in his head rather than sound on his lips. In his drugged state, with his thoughts drifting, that was a disaster waiting to happen around his fraying control.

Jono didn't know what to do or how to help. Then Patrick's shaking fingers grabbed Jono's hand and guided it to his erection. Jono gently pulled his hand free, hating the frustrated whine Patrick let out.

When humans took shine, they normally did it within the arms of a vampire who could help focus their desire for darkness through sex, helping them ignore the pain of the high and the teeth in their veins. Jono wasn't about to have sex with Patrick in the state he was in.

"Not going to help you like that, Pat," Jono said.

"Then why are you here if you won't get me off?"

"Because I'm not leaving you."

And Jono didn't, despite the long, painful night that stretched out before them. The clarity Patrick had at the beginning crumbled beneath the insidiousness of shine. When he wasn't puking up stomach acid or trying to hurt himself, he was trying to get Jono to fuck him, all the while slurring, "I can't see. I can't see. You're too *bright.*"

Holding Patrick against his chest, Jono tiredly leaned his head back against the wall as Patrick jacked himself off with painful whimpers, the scent of sick and semen heavy in the bathroom. Patrick still had his jeans on, though they were shoved down past his hips once more, but at least this time the only hand touching him was his own.

Jono desperately called out to the god. *Help me, Fenrir. I don't want to hurt him.*

The god's presence filled his mind and body, skin itching with the need to shift. Jono resisted, and Fenrir let him. Instead, warmth filled his chest, seeping deeper past his bones to his soul itself. Jono blinked, feeling as if he was being constricted. He didn't know what Fenrir had done until Patrick shuddered through a painful orgasm, head turned toward him and eyes finally cracking open a sliver before closing again.

"Where'd you go?" Patrick asked dazedly.

Jono shifted Patrick in his arms, keeping his breathing steady. "Nowhere."

If Patrick could look at him without being in pain, Jono assumed his soul must have been hidden from sight. Whatever aura Patrick had seen pouring out of Jono's body, he wasn't seeing it now.

That didn't stop shine from wreaking havoc on Patrick.

Listening to Patrick beg to be fucked made Jono furious even as he was helpless to do anything about it. In between his pleading, Patrick's magic would burst out in small, uncontrollable eruptions that he desperately tried to reabsorb. The threshold around the apartment hummed in Jono's ears after each release, getting shriller and shriller. After the fourth miniature explosion that shattered the mirror and broke the bathroom door off its hinges and nearly sent it crashing down on top of them, Jono hauled Patrick to his feet.

"You need to stop," Jono pleaded. "Patrick, please."

"Can't," Patrick muttered, reeling in his arms, bare feet sliding against the floor. Jono had gotten rid of both their shoes earlier after a near miss of the toilet when Patrick got sick. "I can't. Not enough room in me. Can't *think*."

"Then pour it through me. I can handle it."

Patrick frantically shook his head, the motion causing him to get sick again. Nothing came out but dry heaves. Jono braced him over the toilet anyway when he would've sunk to his knees. He pressed his forehead to the back of Patrick's sweaty head, expression twisting.

"You won't hurt me," Jono promised.

He'd done it before, in Central Park, and he knew he could do it again. He could handle it, even if Patrick didn't want him to, because carrying something else in his soul wasn't new to Jono. If Patrick was in a better state of mind, maybe he'd be able to stand firm. But he wasn't, and Jono used Patrick's glaring inability to say *no* to get the mage to agree.

And Jono would always hate himself for doing it.

It took nonstop cajoling for almost thirty minutes to get Patrick to channel his magic inward instead of out on the next outburst. The soulbond burned like fire where it connected in Jono's soul but better that burning pain than the building going up in flames around them. Sprawled now in the bathtub, with Patrick curled up on top of him, Jono refused to let him see how much it hurt.

Far less than what Patrick was going through.

Magic ripped through Jono's soul, cascading downward into a ley line far below that he could sense only because of Patrick. The soulbond acted like a grounding mechanism, stealing away Patrick's magic to channel it somewhere else that could safely absorb it.

Jono suffered through two more bouts of Patrick's uncontrolled magical outbursts while trying to keep Patrick from undoing his own pants. Jono didn't say no to Patrick when he rubbed off on him, coming dry and shaking from pain more than pleasure.

But as the hours ticked over one by one, the chemical smell seeping through Patrick's skin began to fade. When Jono took a breath and all he smelled was Patrick's bitter scent, long-dried cum, and sick, he closed his eyes in relief. He hoped Patrick was finally coming down from his unwanted high.

Jono pushed them both to a sitting position before carefully guiding Patrick to his feet. Jono stripped him with gentle hands, murmuring all the while so Patrick would know it was him. He hadn't opened his eyes yet, and Jono paused every time he flinched. It took a few minutes to get him out of his messy clothes, but once he was naked except for his dog tags, Jono turned on the shower and pushed Patrick beneath the spray once it was warm.

Jono cleaned him up as quickly and carefully as he could, letting the events of the night wash down the drain, knowing it wouldn't be that easy later on. Getting Patrick clean was important, and Jono committed himself to that task even as his own clothes became waterlogged.

Only when Patrick was dried off and wrapped in a towel did Jono get out of his own clothes. He left the mess in the damaged bathroom to deal with later in favor of picking Patrick up and carrying him to the bedroom, wincing as he stepped on broken glass. Jono tucked him under the covers before retreating to dig up a pair of his own sleeping pants and pulled them on.

He meant to get some water or Gatorade, at the very least some medicine, but all of Jono's plans fled his mind the second Patrick murmured, "Jono?"

He returned to the bed, crawling over to where Patrick lay, eyes cracked open and no longer hiding. Jono could still sense the tight hold Fenrir had on his soul, keeping his aura hidden, and he was grateful for the god's interference.

"I'm right here," Jono said, gently brushing back his hair.

"Thought I dreamed you."

Jono's mouth twisted, his anger eclipsed only by his sorrow. "No, love. It wasn't a dream."

Patrick closed his eyes and didn't cry and never reached for Jono.

Jono lay down beside him on top of the duvet, keeping his hands to himself as he watched Patrick slowly fall into a fitful sleep.

14

At the first sound of movement from beneath the duvet, Jono reached for the potion Victoria Alvarez had delivered around dawn before her morning shift as an RN witch at Mount Sinai. He picked it up off the nightstand, holding it with a careful grip as Patrick batted the duvet off his head.

Curled on his side, eyes closed and expression scrunched up in pain and disgust, Jono watched as Patrick carefully touched his swollen nose.

"Something died in my mouth, and I think my nose is broken," Patrick rasped.

"I have something that might help with that," Jono said.

"A gallon of whiskey?"

"Potion."

"Pass."

Jono pressed his lips together, not wanting to push the issue but thinking he should. He watched as Patrick slowly cracked his eyes open. In the midmorning light pouring around the closed curtains, his pupils looked even and normal despite the scrapes marring the skin on his cheeks. Jono reached for him without thinking, then aborted the motion.

Patrick stared at him in silence, watching as Jono slowly lowered his hand. A minute passed before Patrick worked his hand free of the blankets and placed it over Jono's, threading their fingers together. Jono's throat tightened at that action, and he stared at their hands.

"Just so we're clear," Patrick said in a rough voice, looking Jono in the eye, "if you'd have fucked me last night, I would've been okay with it."

Jono didn't know what to say to that, so he said nothing. Patrick rubbed his thumb against Jono's hand before letting out a sigh that proved he probably did need the whiskey to sanitize his mouth, or at least a bottle of Listerine.

Patrick licked his lips, gaze dropping to their joined hands. "Look, I...I'm sorry I put you in that position."

"What? Staying behind?" Jono said, finally finding his voice.

"No. I'm not sorry for that because you found me." Green eyes flicked up to meet his own, and Jono never blinked. "I'm sorry I channeled my magic through you. I never wanted to put you in a position where you had no choice but to let it happen."

"We've talked about this, Pat. The soulbond lets you, and I don't mind. Helping you last night wasn't a hardship. It never will be."

Patrick squeezed Jono's hand, wincing when he turned onto his back. He ran his other hand through his hair. Half of it stuck up, while the rest was plastered to his skull in odd patches.

"It hurts you, and I don't ever want to hurt you."

"You weren't in your right mind last night. I wasn't going to take advantage of you after you—"

Jono broke off, teeth clacking together as he tilted his head back to glare at the ceiling. Remembering the state Patrick had been in when they'd reached SoHo was enough to ignite his temper all over again. He refused to bring that anger into the bed they shared.

"Do you know I've been shot, stabbed, cursed, burned, broken way too many bones, bruised some internal organs, but nothing hurts worse than getting fucking sacrificed to gods." Patrick drew in a careful breath through his mouth instead of his nose, and Jono looked back over at him. "Some god I don't know saved me before Tremaine got very far. I hate owing the gods anything, but I might be okay with this one."

Jono didn't even bother trying to choke back the harsh sound that escaped his mouth. "What happened wasn't your fault."

"I know."

With Patrick's shields down, it was easy for Jono to sniff out the lie. He let Patrick keep it.

"How are your eyes?" Jono asked instead.

"I can't see your soul, so I'm hoping the shine is out of my system. I have a raging headache though. Kind of feel like I have the flu."

Jono cleared his throat. "Come on. Let's get you up. I've a potion you need to take and about a hundred text messages to answer."

Patrick shoved the blankets down so he could slowly sit up, his heart rate picking up in Jono's ears. "Shit. Sage? Kennedy?"

"They're both at Ginnungagap. Sage has your dagger, though I'm not sure why you didn't just keep it on you."

"I knew Tezcatlipoca wouldn't have just let them go. Giving them my dagger was the only way I could get them backup. I figured the gods who make my life a living hell wouldn't want to lose it."

"Next time, I'm going with you." Jono unscrewed the cap on the metal water bottle and handed the potion over to Patrick. "Drink."

"It smells disgusting."

"Drink, and then you can gargle with whiskey."

Patrick took the bottle from him and drank the potion in several long gulps, trying not to gag. He dropped the bottle on the bed after he finished and let go of Jono's hand. Patrick realigned his nose with a quiet scrape of cartilage that made Jono wince.

"Don't want it to heal crooked," Patrick muttered, looking a little queasy. "Ugh. That shit you made me take is foul. Where'd you buy it from?"

"I told Marek it was okay to ring Victoria and have her come by." Jono hesitated before saying, "He seemed to know exactly what you would need and told her so she could brew the appropriate potion."

Patrick sighed as he slid off the bed, not put off by the fact he was nude. "The Norns probably want me in better fighting form for whatever will go down with Tezcatlipoca and Santa Muerte."

Jono set the empty bottle back on the nightstand. "Santa Muerte?"

"A personification of death is running around in the fringe of the veil and the subways." Patrick paused in the middle of pulling on a pair of underwear. "Do you remember where you found me?"

"Yeah. You were outside a building in SoHo with Áłtsé Hashké."

Jono tripped over the name, mangling it. Patrick finished pulling on his underwear and straightened up. His gaze was distant for a few seconds before refocusing. "Coyote?"

Jono shrugged. "One of them?"

"Trickster gods are the worst. Fuck it. I'll let him fight Persephone over me."

"He seemed more pissed at Tezcatlipoca and Quetzalcoatl than about gloating over rescuing you."

"Next time I'll just sell my soul to a pawn shop. It would make my life easier." Patrick yanked a shirt on, making his hair even worse if at all possible. "Did I call Quetzalcoatl Pretzel last night, or did I dream that?"

Jono snorted in amusement. "Yeah, you did."

"Agent Pretzel is forever going on my shit list." Patrick left the bedroom for the hallway, where Jono had tossed their shoes last night. "Tremaine has tunnels in his territory that lead to an abandoned subway platform. They built a shrine to Santa Muerte and fucked with the old subway wards."

"That's not good," Jono said as he got up and headed for the guest bathroom.

"I know, but I think it could be our way into the heart of his Night Court."

Jono let Patrick finish lacing up his boots in the hall while he tidied up the bathroom as best he could. Jono would have liked to burn their clothes from last night, but he settled for putting them in a trash bag, along with the towels, shower curtain, and bath mats. Having the lights on revealed the damage from last night, and it wasn't pretty.

Some of the floor tiles and the sink were cracked. The toilet needed to be scrubbed down with bleach to sanitize it. The door was off its hinges and would need to be replaced. Some of the paint looked scorched, and the glass on the floor from the broken mirror needed to be swept up.

"Seven years bad luck," Patrick said when he peered around Jono at the mess. "Glad we got renter's insurance. Hand me my med-kit, would you?"

Jono bent down to retrieve the field-rated med-kit stored under the sink. Patrick unlocked the case and dug through its contents, coming up with a roll of medical tape. Jono watched as he tore off a strip and very carefully pressed it over his nose. The swelling seemed to be going down, but it would be a slow healing process, and the potion wouldn't heal all the hurts Patrick had come away with last night.

Jono took the medical tape from Patrick and tossed it in the med-kit before leaving the bathroom. Patrick grabbed his wrist before he got very far, and Jono went still. Jono gazed down at him in silence, waiting for Patrick to speak first.

"If I didn't go last night, we wouldn't have saved Kennedy. I wouldn't have found a way to get us inside. I knew you would find me the same way my old team would have," Patrick said quietly.

Jono raised his other hand and touched his fingertips to Patrick's cheek. "You don't leave me behind again."

"I can't promise that."

Jono wanted to argue, but the tired sincerity in Patrick's voice made him hold his tongue. The oaths Patrick had already taken over the years, the bits of himself he'd sold off, all the promises that built him would never be enough to keep him whole. Jono refused to add to the cracks.

"Then do your best to keep me with you when you fight, and I can learn to live with that."

"Okay."

Patrick rose up on the balls of his feet to kiss Jono, slow and careful, the press of his lips a silent apology. Jono accepted it because he could do nothing else. He wouldn't place his anger at the situation on Patrick when all the blame belonged to the gods.

"We're taking down the Manhattan Night Court so you don't owe Lucien shit," Jono murmured against Patrick's mouth.

"A sound plan," Quetzalcoatl said from the living room. "We should get started on it."

Patrick pulled back with a scowl, raking a hand through his messy hair. "You could've knocked."

Jono curled a hand over Patrick's hip to keep him close as he peered over Patrick's shoulder at where the immortal stood, dressed in what passed as a uniform for a DEA special agent. His badge hung from a chain around his neck, and the choker of conch shells gleamed around his throat. The ozone scent that filled the flat made Jono's nose twitch.

"It's almost noon and we need to discuss the case. Lucien wants an update, and so do I. I told your friends I would give you a ride to Ginnungagap."

"Sure thing, Pretzel," Patrick replied. "Right after I make some coffee."

"And eat something," Jono added.

Quetzalcoatl crossed his arms over his chest. "We don't have time for your stalling tactics."

"I'm not stalling. Unlike your immortal ass, I need actual sustenance. I can't survive on prayers," Patrick retorted.

They didn't linger in the flat any longer than it took to brew a pot of coffee and some tea, and for Jono to make a couple of no-fuss sandwiches with leftover lunch meat and cheese.

Jono let Patrick take the front passenger seat once they made it to the SUV that was double-parked on the street in front of the building. Patrick seemed better, but Jono knew from experience the other man was adept at hiding his injuries and exhaustion.

Jono texted Emma and the others in the group chat, saying they were on the way while Patrick conversed with Quetzalcoatl about the case. He was only half listening when Patrick squawked out a "You did *what*?"

"Informed your director we agreed to collaborate on the case," Quetzalcoatl replied.

"You fucking liar, we did *not* agree to that."

"I either covered for you or the PCB took the heat for what happened last night. Considering what prowls the streets, I didn't think you'd appreciate the press sinking their teeth into this story."

Jono let them hash out the legalities of the case and who had jurisdiction for the rest of the drive, knowing his opinion wouldn't matter. It wasn't his job, wasn't his skillset. He focused instead on the steady updates that Emma and Sage were feeding him in the group chat.

"Kennedy's alive," Jono announced during a brief lull in the argument.

"I'm a little surprised about that," Patrick admitted.

"Emma got her to change back to human."

"I don't think she'll look much better."

Patrick spoke with the resigned knowledge of someone who knew what the worst looked like. Jono didn't know Kennedy, had only seen her in passing at the bar, but he knew enough she didn't deserve what had happened to her.

When they finally arrived at Ginnungagap, Quetzalcoatl parked on the street near the construction zone. Jono didn't see any construction workers, and the threshold wrapped around Ginnungagap wouldn't let anything pass through it without approval by the owner, or itself. Jono still wasn't sure how the primordial void functioned in the mortal world.

Patrick's Mustang was parked in the alleyway, the rear bumper crunched a bit on the right-hand side. Patrick groaned as they passed it by. "My premiums are going up and I'm blaming the hells."

A metaphysical wall crashed down between them and the outside world when they crossed the threshold. City noise became muffled, and the skittering feel of magic prickled his skin before fading away. Jono breathed in deep, parsing out familiar and unfamiliar scents. Emma and the others were here. He could pick out the particular scent of a couple of human servants and Carmen's distinct blend of desire and blood from the unfinished mezzanine.

Jono wasn't surprised she was on the premises. Ginnungagap was Lucien's territory, and if the rest of the vampires were sleeping, someone had to keep watch over everyone here.

Quetzalcoatl seemed unbothered walking into a place that technically belonged to a different pantheon. He had good company in Hermes, who was sitting cross-legged in the middle of the floor with someone's head in his lap. Jono couldn't see Kennedy's face, wrapped as she was in a cocoon of blankets, but he could smell her distress and the coppery scent of blood. He didn't realize he'd come to a stop until Patrick nudged him forward.

"Come on," Patrick said softly. "Let's see how she is."

Sage met them halfway, her eyes locked on Patrick. Jono watched as the tight line of her shoulders eased as her gaze raked up and down Patrick, taking him in.

"Are you okay?" Sage asked.

"Bruised, but I'll live. Victoria makes good potions even if they taste like shit," Patrick said. "Where's Wade?"

"Back at my place," Marek said from where he sat on an empty pallet, typing away on his MacBook. "I figured the coin would be enough protection to hide him from a god. Half the pack is home anyway keeping him fed."

Sage stepped close and Patrick got a surprised look on his face when she hugged him. He gamely accepted it though, arms coming around her to squeeze back. Jono left Patrick to get scent-marked in favor of kneeling beside Kennedy. Emma and Leon stood behind the immortal, hovering in that way alphas sometimes did over a wounded pack member.

Kennedy's bald head was mostly covered by a blanket. Angry scar tissue covered her scalp, indicating her wounds had been so bad the change back to human hadn't been enough to heal her. Jono carefully settled his hand on her shoulder. Her entire body jerked weakly against his touch.

"She's in shock still. It took everything I had to get her to change back. We should get her to a hospital," Emma said.

Jono said nothing, gently pulling the blankets down enough to see Kennedy's heavily bruised face, the bones that were slow to reform and heal, and the gauntness to her body that spoke of deprivation no one deserved to endure.

"She was worse at the club," Sage said quietly.

"Not sure this counts as better," Jono replied, trying to keep the anger out of his voice and his scent, not wanting to disturb Kennedy. "She didn't deserve this."

Emma crossed her arms over her chest, fingers digging painfully into her upper arms. "No, she didn't. So tell me what we're going to do about it."

Jono kept his mouth shut, kept his hand on Kennedy's trembling form, and for once couldn't completely ignore the howl ripping through his mind. Patrick was the one to pull him back from a feral edge, his hand like a brand on his shoulder. Jono jerked his head up, blinking at the other man.

"If a rival pack took one of your pack mates or injured someone under your protection, what would you do?" Patrick asked him.

Jono had to remind himself to keep his touch light and gentle on Kennedy's body. "To avenge you? Anything."

Patrick blinked, the hard line of his mouth softening. "Murder is so much better than flowers some days."

"I've got bail money," Marek said absently.

"Well, you've stated we're a pack now, and your eyes and viral strain put us as god pack status. Think that's enough to get Tremaine to accept a challenge?"

"Even if he doesn't, I'll bring the fight to his territory. I'm still not keen on doing it through Lucien," Jono said.

Patrick sighed. "You know what I promised Lucien. I know you don't like it, but if giving him the Manhattan Night Court prevents this from happening to other werecreatures, then it's a promise I won't feel too bad about keeping."

"Not sure trading one master vampire for another even worse one is the best plan here," Leon said.

Patrick shrugged. "Better the devil you know."

"You're the only one out of all of us who knows the fucker."

"Careful how you speak of my love. We take insults to our master very personally," Carmen called from the mezzanine. "You have guests, Patrick."

"Who?" Jono asked sharply.

"Wolves."

The bite in her voice was all anticipatory violence Jono had no problem matching.

"That's my cue to go," Hermes said. "You should take her."

"I've got her, Jono," Emma said.

She settled on the cold cement floor beside the immortal and gathered Kennedy into her arms. The muffled moan Kennedy let out had Jono clenching his hands into fists. He got to his feet, aware of Hermes' eyes on him.

"I think you'll make this fight interesting after all," Hermes said right before he pulled out Patrick's dagger from his inner jacket pocket and tossed it to the mage.

"Jono isn't yours," Patrick warned. He caught the dagger and strapped it to his right thigh with quick fingers.

"Keep telling yourself that, Pattycakes."

Between one blink and the next, Hermes disappeared, sliding through the veil as only an immortal could. Quetzalcoatl remained where he stood, leaning against an iron support beam.

"Not going to join him?" Jono asked.

"The arrogance you mortals carry means you miss what is right in front of you. They will see me as they want, not as I am," Quetzalcoatl said.

"That's some holier than thou bullshit right there," Patrick said as he strode over to the door and yanked it open. "The fuck are you doing here, Estelle? Are you *spying* on us?"

Jono closed the distance between them, coming to stand beside Patrick as they faced down Estelle, Youssef, Nicholas, and half a dozen other god pack werewolves on the other side of the threshold. Estelle's expression was carved from ice, bright amber eyes taking them in.

"I understand you breached vampire territory last night, breaking our treaty yet again. We are here to discuss your transgression," Estelle said.

"How about no?" Patrick replied snidely.

Jono hooked his fingers around the collar of Patrick's leather jacket, hauling him backward. "Let them in. I want them to see what their bargaining has done to those they were supposed to protect."

Patrick scowled, shrugging out of Jono's grip. "I don't got any say if they're allowed in here, but sure, try to cross over."

Jono swept his arm through the air in an exaggerated manner, holding on to his rage with everything he had. Estelle lifted her chin high and stepped inside. Youssef followed, as did Nicholas, but the werewolves they'd brought to use as muscle and intimidation were denied entrance in a rather brutal way. The first one who tried to cross the threshold was picked up and thrown across the alley by an invisible force. He slammed into the opposite building hard enough to dent the wall.

"Watch my car," Patrick yelled, sounding irritated.

"I don't appreciate your treatment of my pack," Youssef snarled, a hint of claws replacing his fingernails. "Let them pass."

Patrick smiled, looking a bit demented with his taped-up nose, healing bruises, and messy ginger hair he hadn't bothered to tame. "I'm not the one keeping them out. What lives here is. If you're too fucking stupid to recognize that threat, you deserve everything coming your way."

The door swung shut on its own. Jono eyed it before deciding it wasn't worth freaking out over. Instead, he turned to face Estelle and Youssef. "You lot got some explaining to do."

"In no world do we owe you anything," Estelle said.

"Yeah?" Jono pointed at where Emma sat with Kennedy in her arms. "That so? Could think of loads you owe Kennedy. You remember Kennedy, right, Estelle? Werelion you sold off to Tremaine?"

Estelle's gaze cut their way, lingering on Quetzalcoatl in his DEA uniform and the badge prominently displayed on his hip. He watched them with an intensity that even Jono found hard to shake off.

"I don't know what you're talking about."

"Sure you don't," Patrick scoffed, already walking back to Emma. "Get your ass over here so we can refresh your memory."

Nicholas looked like he wanted to confront Patrick, but either Quetzalcoatl's presence or Carmen's sudden arrival kept him rooted where he stood.

"You wolves are playing a game you're going to lose," Carmen said as she came down the stairs with Naheed trailing behind her.

Carmen wore the same Kevlar-lined motorcycle bodysuit from last night, her black curls spilling over her shoulders and down her back. As she descended, the glamour she wore like a second skin peeled away, revealing her true form—dark red pupils in the center of inhuman eyes, the twisted horns of her kind, and the push of desire that never seemed to bother Jono.

She was lethal and gorgeous, and as first impressions went, terrifying in a way that all demons were, no matter their status. Jono could hear the faintest uptick in Estelle's heartbeat, and he took that as a win.

"She won't bite," Jono said casually. "Not like her master."

"And who is her master?" Estelle wanted to know.

"You'll learn soon enough," Carmen replied. "Until then, you deal with me, wolf."

"You hold no territory here," Youssef said.

"And that is where you are wrong."

Carmen smiled, showing off sharp teeth. Behind her, Naheed pulled a wooden rod from beneath the back of her shirt and smacked it against her other hand. The bitter smell of aconite drifted through the air, causing Kennedy to whimper frantically. Jono's eyes watered, but he blinked the moisture back.

Youssef's nostrils flared at the scent. "Aconite."

"Pulled fresh from the Old World and bound by a witch to a piece of earth. She was never fond of the four-legged monsters who murdered her children, but the magic she left us is still useful. Some things don't fade with death."

Patrick knelt beside Emma and carefully untucked the blankets from around Kennedy's head. "You deserve to see what your actions have done. How long did Tremaine have her, Estelle?"

Estelle said nothing, and neither did Youssef. Their silence was, at best, a way to not self-incriminate themselves, and at worst, pure guilt.

Patrick stood, fury in his eyes that made Jono proud to know him. "You've failed the people who rely on you to protect them. I don't know how many independent werecreatures have gone missing because of you, but even one is too many."

"Don't put words in my mouth," Estelle told him. "You don't know what you're talking about."

"Really? Because I know how they died, Estelle. I *know* that Tremaine sucked the marrow from their bones. He and his people raped and *ate* yours when they weren't forcing them to fight for their lives. So don't stand there and tell me I don't know what the fuck I'm talking about when you're the ones letting it happen because you bargained for the graves they lie in."

Patrick's voice echoed angrily in the warehouse, the accusations rooted in a truth Jono would never deny, unlike Estelle and Youssef.

"We have bargained for nothing," Estelle finally said.

"Of course not," Patrick sneered. "You only have treaties with the Night Courts you're trying to use to force Jono out. Nothing like a preternatural DMZ on paper to make your conscience nice and clean. But I know a guy who's real fond of saying a piece of paper doesn't give you any rights. Doesn't buy you peace of mind either."

"We are not responsible for what happened to Kennedy," Youssef said.

"Keep telling yourself that."

"Go look at her, then get out," Jono growled. "You aren't welcome here."

"You are here on our allowance. Know your place," Estelle snapped.

Jono barked out a laugh. "Did you forget when I put your dire on his knees? Don't make me put you there as well, Estelle. I won't let you live if you push me."

The brittle tension between them only broke when Estelle stiffly approached the others, doing her best to make it seem as if

Jono meant nothing to her. Youssef joined her. Nicholas stayed where he was, glaring at Jono but making no move to attack. Jono had no use for the dire and made that known when he turned his back on the other man in a clear dismissal he knew would rankle.

Estelle and Youssef stopped near where Emma sat. They said nothing in the face of Kennedy's obvious wounds before Patrick knelt to tuck the blanket back around her again.

"Now, since I know your type and you lie like you breathe, I'm going to say this only once," Patrick said as he stood back up. "When I find the others you sold off, dead or otherwise, the SOA will be dealing with Jono, not you."

"*We* are the New York City god pack," Youssef growled.

"You aren't the only god pack in town now, remember? And I don't trust you at fucking all."

Estelle's jaw worked, her gaze cutting over to Jono. "We have done nothing wrong."

"Be careful with your words all you like. I know the truth, and so do they." Jono flicked his fingers in the direction of Patrick and Quetzalcoatl. "I stand by what I said in the challenge ring, Estelle. I've made my pack, and you can't run me out of town."

"And does your pack include Emma's?"

The threat in Estelle's voice was enough for Jono to take a step forward. Emma spoke up before he could answer *yes* out of sheer spite.

"I adhere to god pack law, but Marek sent us here last night. It wasn't within our legal rights to disobey a vision from a seer. The law is clear on that," Emma said carefully.

"And I am here at the behest of the federal government, who has jurisdiction over the seer," Quetzalcoatl added, finally speaking up.

Marek rolled his eyes at that but said nothing.

"I'm taking over Kennedy's care. If you come near her again, I will fight you, and you won't win," Jono promised.

He couldn't keep the hatred out of his voice and didn't even try.

Estelle narrowed her eyes, but it was telling—oh so telling—that she said nothing in the face of his threat, and neither did Youssef. Jono thought it was a right shame some of her enforcers hadn't been granted entry to see the way their alphas were backed into a corner.

Carmen sauntered closer, all sultry intensity that made both Estelle and Youssef drift toward her before jerking back. Carmen stopped right in front of them, her smile a warning even Jono would think twice about ignoring. Naheed stood some meters away, the aconite rod pointed at Nicholas in a threatening manner to keep him at bay. Tiny swirls of spellwork flared to life on the old wood, hinting at the dangerous artifact it truly was.

"Keep your wolves out of our territory," Carmen said.

"Or what?" Youssef asked in a low voice.

"Revenge is sweet, but regret is bitter on a death bed." Carmen leaned closer, as if sharing a secret. "We will make you regret *everything* if you cross us."

Estelle stared at Carmen for a long moment before she spun on her heels and retreated to the door, Youssef and Nicholas following a second later. Jono let them go. He'd said his piece. Whether or not they accepted it would remain to be seen.

Once the door shut behind the trio, Leon let out a heavy sigh. "We're going to be brought to task because of this."

"If they try, you tell them you've been ordered by the SOA to report any punishment. I'll consider it witness tampering if they lay a hand on you in any capacity," Patrick said.

Jono went to crouch beside Emma and Kennedy. Emma raised her head to look at him.

"Give her to me," Jono said quietly. "I'm going to take her to the hospital. Can you send one of your pack members to sit with her?"

Emma nodded. "Yes, of course."

Jono tried not to take her instant acceptance as loyalty and choosing sides when they both knew that's exactly what it was.

"Can you pick up Wade on your way back, Jono?" Patrick

asked. "I need to stay here and figure out what the hell mess Agent Pretzel here got me into with my agency."

Quetzalcoatl shot him an unimpressed look. "I got you *out* of a mess, remember?"

"No. Áłtsé Hashké got me off that altar, but you're both immortals and the only thing you guys do is make my life a living hell."

Jono ignored their bickering and took Kennedy out of Emma's arms. The way she tucked herself in close to his body told Jono all he needed to know about the decisions he'd made over the last few days.

That they were the right ones because pack should always come first.

15

master vampire Patrick wished he could shoot. Head, heart, dick—
he wasn't picky, any target would do.

"Look, I have described every single fucking detail I can
remember. It's not my fault if none of that lines up with the damn
subway map," Patrick complained around a mouthful of chow
mein. "Maybe if all of you vampires weren't such fucking rats, we
wouldn't be in this situation."

Sergio Lopez looked as if he wanted to reach across the table
and stab Patrick for his disrespect of Lucien, but the Anahuac
Cartel member thought better of it when Jono growled, "Don't
even think about it, mate."

Normally, Patrick would be more than willing to defend
himself, but he was still rattled from last night. Lying on that altar
had jarred loose some memories he'd rather keep buried, and he
desperately wanted another shower. He kept thinking he could feel
Tremaine's hands on him, and the sooner he could forget that
moment, the better.

Lucien seemed unbothered by the pair's byplay, staring intently at the maps and blueprints strewn over the large card table one of his human servants had set up in Ginnungagap. It was past sunset, but even before Lucien's Night Court woke up, there had been a steady stream of visitors.

Patrick had been unaware the Anahuac Cartel was in town until a large group of them rolled up to Ginnungagap that afternoon. They'd brought offerings in the form of money, drugs, and weapons, which Carmen had accepted in Lucien's stead. Patrick had taken one look at the cartel members and mentally revised the story he was going to have to tell his superiors about this case. Nothing said tainted evidence like palling around with a notorious drug cartel.

When Lucien finally arrived with Einar, Irena, and a couple more vampires after sunset, Wade had quietly retreated to a corner to stress eat his way through the gigantic tote bag of snacks Emma had sent along with him. Honestly, Patrick wished he could join the teen.

Sergio glared at Patrick, muscled arms crossed over his chest. He wasn't much older than Patrick, which meant he had to be a goddamn bloodthirsty monster in human skin to be heading up the United States branch of the cartel out of Chicago at Lucien's behest. Sergio's black hair was buzzed short on the side and left long on top, gelled back by thick product. He was clean-shaven, with a strong jaw and hooded eyes. He carried a pistol on his hip made out of gold-plated, warded metal, a sign of his rank more than a nod to stereotypes.

His entire crew were deferential to the vampires on sight, though they gave Patrick and his group a wide berth. They knew what Jono was and treated that threat with a healthy dose of wariness. The fact that a god pack werecreature was sitting at the same table as Lucien and arguing with the master vampire without fear of dying meant they didn't want to step on his toes.

Quetzalcoatl had left Ginnungagap hours ago to help cover Patrick's ass where the case was concerned. They'd finally agreed to pool their resources, something Patrick had been reluctant to do, but with two immortals aligned with the hells stalking the city streets, he'd had no choice. Looping Casale in had been a stressful one-hour phone call out in the alleyway since Ginnungagap still didn't allow signal in and out.

Sage reached across the table to grab one of the blueprints, dragging it closer. "Did Biyu only get blueprints for the building the Crimson Diamond is in, or did she get any of the adjacent buildings as well?"

Biyu was one of Einar's human servants, a petite, charming Chinese dissident and gifted hacker they had apparently pulled out of Beijing ten years ago. She'd learned how to hack within the Great Firewall of China without getting caught—until she did.

Arrested, disappeared into a jail used to extract confessions the Chinese government could parade through the media as a warning, Biyu had been left to rot. Einar rescued her before she'd signed that contract and sold her soul to the government. Biyu had been with Lucien's Night Court ever since, and her hacking skills explained a lot at how Lucien was able to cross international borders so easily these days.

"No. Tremaine doesn't hold those buildings as his territory," Lucien said.

Sage shuffled a few more maps and blueprints together, muttering about tracks under her breath. Patrick watched her while shoving another bite of chow mein into his mouth. The food was cold, having been delivered earlier, but Patrick didn't care. He'd felt hollowed out since waking up that morning, craving something he refused to acknowledge. He'd already smoked a couple of cigarettes, which was more than he'd had in the last few weeks. Jono hadn't said a single word about that, even though he had to smell the nicotine and smoke that lingered on Patrick.

Fighting the desire to ask Lucien for another cigarette was easier than Patrick thought it would be, only because he didn't want to owe the vampire anything more than he already did.

Victoria's potion had worn off hours ago, and the dull throbbing through his head and body made Patrick wish he had another potion to drink, no matter how disgusting they were.

Jono shifted in his seat between Patrick and Lucien, the arm he had draped over the back of Patrick's chair pressing against his shoulders. The line of heat would've been relaxing under any other circumstances, but even with the tension Patrick carried, having Jono with him made things easier.

"All right?" Jono asked in a low voice. He bent his arm and settled his hand on the back of Patrick's neck to gently massage the stiffness there.

"This is a mess," Patrick admitted quietly. He tilted his head to give Jono better access to the knots in his muscles, all the while staring at the maps getting shuffled around on the card table.

"Seems that's normal for us."

Patrick snorted. "I'll take a new normal any day now."

Trying to make sense of the city grid through several different map styles and building blueprints from different decades was tough, but they were doing it. Patrick's memories were hazy from last night, but he remembered the abandoned subway platform, and Jono knew the exact spot he'd been dragged through the veil by Áłtsé Hashké. Tracing back the steps took some work, but it was possible.

All of it painted a mess of unsanctioned tunnels within the fringe of the veil that were laughably not up to code.

Sage uncapped a pen with her teeth and started marking points on the maps, flipping rapidly through the sheets of paper. Lucien let her, watching in silence as Sage traced out a route from the Crimson Diamond to the abandoned subway platform Patrick was almost sacrificed in.

On paper, the abandoned subway platform was probably located between the Canal Street Station and Spring Street Station. The subway had a mere handful of stations it had abandoned over the years, forcing reroutes during the time when it was being built. Most of those reasons hadn't come with the blueprints, but Patrick could make a wild guess. Building structures through the veil was never easy or safe.

"I know you vampires have to hide from the sun, but living in tunnels like rats is a ridiculous way to do it," Patrick said.

"Watch your mouth," Lucien said.

"Are you embarrassed by the truth? My heart bleeds."

"Can we focus?" Sage asked loudly before Lucien could go from contemplating murder to actually doing it. "I still have a brief to write when I get home tonight. I would like to finish up here as quickly as possible."

"What did you find?" Jono asked, leaning forward. He dropped his hand from Patrick's neck to his thigh, giving a squeeze. The gesture was one of support and a warning to not antagonize the bloodsucking bastard.

Sage tapped her pen against the paper. "There's definitely a set of old tracks that run off the R line according to these records. Seems like the extension was scrapped last century when the city decided to give the A line its own route rather than connect the two. Tremaine's been here long enough he could have taken it over with no one knowing."

"The tracks were rusted, but the tunnel looked open. You could still drive a train on them if you were desperate enough." Patrick paused, fork halfway to his mouth. "There's an idea."

"No police," Lucien said.

"Might not get your way on that, but I wasn't talking about the police. I was talking about a train."

"You'd still have to send the request through the PCB," Sage said. "Defense of the subway falls to the MTA and the PCB. You can't loop in one without notifying the other in a situation like this."

"I'll think of something. We need to reach that back door, and we can't get there on live tracks with the amount of people you want to bring down there for the fight, Lucien."

"You said the wards down there were broken. You do not have the skills necessary to diffuse them, nor do you have the strength," Lucien said.

Patrick resisted the urge to look at Jono.

"The SOA would." The look Lucien leveled him was distinctly unimpressed. Patrick shrugged. "My agency has artifacts on hand for situations like this. I can request usage of one."

"You still need to give a reason to them. That reason will not be my Night Court."

"So I'll lie. Won't be the first time."

"If you go through the tunnels, you'll need a distraction on the street level," Sergio said, tapping at the blueprint for the Crimson Diamond. "The bastard will be expecting you."

Jono leaned back in his chair and rubbed his mouth, wolf-bright eyes narrowed in thought. "What about a fight? We talked earlier about issuing a challenge. Think Tremaine would take the bait?"

"Tremaine would bill it as a headliner if you were in that ring," Wade spoke up from behind them. "Tloque Nahuaque would try to kill you."

"He can try," Jono said with a snort.

Patrick glanced over his shoulder at Wade. He'd left his tote bag of snacks over by the stairs and had sneaked up on them. Wade still didn't know how to contain his aura, which meant his soul was a bright halo around his body and always would be until he learned control. Patrick's eyes watered and he blinked rapidly to try to clear his vision.

"Have you ever been down in any of those tunnels?" Patrick asked.

Wade shoved his hands into his jean pockets, shoulders hunched up to his ears. "Yes."

The answer came out in a monotone, the tone telling. Wade was a minefield of trauma Patrick had to carefully navigate. "Did they ever take you to an altar?"

Wade flinched with his entire body. After a moment, he jerked his head in a sharp nod. Patrick wished he could leave Wade's memories alone, but they had a goddess of death skulking around the subway, being courted by another immortal whose chosen gifts came in the form of sacrifices. As much as he wanted to protect Wade, the gods wouldn't let him, not if it interfered with Patrick's ability to finish the task they'd assigned him.

"If you went down there with us, could you lead us up to the club?"

"Patrick," Sage said warningly.

She was thinking about Wade's mental health over the lives of everyone else in New York City. Patrick understood that. He could admire her willingness to protect the teen when he wasn't able to, but Wade had on-the-ground information they needed. Patrick couldn't pass that up. His soul debt didn't allow him the luxury to stop.

Patrick had learned to be ruthless because that was the only way to survive. If Wade didn't want to come with them down into the tunnels, Patrick would have no other choice but to lean hard into General Reed's order for Wade to stay with him. It was a tactic he'd apologize for later, after the fact, when they saw the other side of this fight.

It still left a bad taste in his mouth.

"You've seen who I have to deal with, right?" Patrick asked Wade. "The gods who annoy the shit out of me?"

Wade rolled his eyes. "Yeah."

"Long story short, the Dominion Sect tried to get Tezcatlipoca and Santa Muerte to hand me over to them. Fighting against gods isn't new to me. I just prefer to do my fighting with as much of an upper hand as I can get. That means I need you down there with me. You're the only one of us who can navigate those tunnels. Would you do it with us?"

Before Wade could answer, Lucien's head snapped up, his black eyes locked on the entrance to Ginnungagap.

"We have company," Lucien said, fangs pricking his chapped lips.

Patrick stood, as did Jono. Sage slapped all the maps and blueprints together, rolled them up messily, and darted toward the stairs to hide them up on the mezzanine and out of sight. Wade scrambled after her, grabbing his tote bag of snacks and bringing it with him as he took the steps two at a time.

Einar went to answer the door with Irena at his back. She'd unearthed an AK-47 from somewhere and had it braced against her shoulder with steady hands. She wasn't the only one armed. Patrick watched as cartel members and other vampires reached for their weapons. The human servants placed themselves close to things that could be used as cover, all of them armed with pistols.

Lucien didn't move beyond draping his arm over Carmen's shoulders when she came to stand by his side, a show of force most people knew better than to cross. Carmen tossed her hair over her shoulder, the curls shifting around her horns.

Einar opened the door, keeping his body angled out of the way of Irena's line of sight. The master vampire who stood in the dark alleyway with her inner circle was a surprise that made Patrick lock down his personal shields.

"Greetings, Lucien," Maria of the Bronx Night Court said, not moving a millimeter over the threshold. "I've come to negotiate territory."

"Yours?" Lucien drawled.

The vampires at Maria's back bristled at the implication, but she didn't blink an eye. "Tremaine's."

Lucien didn't invite Maria in. Patrick could sense the threshold around Ginnungagap strengthen in the face of the threat at its door. Lucien walked forward with Carmen held close to his side, the pair of them in lockstep as they approached the local master vampire. Patrick followed, wanting a better view and needing to hear what would be said. Jono joined him.

Maria wore a hoodie instead of a tiara of fangs this time

around, along with plain dark clothes. As disguises went, it was terrible, but Patrick figured this visit was a quick in-and-out run through Manhattan. The gold rings and necklaces she wore prickled with magic that Patrick didn't trust, though he trusted Ginnungagap to keep it out.

"Tremaine owns nothing," Lucien said. Irena stepped aside to give him room but never lowered her weapon.

"Of course. He is yours." Maria's plum-colored lips quirked upward at the corners, pulling at the skin of her face. "As I never will be. I know what your eyes mean, Lucien. I have not lived this long by being ignorant of change. I am here merely to say Tremaine has asked for solidarity amongst our five Night Courts against your presence in the city. We owe Tremaine nothing and will not join his fight."

"You lie well enough, but I know what Tremaine learned from me. Whatever promises you gave him over the years will belong to me. He is my child, after all."

Maria's smile looked tacked on, her eyes cold. "No one owns me."

Lucien moved too quick to follow. Before Maria or her followers could react, Lucien had her by the throat with one hand, nails cutting into her skin until she bled. He pulled her halfway over the threshold, and Ginnungagap reacted to Maria's presence by tossing aside her followers the same way it had dealt with the god pack.

Magic twisted around Maria's feet and legs, rising from the ground like burning vines. Her mouth opened on a scream Lucien choked off with tight fingers. He brought his face close to hers, staring into her eyes and pushing his will through her.

Maria shuddered in his grip, fighting him, but Patrick knew she would lose.

"Stay out of my business," Lucien said in a low voice. "Our mother made me before you ever walked this earth in life or death. I will own you for that reason alone."

With that threat given, Lucien threw Maria into the alley and didn't wait to see where she landed before slamming the door.

"Dramatic much?" Patrick said into the silence.

"Not the time, Pat," Jono muttered.

"Shows what you know."

"Sounds like the other Night Courts are banking on Lucien taking over and are currying favor," Sage said as she came down the stairs, carrying the blueprints and maps. "At the mediation the other night, Tremaine was trying to get them on board with running Lucien out of town."

"Isn't telling us that breaking client confidentiality?" Patrick asked.

"They broke it first when they started killing independent werecreatures."

"Touché." Patrick didn't back off when Lucien turned to face them. "If there's a chance the other Night Courts won't come to Tremaine's defense, then we shouldn't waste this opportunity."

"So eager to help for once?" Carmen asked.

"Eager to pay up and move on," Patrick shot back before waving Sage over. "Leave the maps. Lucien can formulate a plan while I get us a train and some artifacts to deal with the subway wards."

"Don't bring your agency or the cops into this," Lucien warned.

"It's a little late for that."

"What about Tremaine and Tloque Nahuaque?" Wade wanted to know as he hurried their way. The teen still couldn't bring himself to call Tezcatlipoca by his true name.

Patrick sucked air between his teeth. "Lucien? You got his number?"

Lucien's black eyes flickered toward his Night Court. "Biyu."

The woman in question peeled off from the group of human servants at Lucien's call. Her thick black hair was tied up in a high ponytail, showing off the necklace of bite mark scars wrapped around her throat. Patrick pulled out his phone at her approach.

She recited the number from memory in a firm voice and Patrick saved it.

"I'll let you know how it goes," Patrick said as Jono opened the door, peering out carefully in case any vampires had decided to stick around.

"Tonight."

Patrick ignored that order, ducking out of Ginnungagap after Jono. Sage and Wade followed him. He conjured up a tiny mage-globe and let it rest against his palm as they hustled back to the Mustang parked a block away. He'd had to move the car earlier when Sergio and his crew arrived. They weren't ambushed on the way, but the lack of a fight didn't lower Patrick's paranoia any.

"I'll drop you off back home," Patrick told Sage as she and Wade got into the back seat.

"I'll let Marek know we're on the way," she said.

Patrick got behind the steering wheel. Even before he pulled into the street, Jono was calling Tremaine. "Put it on speaker-phone," Patrick told him.

Jono obliged. On the fifth ring, the line picked up but no one spoke. Only the low sound of music filtered through the speaker. Jono was forced to start the conversation. "I don't appreciate you taking what's mine."

Patrick rolled his eyes at Jono's proprietary claim, but it left him feeling warm inside.

"How did you get this number?" Tremaine demanded after a heavy pause.

"You really think you can hide from Lucien?" Patrick asked.

"Ah, the mage. And—" Tremaine paused before continuing with, "The weretiger and my champion."

Wade whimpered. In the rearview mirror, Patrick saw Sage reach over to give the teen a comforting hug. Patrick wasn't surprised the vampire could hear all four of their heartbeats, but he didn't like Tremaine singling out any of them.

"Bit of a predicament you've found yourself in," Jono said,

forcing Tremaine to focus on him. "You've fucked with a god pack, and that shit is just not done, mate."

"The treaties I hold with the New York City god pack still stand."

"Not talking about them."

Patrick braked for a red light, searching the intersection and the surrounding buildings for any threat. He leaned forward to stare up through the windshield, knowing how much vampires liked to attack from above. He didn't see anything.

"You hold no territory here, wolf."

"Name's Jono, and my pack territory is just as valid as Estelle and Youssef's. You owe me for what you did to Patrick."

Tremaine chuckled, the sound dry and amused. "I owe you nothing."

The light turned green. Patrick drove through the intersection, eyes flickering from side to side.

Jono made a thoughtful sound in the back of his throat, but his eyes were clear and hard. "Here's the thing. You got a god pack who will make deals with you and one that won't. You think just because you're a slave to a pair of immortals that means you've got power over us? You aren't the only one who curries favor with the gods."

"Also, you've pissed off Lucien," Patrick added.

"Lucien will regret coming to New York," Tremaine said flatly.

"You've been off your leash a long time if you believe that. Lucien doesn't regret anything."

"Here's what you're going to do," Jono said before Tremaine could get a word in edgewise. "I'm issuing a challenge for what you did to Patrick. Me and you, in that ring, is where we'll settle the score."

Tremaine was quiet for two more blocks before he finally spoke. "I've lived a long time. Killed a great many people, but when this is all over, I think I will enjoy killing you the most."

"You're all talk, Tremaine. If you want to forfeit, just say so."

"Friday night, an hour after sunset for the fight. You will arrive before then so I know *you* haven't forfeited. Under the terms of the challenge you issued, we will settle this in the ring. If you win, I will let you live."

"Aw, mate. That's right generous of you. If I win, I'll return your bloodsucking arse to Lucien."

Jono ended the call and dropped his phone into his lap. Patrick drummed his fingers against the steering wheel. "You don't want to kill him yourself?"

"I figure the threat of being sent back to Lucien might make Tremaine do something stupid. Besides, I wouldn't mind witnessing their reunion again."

"Huh." Patrick shook his head. "I didn't think of that."

"I told you that you make a better alpha than Estelle and Youssef," Sage said from the back seat.

"We don't have enough clout as a pack to make it mean anything," Jono reminded her.

"Yes, well, take down Tremaine and things might change."

"What's a little murder to help make your point?" Patrick mused.

In Patrick's experience, when fighting against the hells, it wasn't a bad thing.

16

Thursday dawned clear and muggy. The low-grade headache that had been Patrick's constant companion the day before had finally faded with the help of sleep and half a pot of coffee. Jono hadn't let him flavor it with whiskey since he had an 0900 meeting with SAIC Henry Ng about the case, which was just unfair.

"You don't want to smell like you've spent the night pissed whilst out at a pub," Jono had said before kissing him and shoving him out of the apartment with a thermos filled with coffee.

Patrick could see his point, but he could also see the point of *whiskey*.

His cravings were through the roof ever since he'd taken shine, and self-medicating was the only way Patrick knew to overcome it. No way was he ever going to touch that shit again of his own free will, but the comedown sucked.

Holding on to his thermos tightly in one hand, Patrick flashed his SOA badge at the security guards on duty in the federal building that housed his agency's New York City field office downtown. He tapped his access pass against the sensor that controlled the closest security gate and walked on through, bypassing the secretarial desk for the elevators.

Patrick took the elevator up to the thirtieth floor. His office was on a lower level, but he hadn't really seen it for almost two weeks at this point. The floor that housed the office of SAIC Henry Ng hadn't changed much since Rachel Andrita had been ousted from her position and arrested for treason. Last he heard, she was being detained at a location only a handful of people knew of, and he wasn't one of those.

Patrick gave it another few weeks before the Dominion Sect caught up with her and she died under mysterious circumstances.

Chugging down some coffee, Patrick waved hello at Henry's executive assistant. The young woman had transferred from San Francisco to New York City, along with a few other support staff. Tiana Martin wasn't a magic user, but she had a steel spine inside her polite demeanor that Patrick knew better than to mess with.

"Door is open," Tiana said with a quick smile, barely glancing away from the computer screen as she typed.

"Thanks."

Patrick still knocked, waiting for the muffled "Come in," before entering.

The corner office seemed more welcoming than the last time he'd stood in it. The furniture remained the same, but the décor had been switched up to account for Henry's taste. The warlock in question was in his late thirties, had an affinity for elemental magic, and could cut someone off at the knees verbally when pressed. It was a trait Patrick could admire when it wasn't directed at him.

"Sir," Patrick said politely as he nudged the door shut behind him with an elbow. The silence ward wrapped around the office hummed to life, a burst of static in his ears before fading out.

"Collins," Henry replied. "You're the source of all my headaches this week."

"Sorry, sir. Can't be helped."

"I'm sure it could if we didn't have a fight brewing in the preternatural world."

"If that stopped happening, we'd be out of a job."

"Some days I think that wouldn't be so bad." Henry gestured at the pair of leather chairs in front of his desk. "Please, take a seat."

Patrick did as he was ordered, setting his coffee thermos on the ground near his feet. "Have you read my report?"

"Yours, and the PCB's. The DEA promised our agency would be read into their current investigation by the end of today. You haven't been answering your phone or emails."

"I've been busy," Patrick hedged. This was the first major case he'd handled with Henry running the field office. The long leash Patrick had been given was probably due to Setsuna's interference, but Henry didn't seem as annoyed about that as Rachel had been.

"I'm aware of how you run your cases, Collins. I also know you've prevented quite a lot of catastrophes if one reads between the lines."

That's one way of putting it. Patrick shifted on his seat. "I'm trying to do that here."

Henry studied him for a long minute before sighing. "I understand this case revolves around a breakdown of treaties held between the Night Courts and the god pack."

"That's part of it."

Henry might have read the reports, but there was nothing like putting a human spin on events. Patrick gave the other man a concise update from yesterday, sticking to the story he knew would be believed—namely, one that didn't revolve around the gods and which skimmed over the fact he'd taken shine but not his escape from Tremaine's Night Court.

"If the subway wards have been compromised, we need to move on that," Henry said with a frown when Patrick finished.

"I understand your concern, but if we move now, I think that will endanger too many people. I have a plan in place, and the DEA has signed off on it for support purposes. I just need your authorization to use an SOA artifact."

"What kind?"

"A barrier ward."

"That won't be enough to contain the damage you're describing in the subway, especially if the wards are damaged further. If you used a barrier ward for containment, you'd need to feed it power on a consistent basis. You aren't capable of doing that."

He said it kindly, but it still stung. Patrick was used to other magic users pointing out his shortcomings. Ignoring the comment was the only thing he could do in a situation like this.

"I can find a workaround. I always have."

"If you were any other agent, I'd tell you no, that I'd want you to find another way. But the director was very clear about letting you run your cases as you saw fit, and I'm not one to disobey her on an issue like this. Not after June. I'll sign off on your request for an artifact, but I'll be keeping some agents on call for backup."

That was the best Patrick could hope for, especially since he was keeping some details back. Lying to his supervisor wasn't the best option, but so long as he made sure the SOA's legal department still had a case to stand on, then his actions were acceptable.

That's what he told himself to sleep at night.

Not that it did any good.

Patrick took his signed-off authorization down to the twentieth floor where the SOA's artifacts were stored within heavily warded walls. Artifacts were portable objects that retained magic even nonmagic users could wield. The SOA regulated theirs within strict parameters. Precautions taken at field offices paled in comparison to those at the Repository, a storage facility housed in a highly classified remote detachment of Edwards Air Force Base. The public knew it as Area 51; Patrick knew it as a headache.

The Department of the Preternatural, the Supernatural Operations Agency, and the Preternatural Intelligence Agency all had equal control over the Repository. The magical and supernatural relics and weapons it contained were all drawn from one myth or another, either new or old. What hadn't changed was their dangerous, destructive capabilities.

Every country had an equivalent of the United States' Repository within their borders. The buildup of magical weapons and artifacts had grown out of the two World Wars and peaked during the Cold War. That hadn't been enough to deter governments from hoarding items capable of mass destruction in some form or another.

Barrier wards were a powerful defensive tool that Patrick had seen deployed in a war zone many times, as well as on home soil. They contained the strongest shields any mage was capable of casting. Patrick had stood behind barrier wards that Nadine had cast and never felt safer. He only hoped they would be strong enough for what he had in mind.

Patrick passed over the authorization and his badge to the agent on duty. While the agent uploaded the authorization and started the retrieval process, Patrick made a phone call.

"Didn't think you would lose the fight with the DEA," Casale said when he picked up.

"The situation changed. DEA Special Agent Delgado," Patrick remembered at the last second to use Quetzalcoatl's alias, "made a compelling argument. I'll be at the PCB within an hour. I need to discuss an update with you."

"We're still sorting out the mess from the other night's run through the streets. Convenient that all of the CCTV cameras or security cameras outside local businesses for the entire route of that chase were burned out."

At least Hermes is good for something, Patrick thought. "Magic does that sometimes. You got eyewitness accounts though."

"Which any good defense attorney will pick apart. We'll talk about it later, Collins."

Casale ended the call and Patrick put his phone away. A few minutes later, he was in receipt of a piece of quartz crystal the length of his palm. The magic resonating from the crystal had the feel of a high-level ward. Patrick breathed a quiet sigh of relief when he wrapped his fingers around the quartz and pocketed it.

Patrick left and took the elevators down to the ground floor. He passed through the security gates and crossed the lobby, heading outside. As he pushed open the glass door and stepped onto the sidewalk, Patrick stumbled over something heavy that got underfoot. Grabbing at the door for support, he looked down at the ground.

And froze.

The black Santa Muerte idol was maybe the length from his wrist to elbow, the scythe and globe painted gold. A chill ran through him as he stared at it, the hairs on the back of his neck standing on end.

Three years since he'd last worn a Mage Corps uniform hadn't dulled his instincts. For all that he lived and worked in the civilian world, Patrick's resting state was war, and always would be.

Patrick shoved the glass door closed behind him and wrenched his personal shields out of his bones. He layered them for strength as the ear-piercing sound of gunfire ripped through the air with the searing intensity of the front lines.

"Get down!" Patrick yelled as he conjured up two mageglobes and sent his magic ripping down the sidewalk.

The federal building was surrounded by wards, and the protections would keep everyone inside its walls safe. The wards wouldn't do anything for those on the outside. Midmorning on a busy Manhattan street meant there were a lot of innocent bystanders ready to take a stray bullet or spell straight to the heart.

One mageglobe tore apart the look-away ward hiding the threat in plain sight. The other raised a secondary shield Patrick shored up with every ounce of concentration and power available to him as he sprinted for what cover he could find. The short cement pillars evenly spaced out on the sidewalk in front of the building had been placed there to stop a vehicular attack on the SOA. Right now, they gave Patrick something to hide behind.

He threw himself at the nearest pillar, grunting from the impact. He got a glimpse of four motorcycles speeding down the street, each carrying a driver and passenger dressed all in black and wearing opaque helmets.

The passengers carried fully automatic rifles with bump stocks that never let up in the assault on his location. Patrick's personal shields remained intact, but the one he'd cast to cover the street buckled against the volley of bullets.

Every single bullet cutting his way was spelled; Patrick could feel the foreign magic of a god chip away at his own with every impact. Each bullet felt like they'd been dipped in literal fire as they slammed into and, in some cases, *through* his shield, only to get stopped by the SOA's protective wards.

Say what you would about federal spending, but the money sunk into those wards were worth the cost.

Defensive magic wasn't his strong point, but Patrick still poured his magic out of his soul to patch up the tears in the only protection available. He hadn't been quick enough to cast a wider shield in the initial volley—people lay on the sidewalk, a few unmoving and more screaming or moaning from gunshot wounds. Cars in the street were braking and swerving as drivers reacted in a frenzied manner. The sound of metal screeching together told Patrick at least one accident had happened, but he couldn't think about that right now.

Patrick conjured up another mageglobe, filled it with raw magic, and sent it after the motorcycles. Normally he wouldn't lob what was effectively a grenade made up of metaphysical energy into the middle of a civilian street, but desperate times called for desperate measures.

The mageglobe exploded between the third and last motorcycles on their drive-by shooting spree. The fourth motorcycle's front wheel hit the pothole that appeared in the wake of the explosion, sending the riders flying into the air as the motorcycle flipped over and crashed. The driver hit the ground headfirst, neck snapping from the force of the landing. The body rolled a couple of times before coming to a stop in the middle of the street as cars swerved to avoid him.

The shooter landed on top of a parked car, shattering its back window. She slid halfway into the vehicle, twitching from the impact—hopefully alive enough to talk because Patrick needed answers.

The three other motorcycles sped away, disappearing with the skill of people who had done this before. They left behind hundreds of bullets and casings scattered across the street and sidewalk, wounded civilians, and a Santa Muerte idol that stood untouched by the building's entrance.

The idol seemed to watch Patrick, plastic skull beneath a draped hood filled with a presence he couldn't look away from. Recognition scraped through his magic, the taste on his tongue like ashes. It left him cold, fingertips numb, as the wind picked up in a gust that rose to gale force speeds.

You should have worshipped me, the wind seemed to scream.

"Fuck you!" Patrick shouted back.

He pressed his back against the cement pillar and sank his personal shields into the sidewalk, digging in as the wind battered the street. The protective wards on the building flared up ice-white, rising upward as the magic in their making reacted to the threat. High above, pigeons took to the air, cooing frantically. A gargoyle on a nearby building reached out and grabbed a couple of birds out of the sky for its lunch.

As quickly as it arrived, the wind disappeared, dirt and paper and bits of feathers drifting down from above in the sudden stillness. Heart pounding in his chest, Patrick stared at the Santa Muerte idol, the feel of a god gone from the street, even if the taste hadn't left his mouth. He swallowed against it, reminded of the chemical saturation of his taste buds when he'd taken shine. It made him sick to his stomach.

Patrick retracted his shields and got to his feet, casing the area. For all that the threat might have vanished, he didn't trust the absence left behind. Patrick conjured up a mageglobe and sent it toward the Santa Muerte idol. He wrapped his magic around the damned thing right as the doors to the SOA building burst open now that the protective wards had gone dormant. He could see through the disappearing brightness numerous agents filling the lobby. Leading the charge outside was Henry, a pissed-off expression on his face.

"What the hell just happened?" Henry demanded as agents scattered to help the wounded and secure the one shooter who was still alive.

Patrick straightened up with the Santa Muerte idol floating between his hands in a mageglobe. "Someone took offense to my lack of tithes at the altar."

"What is *that?*"

Patrick didn't recognize the woman who came to stand by Henry's side. To be fair, he didn't recognize or know many of the agents who worked out of the field office. But the dark-haired woman staring at the Santa Muerte idol with an expression of pure terror in her eyes stood out.

"Evidence for the case I'm working on."

"That's not all it is."

He sighed tiredly, the sound of distant sirens getting louder. "Yeah."

The thing about getting shot at in broad daylight was that it came with the added layer of Patrick being a federal agent. That brought attention. Throw in Patrick being the agent who handled the case in June meant even more attention he didn't want to deal with.

Luckily, Quetzalcoatl was more than happy to cover for him.

Maybe at the expense of the case staying completely in SOA hands, but Patrick had other things to worry about.

"What is with you always getting shot at?" Casale asked in the midst of the crime scene an hour later.

Patrick wiped sweat off his forehead and shrugged. "I can explain."

"That is the worst way to start a conversation." Casale crossed his arms over his chest, his suit jacket pulling at his shoulders. "Care to tell me what's going on?"

Patrick had already spent the better part of an hour giving his statement, arguing with Henry over the Santa Muerte idol still currently in Patrick's possession inside a warded box, and making sure Quetzalcoatl didn't try to take over the case completely. He'd managed one quick phone call with Jono to assure the other man he was all right before cutting the conversation short because of work.

"Things got messy."

"What happened, Collins?"

Patrick conjured up a tiny mageglobe, letting it spin against his palm. He cast a silence ward, his magic encasing them in a bubble of static. Patrick looked Casale in the eye when he said, "There's shit going down between the god pack and the Night Courts. It has to do with independent werecreatures."

"We already know that."

"I pulled proof out of the Crimson Diamond two nights ago, but I had to take shine in order to save her. She's currently under suicide watch at a hospital. I have a pack I trust keeping an eye on her."

"You took *what*? To save who? Why am I only now hearing about this?"

Patrick waved off Casale's questions. "The DEA and SOA are aware of what happened. Both agencies are working to ensure the new information gets added to the case."

"I take it you had no warrant. Again."

"There's an angle that will hold up in court. It involves my criminal informant."

Casale's gaze sharpened. "The same one from June?"

"Yes."

"More vampires. This city doesn't need more vampires, Collins."

"They have unfinished business with Tremaine, and their claim is one that can be legally acknowledged. But this problem isn't just about shine and dead werecreatures." Patrick bent down to flip up the lid of the box he'd been carting around, unwilling to hand it off to anyone else. Inside the wooden containment box was the black Santa Muerte idol. "This showed up before the fun started."

"Been seeing those a lot," Casale said slowly. "Calling card?"

"Of a sort." Patrick flipped the lid closed and rested his hand on top of the box, the wards warm against his skin. "What are your thoughts on the old gods?"

Patrick knew Casale's wife, Angelina, was a priestess in the Crescent Coven, a group of witches and warlocks who had been brought together to worship Hera, the titular queen of the Greek gods. Someone of Angelina's rank, who kept that sort of company, had to believe in the gods who fucked with his life. Patrick knew Casale loved his wife, and sometimes that meant believing in things even his church didn't.

Casale rubbed at his chin, staring at the containment box. "They are stories, but stories have a grain of truth in them sometimes."

"If I told you Tremaine has allied himself with death, would you believe me?"

Casale was quiet for a long minute before finally speaking. "I'd like to say Santa Muerte isn't real. That she's just a false idol certain gangs worship and think will bring them luck when the bullets start flying."

"But?" Patrick pressed.

"I'm Catholic. The Church says there is only one god. That's what I believe, but I know that's not enough for some people. Humanity has prayed to all kinds of gods over the centuries, Collins. I don't believe we'll ever stop."

Patrick nodded slowly as he straightened up. "What protects Tremaine will see us coming if we go through the front door. I'm hoping they'll be so focused on the frontal assault they'll miss us coming up from behind. I know of a different way in, but I can't get there without a subway train."

Casale pinched the bridge of his nose. "You want me to somehow commandeer you a subway train so you can perform a preemptive attack? Christ, I must be out of my mind for even thinking about letting you do this."

"I wouldn't ask if I didn't think it would work."

"Your idea of *working* always leaves the city a mess. If I don't get you the train, you'll find some other way down there, won't you?"

"Marek will," Patrick said, hoping he wasn't lying through his teeth.

Casale sighed heavily. "It's going to take time for me to wrangle a train out of the MTA. When do you need it by?"

"Friday night. After sunset."

Casale turned his head and looked at the street where members of the PCB's Crime Scene Unit were working alongside an SOA team. "No other possible way?"

"No."

Casale clenched his jaw for a moment before nodding. "I'll get you the train."

"Make sure it's on the A line, and you'll want to assign more cops to Grand Central on Friday night as well. The SOA will be deploying agents as well after what happened today."

At that request, Casale's gaze snapped back to him. "Why?"

"Rats like tunnels, and I wouldn't put anything past Tremaine. Grand Central holds the anchor points for the protective wards that run through the entire subway. I don't want to risk what would happen if those break."

It would be worse than a nightmare. The subway system transported over a million riders every single day. If the wards broke down and what monsters lived in the fringe of the veil found their way through, every single subway rider would be at risk, not to mention everyone else who called the five boroughs home.

All told, the dead would be sacrificed to Santa Muerte by Tezcatlipoca, and Patrick would prefer that never came to pass.

Casale's gaze dropped down to the box and his expression hardened. "It'll mean overtime, but I'll make it happen. After June, I haven't gotten as much pushback from the commissioner as I used to."

"Nothing like a terrorist organization and human sacrifice to get you what you need." Patrick nudged the containment box over to Casale with his foot. "I'm leaving this with you. It should be added to the rest of the evidence back at the PCB."

Casale scowled down at it, as if the idol within was the last thing he wanted to deal with. That was a mood Patrick could get behind; he just didn't have the luxury of succumbing to it.

Since he wasn't overseeing the crime scene and his statement had been taken, Patrick left without saying goodbye. Digging out his phone on the walk to the adjacent parking garage, Patrick scrolled through his contacts—a list that had grown over the past couple of months—and highlighted Nadine Mulroney's name for a call. He wasn't sure if she was in the field or not, but it never hurt to try. She'd answer if she could.

One ring in and she answered.

"Special Agent Mulroney, line and location are not secure," his best friend said in a crisp voice.

"Makes two of us. Can you talk?" Patrick said.

"Give me a minute." Patrick waited two before she came back on the line. By that time, he was unlocking his car and getting behind the steering wheel. "Okay, I'm warded. What do you need?"

Patrick slapped his hand against the roof of the Mustang and set a silence ward around the vehicle. It wouldn't interfere with the phone call, but he was taking no chances with anything else. "I'm chasing after some gods I haven't had the pleasure of meeting before now."

"No one finds pleasure in gods, least of all you."

"They're Aztec, and another is a folk deity and goddess of death. Hermes showed up as well. I think he missed me."

"Did you shoot him?"

"Thought about it."

Nadine hummed, the sound coming through the line like static. "My agency will want a formal request from yours if you need me this time."

"I can handle it. Half the problem is Lucien's anyways, and I'm just helping him out. But the gods fucked with the wards in the subway system. I need to patch them or at least contain them before I can bring anyone else down there."

"You can't shield something like that. You've never had that affinity."

"I know, which is why I requested an artifact with a barrier ward from the SOA. When shit goes FUBAR, think it'll work?"

"I can't make that call, Collins."

"Ballpark it for me, Mulroney."

"Subway wards are *old*. They always are. If the gods have already broken some of them, you have a bigger problem because that's damage which has already weakened the whole spellcasting."

"I know that. But I can't fix it until the gods are taken care of and Lucien kills his rat problem."

"It'll be a stopgap if you're planning on using it how I think you are. It won't last long," she warned.

"I'll have SOA agents standing by to access the area once it's safe."

"Then tie it to the broken edges of the spellcasting. I'll email you sigils I would use. It should buy you some time, I just can't tell you how much."

Patrick let out a breath and shoved the key into the ignition. "Thanks. I owe you one."

"Let me know how it goes."

"Probably badly, knowing my luck."

Nadine snorted. "Murphy's Law has a hard-on for you."

"I'm taken."

Nadine's laughter in his ear only stopped when Patrick ended the call.

17

“I don't like this.”

Jono looked up from tying his trainers—a pair he wouldn't mind losing—to find Patrick staring at him from the short hallway that led to their bedroom and the still-damaged bathroom. Jono's gaze slowly traveled up and down Patrick's body, taking him in.

I wouldn't mind seeing him in an actual uniform.

Patrick wore black tactical pants tucked into his combat boots, which were laced up tightly. A black, fitted long-sleeved shirt was tucked into his pants. His tactical pistol was holstered on a heavy-duty belt, dagger secured to his right thigh. He wore fingerless gloves and carried a fully assembled M4A1 carbine in his hands with a familiarity that wasn't lost on Jono. A few extra magazines were secured to his belt, and he carried a duffel bag over one shoulder big enough to hide the assault rifle in. The shoulder strap of a tactical vest peeked out from it.

“This was the plan, remember?” Jono said, leaning forward to rest his elbows on his knees. Personally, he'd rather spend Friday night working or at home with Patrick, not fighting to the death.

“I still don't like it.”

Patrick came closer and dumped the duffel bag on the coffee table with a loud *thump*. Jono watched as he placed the assault rifle inside and zipped the duffel bag closed.

"I'm the distraction."

"You're the bait."

"That, too."

Patrick crossed his arms over his chest and scowled at Jono, brows furrowed. "You don't have any backup."

"Now you know how I feel when you go haring off on your own," Jono pointed out dryly. "And that's a load of bollocks. I have you."

"I don't trust Tezcatlipoca. If it was just Tremaine I wouldn't be as worried."

"Makes two of us." Jono got to his feet and moved around the coffee table to where Patrick stood. Jono curled a finger through a belt loop and tugged him closer. "There's Fenrir if things go pear-shaped."

Patrick tilted his head back so he could look Jono in the eye, hands coming up to rest on Jono's shoulders. "You can't let him out. Word might get back to Estelle and Youssef, and we don't want them to know about him yet."

"Word already is out. Lucien knows."

"And if he tries to use that against us I'll kick his ass."

"You're still in debt to him."

A fact Jono absolutely loathed and which Patrick waved off. "We succeed with this coup and give him Manhattan, then I'll have kept my promise to him. Debt erased."

Jono kissed Patrick on the mouth, biting gently at his bottom lip before pulling away. "No more making deals with a devil unless Sage is the one working out the details."

Patrick hooked his hand around the back of Jono's neck and drew him back down for a deeper kiss. Jono obliged, drinking in the taste of him until Wade interrupted them when he walked out of the bedroom.

"Gross," Wade said. "Stop making out where I can see."

Jono broke the kiss and rolled his eyes. "You can sod off if you don't like seeing two blokes kissing."

Wade made a face. "I don't care that you're two guys. I just don't like seeing adults make out. It's like watching my mom kiss her boyfriend when she was still alive. No one wants to watch their parents make out."

"We aren't your parents but guess that makes you a kid if you're complaining about adults," Patrick said.

Wade scowled before slinking into the kitchen to open the cupboard Jono had stocked with a new supply of snacks. "I'm not a kid."

"Good to know since you're coming with me."

"You sure about bringing him along?" Jono asked quietly, well aware Wade could still hear him.

"I can't leave him here alone, and Hermes took back the coin he'd left in Marek's apartment. There's no safety topside here for him, and Wade knows the way through those tunnels." Patrick ran a hand through his hair and sighed. "It's not my first choice. Believe me, if I could spare him this trauma, I would, but he agreed to come."

"After you pressured him."

The talk at Ginnungagap the other night had continued back at the flat. Jono thought at the time, and still did, that it was a bit too much manipulation happening on Patrick's part toward Wade, but he'd held his tongue.

Patrick winced. "I'm not proud about that, okay?"

"Patrick asked, and I said yes," Wade said as he came out of the kitchen with a Pop-Tart in one hand and crumbs on his lips. "That's more autonomy than Tloque Nahuaque ever gave me."

"You know, you don't have to call him by that title," Patrick said. "Asshole works just fine. Also bastard and fucker, depending on your mood."

Wade shrugged and took another bite of his Pop-Tart. Jono

figured it would take a few therapy sessions before the teen would be willing to call Tezcatlipoca by any other name.

Jono's mobile buzzed on the coffee table and he leaned over to retrieve it. The text message from Sage informed him she was outside.

"Ride is here." Jono handed his mobile to Patrick since he wasn't taking it to the club. "I need to go."

"You know the plan."

"You know you can use me for your magic," Jono reminded Patrick. "I want you to."

Patrick pressed his mouth into a hard line before shaking his head. "I can't."

"Sometimes we don't get a choice. I'm telling you it's okay." Jono reached out and cupped Patrick's face, stroking his thumb gently over the freckles on his cheek. "Don't hold back tonight."

"I don't want to hurt you."

"You never could, love. See you on the other side."

They didn't say goodbye, a superstition Patrick clung to from his time in the Mage Corps that Jono was fine with adhering to. He just pressed one more kiss to Patrick's willing mouth before leaving the flat for where Sage waited in her BMW on the street. He was surprised to see Marek keeping her company.

"Ready?" Sage said as Marek opened the car door, a blast of cold air pouring out to mix with the summer heat. Marek moved the seat forward and climbed into the back, ceding the front to Jono.

"Yeah," Jono replied.

Like Patrick, Sage was dressed all in black. Like Jono, she wore old clothes she wouldn't mind losing when she shifted. Her thick hair was braided back to keep it out of her face. As soon as he closed the door and buckled up, Sage stepped on the gas pedal.

Jono craned his head around to look at Marek. "Thought you'd be at home?"

The color of Marek's hazel eyes seemed more washed-out than

usual. "I'll drop Sage off at Ginnungagap after we take you to the Crimson Diamond."

Ginnungagap was the staging ground for the attack tonight. Jono knew Patrick still had some last-minute coordination with the SOA and the PCB to handle before he met everyone over there.

"Got something to tell me?"

Marek blinked, and his eyes washed out to a pure white. The ozone scent of a god filled the car, setting Jono's teeth on edge. The feminine voice that came out of Marek's mouth made Sage tighten her hands on the steering wheel.

"*We cannot see the end,*" one of the Norns said. "*But neither can the Morai.*"

"What good are a bunch of Fates if you can't see the future?" Jono asked.

The Fates driving Marek leaned forward, the intensity of their gaze making Jono freeze. "*There is more at stake than you know. Death takes many shapes, but it always follows war. The Dominion Sect must not claim either.*"

Marek blinked, his eyes fading back to hazel. Jono watched as he hunched over, lacing his hands together over the back of his head.

"Fuck. Verðandi is worse than Skuld when she wants to make a point," Marek mumbled.

"Need me to pull over?" Sage asked.

Marek swallowed audibly. "No. I'll be fine."

Jono and Sage shared a disbelieving look, but neither called Marek out on the obvious lie. He never fared well for a few hours after he had a vision or channeled the Fates who owned him.

"You're not driving home from Ginnungagap. I'll text Emma and have her pick you up."

Marek said nothing, which was an answer by itself. Jono faced forward again, keeping an eye on the traffic as they left Chelsea behind for SoHo. Both neighborhoods were thick with early Friday-night crowds, and their numbers would only increase. Jono tried not to think about how many people were using the subway tonight and what might happen if their plan didn't work.

When Sage finally braked to a stop in front of the guarded door of the Crimson Diamond, she looked Jono directly in the eye and showed her throat. "I will keep the pack safe," she promised.

Jono reached out and pressed his hand to her throat, scent-marking her. "Dire."

The god strain of the werevirus didn't run in her veins. Sage didn't have his eyes, but she had the heart and fortitude any god pack would welcome. The rank he bestowed on her was only proper. The wide-eyed, pleased look she gave him was one he would always remember.

Jono got out of the car and helped Marek return to the front passenger seat before he closed the door. Then he headed for the entrance to the Crimson Diamond and didn't look back.

Human servants guarded the door since sunset was still thirty minutes away. Neither stopped him when Jono reached for the door handle and let himself inside. A pair of human servant host-esses and two cartel members stood in front of the flower wall with its neon sign.

"Jonothon de Vere," the blonde woman said. "Our lord is expecting you."

Jono highly doubted Tremaine had Lucien's ability to walk in daylight and was here to greet him. "Is he now?"

The taller cartel member cracked his knuckles in a cartoonish sort of threat Jono ignored. "This way," the man ordered.

Unlike the hostess, the cartel members didn't wear bite mark scars around their throats, but they carried pistols like an exten-sion of their arms. Jono followed them deeper into the club, taking in the crowd. The main floor was full of well-dressed people getting drunk or high, placing bets for the fight, or getting off as they waited for the vampires to wake with sunset and the night's entertainment to begin.

At the edge of the marble dance floor, a cluster of low tables and leather chaises were guarded by heavily armed cartel members. Some of the men and women faced outward, eyes on the club, while others kept watch over their charges. Jono drew in a deep breath, taking in the scents around him—chemical, sweat, metal, gunpowder, and the electric tang of gods coming together in a toxic mixture.

Tezcatlipoca greeted him with a smile and a raised glass of tequila. Dressed in a tan linen suit, wearing an overabundance of gold and obsidian jewelry, the god had his arm around the shoulders of an emaciated woman. Her bones pressed sharply against paper-thin skin, the black, off-the-shoulder evening dress she wore barely clinging to her arms. Even in the dim club lighting, Jono could make out the embroidery along the long skirt that covered her feet, a pattern of skulls and crossed scythes.

Shiny black hair was pulled up in an intricate braided updo studded with obsidian pins and a cluster of marigolds. Her face was more bone than flesh, the skin there painted in the style of a sugar skull—deathly white, with black and red detailing around her eyes and mouth. She looked at Jono with pitch-black eyes, no sclera showing at all, and the only scent he got off her was death.

"Tezcatlipoca," Jono said, never taking his eyes off the deity. "Santa Muerte."

"*Nuestra Señora de la Santa Muerte,*" one of the men who had led Jono to the table said. The tone in his voice was that of a believer as he knelt and crossed himself, head bowed in obeisance.

Santa Muerte extended her hand toward the man, and he crawled forward in order to kiss the obsidian ring sitting prominently on her middle finger.

"I assumed you would forfeit," Tezcatlipoca said.

Jono took a seat on an empty chaise without being invited. He ignored the furious looks thrown his way by a handful of Tezcatlipoca's faithful. "You don't know me."

"I know you stink of the mage who didn't tithe properly."

Jono's lips peeled away from his teeth. "Patrick doesn't belong to you."

"I suppose you think he belongs to you?" Tezcatlipoca took a sip of his tequila, gaze hooded. "He is owned by Persephone."

"You think that makes him fair game? Some toy for the gods to fight over and use?" Jono leaned forward and picked up the bottle of AsomBroso Reserva Del Porto and pulled out the glass stopper. "Patrick is part of my pack. You don't get to touch him, you fucking twat."

Jono took a swig of tequila straight from the expensive bottle. The taste was smooth on his tongue; top shelf for sure. When one of the cartel members tried to yank it out of his hand, Jono grabbed the man by the throat and squeezed hard enough to completely cut off his air. Jono tossed the man onto the dance floor, not bothering to watch where he landed.

"My challenge was to Tremaine. You want in on it?" Jono asked as he leaned back on the chaise and gestured at Tezcatlipoca with the bottle. "Then get in. Or are you too bloody scared?"

The quiet click of a gun's safety being undone and the cold press of a muzzle against the back of Jono's skull didn't bother him at all. He just took another sip of tequila and kept his eyes on Tezcatlipoca.

He needed to keep Tremaine and the gods occupied so Patrick and the others could find their way inside and go unnoticed for as long as possible. If it meant antagonizing a god, well, he'd watched Patrick do it enough. Jono figured it couldn't be that hard.

Santa Muerte placed one bony hand on Tezcatlipoca's knee. *"My love will tear you apart."*

Her voice reminded Jono's of the Norns: inhuman and not meant for this world. It was nothing compared to the one that howled in the deep recesses of his mind.

Jono pointed at her. "You're on. State your terms."

Santa Muerte smiled, the expression hollowing out her cheeks with shadows. *"Your soul belongs to me when you die."*

"Sorry, taken. Try again." Jono went to take another sip of tequila when the person holding the gun to his head shoved hard at his skull. He looked over his shoulder and scowled. "You mind, mate? Trying to drink here."

"Respect your betters," the man snapped.

"I would if anyone was better than me."

"Do not kill him before the fight begins," Tezcatlipoca said, casually lifting a hand to forestall the man from shooting Jono in the back of the head.

The gun lifted away, taking the threat with it. Jono's heartbeat remained calm and steady as he went for that sip of tequila. "So is it going to be a twofer? Tremaine, then you?"

"You think highly of your chances when you are here alone."

Jono shrugged. "I'm god pack. It's my right to issue the challenge, not theirs. This, right here, is on me."

"Ah, but you have already issued your challenge to Tremaine, and our guests are interested in watching you die."

"And if I don't?"

"Then you and I shall fight. If you win, you may leave. If you lose, you will be a gift to my greatest love."

Patrick's grumblings about being sacrificed to gods flashed through Jono's mind. Jono knew he would die if he lost, but it was a risk he was here to take.

Jono sipped at the tequila a few more times before setting the bottle aside. He wasn't here to get pissed, but to fight. Tezcatlipoca and Santa Muerte ignored his presence as they accepted gifts and prayers from what followers had come tonight. Jono didn't recognize any of the men or women on sight, but he recognized the wealth they carried.

Almost everyone who approached was human, though there were several who had the scent of magic on them. None were mages, and almost all were cartel members, their alliance to the gods holding court by the dance floor and not the Dominion Sect, as far as Jono knew.

Sunset came and went. The excited air of the club shifted when the employees-only doors past the dance floor finally opened. Several human servants tottered out with fresh bite marks on their throats. The vibe of the crowd shifted into something more anticipatory, almost predatory.

Jono remained where he was, watching as members of Tremaine's Manhattan Night Court arrived. They trickled through the door in ones and twos, gliding into the crowd freshly fed but still hungering for blood. Jono didn't care about them, only their master.

They'd agreed on the fight happening an hour after sunset. Jono knew, after Maria's visit at Ginnungagap, that Tremaine had probably set that start time to ensure the other Night Courts had time to arrive. It worked in their favor in that it gave Patrick and the others time to implement their attack.

Jono kept an eye on the crowd, and his hearing dialed up to pick out distant conversation. Guests were still arriving, but none were vampires from rival Night Courts. Over the course of the following hour, he picked up agitated whispers amongst Tremaine's vampires. The frustrated worry in the bits and pieces of conversation he overheard told Jono no representatives from the other Night Courts in the five boroughs had arrived.

Jono kept his expression impassive and his heartbeat steady, glad no other werecreatures were in the club to smell his emotions. Not for the first time did he envy Patrick's magic and ability to shield so tightly scent couldn't get through. The trick was useful when it wasn't being used against him.

Sunset was nearly an hour gone when Tremaine finally deigned to grace the Crimson Diamond with his presence. The master vampire of the Manhattan Night Court came out to welcoming applause from the crowd, raising his arms to accept their adoration like he was some posh lord who thought he deserved it. His white-blond hair was slicked back, blue eyes unblinking as he stepped onto the dance floor in a tailored suit Jono hoped would be ruined by the end of the night.

"Ladies and gentlemen," Tremaine said, pitching his voice to be heard over the bass thump of the music still pouring out of the speakers. "You are my specially chosen guests for tonight's entertainment. A once-in-a-lifetime experience involving myself and a god pack werewolf. I do hope you have placed your bets."

The excited murmur of the crowd grew louder. Jono ignored the glances thrown his way in favor of raising two fingers and flashing them at Tremaine in a greeting the master vampire couldn't miss.

"And when I kick your arse, your guests will get the pleasure of watching me tangle with your business partner over here," Jono said in a bored voice.

Tremaine's eyes cut away to Tezcatlipoca for a brief second before returning to Jono. "A grand event that would be, but it will never happen."

"Bit full of yourself, aren't you?"

Jono stood and walked onto the dance floor. The marble beneath his feet was smooth, offering little traction. He couldn't decide if he wanted to shift first or not, but ultimately decided against it. Jono needed to prolong the fight to buy Patrick time.

Besides, Jono wanted the bastard to suffer for putting his hands on Patrick.

Tremaine stood his ground as Jono came closer, an amused twist to his mouth that couldn't hide his fangs. "You think highly of yourself for an animal."

"More highly than your master thinks of you," Jono drawled. "I'd say Lucien sends his regards, but that would be a lie."

The hate in Tremaine's eyes brought a smile to Jono's face. "I have no master."

"Seems like you have two. Me? I don't have any."

A human servant came forward at a snap of Tremaine's fingers, silently removing his suit jacket, cufflinks, and tie before retreating again. Tremaine casually rolled up his sleeves, revealing pale forearms.

"That will change tonight."

Jono shrugged. "Doubt it."

"Pity you brought no one to watch me bring you to your knees and beg. I'm sure you'll go down just as prettily as the mage."

Jono had to check his rage before speaking. "You think I'd let my pack be around you after the shit you pulled earlier this week? Wasn't gonna happen."

"Then I'll send them your heart to remember you by."

"Won't be mine they'll get as a gift after tonight."

Tremaine raised a hand and snapped his fingers again. A vampire appeared at his side, so quick Jono's eyes could barely track him. Jono recognized him from the previous weekend.

"Yes, my lord?" the vampire asked.

"Where are Devon and the others?"

If vampires could sweat, Jono thought the messenger would be drenched. "They have not yet responded to the invitations. All calls to their Night Courts are going unanswered."

Jono hoped Maria hadn't been lying when she told Lucien she and the other master vampires wouldn't be coming tonight. If they did show up to support Tremaine at the last minute, he only hoped Lucien brought enough weaponry to deal with the bloodsuckers.

"I came for a fight. So did your guests. You going to disappoint us all by delaying it? Or are you that scared?" Jono mocked.

"I fear nothing, least of all you," Tremaine snapped.

"I'll be sure to tell Lucien that." Jono backed up a couple of steps and spread his arms. "Well? I'm ready. Are you?"

People in power were all the same. They hated having their authority challenged, hated not being the one in charge. Jono knew how to play that game in the werecreature community. Watching Patrick and Lucien go toe-to-toe told him it wasn't much different in a vampire's Night Court.

Challenges weren't liked in any corner of the preternatural

world for the sole reason they almost always ended with someone dead.

Hope you're getting close, Pat.

Jono refused to pull at the soulbond between them. He wasn't sure if the gods here could feel it, and he didn't want to bring attention to it or Fenrir. Jono focused on Tremaine instead.

Vampires were long-lived. That didn't necessarily mean they became more powerful with every century they survived. Tremaine was an exception Jono knew not to underestimate. He was Lucien's child, two steps removed from Ashanti herself. A monster in human form who wouldn't hesitate to pry open Jono's rib cage and rip out his heart.

In turn, Jono couldn't wait to tear the fucker apart.

Fenrir licked at his thoughts, the need for blood, for war, creeping through his veins. Jono did his best to ignore that siren call, but it was difficult with Tremaine standing in front of him.

Then Tezcatlipoca stood, drawing every eye in the room. The rest of the clubgoers might have only seen a rich cartel gang member, but those who only had one foot in the mundane world knew the truth. Jono saw a few human servants put distance between themselves and the gods in control of the evening.

"Shall we begin?" Tezcatlipoca said.

He extended a hand over the dance floor and snapped his fingers. Gold fire burned into existence around his hand before falling like embers to the marble below. The magic spread rapidly, forming the same circle used during the fight Jono had broken up last weekend. Fiery golden lines formed the great circle, the wide face of a warrior rising in the center between Jono and Tremaine. The four quadrants formed, along with the sunbeam spikes. Once all the circles sealed together, the outermost one rose up in a wall, barricading Jono inside with Tremaine. There was no way out of the gods-built magic cage except through death.

This time, Patrick wasn't up on the mezzanine with his gods-given dagger capable of breaking the spellwork. Jono had only what he'd carried into the fight—everything that could give him an edge.

Tremaine, for his part, didn't look nervous at all. He'd come to this fight dressed for a night on the town, clearly believing Jono was an easy mark when the only person Jono was easy for was Patrick.

Tremaine flexed his fingers, his presence filling the fight ring while the roar of the crowd filled Jono's ears. "I'm going to enjoy killing you."

"Lucien was right. You're all talk," Jono said.

At the mention of his master, Tremaine snarled out a command that Jono sensed deep in his soul, the push of power behind it familiar.

"*Change.*"

Black magic plucked at the werevirus running through his veins, but Fenrir kept hold of his soul so Jono could stay in human form. Tremaine's power rushed through him and dispersed, the order nothing but sound in Jono's ears.

Music filled the space between them. The crowd seemed surprised that Jono hadn't shifted on the command of a master vampire, the murmur of their voices white noise through the magic caging them in.

Jono smirked, meeting Tremaine's surprised gaze. "That all you got, mate?"

Tremaine snarled and rushed forward so fast he was only a blur in Jono's sight. Jono moved, but not quick enough to escape the glancing punch to his face. He caught it on the chin, the speed and force of the blow making his jaw ache. He lashed out, fingernails shifting into the beginning of claws, and caught the edges of Tremaine's shirt.

The fabric ripped as Tremaine blurred out of reach. Something wet trickled over Jono's bottom lip, the taste of blood on his tongue. He wiped it away with the back of his hand, eyeing Tremaine as he mentally noted how fast the master vampire could move.

Pretty fucking fast.

But not fast enough to escape Jono's claws.

The thick black blood staining the edges of the torn dress shirt put them at a draw for first blood. Tremaine's expression twisted into something monstrous, all vestiges of humanity leaving him as the master vampire crouched low to the dance floor.

Jono widened his stance and braced himself for the next attack, anticipation thrumming through his veins. "Best get on with it. I don't have all night."

In reply, Tremaine lunged forward, and Jono met him halfway with a snarl that was more wolf than human.

18

"I got you a train," Casale said. "Special express, straight into crazy."

Patrick closed the car door and hiked the duffel bag higher onto his shoulder but didn't head inside Ginnungagap. "I'm duly impressed with your bargaining skills."

"The MTA was a hard nut to crack, but they finally agreed. The train will stop at West Fourth Street-Washington Square Station twenty minutes after sunset. It's a special, so look for that on the signs. Police will be on the platform to ensure only your group gets on. Detective Specialists Guthrie and Ramirez will be your contacts there. They will redeploy to Grand Central after you leave the station."

"The SOA has agents stationed at Grand Central as well. SAIC Ng is coordinating their defense. You should probably call him."

"We've been in touch. I'm providing a few officers, but the DEA is handling the majority of surveillance at the Crimson Diamond."

"I know," Patrick said, thinking of the argument he and Quetzalcoatl had worked their way through over a conference call earlier in the day. "I already told Special Agent Delgado not to prematurely breach the club and to wait for my signal."

"If your signal is a destroyed building, you're talking to the commissioner in my stead."

"I'll give him my director's direct number. Thanks for the train, Casale."

"I hope you're wrong about this, but my gut says you aren't. We'll start closing stations as soon as we get word you've been dropped off in the restricted area."

"Understood. I need to go."

"Good luck."

Patrick ended the call, mind churning as he headed for the entrance to Ginnungagap in the alleyway. Wade was holding the door open for him, chewing on a granola bar and eyeing him worriedly.

"I thought we weren't bringing in the cops?" Wade asked.

"Red tape is a bitch, and I want my ass covered." Patrick shouldered past him and squinted through the bright light at everyone gathered in the center of the warehouse around construction tools. "Suck it up, Lucien, okay?"

In response, Patrick found himself grabbed by the throat and slammed against the wall by the door, Wade's frightened yelp ringing in his ears. Patrick's head smacked hard against the wall, and he scowled through the pain.

"Fuck, at least let me put on my hard helmet before you start knocking me around," Patrick got out around Lucien's heavy grip.

Lucien was so close his face was a blur in Patrick's eyesight. "I *said* no cops."

"We need the backup, and Quetzalcoatl agreed. You mind letting me breathe?"

Lucien only tightened his grip until Patrick gagged.

"Let him go."

The voice wasn't familiar, but the electric recognition of a god burning through his magic was. Patrick looked askance at where

Áłtsé Hashké stood so close he could reach out and touch the immortal if he wanted.

Patrick kept his hands to himself. He wished Lucien would do the same.

"This isn't your business, Áłtsé Hashké," Lucien warned.

"It has been my business since Tezcatlipoca first started sacrificing werecreatures. Let Patrick go. The debt he owes us supersedes the one you brokered out of him."

Lucien loosened his grip by degrees but didn't immediately let go. Patrick sucked in a breath around the fingers still wrapped around his throat.

"The cops and the feds don't know who you are, Lucien. I said I'd help you take over the Manhattan Night Court. You didn't specify *how*," Patrick said.

"Details matter," Sage said as she suddenly appeared by Patrick's side, smiling grimly at Lucien right before she yanked the vampire's hand off his throat. "Don't touch him again."

Lucien didn't seem put off by either Sage or Áłtsé Hashké. His attitude would be called careless in anyone else, but Patrick knew this was just the way Lucien was. The master vampire was capable of analyzing what happened around him, pick apart the weakness in everyone, and twist events to suit his exact purpose.

Lucien wasn't careless, he was *calculating*.

Patrick rubbed gingerly at his throat as he bent down to retrieve his duffel bag from where it had fallen off his shoulder. "Admit it. The cops are a good idea."

"I won't make a distinction of sides if they get in my way." Lucien's black eyes flickered between the three of them before he raised a hand and gestured sharply at the door. "We're on a schedule. Get moving."

As much as Patrick would give anything to not be part of this coup, he had promises to keep, places to be, vampires to kill. His life could be called a lot of things but never dull.

Sunset was five minutes in the past, but Lucien's vampires were all fed and ready to fight. They gathered up the duffel bags containing their gear and filed out of Ginnungagap. Patrick raised an eyebrow at Áłtsé Hashké.

"You coming?" he asked.

The trickster god stroked a hand down the breastplate made out of white bone beads tied together by black leather strips. "I will see this to the end."

"Hate to break it to you, but the Fates can't see that."

Áłtsé Hashké smiled, yellow eyes crinkling at the corners. "They are not my Fates."

Honestly, Patrick wished they weren't his either.

He corralled Sage and Wade, hustling them out of Ginnungagap after Lucien. Members of Lucien's Anahuac Cartel, led by Sergio, were waiting for everyone out on the street in a line of SUVs two lanes deep that didn't look suspicious at all.

"It's like they want to be noticed," Patrick muttered under his breath.

Sage huffed out a small laugh but kept her opinions to herself.

Patrick hastily conjured up a mageglobe and cast a look-away ward over the area. Everyone was piling into the SUVs with their gear, all seats taken. Patrick found himself riding shotgun in an SUV with Sage, Wade, Irena, and a couple of cartel gang members. Their driver was a petite woman dressed like she was ready to rob a bank and take a selfie at the same time judging by her pristine makeup.

He kicked absently at the duffel bag between his feet. Patrick didn't know where Áłtsé Hashké wandered off to. The immortal didn't join them in their chosen vehicle as the convoy of SUVs broke up to take different routes to the West Fourth Street-Washington Square Station. Patrick dropped his look-away ward as everyone drove off, drawing down his magic.

Patrick tried not to think about Jono on the ride to their designated subway station, but it was a losing battle. Patrick resisted the urge to tug at the soulbond, not wanting to distract Jono in case he was in the middle of something important—like fighting for his life.

He closed his eyes, unable to push aside the memory of what Jono had looked like walking out of the apartment without a backward glance. Jono had Fenrir's support, but that wasn't a forever guarantee, and Patrick knew how capricious the gods could be. Patrick had to believe Jono would survive whatever he would ultimately face at the Crimson Diamond.

Maybe Jono is right. Next time we should stick together.

Patrick didn't know what he would do if Jono didn't make it out alive tonight. His concern had nothing to do with the soulbond and everything to do with the fact that Jono was becoming important to him. Jono was a risk and a weakness in a way Patrick couldn't bring himself to let go of.

He opened his eyes, staring at the street. Patrick would deal with all the emotions Jono stirred up in him later, preferably when the other man was within reach to kiss.

The convoy of SUVs reached the subway station in waves, with drivers stopping only long enough to discharge their passengers before continuing on. Patrick was leaving the SUV before it even rolled to a stop, hauling his duffel bag over his shoulder as he hustled to the sidewalk.

A look-away ward could only hide so much, but Patrick cast one anyway. If word got back to Tremaine about their movements, it would hopefully be too late for the master vampire to react. Sage and Wade hurried after him, keeping pace. They made their way down into the subway, where a police officer from the SOA was posted at the fare gates.

The officer took one look at them before rapping his knuckles against the bulletproof glass surrounding the booth agent. "Let them through."

Seconds later the faregates unlocked at the same time with loud *ka-thunk* sounds. Patrick and the others went through unimpeded while the officer kept a dozen general commuters back.

"This isn't staying undercover," Sage mused on their walk down to the platform.

"Biyu hacked the subway CCTV for this station and the train we're taking. We aren't being monitored," Patrick said.

Lucien's hacker was holed up wherever his Night Court lay low during daylight hours. Patrick didn't know where that place was and doubted he ever would. He just knew her job was to keep Lucien and his Night Court off the police's radar as much as possible.

"You are a lawyer's worst nightmare, in case anyone hasn't told you that lately."

"You're not the first to say that."

As much as Patrick would have liked to abide by mortal laws, the gods and their expectations wouldn't let him.

True to Casale's word, Allison and Dwayne waited for them on the subway platform, the two detectives eyeing the crowd.

"Nice friends," Allison said, arms crossed over her chest, badge prominently displayed on her belt.

"We're not friendly," Patrick replied. "How long until the train arrives?"

Dwayne looked at the watch on his wrist. "About five minutes."

"Great."

By the time the train in question was set to arrive, the platform was filled with everyone who had agreed to join the fight. Mixed in with the crowd were clusters of civilians who Allison and Dwayne made a point to speak to. Lucien and Carmen kept their distance from the detectives.

The electronic signs overhead started to flash SPECIAL on their boards. The sounds of the subway train approaching filled the tunnel, the squeal of metal on metal echoing in his ears. A surprisingly short three-car train pulled into the station with a screech of brakes, rolling to the center of the platform.

"This train is a Special for NYPD use only!" Dwayne called out loudly, cupping his hands around his mouth. "It will not be stopping at any station. Remain on the platform if you haven't been cleared to board."

"Good luck," Allison said as the train carriage doors opened up. "Don't die."

"I don't know if you've seen the odds but—" Patrick broke off with a grunt as Sage shoved him onto the first car of the subway train. "Rude. I was having a conversation."

"And now we are having a coup," Sage responded calmly as she settled into a subway seat.

The train lacked an operator, but the conductor opened his door and poked his head out, gaze landing unerringly on Patrick. "Hey. You. The redhead."

"Collins," Patrick replied helpfully.

"Whatever. I got orders to stop at a switch point and drop you off. This everyone?"

"Yeah."

The man grunted. "Great. I'm closing the doors."

He ducked back into the control booth, and moments later all the doors slid closed. Patrick took a seat beside Sage and dropped his duffel bag between his feet. He unzipped it and started pulling out his field gear, strapping it on piece by piece. Armored joint pads for knees and elbows, a Kevlar-lined tactical vest streamlined for a breach procedure rather than patrol, a hard helmet, night-vision goggles, and his M4A1 carbine.

He'd worn his dagger and tactical pistol out of the apartment, with the quartz crystal artifact tucked into his front pocket. The only other thing he carried was his phone and car keys secured in a pouch on his belt.

Patrick took a moment to calibrate the ACOG scope on the rifle to his eyesight before clipping the strap to his tactical vest. The weight of the rifle was a comfort that steadied him in a way little else did these days except for Jono.

The vampires in Lucien's Night Court were donning their own gear, with several pulling on balaclavas, including Lucien. Considering the police force they might be dealing with at the end of the night, hiding their faces was a good decision.

He leaned back and stared at the opposite window across the subway car. Hints of magic swirled at the peripheral of his vision as they passed through the tunnel. Wade sat on the other side of Sage, pale-faced and nervously tapping his fingers against his knees. The bulletproof Kevlar-lined vest he wore was almost too big for his skinny frame. Sage reached over and grabbed his hand, giving it a gentle squeeze.

"Hey. We won't let anything happen to you," Sage said.

"They'll know we're coming," Wade said quietly, sounding more like a child than a teenager.

The fear in his voice, in his eyes, made Patrick feel guilty about dragging him down into this nightmare but not enough to leave him behind. Wade had wanted to come, but that didn't make this situation easier.

If he was a better person, maybe he would've put Wade's trauma first. If they weren't fighting against gods, then he could have. But weighed against a city of millions, one teenager's shitty past wasn't enough to make Patrick change his mind. In war, there was no such thing as the greater good, only good enough for now. Patrick couldn't always be a good person.

He hated that about himself sometimes, especially right now.

"Probably," Patrick said. "Doesn't mean they're prepared. And Sage is right. We'll do our best to keep you safe."

Patrick could only hope Tremaine's arrogance would leave them a couple desperately needed openings to take him down.

The ride to the drop-off point was quick, with the train rolling to a stop before it entered the Spring Street Station. The doors opened, the darkness in the tunnel beckoning them forward. The conductor poked his head out of the booth again.

"I'll radio that you're dropped off," he said.

Patrick flashed him a thumbs-up before tugging his NVGs over his eyes and leaving the train with everyone else. They walked forward down the track to where the headlights illuminated a set of rusted tracks curving off the main line. The tracks led into a separate tunnel walled off by an iron grate over the entrance, with a door built into it.

When Patrick placed a gloved hand on the grate, magic flickered alive in the iron, protective wards that should have been whole but weren't. He looked over his shoulder, the world tinged green through the goggles, but Lucien was easy enough to find.

"The damage extends out here. I need to set the barrier ward at the source of the damage," Patrick said.

"Someone get us through," Lucien ordered.

Sage stepped forward and wrapped her fingers around the rusted lock and door handle. With a grunt, she broke it off, easily shattering the iron. The wards sputtered and sparked around the damage but didn't lash out at her. It told Patrick in no uncertain terms the damage went deeper than was safe.

With the way open, everyone continued on. Like Patrick, Sergio's cartel members wore NVGs to help them navigate the darkness. The vampires, Sage, and Wade didn't need that kind of external help. The group walked nearly three-quarters of a mile down old rusted tracks through the dark, damaged magic scraping against Patrick's shields with every step he took.

When they reached the abandoned subway station, Patrick had to force his heart to remain steady, his mind flashing back to unwanted hands on his body and the way the world had tilted in the light of a thousand candles.

Now, the candles were snuffed out, the altar where Santa Muerte had sat on her framed throne empty of the goddess. The flowers had all dried out to husks, the floral scent buried beneath the musty air that filled this area of the subway system.

Patrick took it all in with clear eyes and mind. He reminded himself that he hadn't died down here thanks to the god who sat in coyote form in front of the steel vault door that led to the heart of Tremaine's Night Court.

"Okay, someone needs to say it. This is too easy," Patrick said.

Lucien approached the vault door, assault rifle held in his hands. "Tremaine always had a blind spot when it came to his defenses."

"Like what? Not having enough?"

"By thinking walls were enough on their own. I see no trip-wires or bombs. He's just barricaded his back door." Lucien paused before shaking his head. "Ah. Stănileşti."

Einar looked at Lucien with a mildly disapproving expression on his face. "That was not one of your better plans."

Patrick dug out the quartz crystal from his pocket and gripped it tightly. "Care to explain to those of us who haven't lived through history?"

"The Ottomans won the battle with Russia, though not the war."

Carmen went to stand beside Lucien, studying the vault door. "Irena? Come take a look."

Irena came forward on silent feet, pacing back and forth in front of the vault. "Stainless steel and concrete make. Probably built into the surrounding support walls of the station. It can't have a time lock on it if they use it on a regular basis or if it's their bolt-hole."

"Dual control?" Lucien asked.

"Doubtful. I'd go with a combination lock. We can drill through the panels to get to the locking mechanism if you want to stay unnoticed for as long as possible."

"How long will that take?"

"Not quick enough to make you happy."

"Use the thermal lance. I don't care about the noise it will make."

"And the wards?"

"We brought artifacts. Use them."

A pair of Lucien's vampires carried over a heavy-looking crate and deposited it near Irena. Between the three of them, they rapidly put together the tool Irena would need to cut through the vault door. She donned a protective suit and helmet that could withstand high heat from the backpack she had carried into the tunnel and got to work.

Patrick left them to it, retreating to the tunnel entrance, artifact in hand and sweat sliding down his spine. A loud yip drew his attention to where Áłtsé Hashké pawed at the wall of the tunnel, magic sparking like miniature Vesuvius flames in Patrick's NVGs with every scrape of his paw.

"If you say so," Patrick said with a shrug.

Áłtsé Hashké moved out of the way, and Patrick knelt in front of the curved brick wall. He moved his goggles onto the top of his hard helmet, the sudden change to darkness making him blink rapidly to adjust his eyesight. Magic burned bright, and modern technology couldn't always block it out.

He pressed a gloved hand against the brick, watching as the damaged wards flared into existence at his touch. Patrick studied the way they linked together, running his hand over the wall, tracing out the power that had warped the magic into something ugly and dangerous—a hole for all the hells to walk through.

Áłtsé Hashké yipped again, sounding impatient. Patrick rolled his eyes. "Defensive magic isn't my affinity, and I can't tap a ley line."

Another yip.

"Yeah, well, fuck you, too."

Patrick pressed the tip of the quartz crystal against the brick, the artifact warming rapidly. He could feel the heat of borrowed magic through his glove, pricking at his own shields. Áłtsé Hashké watched with eerie yellow eyes as Patrick reached with his magic for the *command* buried within the artifact. A nonmagic user would've been given a set of spell words to speak, but Patrick didn't need those in order to access the magic held inside the artifact.

Power poured out of the crystal, the barrier ward etched in its depth set by a mage of considerable strength. Patrick carefully wrote out a series of linked sigils that Nadine had given him. Then he used his entire body weight to force the quartz crystal into the brick wall, magic easing the way.

The barrier ward spiderwebbed away from the artifact, bright lines overwriting the wards in the tunnel in a different pattern, one meant to contain the damage. It was a stop-gap measure Patrick only hoped would last long enough until SOA agents could get down here and find a permanent fix.

Áłtsé Hashké gape-grinned at Patrick, then trotted off back into the depths of the abandoned station. Patrick rose to his feet and pulled his NVGs down over his eyes once more before following after the immortal. He pushed his way to the front of the crowd, taking in the scene.

The vault door had been sliced through in segments, though the entire thing was still standing as Irena cut the last line to the final corner. The heat was intense from the thermal lance, and there was a good amount of space between her and everyone else. When she finished, she disassembled the thermal lance and put it back into storage.

Lucien approached the vault door and studied it for a few seconds before he pressed both hands against the segmented pieces and *pushed*. The sections that Irena had cut through toppled over with a crash that reverberated through the ground.

"They'll have heard that," Carmen said.

Lucien flashed her a smile that was all fangs from beneath his balaclava. "Good."

Patrick clicked the safety off his weapon and conjured up a mageglobe, letting his magic hover near his left shoulder. "Plan Let's Get Ready To Invade These Assholes is a go."

Lucien ducked through the hole, and the rest of them could only follow the master vampire into the unknown.

19

He ducked his head, shielding his face from pieces of the cement wall that bullets tore up across the way. The T-intersection of the corridor he and a handful of others were hunkered down in was looking more and more like a corner with no way out. Patrick ejected the empty magazine in his M4A1 carbine and slammed in a new one, feeling it lock into place.

"This was a shitty idea!" Patrick shouted.

Across the distance separating them, Lucien pulled the release on a flashbang grenade with his teeth and tossed it around the corner. "No one asked you."

Patrick squeezed his eyes shut, his NVGs shoved up onto his hard helmet since Tremaine hadn't yet cut the lights down where they were. The grenade blew—sound, light, and smoke exploding in the adjacent corridor. Patrick moved, using those few precious moments of distraction to shoot around the corner.

The recoil against his shoulder was easy to resist. Patrick went for maximum damage over clean shots, cutting through bodies before they could retaliate. His spelled bullets made a dent in the handful of vampires trying to hold them off, but the too-human members of the Omacatl Cartel suffered more.

Patrick didn't care.

He pulled back, finger lifting off the trigger, and Lucien blurred into the fray, leaving Sergio to guard his old spot. Patrick looked over his shoulder at where Wade crouched behind him, Sage's huge orange and black striped head hooked over the teen's shoulder in a protective manner. She'd changed forms the second they'd crossed the vault door and had stuck close to Wade.

"How are you holding up?" Patrick asked.

Wade blinked at him, slow and measured. Dried blood that wasn't his was spattered over one cheek, but he didn't seem to notice. "I can't believe you do this for a living."

"Technically, I don't do this anymore."

"What? Mass murder?"

A meaty smack drew Patrick's attention. He turned around, watching as a severed head bounced off the wall before rolling to a stop.

Patrick didn't know how to tell Wade that there were things he thought he'd never have to do. That there were lines he thought he'd never have to cross. Patrick used to believe that once, but he learned the hard way—a long, long time ago—that *never* was just another word for *until*.

"Off-the-record missions." Patrick chanced a look around the corner, saw that it was clear, and ducked into the corridor, weapon raised. "We're going to need some witnesses."

Lucien dropped the head he'd twisted clean off a body. It landed with a dull thump by his feet. "I have no use for the garbage that bows to Tremaine."

He licked blood off his fingers as the rest of the group moved into the narrow corridor. The tunnels that made up the Manhattan Night Court were more extensive than Patrick remembered. Wade knew the way and had been leading them to the underground stairwell Patrick knew would bring them directly to the club with unfailing accuracy.

Patrick looked over his shoulder at Wade. "How much farther?"

"Two more turns, then the main corridor," Wade replied, keeping his eyes averted from Lucien. "The other groups should reach it soon.

The tunnels, while tightly packed, were spread out beneath the city block. They went as deep as the subways, if not deeper in some areas they bypassed. They'd posted sentries at those intersections, one or two vampires or cartel members at each post to keep watch. The fringe of the veil was a strange place without protective wards, and they needed a rearguard to watch their six.

"They'll be waiting for us at the stairwell. It's a chokehold there," Carmen said.

Unlike Patrick, she wasn't wearing a helmet and her horns were on full display. Her dark red pupils seemed to burn in the bright halogen lights lining the ceiling as she strode through the mess Lucien had made.

Patrick flexed his fingers against the grip of his weapon. "I've got a spell or two that will clear them out."

They'd been at this for twenty minutes now, pushing forward into uncharted territory. Up until now, they'd gone for stealth over announcing their presence but it seemed Lucien was done with fucking around.

The smell of blood hung heavy and thick in the air as they advanced down the long corridor. Patrick's boots squelched through blood and bits he opted not to think about. He didn't have time to dwell on the dead or undead.

It was the living who mattered.

They made it to a cross-corridor intersection that branched off into four separate directions. Irena and Einar were already there, pinned down by suppressive fire that rang loudly in Patrick's ears.

He didn't know if Tremaine's people were getting desperate or finally figuring out they had a problem because their defense this time around was more like an offense.

Bullets bit off chunks of concrete at the corner, forcing them to remain farther back from the cross-section than they liked. Ricochets were a dangerous problem that Patrick dealt with by raising a shield between their position and the only way out.

"You need to stop teaching your children bad habits. They don't need to grow up to be like you," Patrick said to Lucien.

Lucien calmly reloaded his M4A1 carbine. "Get us a way through."

Patrick conjured up a mageglobe, the washed-out blue sphere spinning in the air at shoulder level. He filled it with raw magic, going with brutal force over a targeted attack. Military grade spells weren't supposed to be used in civilian areas, not to mention they had an entire building above them that Patrick didn't want toppling down. He had no desire to be buried alive. That meant tailoring the blast to something less powerful but which would give them room to maneuver.

Patrick sent the mageglobe spinning around the corner. He counted to three before igniting it. The resulting explosion ripped through the air, followed by screams that rang in Patrick's ears. Across the way, Irena and Einar blurred into the fight, followed by other vampires and cartel members. The screams ahead were loud, but it was the faint cry that came from the rear that had Wade grabbing onto Patrick's arm with too-strong fingers.

"They keep the fighters on this level," Wade said.

Carmen tilted her head to the side. "They're getting rid of the evidence."

Before Patrick could open his mouth and respond, Wade took off on fast feet. Sage twisted around to follow him. Patrick dropped his shield and scrambled after them. "Wait!"

Too late—Wade and Sage both disappeared around the far

corner. Patrick swore and double-timed it down the corridor and past the sentries they'd posted. He veered right, seeing a flash of orange and black turn left at the next cross-section up ahead.

Patrick followed because he refused to lose track of either of them. Seconds later Sage's snarl reached Patrick's ears, the rage in it impossible to ignore.

Evidence, Patrick thought bleakly as he followed them to a room whose door had been shattered upon impact.

Inside was a gruesome scene, one which Patrick wouldn't be able to scrub out of his mind anytime soon. His combat boots, even with their gripping tread, slipped on a floor coated in blood. He got his balance back in time to put two spelled bullets in the chest of the vampire that came at him. When that didn't stop the creature, Patrick yanked his dagger free of its sheath and stabbed it into the vampire's skull.

The vampire shuddered, going limp and hanging off his dagger for half a second before sliding free of the blade. Patrick stepped over the body, swallowing reflexively against the churning in his stomach.

His mind didn't want to process what had happened in that room. Not right away.

Where Tremaine and Tezcatlipoca had sacrificed people to Santa Muerte on that altar through rape and exsanguination, the fights to the death had been the money draw. Now, they seemed to be cutting their losses by killing the werecreatures they had trafficked to entertain the rich.

Eight people were chained to the walls of the room by way of silver manacles. All but two were dead. One body's head had been torn off completely, the skull crushed like a melon before getting tossed aside. Every corpse was naked and missing limbs, the amputated appendages sewn closed with barbed wire. Silver collars encircled their necks, ensuring they couldn't change form. Their bodies were covered in bite wounds, chunks ripped out from a feeding frenzy that could have happened today or yesterday or a week ago.

The two who were still alive had a look in their eyes Patrick had seen in Kennedy's—little sanity, and only enough awareness left to understand that dying would be better than living like this.

Patrick readjusted his grip on the dagger right as a vampire slammed him to the ground, its teeth biting down on his neck. Only his personal shields saved him from getting his throat torn out. Patrick grunted, sliding in the tacky blood on the floor, and drove his dagger into the vampire's back.

The vampire screamed around his throat, the sound ear-piercing. Patrick winced as he shoved the twitching body off of him. Unlike conventional blades, his dagger provided a true death vampires couldn't come back from. Tearing out their hearts and cutting off their heads weren't required.

Patrick got to his feet in time to see Sage eviscerate a pair of vampires she'd backed into a corner. They would be hard-pressed to heal from those wounds before dawn, so Patrick put them out of their misery by cutting off their heads. The double-edged blade was sharp enough to saw through bone with little effort. The gods-forged weapon came in handy for situations like this.

Patrick wiped the blade clean on his pants, then shoved it back into its sheath. He approached where Wade had his arms wrapped around one of the survivors. The teenager was snarling in a way that made the hair on the back of Patrick's neck stand on end. Small patches of iridescent red scales had broken out along his hairline and neck. Wade's aura burned like a halo around his body, so bright Patrick had to cover his eyes.

"Pull yourself together, Wade. You can't shift down here. You'll bring everything down around us," Patrick said.

Patrick peered through his fingers as he knelt between the two survivors. Wade seemed to get control over himself, the brightness of his aura fading, but not completely. The scales on his face and neck mostly faded, but Patrick could see the shadow of them. He didn't have time to think about Wade's tenuous control. They needed to get out of that hellhole and back to the main group.

Patrick used his dagger to cut through the collars that kept the werecreatures connected to the walls. The silver-coated collars, etched with a binding ward, broke apart beneath Patrick's dagger. Beneath the metal were open wounds and burns on their necks. Suddenly being free didn't snap the pair back to reality. Both victims remained where they were.

"Sage, get over here. You'll have to carry them topside," Patrick said.

There was no way either survivor could walk, even with the binding ward broken and their ability to change forms returned to them. The woman was missing a leg up to the knee, and both of the man's feet had been chewed to ragged bits up to the ankles. The barbed wire dipped in aconite embedded in their skin to close up the wounds would need to be removed by a medical professional. Patrick hoped they survived long enough to reach a hospital.

They were werecreatures, capable of regenerating missing limbs and flesh, but he knew what gangrene looked and smelled like. Patrick wasn't sure if either of them would ever fully recover from this torture.

Sage crouched beside him, nose twitching from her heightened sense of smell. Patrick and Wade carefully deposited the two survivors onto her back. Patrick cast a binding ward around them, ropes of magic securing the pair to Sage's body.

"Let's get the fuck out of here," Patrick said, taking point and heading for the door. Sighting down his rifle, half a dozen tiny mageglobes floating near his shoulders, Patrick eased into the corridor. "Clear."

Sage carefully maneuvered through the door, with Wade following after her. They hadn't gone more than a handful of steps when an animalistic roar echoed in the air. Patrick didn't freeze—he started running.

"Sounds like Tezcatlipoca hit the field," Patrick tossed over his shoulder. "*Move*."

They moved, as quickly as they could, which wasn't as fast as Patrick would've liked. Sage and Wade were both trying to make sure their charges weren't hurt in the process but when they were all trying to outrun a pissed-off god, pain was unavoidable.

Patrick retraced their steps back to the main corridor. Lucien's sentries were still alive, but most of the group had gone up the circular stairs that led aboveground. Einar stood by the entrance, weapon in hand and impatiently waiting for them.

"Áłtsé Hashké cleared a path after you ran from your duty," Einar said.

Patrick flipped him off. "Oh, fuck you. I wasn't leaving anyone behind."

"The police will have evidence whether it is alive or dead. The animals aren't worth the trouble."

"Get the fuck out of my way before I stab you and tell Lucien my hand slipped."

Einar was unimpressed with Patrick's attitude, but whatever he wanted to say was drowned out by the thrumming of a dozen heavy feet against the flooring. Screams—distant and garbled—echoed underneath the noise. Shadows blurred at the peripheral of Patrick's vision as the vampires Lucien had stationed in the corridors behind them rallied to the only way out.

"Jaguars," a vampire got out as he stumbled into view, hanging off the shoulders of his dark-haired partner while trying to keep his intestines inside his body. "They came from behind."

Einar ducked through the doorway. "Get topside."

The vampires moved quick, blurring out of Patrick's sight. He swore, gesturing for Sage and Wade to go first. "I'll cover your six."

They went first, disappearing into the stairwell. Patrick had one foot on the stairs when the pack of jaguars raced around the corner. He sent three mageglobes filled with explosive raw magic at the extension of Tezcatlipoca's power and set them off. Patrick kept his footing as the mageglobes exploded, shaking the walls around them.

From above, Wade shouted, "I thought you said don't bring down the building? Is this some do as I say, not as I do bullshit?"

"Shut up and run!" Patrick yelled.

Fucking *teenagers.*

Patrick dropped mageglobes on every landing, timed to explode every five seconds. His ears were ringing from the noise by the time he reached the last step, pitching himself into the room he remembered that used to house a vault.

The vault was gone now, pieces of it embedded in the walls, ceiling, and floor all around them. Sage had leaped over the shrapnel and through the doorway, the heavy steel door having already been torn off. Wade had run after her, his footsteps having melted the metal beneath them. That little detail was slightly more worrisome than the jaguars hunting them—but only slightly.

"Sage, I'm gonna need you in this fight," Patrick yelled at her as he followed in Wade's exact footsteps. "Put those two in a storage room, and I'll ward the doors."

Sage darted toward the broken open employees-only door at the end of the hallway that led into the club proper. Standing in human form between them and the fighting happening in the Crimson Diamond was Áłtsé Hashké.

"I will safeguard them," the god said. "Go."

The binding ward that had kept the two werecreatures secured to Sage on their mad dash out of the tunnels broke by way of a single touch from the god. Pain spiked through Patrick's head as his magic disintegrated. He'd be angry about the god's lack of care, but the furious snarls coming from behind him overrode his thoughts.

One quick glance over his shoulder proved the jaguars had made it topside.

"Run!" Patrick yelled, racing for the club.

Áłtsé Hashké pulled the werecreatures off Sage and carried

them into the storage room. The door slammed shut and sealed with a burning light that made Patrick's eyes water. Patrick, Sage, and Wade ran out of the back room and into the screaming mess of a fight between two Night Courts and the gods that oversaw it all.

20

PATRICK TOOK IN THE FIGHT WITH A SWEEPING GAZE. DESPITE THE screaming guests huddled behind what cover they could find, and the bullets flying through the air from both sides, what caught and held his attention was Jono.

Relief washed through Patrick like a head rush. *Oh, good. He's not dead.*

The cage made out of magic on the dance floor was still intact. Inside, Tremaine and Jono were squaring off, and it looked like Tremaine was on the losing side of the fight. The master vampire's clothes were torn in multiple areas, his pale skin peeled open from slashes given by Jono's claws. Tremaine wasn't close to true death, but not for Jono's lack of trying.

Werecreatures, when they shifted into their animal form, never resembled the animals from nature. Bigger, more monstrous, no one would confuse a werecreature with their mundane counterpart. That went double for Jono, whose wolf form was significantly larger than other werecreatures, wolf-bright blue eyes of his god pack heritage prominent in his huge head.

Patrick grabbed Wade by the arm and hauled the teenager with him across the dance floor. He laid down a wide spray of suppressive fire at a pair of Omacatl Cartel members to keep them at bay. Sage threw herself into the fight with a roar, and Patrick didn't try to stop her. Skidding to a stop by the cage, he yanked out his dagger and slammed it into the magic.

Tremaine's eyes barely flickered Patrick's way, too intent on the threat right in front of him. The master vampire's face was twisted into something monstrous, fangs bared and slick with Jono's blood.

"Hey, asshole," Patrick said as the magic started to disintegrate, heavenly white fire burning around the dagger's matte-black blade. "Lucien wants a word with you."

Wade pressed himself against Patrick's back, fingers shaking when he grabbed at Patrick's arm. "I don't feel good."

Tremaine lunged toward them, a blur Patrick couldn't track. Before the master vampire even reached them, Jono was there, knocking the fucker out of midair with a headbutt that sounded like it hurt. Tremaine went flying, no longer trapped by a god's magic, and landed in the scrum happening around them.

Patrick looked over his shoulder at Wade, his aura blinding. It felt as if Patrick had taken another hit of shine. Squinting, he watched as iridescent red scales flowed over Wade's face in waves, leaving behind scaly patches. Bits of gold seeped into his brown eyes, pupils more oval than round now.

"*Don't* shift," Patrick said.

A panicked look crossed Wade's face. "I'm not!"

The scales pushing through his skin proved otherwise.

Patrick wrenched his personal shields out of his bones and pushed his defense outward, far enough to encase Wade as well. Patrick let go of his rifle, the weight hanging heavily from the strap connecting it to his tactical vest. He averted his face as he reached behind to grab Wade by the arm with one hand and flipped his dagger around for a better grip in the other.

"You're *shifting*, Wade. You need to stop."

"I don't know what's happening!"

He sounded frantic, one heartbeat away from panicking and losing all control—which would be an absolute *disaster* in an enclosed space. Patrick tightened his grip on the teenager and dragged him forward. "I'm getting you out of here."

Wade whimpered, but he didn't dig in his heels. "My body doesn't feel right."

Patrick looked straight ahead at Jono, meeting the bright blue eyes staring back at him. "Make a hole to the exit."

Jono growled an affirmative, then leaped forward, straight into the fray. A cartel member wielding an AK-47 screamed when Jono's jaws clamped around his waist, and he was tossed into the air with a fierce shake of Jono's head.

Patrick stayed on Jono's six, pouring his magic out of his corrupted soul and into the shields wrapped around himself and Wade. The shields were invisible to the naked eye until spelled bullets impacted them, causing ripples of light to flash through the air. Patrick grunted, feeling the hits in his soul, but he kept moving.

They got past two tables and three clusters of vampires tearing the shit out of each other when two jaguars cleared downed bodies in a huge leap to land between Patrick and Jono. He skidded to a halt, never letting go of Wade. Raising the dagger, Patrick pointed it at the jaguars. Heavenly fire erupted from the double-edged blade in a warning.

Jono paused, half turning, but Patrick violently shook his head. "Keep going."

Jono stayed put. Patrick could've throttled him.

Wade huddled behind Patrick, shivering in his grip. "Tloque Nahuaque is gonna kill me."

"He's gonna have to go through me first," Patrick promised.

"That should be easy," Tezcatlipoca said from behind them.

Patrick moved, wrenching Wade around and hopefully out of

reach, but he wasn't quick enough. Tezcatlipoca slammed through Patrick's shields, breaking through the layers without care. Patrick grunted in pain as his soul took a hit he couldn't afford right now. The immortal grabbed Wade's other arm, his touch drawing a scream from Wade that shouldn't have come from human-sized lungs. Patrick's ears rang with it, throbbing with the need to block out the sound. Behind him, Jono howled, adding to the cacophony.

Tezcatlipoca was dressed as a warrior-god of old instead of a modern man. Gone was the linen suit, and in its place was a loincloth and obsidian studded armbands decorated with feathers. The burnished gold chest plate seemed larger, matching the grandeur of the heron-feather headdress he wore. The god's long black hair fell loose to his waist, while black and yellow paint bisected his face over his cheeks and nose.

On his left foot was a leather sandal, the ties twisted around his ankle. His right foot remained the polished obsidian Patrick remembered, the glass shiny as a mirror, stretching halfway up his leg before melding with flesh.

"*This*," Tezcatlipoca said, giving Wade a hard shake, "belongs to me."

"Over my dead fucking body," Patrick bit out right before he twisted around Wade and tried to stab Tezcatlipoca in the ribs.

It didn't work.

Patrick was blown backward by a magical hit that was like taking a sledgehammer to the chest. He lost his grip on Wade, fingers closing on nothing. Patrick flew through the air and landed on a broken chair, a piece of the wooden leg cracking beneath him, or maybe it was a rib. Patrick couldn't tell with the way all the air had been driven out of his lungs. His shields were like so much shattered glass around him.

He fucking *hated* gods.

A jaguar lunged at him, and Patrick couldn't make his limbs work fast enough to get the fuck away. Then Jono was there, standing over Patrick in a protective manner that blocked out everything happening in the club. Patrick rolled to his side, sucking in a painful gasp of air as his lungs finally unlocked.

Jono's hind paws dug into the floor, claws tearing up the carpet. Patrick froze as Jono lunged forward to get his jaws around the jaguar's throat. With a wrench of his head, Jono sent the beast flying before retreating back to Patrick's side. Patrick shoved himself to a sitting position, ignoring the ache in his chest beneath the tactical vest he wore.

"Wade!" Patrick coughed out.

Tezcatlipoca had one hand tangled in Wade's hair, the other around his throat, but his eyes were focused somewhere else. "Let me gift you a life you have yet to experience, my love."

Patrick dug his free hand into Jono's fur and hauled himself to his feet. He followed Tezcatlipoca's gaze across the club to a skeletal woman dressed all in black with her face painted like a Mexican sugar skull and wearing marigolds in her hair.

The smell of those flowers blossomed on Patrick's tongue, sudden and floral, making him gag with the memories it brought. He froze, and he'd hate himself later for that, but Áłtsé Hashké didn't hesitate.

"You have done enough harm to the children, cousin. I will not let you have this one," Áłtsé Hashké said.

Patrick watched as the god reached around Tezcatlipoca and pried his hands off Wade with a strength none of them had. Jono lunged forward to grab Wade by his tactical vest and haul him out of reach. That left them both open to an attack by the jaguar on their left. Patrick put himself between them and the extension of Tezcatlipoca's power, dagger at the ready. Bright heavenly fire reflected in the jaguar's eyes.

"You have chosen the losing side, cousin," Tezcatlipoca said, sounding furiously betrayed.

Tezcatlipoca wrenched free of Áłtsé Hashké's grip, eyes

glowing from an inner light. He twisted around to face off with the trickster god, only Áłtsé Hashké was no longer there. Tezcatlipoca let out a war cry that shook the building until Patrick realized the source of that reverberation came from the front of the club, not the rear.

"DEA!" someone shouted from behind a row of riot shields etched with protective wards as their backup swarmed the building. "Lower your weapons!"

Quetzalcoatl's raid had begun.

As Patrick faced off with the jaguar, trapped between two gods allied with the hells, he made the decision to run because surviving was all that mattered.

Patrick grabbed Wade by the arm and held on tight. "Let's go."

It was like working with his old team again, the way he didn't have to explain himself. Jono knew what he wanted, and maybe that was because of the soulbond tying them together, but Patrick didn't care. Jono put himself between them and the threat with a growl that was only cut off when he got his jaws around the jaguar's throat.

Wade was too warm in Patrick's grip, even through gloves. The teen's eyes were solidly gold now, the black pupils reptilian slits. Iridescent red scales covered his face and neck, his hair disappearing in patches. Patrick's M4A1 carbine banged heavily against his hip as he dragged Wade forward, struggling to piece together his patchwork shields. The anchor points in his bones weren't damaged, but that hit from Tezcatlipoca had siphoned off more of his magic than he liked to think about.

He needed to get Wade out of the Crimson Diamond.

Tremaine, like with Tezcatlipoca, didn't want to let Wade go.

The master vampire slammed into them from the side, his sharp nails scraping over Patrick's weakened shields. Patrick grunted as he twisted in between Wade and Tremaine, expanding his shields. Standing between the two brought the remembered smell of marigolds to his nose. Patrick swallowed against that unwanted memory and brought up his dagger, hoping for room to strike.

"Get the fuck out of my way," Patrick said.

The cold itch at the edges of his mind was all Tremaine. This time, Patrick wasn't half out of his mind while high on shine. He blocked Tremaine out of his thoughts by altering his shields, the pressure easing.

"*That* is not yours," Tremaine said.

Patrick took a step to the side, bringing Wade with him. "He has a fucking name."

Sage barreled her way through a pair of vampires on his left, aiming for Tremaine. The master vampire leaped out of her way—straight into Carmen's painful right hook.

"Oh, child," Carmen purred, the venom in her voice as she shot Tremaine in the back while he was on his knees impossible to miss. "Your daddy wants a word."

Tremaine wasn't crippled by the bullet. Patrick could see a bulletproof vest beneath his torn dress shirt as the vampire looked over his shoulder.

"I owe him nothing," Tremaine snarled.

"Of all the things to get with the times on, you had to go for body armor."

Tremaine moved out of the way of Carmen's next bullet, a shadowy blur who would rather run than face what passed as his family.

"You're a fucking coward, Tremaine," Patrick yelled.

The fact that he was running headfirst toward Quetzalcoatl and a defensive line of federal agents and NYPD officers just made Patrick's day worse. He needed Tremaine *out* of police custody in order to keep his promise to Lucien.

A shudder ran through Wade's entire body, muscles fighting against Patrick's grip. He looked at the teen in his custody and made a choice he knew he wouldn't regret. Making sure Lucien got Tremaine's head on a proverbial platter was relegated to second place. Wade came first.

"Sage!" Patrick shouted, gaining her attention.

That large, monstrous head whipped around, the curved fangs in her mouth glistening with blood. Her teeth resembled a saber-tooth tiger's rather than a modern one, and Patrick was thankful she was on their side as Sage quickly closed the distance between them.

Wade felt heavier in his hands than a teenager had any right to be. All the hair was gone from his head now, and the fingernails on each hand had turned black. The frightened expression on his scaly face made Patrick wish he could give the kid a normal life.

"You know what? Don't fight it," Patrick said as he helped Wade onto Sage's back. "Sage, you stay with him for as long as possible."

Wade wrapped his arms around Sage's neck, her fur too short for him to hang on to. Wade opened his mouth to talk, but whatever he was going to say was drowned out by the collective roar of jaguars from behind them. Sage didn't wait for Patrick's order, she just ran.

"Delgado, clear the exit!" Patrick yelled, pitching his voice loud enough to be heard over the fighting and gunshots. This was just another battlefield they all had to survive, and the only way they'd live was if the building didn't come down on top of them.

That meant getting Wade to the street.

Which would have been so much easier if they didn't have gods in the mix.

Jono landed next to him and crouched low on his front paws. Patrick took the hint and scrambled on top of Jono's back after sheathing his dagger. Patrick barely got a good grip on Jono's shaggy fur before Jono leaped forward, intent on chasing after Sage.

Patrick looked over his shoulder only once, seeing Tezcatlipoca's jaguars coming straight for them. Refocusing ahead, Patrick wrapped his shields around the both of them. He thought maybe they'd actually make it, but Patrick was never that lucky.

Up ahead, Sage went down, and Wade went with her. Patrick's heart crawled into his throat, thinking they were dead, when a long reptilian tail cut through the air before slamming into the floor. Broken pieces of tables and chairs went flying as a large, leathery wing unfolded into the air, the leading edge dragging over the floor.

Patrick threw himself off Jono, crashing to his knees. He conjured up a mageglobe and tossed it to Sage and Wade's position, creating a wide shield around them to keep the bullets at bay. He couldn't do anything about the jaguars on their six.

Quetzalcoatl was a different story altogether. The immortal barreled his way forward from the left, a bullet-proof vest beneath his DEA windbreaker and not caring about cover at all. If he was human, Patrick would've been furious, but gods could survive anything save their last follower dying and taking their name with them.

Brown eyes glowed in his face as Quetzalcoatl ignored his gun and instead tackled the leading jaguar, punching clean through the creature's ribcage. Blood exploded out of the jaguar's mouth, nose, and eyes as it shuddered and died, its life fading and returning to Tezcatlipoca. The rest of the jaguars howled a challenge but didn't stop, intent on escaping in the same direction Tremaine had gone.

Patrick could only hope they'd eat the fucker.

Quetzalcoatl stood, pulling his arm free of the jaguar's body. Blood coated his hand and forearm, fingers clenched around a still-beating heart that dripped blood. Fire flickered at Quetzalcoatl's fingertips, engulfing the muscle and burning it to ash in seconds.

"The fledgling needs to spread his wings," Quetzalcoatl said.

"He's never shifted mass before, much less flown," Patrick replied.

"You can't keep him from his heritage. This is instinct."

"I'm not the one who kept him for cage fights."

"I am aware of that. Drop your shields."

Patrick didn't want to, but he knew if he didn't, the god would rip them down himself. He drew down his magic, wincing at the rawness in his soul as he did so. Jono growled but Patrick refused to look at him, to use him, ignoring the way the soulbond tightened in his soul.

Quetzalcoatl threw back his head and let out a roar that sounded like nothing else on earth. It made every hair on Patrick's head stand on end, caused the nerves in his teeth to tingle. Jono echoed the roar with a howl that Sage answered. Patrick was relieved to discover she wasn't dead.

His relief was short-lived as Wade reacted to Quetzalcoatl's call by shifting mass completely in a way the building couldn't handle.

"Get to the street!" Patrick yelled as Wade's back arched, body growing, his wings flopping with every thrashing step he took.

A blur of orange and black darted out from beneath Wade's clawed feet, dodging the long tail that smacked against the floor. People screamed, almost everyone's attention on the dragon shifting in their midst. Shots rang out as pistols and rifles alike were trained on Wade, but not even spelled bullets could pierce a dragon's scaled hide. All the bullets served was to irritate Wade, and in his panic, the teenager in a fledgling dragon's body hurtled himself toward the front of the club.

The door definitely wasn't big enough for him now.

Jono shoved at Patrick with his head and they started running, with Sage right beside them now. He kept his shields up as Wade ran straight through the front wall of the building, creating a hole that took out a good chunk of the first- and second-floor wall in that area, along with the wards. The entire building shook, plaster falling down around them from the ceiling high above.

Quetzalcoatl's voice drifted out from the depths of the club behind them, sounding like the roar of a tornado. *Brother, I have missed you.*

They raced out of the building through the hole Wade had made. The flashing lights from police cars at either end of the block and in the street flickered in Patrick's eyes. His group wasn't the only one racing to escape the hellhole the Crimson Diamond had become. Cartel members, vampires, and traumatized guests were right behind them. Every cop, DEA, and SOA agent around them didn't know where to fucking shoot first—but when in doubt, go for the biggest target.

Wade's center mass was the size of a bus, the long type with six wheels and a center accordion-style connection. Add in his tail, which was just as long but tapered to a pitchfork point, and Wade was *big*. His wings stretched out and away from his body, the leading edges banging against the buildings on either side of the street as he turned, gouging through the structures. Debris fell to the street, causing officers to scramble to safety.

His wedge-shaped head at the end of a long neck ducked down, one big golden eye with its reptilian pupil staring right at them. Wade opened his mouth, but instead of words coming out, a ball of fire erupted from between his sharp teeth to explode on the street between where they stood and the first responders who were looking like prey to the jaguars.

Wade, for all that he was a fledging dragon impervious to bullets, was still a scared teenager who didn't deserve to be tormented like this.

"Fly!" Patrick yelled over the burst of gunfire that ricocheted off Wade's scaly body.

Wade twisted his body, tail slamming against the opposite building and sending chunks of the façade and glass raining down on the sidewalk. He folded his wings in tight before snapping them out again, eyes locked on Patrick as smoke drifted out of his nostrils.

Like Quetzalcoatl had said, it was all instinct, and the body knew what to do even if the mind didn't. Wade launched himself into the air with furious flaps of his large wings, escaping gravity despite his size. The police and federal agents seemed to think twice about firing into the air after him. Patrick could only hope no one would corner the kid before he could—somehow—find Wade again.

Someone landed in front of Patrick, startling him badly. Jono jerked his head around to bite them, but his teeth never made contact. Lucien slammed the butt of his rifle against Jono's nose, causing the werewolf to jerk his head aside, blood pouring from his nostrils from the unexpected hit. Lucien was covered in blood, his mouth smeared with it in the balaclava's opening, testimony to however many throats he'd torn out in the club and below.

"Back the fuck off," Lucien snapped.

"*You* fuck off," Patrick shot back, resting his hand on the top of Jono's huge head in a comforting manner.

Lucien's attention wasn't on them but the master vampire standing across the street. Wade had hidden Tremaine from sight, but there was nothing separating them now. The master vampire stood beside Santa Muerte, a worshipper given the blessing of death herself and all the favor that entailed.

"Is this how you turn your back on your mother, Tremaine?" Lucien said, voice carrying over the noise of the crowd. "Offer yourself to the first god who would accept your lies?"

"Ashanti hasn't spoken to me in decades. What use is a mother who disappears when death herself favors me?" Tremaine spat back.

The wind picked up, the heavy heat in the air disappearing in the face of a chilly breeze that got stronger. It reminded Patrick of the drive-by shooting and the gale force winds that had blown over him. Santa Muerte's dress rippled in the wind, stretching into shadows that turned into a shroud. It wrapped itself around Tremaine's body, hiding him from view and the bullets Lucien shot in their direction.

The jaguars at the perimeter roared in tandem, but they

couldn't drown out the sound of the wind building all around them.

Coming from behind them.

Patrick's eyes widened as the wind picked up, screaming in his ears. He threw himself at Jono, getting a tight grip on the scruff of Jono's neck. *"Get clear!"*

Jono leaped forward, Sage right by their side, putting much-needed distance between them and the Crimson Diamond. Patrick held on for all he was worth as the crowd panicked even more.

Lucien ran, a shadowy blur that beat them to the outskirts of the police line. Jono's paws crunched a few squad car hoods and trunks as he got them out of the danger zone. Other members of Lucien's Night Court appeared on the street around them, their arrival drawing attention from the police, but not for long.

Wind exploded over the street as if a tornado touched down, the force of it driving everyone to their knees or bowling them over completely. It was powerful enough to move vehicles, sending more than one squad car screeching over the asphalt. Jono and Sage leaned in close to protect Patrick from the supernatural strength of it, their claws biting into asphalt. Even Patrick's shields couldn't keep it out because it was no ordinary wind.

The roaring sound got louder, hitting a decibel that threatened to rupture eardrums. Then the roof of the Crimson Diamond exploded outward, a golden light as bright as the sun shining through the opening. Debris rained down on the street as people struggled to find cover, and Patrick wasn't the only magic user who cast shields over those who couldn't.

Rising out of the damaged building in a vortex of air came a shining, writhing feathered serpent wrapped tight around a huge jaguar clawing at its body. Both were twice the size of Wade's dragon form, the auras of gods pouring out of their bodies.

Quetzalcoatl and Tezcatlipoca, locked in combat, rose into the sky above Manhattan. Patrick couldn't be sure if the sound in his ears was the wind or their screams. He shielded his eyes from the sight, the primordial power pouring out of the pair painfully bright against the night sky.

Then the two gods exploded with a sonic boom heard in all five boroughs, rings of magic rippling like a shock wave through the air high above New York City.

21

THE FURIOUS ROAR OF THE WIND ABRUPTLY STOPPED, DRIFTING INTO a breeze that barely ruffled his clothes. Patrick let go of Jono and got to his feet, holding his rifle close.

"Did all your people get clear?" Patrick asked Lucien.

The master vampire ejected the magazine in his M4A1 carbine and reloaded, ignoring the question. "This isn't over. Your promise to me hasn't been kept."

Tremaine was still out there. Standing with Santa Muerte, he'd chosen his side despite being Lucien's once and—

Patrick's thoughts came to a screeching, brain-rattling halt.

"Tremaine is yours."

Lucien gave him a scornful look. "Yes."

Tremaine was Lucien's, whether on the run or not. They'd cornered him, and Patrick knew from painful personal experience just how much Lucien hated to be cornered.

"What happened in Stănileşti?" Patrick demanded, taking a step forward.

Lucien's black eyes narrowed to slits. "We burned the buildings to the ground with all the soldiers in them, but they had mage priests we could not fight against and win."

Tremaine didn't have any manpower left for him to wreak havoc like that, but he had a god. One god, one powerful god who personified death, along with his own sadistic upbringing. Tremaine's words and his raw pride flashed through Patrick's mind.

He could barely get his numb lips to shape the syllables. "He learned that lesson well."

"And what lesson is that? I taught him many."

Raze and ruin and Stănileşti.

Lucien was known in history for his salted-earth policy. For leaving nothing behind that his enemies could possibly use while he moved on—exactly what Tremaine was doing now. Only tonight it wasn't about a town where two armies went to war against a Night Court but a huge metropolitan city held up by tunnels that could bring it tumbling down around the lives of millions of people.

The body count this time would be one for the history books.

"He's still in the fucking subway tunnels. The barrier ward won't be enough as a patch if they break the anchors," Patrick said, mouth gone bone-dry.

He fumbled out his phone from his pocket, dialing Casale's personal line. It picked up almost immediately.

"What the fuck was that light show just now?" Casale demanded. "And was that a *dragon* that just flew overhead?"

"Evacuate the subways and Grand Central. Don't let anyone inside. I'm coming to you," Patrick said.

"Collins—"

"Santa Muerte is still *here*, Casale. She's still looking for sacrifices, and they're going to blow the fucking protective wards in the subway to sacrifice everyone in it to power their prayers to her. I need to know where the central anchor point for the protective wards is located."

"It's in the M42 sub-basement here in Grand Central. I'll send—"

"You'll send no one. I just said keep everyone the fuck out of there. I'll deal with Tremaine and Santa Muerte." Patrick ended the call. "Rats and their fucking tunnels."

"We need transport to Grand Central," Lucien said.

Carmen slipped past Einar, nodding at the squad cars closest to them. "Keys are still in the ignition."

Looked like they were stealing a couple of cop cars.

They'd be noticed instantly, and Patrick didn't have time to talk about why he and a bunch of vampires needed the vehicles. Áłtsé Hashké made sure he didn't have to.

"They will not see you leave," the god said.

The world slowed around them, as if time was standing still when Patrick knew that was impossible. Áłtsé Hashké stood on the outskirts of the crowd of frozen police officers and federal agents. The trickster god watched them with unblinking yellow eyes, mouth quirked at the corners, as if he knew a secret none of them were privy to.

"That building is about to come down. The werecreatures we saved don't deserve to die in it," Patrick said.

"The children will be kept safe."

Patrick knew better than to ask for a promise from a god, so he kept his mouth shut. He looked at Jono and Sage, realizing their bulk wouldn't fit in the back seat of any car.

"Can you keep up?" Patrick asked.

Both of them nodded their large heads, and Patrick took their silent confirmation at face value. He climbed into the driver's seat of the nearest cop car, unsurprised when Lucien joined him. Lucien didn't bother with a seat belt, too interested in the computer setup hooked to the dash.

Patrick put the car in reverse, slammed his foot on the gas pedal, and hit the sirens. The world snapped back to normal once he hit the cross-street with Jono and Sage pacing the vehicle.

The drive uptown to Grand Central was chaotic, but they got there. Jono and Sage easily kept up. The three cop cars and two werecreatures made a strange sight on the street, but the white vehicles with blue-striped NYPD detailing were enough to keep everyone out of their way.

Manhattan was a grid laid out in one-way streets. They took Sixth Avenue all the way up to East Forty-Second Street. The closer they got, the more crowded it got. A sea of people was moving away from the transit hub on order of the police. Some of them started panicking once they caught sight of Jono and Sage, and that was a stampede Patrick didn't need to deal with.

Patrick parked and left the keys in the ignition. Jono and Sage moved up to stand beside him as Einar, Carmen, and half a dozen other vampires who'd ridden in the other two cars joined them.

"You're gonna get shot with that balaclava on your face," Patrick said as he started forward.

"Then you better make sure we don't," Lucien replied.

Patrick conjured up a mageglobe, filling it with a look-away ward. He pushed his magic out of his soul, the familiar twisting sparks of the spell drifting all around them. It wouldn't make them invisible, but it would hopefully keep anyone from thinking Lucien and his vampires were the enemy and shooting them on sight.

Patrick kept himself, Jono, and Sage, outside the spell, needing to be seen. Jono lengthened his stride to take point, his massive bulk clearing them a way through the crowd faster than Patrick could have on his own.

Up ahead, the windows lining the walls of Grand Central were completely dark, as if all the light inside had gone out. The pitch-blackness pressing against the glass didn't look right. Patrick held his M4A1 carbine close against his body as he ran, yanking his SOA badge out from beneath the tactical vest he wore as he did so.

As they got closer, the crowd of commuters thinned out into lines of police. He raked his gaze over the officers working crowd control, trying to find Casale. Over the noise of people yelling, distant sirens and honking horns, the sharp *caw* of a raven sent a chill down his spine.

Patrick's gaze snapped up, locking on the pair of ravens perched on top of the statue of Mercury above the Tiffany clock on the building's façade. Larger than normal ravens, with wings half-spread, they looked right at him, right *through* him. Unlike with Tremaine, Patrick couldn't keep Huginn and Muninn out of his mind.

They desire what only war should carry, the ravens said, their voices cracking open a headache in his brain. *The dead will not rest.*

"Collins!"

Casale's shout had Patrick shaking his head hard to clear it. When he looked back at the statue, the ravens were gone. As warnings went, those two were damn unhelpful.

"Casale," Patrick yelled back, flashing his badge at a couple of cops standing at the perimeter on the intersection to get by. "Is Grand Central evacuated?"

Casale stood at the southwest entrance into the terminal, a statue of an eagle with its wings spread situated above the doors. The shadows that Patrick could see through the doors pressed right up against the threshold, so black he couldn't make out anything inside.

"We don't know how many civilians are left inside," Casale said in a tight voice, one hand gripping a radio. "Everything just went dark about five minutes ago. Anyone who goes in doesn't come out, and radios go to static. MTA officials are still in the master control room, but we can't reach them."

"Trains are still running?"

Casale gave a grim nod. "Still running to offload their passengers into the nearest stations if possible."

Patrick tightened his grip on his rifle before unclipping the strap from his tactical vest. "Take this. It's only going to get in my way."

He needed his hands free for what he was going to find inside Grand Central Terminal. After all, bullets wouldn't kill a god.

Casale took the rifle with a dubious expression on his face. "What are you doing?"

"My job."

"You aren't going in there without backup."

Patrick let his look-away ward drop as he unsheathed his dagger. Casale did a double take at Lucien and the others' seemingly sudden appearance.

"I have my backup. I just need to know where the entrance to the M42 sub-basement is."

Casale looked like he wanted to argue when Hermes slipped between two police officers and jogged over. He wore the same DEA uniform as before, and the smirk he directed at Casale made the PCB chief scowl at him.

"I'll take them," Hermes said, grabbing Patrick by the arm and hauling him down the sidewalk to the main entrance on East 42nd Street.

"You just don't want your statue to get blown up," Patrick said under his breath.

Hermes shrugged, though he didn't let Patrick go, eliciting a warning growl from Jono. "They got my name wrong when they built it. Here. You'll need this."

Hermes took Patrick's free hand and pressed a single Greek obal against his palm. Patrick curled his fingers around the gold coin, heart beating fast in his chest. "This feels all kinds of familiar."

"The coin was taken from the seer's home. It is the only one I am giving you."

Patrick looked down at the coin and the massive amount of magic it carried in its tiny form—enough to power a barrier ward.

"Why?"

Hermes smiled grimly as he hauled open a door, the shadowy

blackness behind it reaching for them. "Because Persephone isn't pleased with Santa Muerte trying to take your soul."

"Yeah, whatever. She owns it. Everyone else can get in line, is that it?"

"Exactly."

Steeling himself, Patrick walked into the darkness, the blade of his dagger lighting the way. He blinked, able to make out the foyer, though everything was shadowy and dim save for the millions of marigold petals that covered the floor.

"Okay. This looks bad," Patrick said as everyone else joined him in the foyer.

Lucien yanked the balaclava off his head and tossed it aside. "Try to have some fun."

"Dying isn't fun, asshole."

They walked through a second set of doors, entering the Vanderbilt Hall. Everything was shaded-out gray and wrapped in shadows. Even the grand chandeliers up above didn't let out any light. Straight ahead was an arched opening that led to the Main Concourse. Patrick could see the golden glow of the clock straight ahead against the darkness, shrouded in magic that seeped up from far below.

Marigold petals puffed up with every step they took, the smell of the flowers something Patrick wished he could forget. Jono and Sage marched on either side of him, heat pouring off their bodies, but Patrick couldn't shake off the cold.

They passed swirls of heavy shadows that looked almost like fog until faces appeared in the grayness. Patrick realized they were people—souls—trapped in this strange darkness flowing up out of the fringe of the veil. Not quite dead, not quite alive, but some weird in-between brought on by the power of an immortal.

As they entered the Main Concourse, Patrick's gaze was drawn to the skeletal goddess standing in front of the information desk beneath that famous golden clock. Her black dress fell past her feet to the floor, disappearing into the marigold petals like an inky waterfall. Santa Muerte watched them come with a smile on her painted face, her scythe held in one hand, though the globe was missing.

Death, in all her glory, was strangely beautiful.

Santa Muerte extended an arm, pointing at Patrick. *"You will lie down on my altar."*

"I don't fucking think so," Patrick shot back. "Hermes, get us below."

Hermes made an exaggerated gesture at Santa Muerte. "You might want to deal with her first."

"Do I look like I'm immortal? You play bait this time."

Santa Muerte slammed the butt of her scythe against the floor. The shock wave barely made the marigold petals flutter, but it sent Patrick and everyone else flying through the air. He landed hard, rolling with the hit, petals filling his mouth and nose. He spat them out and shoved himself to his feet, dagger still in hand.

The blade of the scythe glinted brightly, even in shadow, as it cut through the air toward him. Patrick twisted to the side and raised his dagger instead of his shields, locking his elbows. The dagger scraped against the head of the scythe before catching at the point where it attached to the black snaith. Patrick stared up into Santa Muerte's grinning, skull-like face and hoped the prayers in his dagger would be enough to keep him from dying.

Santa Muerte suddenly spun around, twisting the snaith in her hands. The curved blade cut through the air around her in an arc. Jono ducked beneath the blade and clamped his jaws around the black wood, white fire seeping out of his wolf-bright eyes.

"Cousin, you are on the wrong side," Santa Muerte said.

Jono growled around the weapon caught between his teeth and didn't let go.

A hand grabbed Patrick by the back of his tactical vest, hauling him to his feet. He twisted in the grip, bringing his right arm around to stab whoever was behind him. A too-warm hand grabbed his wrist as an amused chuckle filled his ears.

"That blade does not need my blood again," Áłtsé Hashké said.

Patrick stopped fighting, letting the trickster god pull him away from where Jono and Santa Muerte fought over control of the scythe.

"I can't leave him behind," Patrick protested.

"He will stay with you. The lady and I will have words about her desecration of the children."

"They aren't of your people."

Áłtsé Hashké shook his head. "The beasts they carry are. All beasts belong to the Creator. Those are the souls I care about."

Lucien dropped down beside them, a shadow amongst all the gray as Áłtsé Hashké went to argue with death.

"Tremaine is not on this level," Lucien said.

Patrick took a breath, held it, then let it out to clear his mind. "Then let's get the fuck below."

He didn't know which exit they needed to take, but with Áłtsé Hashké confronting Santa Muerte, they had a five-second window to escape.

"This way," Hermes said, sliding out of the shadows.

Santa Muerte screamed her fury behind them, but no one looked back.

Jono and Sage caught up to Patrick in their race through Grand Central for a side route off-limits to the general public. They bypassed an old elevator with an Out of Service sign on it, following Hermes to a nondescript door with a scan-card access. It should have been locked, but the fringe of the veil that Santa Muerte had called forth meant the electronics weren't working right. The door opened onto a dark stairwell, every step covered in marigold petals.

"I am so sick of going underground," Patrick said.

Hermes stepped aside, waving at the stairwell. "I'll stay up here. Santa Muerte might listen to me if Áłtsé Hashké can't talk sense into her."

"She strikes me as a goddess who doesn't listen to anyone."

"She listened to Tezcatlipoca."

Patrick remembered the altar they'd put him on and shook his head. "She listened to the prayers, not to him."

Patrick took point, with Jono right behind him, heading down into the bedrock of the city. A mageglobe formed against the palm of his free hand, the washed-out blue glow the only hint of light in the shadows they descended through.

Patrick kept track of the landings, the walls changing from cement to ancient Manhattan Schist in the last few stairwells. The door on the final landing was broken open; a man in an MTA uniform lay beyond the damaged metal barrier. His head was twisted at a sharp angle, the vertebrae in his neck broken from the attack.

Lying near the body, surrounded by marigold petals, was a black Santa Muerte idol.

"Tremaine is here," Patrick said quietly, giving the idol a wide berth as he entered the M42 sub-basement.

Lucien and his Night Court advanced into the space, blurring into the shadows as they searched for their wayward rat. Patrick swore and followed them deeper into the sub-basement. It was brighter down here than up above, even with the shroud around them. The reason for that was the protective wards.

The machinery around them was from early in the last century. The old rotary convertors that once channeled electricity and magic were now solely used as the anchor points for the large-scale protective wards snaking through the New York City subway system. The solid-state convertors currently in use to power the trains were in a different section of the sub-basement.

Patrick turned his back on the area with modern machines, focusing on the ones that mattered. Magic seeped through the old iron, shining through the dark with a persistence that hadn't dulled in over a hundred years.

On top of every single rotary convertor, tied to an anchor point, was a Santa Muerte idol.

"Oh, fuck me," Patrick breathed.

He eyed the intricate protective wards that linked each anchor point together, the powerful base that connected some of the city's oldest, most continuously running magic. The magic bowed around where the idols touched, the wards there changing color from the threat of multiple artifacts. Magic needed guidance, and the wards down here provided it for the entire subway system.

Tremaine, at the behest of Santa Muerte, was intent on ripping all of it away.

"We need to—"

Patrick broke off with a grunt as Sage slammed into him, knocking him over. His arm was caught in Jono's mouth and Patrick was quickly dragged in between two of the rotary convertors. He looked back at where he'd stood, seeing Sage squaring off with empty air.

Then the shadows sloughed away, Santa Muerte's shroud retreating to reveal her favored disciple. Tremaine stood in the walkway, one hand holding a golden globe that crackled with electric magic backed by a god.

"Command trigger," Patrick yelled, yanking himself free of Jono's teeth and scrambling to his feet, panic choking him. "Don't let him drop it!"

Sage lunged forward, but it was too late.

Tremaine let the globe fall.

Patrick lashed out with his own magic, but it was useless. The globe easily deflected his attempt to erect a shield around it. When the globe hit the ground, the world exploded with magic powered by a god, driven by a strong, cold wind that should not have reached them underground.

Jono was lifted clean off his paws and slammed against the far wall. Patrick was thrown backward and skidded over the floor. Patrick grunted and hooked an elbow around the nearest railing that surrounded a rotary convertor.

Marigold petals swirled through the air, making it difficult to see. Patrick used the railing to haul himself to his feet beneath the force of the wind. His feet skidded a little on the floor, the world tinged in orange against the shadows. Patrick dug out the coin Hermes had given him and squinted at the idol situated on top of the massive anchor point.

The gears of the rotary convertor rose out of the floor like a ship's propeller, encased in a metal support structure taller than Patrick. The idol sat on the highest point of the arch, Santa Muerte's magic seeping into the intricate wards like poison. Despite the supernatural wind, Patrick didn't hesitate to throw the coin at the idol, knowing that whatever magic Hermes had imbued it with, the coin would find its way to where it needed to be.

Patrick only had a second to confirm the coin hit its target when Jono howled a warning—all that saved him from a broken arm. Patrick loosened his hold on the railing right as Tremaine slammed into him, driving him to the floor. All the air left his lungs with the impact, marigold petals rising in a cloud around him. Some slipped past his lips to twist against his teeth and tongue. The taste made Patrick want to gag.

Jono snarled, but the threat went unheeded by Tremaine. The master vampire loomed over Patrick in a way that reminded him too much of the altar in the subway. One cold hand wrapped around his throat so tightly Patrick couldn't breathe. The strength behind that grip was capable of snapping his neck and Patrick didn't try to pull free.

Before Patrick could get his bearings and stab Tremaine, the master vampire pinned his right wrist to the floor. Tremaine's cold fingers dug into the tendons in his wrist, forcing his own fingers to loosen around the dagger's hilt. Tremaine jerked his hand to the side and the dagger clattered free of his grip.

"This feels familiar," Tremaine said, smiling down at Patrick, revealing red-tinged fangs.

Patrick wished it didn't. He would've said as much if he could speak. Only he didn't have enough air to get the words out, much less the scream that wanted passage through his throat when Tremaine placed the black Santa Muerte idol from the door on his chest.

Black lightning erupted from the artifact, slamming through his shields and his body with enough power to make his spine arch on its own accord. Patrick's heels slid against the floor as he convulsed from the shock of Santa Muerte's magic coursing through him. His shields frayed at the edges, skin hot beneath his tactical uniform.

Black spots ate away at the edge of Patrick's vision, the burn in his throat—in his lungs—hotter than the foreign magic assailing him. Above him, ugly satisfaction twisted Tremaine's face into something monstrous as the wards popped around them, going off like fireworks. Santa Muerte's magic embedded in the artifacts warred with the lone barrier ward erected by the coin—but Hermes' magic was holding.

Patrick couldn't reach his dagger, and Santa Muerte's magic was like a binding ward around him. What magic was left in his soul wouldn't be enough to defend himself.

Except Patrick's soul wasn't the only one he had access to.

He closed his eyes to block out Tremaine's face and focus on the howling in his ears that wasn't the wind, but Jono. The soul-bond resonated between them, a link to power Patrick had lost three years ago and never thought he'd find again.

He'd never wanted to find it like this.

It reminded him too much of what Ethan had done to Hannah —tying souls together for power they each had no right to take. Patrick's tainted soul was scarred and broken in ways he'd learned to live with. He had never wanted what now tied him and Jono together.

He'd never wanted to be like his father.

I'm sorry.

The silent apology rattled through Patrick's brain even as he cracked open both their souls.

It hurt, like stretching long unused muscles for the first time in ages. Patrick reached through the soulbond connecting them, Santa Muerte's magic incapable of keeping their souls apart. Patrick poured his magic through Jono's soul in search of the ley lines that fed the nexus that lived deep beneath New York City.

Ethan hadn't completely damaged the nexus back in June, but Patrick didn't trust his control enough to access that deep reservoir of wild magic. Instead, he tapped a ley line, the rush of external magic like the best high as he drew it out through Jono's soul and formed a mageglobe with it.

His magic crackled to life between himself and Tremaine. He opened his eyes, seeing the shine of his magic reflected in Tremaine's blue eyes for an instant before Patrick exploded the mageglobe.

Patrick's thinned-out shields held.

Tremaine wasn't so lucky.

The master vampire threw himself off Patrick, but he wasn't quick enough to escape the blast radius. The blast caught him in the arm and his side, sending him flying through the air. Patrick drew in a harsh lungful of air, his throat burning with it.

"*Fuck*," he coughed out.

Shoving aside the pain, Patrick solidified his shields and rolled to his side, soul still open to the ley line. The motion dislodged the idol and it clattered to the petal-covered floor, its eyes staring right at him. Santa Muerte's magic sloughed off his shields. Patrick made a sweeping gesture with his arm and sent the figurine careening away from him with the help of magic.

Breathing hurt. His entire body hurt, nerves doing that annoying pins and needles sensation in every limb. It left him clumsy and shaky, but he still had enough coordination to wrap his fingers around his dagger.

The unearthly wind hadn't died down, the force of it still keeping Patrick and Jono physically separated. The soulbond hummed between them, and Patrick sank into it, letting its stability help clear his head. He got his knees underneath him and shoved himself upright. He stared at the magic above arcing from anchor point to anchor point like some demented Tesla oscillator.

If it exploded, they—and too many others—would die.

The idols needed to be destroyed all at once to ensure the damage to the protective wards didn't get any worse. The magic in Hermes' coin had slipped between one of the idols and the anchor point, disrupting Santa Muerte's power, but it couldn't cover all of them.

It was still a weakness in the goddess' power that Patrick intended to use.

He conjured up another mageglobe, casting a spell through it that he hadn't used in three years and counting. A military grade fusillade spell could be rated up or down a scale of power depending on the target, but the underlying framework of the spell within the mageglobe was something only a mage could keep stable. It required a lot of magic to power because a spell like that was meant for a precision attack with a continuous flow of magic to ensure eradication of the target.

If Patrick needed to be precise about anything, it was this.

Santa Muerte's magic arced between the rotary machines, the damage it caused in the protective wards spreading. Patrick focused his magic and released the fusillade spell on a silent command. Magic poured through Jono's soul into his, feeding the spell with power and bolstering Patrick's strength.

His magic targeted every single Santa Muerte idol standing on top of the anchor points at once, pouring his magic into them. Drawing power from the ley line gave the spell enough of a boost so that Patrick could overload Santa Muerte's idols.

It took effort, and a focus Patrick fought to keep on his target, but he could feel the idols crack beneath his attack. Pinned between the barrier ward and Patrick's magic, every last idol exploded in a riot of brightly colored light that cut through the shadows. The sound of their destruction echoed loud enough in the sub-basement to make Patrick's ears ring.

White lightning erupted from the Greek coin and crackled over every rotary machine. The barrier ward embedded in the gold coin spread over the damage on the anchor points like a tsunami, holding the base of the protective wards together.

The shadows melted away, taking with them the marigold petals that covered the floor. Fluorescent light gradually shone down on them, revealing bright wards that covered the walls and floor all around them in a cascade of old magic.

In the sudden echoing silence, Patrick heard Lucien speak.

"Santa Muerte was no mother to you, Tremaine."

Patrick looked over his shoulder, wincing at the pain in his neck. Tremaine knelt on the floor in the spot he'd landed in after Patrick's attack. His left arm was blown apart to the elbow, thick black blood dripping from the stump around shattered bone and ragged flesh.

Lucien knelt behind him, digging his fingers deep into the side of Tremaine's neck. Black blood flowed from the wound like a waterfall. The sound of breaking bone and tearing flesh indicated Lucien was going for Tremaine's heart with his other hand. Tremaine's mouth moved soundlessly as Lucien worked a hand through his rib cage from behind, his entire body jerking from the internal excavation.

Lucien pressed his mouth to Tremaine's ear, his voice rough and unforgiving as the space around them was suddenly filled with the vampires who'd joined them underground. "If you had stayed, I wouldn't have punished you like this. If you had come crawling back on your knees, I would have welcomed you home. But you chose to run, and you didn't run far enough. That's one lesson you never learned, child."

Lucien wrenched his hand free from Tremaine's back, pulling out his child's heart in one easy motion. His other hand tore upward through Tremaine's neck until his fingers caught on bone. Lucien ripped Tremaine's head off his body with a meaty *crack*.

Tremaine's body collapsed to the ground. Lucien tossed Tremaine's head on the corpse and got to his feet.

"Leave the body," Patrick rasped. "We need it as evidence."

A cold nose prodded his shoulder, followed by the warmth of a body Patrick tiredly leaned against. Jono held him up, a rock Patrick didn't want to let go of.

Lucien looked around at the protective wards and the dark areas in the barrier ward where Patrick's magic had shattered every idol.

"You haven't had the strength to use that spell since the Thirty-Day War," Lucien said, black-eyed gaze pinning him with a knowing look. "You're just full of surprises these days."

Patrick gave him the middle finger. "Fuck off."

He was tired and aching, and still had thirteen stories of underground stairs to climb. The relief coursing through Patrick's body left him feeling almost numb. They needed to get magic users down here with an affinity for defensive magic, but he knew the barrier ward would hold until then. A god's magic was worth its weight in gold.

They climbed their way out of the sub-basement for the world above, leaving the dead behind for later processing. Tremaine's death was a true death this time, killed twice by the one who had made him, his business empire broken and his throne empty. The remains of what Tremaine had built in New York City belonged to Lucien now.

They always had.

Patrick wasn't surprised when Lucien disappeared with his Night Court the moment they reached topside. The breeze of their passage was the only goodbye he got. Patrick, Jono, and Sage made their way back to the Main Concourse, the lights back on in Grand Central and the shadows gone.

The scars of Santa Muerte and Áłtsé Hashké's fight lay carved in the floor of the terminal, but that was the only damage in the area. Those commuters who hadn't been able to evacuate in time weren't dead. Freed of the shadows, they huddled together in shock or headed for the exits on stumbling feet. The fearful looks thrown his way reminded Patrick he was a bruised mess while walking between two werecreatures. He probably looked like a threat, but Patrick didn't have time to stop and explain away his appearance.

He let everyone think whatever they liked as he took in the Main Concourse, the chandeliers and other lights illuminating the space. The clock in the center glowed with magic, same as it had in the shadows cast by death's shroud. Tiny sparks floated away from it up to the ceiling in a shining ribbon of light that defied gravity.

Every constellation painted on the turquoise background of the mural high above them glittered like actual stars. Magic crawled across the ceiling in unstoppable waves. Protective wards became visible, flowing down the gold roof arches to the walls and the floors, spilling down stairs and ramps to the tracks below and the subway tunnels that crisscrossed the city.

Patrick's shoulders slumped in relief at the sight of working magic. Jono bumped his hand with a cold nose and Patrick absently scratched his muzzle.

The wards would hold.

"Let's finish this up."

22

The summer sun beat down on Patrick's shoulders through the tree branches above. Sweat trickled down the back of his neck, making his skin itch. The Yankees baseball cap he wore matched many others in the midday weekend crowd in Central Park, helping to hide his hair. The aviator sunglasses he wore cut down on the glare of sunlight as he stared at the line of people snaking away from the hot dog cart farther down the pathway.

Patrick could easily make out Jono's tall form in the line, arms crossed over his chest as he either listened to or ignored whatever Wade was telling him that required such dramatic gestures from the teen. Patrick's eyes watered as he stared at Wade, the teen's aura still far too bright to look at. It had gotten worse since last Friday.

Wade had flown partway across the city after the attack on the Crimson Diamond, crash-landing in The Great Lawn in Central Park. Marek, Emma, and Leon had been waiting for him, sent by a vision that none of them were willing to ignore. Emma and Leon had talked Wade through shifting mass until he was human again.

Then they'd spirited him away through the park and back to their apartment in the Upper East Side before the cops arrived.

Wade had made national and international news with that stunt, even if no one knew his identity. It wasn't every day a dragon showed up, much less a fledgling, and the excitement hadn't died down. Neither had the conspiracy theories. Patrick had forbidden Wade from leaving Marek's apartment unless officially summoned by the police at the PCB or agents at the DEA. The lack of ability to hide his soul made him too big of a target for Patrick's peace of mind.

Quetzalcoatl had done his best to run interference with the DEA when it came to Wade, but with a case this big, stonewalling wasn't going to work forever. Patrick owed the immortal more than he liked, even if Quetzalcoatl didn't see it as a debt in deference of Persephone's claim. Using his position as a special agent with the Organized Crime Drug Enforcement Task Force, Quetzalcoatl had taken control of the investigation against Tremaine with the full support of the SOA and PCB.

The investigation into Tremaine's Night Court and the werecreature trafficking for cage fights was still bringing in witnesses. The werecreatures Áłtsé Hashké had saved, along with Kennedy, were being cared for in Bellevue. Jono had power of attorney over their treatment, and he spent a couple hours every day sitting by their bedsides, offering his support. No one had questioned his presence or called Estelle and Youssef after Patrick had banned the hospital from reaching out to the god pack alphas.

Right now, Patrick was more than happy to let Quetzalcoatl take the lead on everything. SAIC Henry Ng wasn't pleased about Patrick ceding the final investigation to the DEA, but the case would most likely be bifurcated at trial. Either way, the federal government would get its day in court against Tremaine's decimated Night Court. Not many of those vampires were left, but Omacatl Cartel members who had been arrested were more than willing to sell out the remaining vampires for a plea deal.

Lucien's Night Court had extricated themselves from the fight with no one dead or arrested. Sergio had escaped, though he'd lost quite a few of his people in the fight, either to bullets or the police. He had excellent lawyers on retainer to fight for their release. Patrick knew he would be speaking to the New York State attorney general at some point about plea deals for the Anahuac Cartel members in relation to the SOA portion of the case. Lucien would be annoyed if he didn't.

Patrick shifted on the bench, gaze skimming over the crowd of walkers, joggers, bikers, locals and tourists alike. The trees didn't provide as much shade as Patrick would have liked, but he wasn't out here for an aimless walk. The reason he had ventured into Central Park was walking down the pathway with the straight-backed stride of a military man, despite the fact that General Noah Reed wore civilian clothes.

Patrick stood, resisting the urge to salute, though he couldn't stop himself from unconsciously settling into parade rest as the general approached. "Sir."

General Reed extended his hand. "Collins. I understand you've had an exciting couple of weeks."

Patrick gripped his hand for a firm shake before letting go. "That's one way of putting it, sir."

Reed took a seat on the bench, pulling a pack of cigarettes out of the inner pocket of his suit jacket. With an appearance of a man in his midfifties, Reed was short and barrel-chested, his salt-and-pepper hair trimmed to exact regulations. He always carried a hint of smoke around him. Most people attributed that to his chain-smoking habit, but Patrick was one of the few who knew that was a cover.

"Take a seat and ward us, Collins." Reed waved the pack of ciga-rettes at Patrick. "Want one?"

Patrick's nicotine patches hadn't been used in over a week, but he'd gone through three packs of cigarettes since lying on that altar. He didn't have it in him to say *no* right now and took what was on offer. "Thank you, sir."

Reed tapped out two cigarettes, and Patrick lit both with a snap of his fingers and a bit of mage fire. Then he wrote out a silence ward on the wooden bench slat. Static flowed over their area, a bubble of silence encasing them. They smoked for a minute or two, watching the crowd, before Reed spoke.

"I'm giving a speech at the United Nations tomorrow morning about promoting shared defenses against the hells." Reed took a hit off the cigarette, blowing smoke out of his nose that smelled more like sulfur than tobacco. "It's irritating how human memory fades even after a few years."

Patrick said nothing, keeping his eyes on Jono and Wade, who had finally reached the front of the line and were receiving their hot dogs. "Some of us don't forget."

"I know you don't. How is the fledgling?"

"A mess." Patrick flicked ash off the tip of his cigarette. "Trauma does that."

"He has learned bad habits. I saw his soul from a kilometer away."

"He never learned anything. Kid didn't know what he was for years. I would appreciate it if you could teach him how to hide before you leave."

Reed leaned back against the wooden bench, eyeing Patrick. For a moment, his brown eyes flashed golden in the sunlight. "You speak as if he will be staying."

Patrick looked away from the dragon's intense gaze, attention drifting back to Jono and Wade, who were now heading their way. "Wade needs therapy, not war."

"He is of my kind."

"Yeah, well, he's part of my pack, sir. Jono would fight you over him."

"Gods are meddlesome and annoying, as are their vessels." Reed took another drag off of his cigarette, the tip glowing orange.

"You are human and mortal. You can't give the fledgling what he needs."

Patrick's mouth twisted. "You told him to stay with me. He's staying, sir."

He didn't want Wade to leave here today, pressured into signing a contract with the US Department of the Preternatural. Patrick remembered the feeling of hopelessness he'd experienced when he signed his own contract all those years ago, but he'd known what he'd been getting into back then. At least, he thought he had.

"You think so?"

"Wade has been held captive, tortured, and forced to fight for his life since he was fourteen. He's had his entire world upended for the second time last week when he learned what he was. No professional psychiatrist would approve him for basic training, much less active duty."

"He would be better off with his own kind."

"Kid is better off with his pack," Jono said as he and Wade breached the silence ward, Patrick's magic making room for them. "You aren't taking him."

Patrick winced at the antagonistic tone in Jono's voice. "Jono."

"Nah, Pat. We already discussed this. You want me to ring Sage and tell her to come down here to argue with this bloke?"

"He's not some *bloke*, Jono," Patrick said, pinching his now fully healed nose in aggravation. "He's a three-star Army general."

Wade unsubtly hid behind Jono as he scarfed down a hot dog while juggling three more. He didn't stop eating. Jono stayed where he was and shoved his sunglasses on top of his head to glare at Reed.

"You aren't taking the kid."

"Not a kid," Wade muttered from behind him.

Patrick covered his face with one hand before shaking his head in frustration. "Sir—"

Reed held up a hand and Patrick shut up. The general

breathed out a curl of smoke, his cigarette half burned out between his thick fingers. "You can't give the fledgling what he needs."

"And you can?" Jono shot back. "I know your sort, all you blokes in uniform. They'd come around the block back home looking to recruit us. They'd promise a way out and a way off the dole. All we had to do was stand on the front lines and die."

"I take it you didn't accept their offer since you are here."

"How I came here isn't your business. Neither is Wade. You might be hiding as some hotshot general, but that doesn't change your way of thinking. All you lot care about is winning." Jono's eyes cut to Patrick, the anger in his gaze tempered by concern. "You don't care about what's left behind when war gets peeled away."

Patrick bit the inside of his cheek, chewing on skin rather than the words tumbling through his mind. This wasn't how he expected the meeting to go.

"Mortal lives are short compared to ours. The fledgling will outlive you by ten lifetimes and more."

Jono shrugged. "Wade will always be pack."

Reed grunted loudly as he stood. "Walk with me, Collins."

Patrick transferred the silence ward from the bench to a mage-globe and spun up a look-away ward as well before getting to his feet. He glanced at where Jono and Wade stood before facing Reed. "Sir?"

"Your pack may follow."

Patrick wasn't sure if the general included Wade in that count. He matched his stride to Reed's as Jono and Wade fell in behind them. The pace was casual as they meandered down the pathway, heading east as the sun shined overhead.

"I wished you would have stayed with the Mage Corps," Reed said after a couple of minutes. "This would be easier if you had."

Patrick swallowed dryly. "Sir?"

"Back in June, Congress authorized another audit on the

Repository once it was confirmed Ethan Greene and the Dominion Sect were behind the attack here in New York City."

A chill went down Patrick's spine, despite the summer heat. His fingertips brushed against the hilt of the dagger strapped to his right thigh, but it didn't provide any comfort. "What did they find?"

"It's what they didn't find that is the problem."

Patrick clenched his hands into fists. "*Fuck*. What did Ethan take?"

"Back in World War Two, the United States came into possession of a staff," Reed said after a long pause. "It was recovered from the Nazis toward the end of the war. We found it at Auschwitz II–Birkenau."

Patrick opened his mouth, then closed it with a snap, his stomach twisting. "Sir?"

"Hitler would never subject his own people to the atrocities the Nazis committed during the war, but he still needed souls to power the dead. At the time, Allied forces never publicly disclosed how he created the number of zombies he deployed, but we couldn't hide from history where he procured the bodies."

The Holocaust was a tragedy on a scale that was difficult to comprehend, even for those who had lived through that war. The horrific genocide committed by the Nazis was a reminder that monsters could be all too human in the worst way.

"Our government kept the staff?"

"We didn't know what it was back then. Neither did any of the Nazi war criminals hunted down in Brazil. Those who were captured after the war and extradited back to Germany for trial said Josef Mengele was never seen without it beyond the range of most cameras."

"Mengele," Patrick echoed hollowly. "The necromancer?"

"The bastard died a free man before he could be brought to justice to pay for his war crimes. We know he used the staff, we just don't know how. He carried the answers we needed to his grave, and no one has been able to raise his soul." Reed pulled his phone out of his pocket and unlocked it. He tapped at the screen a couple of times before passing it over. "For decades we thought it was an artifact, not a weapon. We were wrong."

Patrick took the phone and stared at the screen. The picture was of a grainy, black-and-white archival photograph, torn and yellowed at the edges. Faded pencil marks listed out a serial number on an old tag pinned beneath it. Patrick zoomed in on the man in the center of a group of SS officers. His face wasn't looking at the camera but at someone else, the wooden staff gripped in one hand.

Reed took another drag of his cigarette. "Look at the next one."

Patrick dutifully swiped to the next picture, this one crisper and clearer than the other one. Taken in color, the wooden staff was long, the tip shod in iron and the head a twist of Celtic knotwork depicting leaves, ravens, and three phases of the moon linked together. It all wrapped around a dull quartz crystal that could barely be seen between the open spaces of the knotwork. The wood itself seemed rough rather than sanded smooth. Patrick assumed it was the quality of the picture before he zoomed in and saw that hundreds of tiny marks were notched into the staff.

He stared at the picture for a few seconds longer before passing the phone back to Reed. "This is what's missing?"

"Yes. Since June."

"What is it?"

Reed put his phone away, staring straight ahead. "Research back in the nineteen-nineties finally pinpointed a possible origin. We believe it belongs to the Morrígan."

Patrick bit down on the inside of his bottom lip until it bled. He remembered what Huginn and Muninn had warned him about before the attack in June, and again last week. Some nightmares took time to form, but when they did, they were all-consuming.

"War is owed what was stolen from her," Patrick said in a hollow voice.

Reed glanced at him, seemingly unsurprised at Patrick's words. "Ethan has a couple of months' lead on us—"

"Try a couple of years." Patrick breathed in sharply, fingers itching for another cigarette. "Odin's ravens warned me back in June before things went FUBAR about something being stolen. I didn't know what they were talking about back then."

He did now.

"You think Ethan and the Dominion Sect stole it during the Thirty-Day War and not this summer?"

"Better double-check the audit report back then and find out who was in charge of confirming the staff's placement in the Repository."

Reed let out a heavy breath that smelled like sulfur. "I'll adjust the time frame of when it went missing. I have people and teams I trust searching for the staff, as does the PIA. Setsuna has kept the SOA in the dark for obvious reasons."

Because Ethan and the Dominion Sect had corrupted Patrick's agency to the bones in the past, and cleaning house was a monumental task no one person could complete in a single directorship. Trust was hard to come by in something like this, and Patrick knew very few people would have made the general's list for the search. That Setsuna hadn't told Patrick of the problem was a conversation he intended to have with her later.

"You sent the Hellraisers after the staff, didn't you?"

"Yes," Reed said, abruptly stopping so he could face Patrick and look him in the eye. "And now I am sending you."

"I haven't worn a uniform in three years, sir. I'm no longer under your command."

"What I and the US government want aligns with what the gods you serve want—Ethan dead and the Dominion Sect crippled. We don't know who got into the Repository to steal the staff, or how they went about doing so, but we need to locate it before they learn how to use it."

"I can't leave my post."

"Setsuna is willing to look the other way and cover for you when the need arises."

"How helpful of her."

Reed didn't blink, his eyes gold instead of brown with slit-black pupils in a too-human face. "You know what is at stake more than anyone else. I wouldn't ask this of you if we weren't desperate, Collins."

Patrick didn't speak until the coppery tang of blood on his tongue was just an aftertaste. "Off the record, sir?"

"For now."

Patrick was acutely aware of Jono and Wade standing just beyond arm's reach, watching him. He knew whatever he chose, his pack would follow him down that road, and they would all have to live with the consequences of his actions.

"Wade stays with us," Patrick said.

Reed glanced over at Wade, who had finished all of his hot dogs and was only half hiding behind Jono now, though his soul still shone too-bright to look at. "He carries bad habits."

"Then teach him better ones before you go."

They stared at each other for a long few seconds before Reed gestured at Wade. "Come here, fledgling."

Wade gave Patrick a panicked look before reluctantly shuffling forward. Patrick stepped aside, letting Wade take his place. The teenager flinched when Reed placed his hands on Wade's thin shoulders.

"Look at me," Reed commanded.

Wade could do nothing but obey, locking eyes with the elder of his kind. The pair stood frozen in the midday sun, statues no one paid any attention to thanks to Patrick's look-away ward. Five minutes passed, then ten. With every second that ticked by, the glaring brightness of Wade's soul shrank until it disappeared beneath his skin. His aura became nothing more than a faint human sheen to Patrick's senses.

The general finally let him go and Wade stumbled back into

Patrick's arms. He was shaking, hunching in close, and Patrick let him.

"*Ow*," Wade muttered.

"I will be here when they no longer are," Reed said, his voice a rumble in his chest. "Remember that."

Wade scowled down at his feet and didn't reply. The general didn't seem put off by his attitude. Patrick gently prodded Wade to go stand by Jono.

"I'll need a full report on the staff and the status of the search," Patrick said.

"I'll see that you get it." Reed smiled grimly, blowing smoke out of his nose, no cigarette in sight. "Good hunting, Collins."

The general walked away. Patrick watched him go for a few seconds before collapsing the tiny mageglobe spinning against his palm. Sound rushed back in around them, the summer day filled with the buzz of people talking, dogs barking, and the distant hum of the city beyond the urban greenery.

Jono stepped closer, wrapping an arm around Patrick's shoulders. "Come on, mate. Let's head back to Marek's flat."

Walking between Jono and Wade out of Central Park, Patrick carried the weight of an uncertain future with him, chilled down to his bones.

23

Jono reached over the back of the sofa and pulled Patrick's mobile out of his hand, ignoring his protest.

"Hey, that's mine," Patrick said.

Jono got a glimpse of a news article about the mayor's latest press conference. He wouldn't have thought anything of it except the picture beneath the headline made him freeze.

Patrick leaned his head back so he was looking at Jono upside down. "You look like you've seen a ghost."

Jono turned the mobile around so Patrick could see the screen, with its picture of the mayor surrounded by other officials and aides. "I know that woman."

Patrick reached up and took his mobile back. "Which one?"

Jono pointed at the blonde woman standing off to the side behind someone else, her face visible over their shoulder. "She was with Ethan when they had me, and I saw her again at the Crimson Diamond."

Patrick's grip tightened on his mobile, but he didn't say anything. He saved the picture though before locking his phone. "I'll head home and look into it."

"I came down to tell you supper is ready, not to run you out. They've got the table all set up on the roof."

"I'm not hungry."

"Wade will eat your plate if you don't join us."

"He can have it. Considering how many hot dogs he had at the park today, I'm surprised he still has room in his stomach. Think we should enter him in the Nathan's Hot Dog contest at Coney Island next summer?"

"You're changing the subject." Jono stroked his knuckles over Patrick's cheek. "Stay. You need to eat."

"I can eat later."

Jono stared down into Patrick's eyes before pulling his own mobile out of his pocket. He texted Emma, letting her know they were leaving. "Right, come on. Let's go."

Patrick sat up, eyeing him. "Where?"

"Home, like you said. Sage will make sure Wade gets enough grub. We have leftovers back at the flat if we get hungry."

"You don't have to leave because of me. You can stay here."

"I don't want you gone, I just want you back." Jono smoothed his hand over Patrick's messy ginger hair. "You've been lost in thought since the meeting in the park earlier today. This news article isn't helping. I hate seeing you like this."

Patrick sighed tiredly, the troubled look in his eyes something Jono wished he could wipe away. "I didn't mean to drag you into this."

"We're a pack. Where you go, I go."

"Yeah, that's what I'm afraid of."

Jono ignored Patrick's mutterings. The past week had been hellishly long, with Patrick working loads of overtime to deal with the cleanup and the case. The dark circles beneath his eyes weren't due to getting punched but from lack of sleep. Jono wanted to lock Patrick up and feed him before letting him sleep for a week straight.

He settled for taking Patrick home.

Patrick spent the drive there with his head resting against the window, staring blankly at the street traffic passing them by. Every line of his body screamed *leave me alone*, and Jono had no clue how to keep Patrick from chewing on the latest problem. Before the mess with Tremaine and Tezcatlipoca, Jono wouldn't think twice about using sex to distract Patrick, but they hadn't had sex since before the night Patrick came down from his drugged-out high.

He was pulled out of his thoughts by his mobile going off, the *Psycho* ringtone filling the car. He and Patrick shared a look.

"Are you going to answer?" Patrick asked.

"I haven't answered them all week."

"Maybe you should. I know the PCB has been in touch with their lawyers."

Jono made a face before giving in and letting the call sync to the Bluetooth in the Mustang. "What do you want?"

"We need to talk," Estelle said.

"I'm not going to help you get your story straight if that's why you rang."

"Maria summoned us tomorrow to the construction site in the Meatpacking District. That isn't her territory and never has been. She said you would be there as well. I want to know what's going on."

Patrick raised both eyebrows in surprise at that revelation. "Huh. Didn't take Maria long to grovel."

"What?"

"We'll see you tomorrow," Jono said before ending the call without giving Estelle the answer she so desperately wanted. Even if he knew it, Jono wouldn't have helped her.

Patrick already had his mobile out, typing away. "I'll text Carmen and see what's up. The meeting tomorrow is news to me."

Jono left him to figuring out when the meeting was going to happen and what it would be about. He focused on getting them home.

Finding parking on a Saturday night was difficult but not

completely impossible. Jono ended up parking a block away, and they walked home in silence. Their hands brushed together, and Jono sighed quietly when Patrick reached for him, tangling their fingers together. Patrick didn't let go, not even when they made it inside the flat and Jono was pushed up against the closed door.

Patrick's free hand curved around the back of his neck, fingers running through the short hair there. Jono settled his other hand on Patrick's hip, staying where he was put.

"You've been keeping your distance," Patrick said, his eyes searching Jono's. "Is it because of what I did to you at Grand Central?"

Jono shook his head. "I already told you how I feel about you tapping a ley line through the soulbond. It doesn't bother me."

Patrick didn't look like he believed him, so Jono kissed the doubtful expression off his face. Patrick chased after his mouth when Jono broke the kiss, stepping closer. "Then why don't you want to fuck me? And don't say it's because work is getting in the way. We've always found time before, but you've pulled away every time I've tried to initiate something."

Jono lifted both hands to cradle Patrick's face, stroking a thumb over his cheekbone. "You weren't dealing with the aftermath of assault all the rest of the times. You've gone back to cigarettes, and don't think I haven't noticed the whiskey bottle was replaced twice this week."

Patrick went still in his arms. "Tremaine didn't rape me."

"Doesn't need to be rape to hurt, love."

They stood there in silence for a long moment before Patrick spoke. "Most days I'm a living reminder of things I want to forget."

"Drowning yourself in smoke and liquor won't take the memories away."

"I see a therapist."

"I know you do. All I'm saying is don't come to me because you think you need to prove something to yourself. I'm not going anywhere, and I'll wait however long you need to feel okay again."

Patrick tightened his fingers in Jono's hair, holding on. His shields that had been raised ever since leaving Central Park slowly disappeared. Jono drew in a breath, smelling exhaustion and weary resignation beneath the bitter scent Patrick carried on his skin, but no fear, no apprehension.

"This isn't—" Patrick broke off, pressing his face into Jono's hands. "I don't want you to fuck me just to prove something to myself, Jono. I want you because that's what I want. Because that's *my* choice. If you don't want me, then just say so."

The truth in his words was bright and clean in his scent. Jono pushed away from the door, his hands dropping down to Patrick's hips, then his thighs, hauling the shorter man into his arms. Patrick wrapped his legs around Jono's waist, arousal seeping through his scent, slow and thick like molasses.

"Never going to not want you, love."

"You sure?"

Jono thought about the soulbond that tied them together but knew it didn't dictate his heart. "It's not magic that makes me want you, Pat."

"If you say so."

"I do." Jono gently squeezed Patrick's ass, looking him in the eye. "Now, I'm going to take you to bed, like you want. And if you tell me to stop, I will."

Patrick laughed tiredly against his mouth, fingers tangling in his hair. "Just make me feel good and I'll never have to."

Jono carried Patrick to the bedroom and took him at his word, attuned to Patrick's body and scent in a hyperaware way. Depositing Patrick on their bed, Jono set about undressing him until he wore nothing but his dog tags, the scars on his body prominent against his skin. Jono kissed his way down Patrick's chest, tracing over scar tissue with his tongue, mouth drifting down warm skin until he could wrap his lips around Patrick's cock.

Patrick let out a groan that sounded like it hurt, bucking into

Jono's mouth. Jono gripped his hips and held him in place, taking his time in familiarizing himself with Patrick's scent and taste. Fingers gripped his hair and pulled, but Jono ignored the desperate tugging in favor of swallowing Patrick's cock down to the root.

Patrick slid his leg over Jono's shoulder to dig his heel against Jono's back. Jono hummed at the pressure, and Patrick made a strangled sound in the back of his throat. "Holy *fuck.*"

Jono swallowed around the thickening length in his mouth before pulling off, his tongue dragging against sensitive skin the entire way. Patrick breathed in deep, unclenching his hand from Jono's hair. His pupils were blown wide, a flush coming up on his cheeks.

"Need a moment?" Jono asked with a teasing smile, stroking Patrick's cock.

"Shut up and get out of your goddamn clothes so you can fuck me. I've missed your cock."

Jono laughed as he stood, already stripping off his T-shirt. "Whatever you want."

"Exactly."

He shed his boots and the rest of his clothes, crawling onto the bed after Patrick. Jono kissed him again, letting their cocks slide together as they rocked against each other. Patrick's hands stroked down his back to grab his ass and pull him in. Jono settled heavily against the cradle of Patrick's hips, seeking out that plush mouth for a kiss.

"How do you want me?" Jono murmured.

Patrick arched beneath him, panting as Jono sucked at the sensitive skin just beneath his ear. "I want you in me."

Jono licked his way down Patrick's throat, biting gently at his collarbone and the thick edge of scar tissue there. "Didn't answer my question."

"The hell I didn't."

Jono shifted against him, sliding lower so he could lick at Patrick's left nipple, knowing it had better sensitivity than the other one. "You want me to fuck you like this and take my time? Or put you on your knees and make you scream my name?"

Patrick groaned, his fingers scratching at Jono's skin. "Both?"

Jono sucked at the nipple until it hardened into a nub, tugging at the other one with firm fingers. Patrick moaned, the sound vibrating against Jono's lips. He pulled back, the nub caught in his teeth and stretching before he let it go. He grabbed the bottle of lube from the nightstand before stacking up the pillows and lying down beside Patrick.

"Come here."

Jono coaxed Patrick onto his lap, knees on either side of him, lean body rising over him. He hooked a finger around the dog tags, pulling Patrick down for a long, deep kiss that left them both gasping for air when they broke apart.

Jono uncapped the lube and poured it over his fingers. "Hold yourself open for me."

Patrick's eyes darkened at his request, but he didn't argue. He merely reached back with one hand to grab his ass and open himself up while bracing himself against Jono's shoulder. Jono slid one finger inside, pushing past the initial resistance. Patrick's eyes fluttered closed, mouth dropping open a little.

Jono nipped at Patrick's bottom lip, hooking his other hand around the back of Patrick's knee. "There's a love. I'm going to get you ready, and then I want you to ride me."

"Didn't think I'd be the one doing all the work here," Patrick muttered as he pushed back against Jono's finger.

"It's not about work. It's about control, and what you want."

Patrick opened his eyes, staring at Jono. He didn't say anything, but neither did he stop rolling his hips onto Jono's finger. Jono didn't look away, breathing in Patrick's scent and cataloguing every twitch of his body.

Patrick leaned in, his lips barely brushing over Jono's. "You're something else, you know that?"

Jono licked his way into Patrick's mouth at the exact same moment he slipped a second finger inside him. Patrick shuddered against him, biting into the kiss with a needy moan that made his own cock twitch.

"Never met anyone else like you," Jono said against his lips. "Don't want anyone else but you."

Patrick pulled back, face flushed and eyes more black than green. "You mean it?"

"Always. I'm not leaving you."

Patrick surged forward, nearly pulling free of Jono's fingers completely as he kissed Jono hard enough their teeth scraped together. It'd been roughly two months since Patrick had walked into Tempest and into his life, and despite everything that had happened, Jono wouldn't give up what they were building between them for anything.

He reached up with his free hand and got a good grip on Patrick's hair, pulling his head back. Patrick arched backward, and Jono sucked a bruise against the pulse in his throat.

"Get on my cock."

"Fuck, yes," Patrick groaned, flailing for a moment on his knees before he found his balance again.

Jono pulled his fingers free and poured more lube onto them. He slicked up his cock with a few hard strokes. Patrick finally batted his hand away and gripped his cock, giving it a good squeeze. Jono dug his fingers into Patrick's hips and lifted him higher. Patrick took the hint and shifted back, guiding Jono's cock to his hole.

Jono held still, his fingers pressing bruises into Patrick's skin as he slipped inside that tight heat. Patrick slid onto him slowly, opening up just a little more with every roll of his hips. Jono fought against the desire to thrust up into Patrick and have that clenching warmth surround him.

Patrick finally seated himself fully on Jono's cock, one hand resting on Jono's chest for balance. His head was tipped back, and

Jono raised a hand to stroke his fingers over Patrick's throat, scent-marking him even if the other man couldn't smell it.

"Come on, love," Jono said, voice rough with want. "Fuck yourself on my cock."

Patrick swallowed, Jono's thumb following the motion, as he rose up on his knees and sank back down. Slow at first, every roll of his hips loosening him up, then faster, the sound of their skin slapping together echoing in the bedroom.

Jono didn't let Patrick go, following the motions of his body with careful hands. Patrick picked up the pace, the flush of arousal spreading from his face down to his neck and scarred chest. Jono's fingers followed the warmth, then drifted lower, wrapping around Patrick's cock and making him lose his rhythm.

Fingernails bit into Jono's skin as Patrick cried out, working himself between Jono's cock and hand. The whine that fell from his lips had Jono's hips snapping upward, driving his cock deep into Patrick even as he pulled him down.

"Oh, *fuck*," Patrick moaned, shuddering as he clenched around Jono. "Right there. Do it again."

"Yeah?" Jono grunted, thrusting into him again.

The wordless sound Patrick let out made Jono smirk. He kept stroking Patrick's cock, drinking in the sight of the other man taking pleasure because it was what Patrick wanted. Jono could smell his desire, the heady scent of it filling his nose. He dragged his thumb over the tip of Patrick's cock, smearing the precum over the sensitive skin there. Patrick swallowed loudly, driving himself down onto Jono's cock.

Patrick's pupils were blown wide, but the clarity in his eyes was all that mattered to Jono. "Don't stop."

Jono stole a kiss, sweet and fierce. "Never."

Jono met him halfway because that's what Patrick wanted. He guided Patrick to the perfect angle that allowed Jono to hit his prostate with every thrust. Sweat made holding on to him difficult after a while as Patrick writhed above him, working himself over on Jono's cock with a dedication Jono could appreciate.

"I can't—" Patrick gasped out, losing the rhythm. "I'm gonna come."

Jono dragged him down onto his cock as he thrust up and didn't stop, keeping Patrick *right there*. Patrick leaned forward, keening through clenched teeth as Jono fucked him hard enough to shake the bed. His cock pulsed against Jono's tight fingers, and Patrick came with a yell, shaking apart above him.

Jono milked every last drop of cum out of Patrick, the warm wetness sticky on his chest. He hooked a hand over Patrick's shoulder, pulling him down onto his cock even as he rolled them to the side. Jono got Patrick beneath him, and he drove into that tight heat with a growl.

Patrick moaned in his ear, fingers tangling through Jono's sweaty hair. "Keep going. Keep—*gods!*"

Jono grabbed one knee and hooked it over his shoulder, giving him more room to fuck Patrick, chasing his own orgasm. Patrick blinked dazedly up at him, sweaty and shaking and fucked out, smelling happy in a way he rarely was, despite everything that had happened.

Jono groaned, burying his face against the curve of Patrick's throat, biting on the skin there as he came. His hips snapped forward, driving into that clenching heat half a dozen times as he spilled his release inside Patrick.

They lay like that for a minute or two, breathing hard as they recovered from the intensity of their lovemaking. Jono pressed his nose against the heated skin of Patrick's neck, running his lips over the bruise there.

Eventually, he pulled away, easing Patrick's leg off his shoulder and pulling out. He stroked his fingers over the too-sensitive skin of Patrick's hole, catching some of the cum that trickled out. He smeared it between Patrick's legs before going back for more, rubbing his scent where no one else would ever touch again.

Patrick watched him through half-lidded eyes, hands loose, biting his lip every now and then. When Jono finished, he patted the bed beside him. "C'mere."

"I should clean you up first."

"No," Patrick said, sleepy and loose in a way Jono was proud of making him feel. "I'll shower in the morning. I want you to stay on me."

Jono wasn't going to argue with that request, even though he knew Patrick would bitch about dried cum and itchy skin in the morning. For now, he got them under the covers, pulling Patrick close as the air-conditioning clicked on, the quiet hum chasing them into sleep.

24

"I'm hungry," Wade complained from the back seat.

"I told you we'd get lunch after the meeting," Patrick said as he drove through a yellow light.

"I don't know why I have to go to this thing when I could've stayed at the apartment to eat."

"Because you're pack, and pack sticks together," Jono replied.

"Pack should get better at leaving snacks around."

"Here." Sage rifled through her Birkin and pulled out a protein bar. "Eat this and stop complaining until after the meeting is over."

Wade snatched the protein bar out of her hand with a muttered "Thanks."

Patrick rolled his eyes as the familiar sound of Wade eating filled the car. With the amount of food Wade could consume in a day, he was glad Emma and Leon had offered Jono a raise. Bad enough they had to feed two werecreatures, but throw in a fledgling dragon and Patrick's paycheck would be stretched thin.

The rest of the drive to Ginnungagap happened without Wade complaining about the lack of snacks. Patrick pulled into the familiar alley, seeing a motorcycle he recognized and a group of god pack werewolves gathered outside the side entrance. The construction workers had the day off again, or at least the morning. Patrick didn't know what work schedule they were running on, he just knew the club was getting closer to completion every time he dropped by.

Patrick parked and everyone got out of the car, eyeing the group by the door with undisguised disdain on all their faces.

"You're late," Youssef said.

"Meeting won't start without us. You could've gone inside," Patrick retorted.

"The door is locked."

"Should've knocked."

"We did," Estelle replied testily.

"Should've knocked louder."

To prove his point, Patrick approached the door and pounded on it with a heavy fist. A couple of seconds later, the handle turned and the door opened. Carmen greeted him with a smile on her face, red-pupiled eyes staring at him. Her curled horns nearly scraped the door when she tilted her head.

"*Bastardo,*" she purred.

"I know your master likes his games, but Wade is gonna chew off his arm if we don't feed him soon. Can we get this over with?"

"I'll chew off *your* arm," Wade muttered.

Jono pushed him forward. "Get inside."

Wade dragged his feet as he shoved his way through the god pack to get to the door. He crossed the threshold with a scowl, sulking like only a teenager could. Sage followed after him, head held high, and didn't once acknowledge Estelle and Youssef. The growls from the werewolves the god pack alphas had brought with them were met by a smile full of teeth from Jono.

"Piss off," he told them as he walked inside.

Patrick crossed the threshold and watched as Carmen pushed the door open wider, staring Estelle and Youssef down. "I won't ask for hospitality because you aren't worth it. But you will pay in blood if you disrespect my master."

"And who is your master?" Youssef asked.

Carmen smirked, gesturing lazily with her hand. "Come inside and find out."

"Maria was the one who called us here."

"Because we told her to."

A look of unease flashed across Estelle and Youssef's bright amber eyes. They kept whatever they were feeling to themselves and stepped inside. Patrick expected the rest of their party to be blown backward like the last time but was surprised when that didn't happen.

The door slammed shut, and Carmen strode over to the bar where Naheed sat on top of the tarp-covered counter, pointedly cleaning two SIG Sauers. A third pistol, fully assembled, sat within reach. She was, as always, ever the attentive bodyguard during the day.

"The other Night Courts had treaties with Tremaine's. They still hold treaties with us. Is that why we are here?" Estelle wanted to know.

"A piece of paper doesn't give you any rights," Lucien said as he came down the stairs from the mezzanine. "I hold treaties with no one."

Patrick always found it interesting how people reacted to seeing Lucien in person for the first time. Most didn't recognize who he was, not immediately, though they never missed *what* he was. Wearing faded black jeans, a black T-shirt, and scuffed combat boots, his pale skin stood out against the dark clothes. Lucien didn't hide his fangs when he smiled at the pair of god pack alphas, black eyes watching as all the blood drained from their faces.

"Daywalker," Youssef said, dragging the word out. He never took his eyes off Lucien as the master vampire approached.

"In the flesh."

"You killed Tremaine," Estelle said slowly.

"I don't care for disobedient children."

Everyone heard the breath Estelle sucked in past her teeth, a tell—a weakness—her side couldn't afford to give up. "He was your child?"

"I made him, and I put him down as was my right, the same way I'll put you down if you get in my way."

Patrick knew the moment Estelle figured out the identity of the monster walking her way. The way her body went stiff, the faint tremble of her bottom lip as her eyes widened, proved she wasn't completely stupid.

"Lucien," she breathed out.

The master vampire's smile was all the answer she got, but it was enough. No vampire would attempt to impersonate Lucien, and his reputation spoke for itself.

Lucien didn't stop until he stood toe-to-toe with Estelle, the pack members she'd brought silent in the face of a predator more dangerous than all of them combined. "I wanted the Manhattan Night Court, so I took it. Whatever treaties Tremaine held with your god pack are null and void. Stay the fuck out of my territory."

Estelle opened her mouth, then shut it, her eyes never leaving Lucien's face. "We have pass-through rights."

Patrick didn't see the Ka-Bar in Lucien's hand until he had it shoved between Estelle's teeth, cutting into the corners of her mouth. His other hand had a gun raised and pointed at Youssef's head before their pack could even think about moving.

"You have nothing but what I give you. I'm letting you leave with your life because the police irritate me and I don't need them looking my way. Consider it a warning."

He yanked the knife out of Estelle's mouth, slicing open her cheek with the motion. Blood gushed down her face and throat, staining her silk blouse. Estelle covered the wound with her hands, stumbling backward. Youssef caught her before she fell, fear and hatred warring in his gaze as he stared at Lucien.

Lucien gestured at the door with his gun. "Get out."

The other god pack members swarmed their alphas and hustled the pair out of Ginnungagap in seconds. The door slammed shut behind them on its own accord.

"Was that the only reason you brought us here?" Patrick asked.

Lucien licked Estelle's blood off his Ka-Bar, careful of the serrated edge. "Does it matter?"

"If I wanted to see a show, I would've gone to Broadway."

"Your life choices remain terrible."

"Yeah, about that. I kept the promise I made to you. Tremaine is dead and the Manhattan Night Court is yours. What more do you want?"

"Yes, your debt is paid. For once."

Patrick flipped him off. "Fuck you."

"Get out before I shoot you."

Patrick opened his mouth, but Jono quickly covered it with his hand. "That's enough, mate. Let's be off."

Patrick scowled against Jono's palm, but Wade was already hurrying toward the exit. Sage followed after him at a sedate pace, pausing only when she was in Lucien's line of sight.

"When you're ready to talk territory boundaries, call me." Sage plucked a business card from the little pocket on the back of her phone case and held it out. "I'll set up a meeting with my alphas."

Patrick stiffened as Lucien approached Sage, but the master vampire didn't try to slice a second smile into her face. Lucien smirked at her and took the business card, crumpling it up before dropping it on the ground.

"If I need to speak with Patrick, I'll call him," Lucien said.

"You'll call *me*. I'm his dire, which puts me on par with Carmen. Don't disrespect me or my pack, Lucien."

Jono had a proud look on his face as he watched Sage turn her back on Lucien and walk out of the warehouse. "Knew I chose right when I gave her that rank."

Patrick batted Jono's hand away from his mouth and headed

after the other two, knowing Jono had his six. They left the warehouse for the alleyway, finding it empty of the god pack but not empty of gods.

"Your car hasn't been fixed," Hermes said from where he sat on the hood.

"I'll fix your face with my fist if you come closer," Patrick said, scowling at him. "Get off my car."

Hermes grinned and stayed where he was. Quetzalcoatl snorted, pushing away from the driver's-side door he'd been leaning against. The immortals were in their DEA uniforms but weren't sweating from the heat in their jackets with the agency lettering on the back.

"Hello, Patrick," Quetzalcoatl said.

"I have a dragon to feed. If you need to talk about work, it can wait until tomorrow."

"I've heard from Áłtsé Hashké. I thought you'd like to know what he had to say."

"That's what phones are for."

"True, but if we left personal greetings by the wayside, Hermes would be out of a job."

"Never," Hermes retorted as he jumped off the hood of the car.

Quetzalcoatl shrugged. "Santa Muerte will follow her worshippers, not the Dominion Sect. She has gone south, at Áłtsé Hashké's request. He does not want her in his lands."

"How long will that last?" Jono asked.

"A few weeks. A few centuries. Who knows? Death goes where she likes."

"And your brother?"

"Ah. A little more complicated, as all families are. He has left New York City, but the Omacatl Cartel can't be carved out of these streets. I'm sure Tezcatlipoca will find his way back at some point."

Patrick shared a look with Jono before shrugging. "Maybe by that point we'll all be dead. Either way, not our problem."

Quetzalcoatl ran his hand over the top of the car. Power

scraped against Patrick's magic before receding as quickly as it had arrived. "I will do what I can to make sure you don't have to worry about the case. It's the least I owe my cousin for my brother's transgression against a soul debt he never owned."

"He comes after Patrick again and I'll tear him to pieces," Jono promised.

Hermes smirked. "So feisty. I'll remember to bring popcorn."

The immortals disappeared, slipping through the veil as if they were never there. Patrick waved a hand at his car, taking down the ward that had hidden the damage accrued from jaguars. The metal, once shredded by powerful claws, was now whole, and the paint job had returned to a pristine black.

"That was nice of him," Sage said dubiously.

"I'd rather submit a claim to the insurance company and let my premiums rise. I hate owing gods anything," Patrick grumbled.

"I'm hungry," Wade whined as he rifled through three stolen wallets. "Can we eat?"

Patrick snatched the wallets out of his hands, checking the identification inside. Each license matched the face of a werewolf Estelle had brought with her. "Goddamn it. I can't take you anywhere."

Wade held up a wad of cash. "Lunch is on me."

"With stolen money."

Jono took the wallets from Patrick and chucked them at the far end of the alleyway. No one watched where they landed. "Lunch sounds great. I'm famished."

"Fine. All of you get in."

Everyone climbed into the Mustang and buckled up before Patrick started the engine. He took a moment to look at everyone, this pack of family he never thought he'd get to have, much less keep. Nothing was ever certain, least of all war, and Patrick knew all too well what could be lost in the shadow of conflict.

"Ready?" Jono asked, arching an eyebrow.

Patrick put the car into reverse and hit the gas pedal. "Yeah."

Jono's hand settled on his thigh, his touch warm and heavy and *there*. Patrick let it ground him, refusing to pull away. Sometimes peace could be found in the chaos of a life unconstrained from the walls people built. Jono, Sage, and Wade were a weakness, he knew that, but one Patrick was determined to fight for.

No matter what.

~~~

Patrick and Jono's adventure continues in *A Crown of Iron & Silver.*

Don't miss out on sneak peeks, exciting news, and more! Sign up for Hailey Turner's newsletter to stay up-to-date on her upcoming books.
~~~

GLOSSARY

Short descriptions of words, acronyms, and phrases used in the story that weren't readily explained in text. Included as well are character names.

Áltsé Hashké: (Pronunciation: Aht SEH hash KEH) Immortal. Diné (given English name: Navajo) trickster god.

Abuku, Setsuna: Witch. Director who oversees and leads the Supernatural Operations Agency.

Academy: K-12 school that teaches magic to practitioners of all affinities and designations. All provide boarding options to students.

Ashanti: Immortal. Goddess and mother of all vampires. Takes the shape of an Asanbosam vampire out of West African myths.

Beacot, Sage: Weretiger. A Diné lawyer who works for the fae law firm Gentry & Thyme. Dire to Jono and Patrick's god pack.

Carmen: Succubus. First known recorded appearance was in Venice, Italy.

Casale, Giovanni: Human. Chief of the NYPD's Preternatural Crimes Bureau.

Citadel: United States military academy for magic users.

Located in Maryland. All Academies across the nation feed into the Citadel. Mages get automatic inclusion. All other kinds of magic users need recommendations.

Collins, Patrick: Mage. Former combat mage with the Mage Corps, currently an SOA special agent. Has a tainted soul and crippled magic. Is technically a mage in name only due to a soul wound.

de Vere, Jonothon: God pack werewolf. Originally from London, England, currently resides in New York City. Alpha of a god pack he co-leads with Patrick.

DEA: Drug Enforcement Administration. A US federal law enforcement agency tasked with combating drug smuggling and distribution. It shares jurisdiction with the FBI and the SOA.

Devon: Master vampire. Heads up the Staten Island Night Court.

Dire: A rank held only within a god pack. The moniker is taken from the dire wolf, but has been shortened to account for different werecreature species. Essentially a rank held by a loyal pack member who helps enforce the alphas' orders.

Dominion Sect: A shadowy terrorist group consisting of mundane humans, rogue magic users, immortals aligned with the hells, and other preternatural creatures intent on destroying the veil between worlds so that hell and its denizens can reign on earth. Some members are attempting to steal godheads in order to ensure their hold on power in the new world they hope to create.

Einar: Vampire. Oldest child and second-in-command within Lucien's Night Court. His sire is Lucien.

Espinoza, Wade: Teenaged fledgling fire dragon. Part of Jono and Patrick's god pack.

Fenrir: Immortal. Wolf in the Norse pantheon. Patron to a god pack.

FUBAR: Fucked Up Beyond All Recognition/All Relief. Military slang.

Ginnungagap: Primordial void. Belongs to the Norse myths.

Godhead: Primordial power belonging to immortals that gives them life. The strength of their power can be altered by worship, or lack thereof.

God pack: A pack of werecreatures infected with the god strain of the werevirus. They act as spokespeople for hidden werecreature packs in their territory. They are supported by monetary tithes from the packs under their protection. Very few retain a connection to their animal-god patrons.

Greene, Ethan: Mage. Was a double agent formally employed by the SOA. Is currently a mercenary and allied with the Dominion Sect.

Greene, Hannah: Mage. Currently a vessel. Spiritually deceased.

Hades: Immortal. Greek god of the dead and the Underworld.

Hellraisers: A US Department of the Preternatural Special Forces team Patrick once belonged to.

Hera: Immortal. Greek goddess of women and titular queen of the Greek pantheon.

Hermes: Immortal. Greek messenger god and god of trade, thieves, travelers, sports, athletes, border crossings, and guide to the Underworld

Hernandez, Leon: Werewolf. Partner to Emma Zhang and co-leader of the Tempest pack.

Huginn: Immortal. One of Odin's ravens in the Norse pantheon, whose name means "thought."

Jamere: Master vampire. Heads up the Brooklyn Night Court.

Kavanaugh, Nicholas: God pack werewolf. Dire of the New York City god pack.

Khan, Youssef: God pack werewolf. Alpha of the New York City god pack.

Ley lines: Metaphysical rivers of powers that drain into nexuses.

Lucien: Master vampire. Was a soldier in William the

Conqueror's army before being turned by Ashanti. Currently a weapons and magic trafficker. Is wanted by many governments.

Macaria: Immortal. Greek goddess of the blessed death and Hades' daughter.

Mage: Highest rank of magic users and the only practitioners who can tap external power from ley lines and nexuses.

Mage Corps: Military branch under the purview of the US Department of the Preternatural. Accepts only mages.

Magic: Emanating from and powered by a person's soul. Roughly one-quarter of the world's population has magic. Strength varies, with different titles being bestowed depending on a person's magical reach. Casting is divided into defensive wards and offensive spells.

Maria: Master vampire. Heads up the Bronx Night Court.

Moirai: Immortals. Greek Fates.

Morrígan: Immortal. Sometimes depicted as an individual Celtic goddess, or more commonly as a triple goddess, of war and fate. She is particularly affiliated with foretelling of death or victory in battle. Often described as a trio of sisters sometimes given the names of Badb, Macha, and Nemain.

Muginn: Immortal. One of Odin's ravens in the Norse pantheon, whose name means "memory" or "mind."

Mulroney, Nadine: Mage. Works counterintelligence for the PIA. Is fluent in French and based out of Paris, France.

Necromancer: A magic user who can be of any rank. Their magic has an affinity for the dead, allowing them to raise the dead, control zombies, and manipulate the lingering souls of the deceased. Their kind of magic is heavily restricted in use in the United States and in most countries.

Necromancy: A family of magic that deals with the dead, usually involving blood magic and sacrifices. Predominately illegal or restricted in most countries.

Nexus: Metaphysical lake of power beneath the earth. Usually located in sacred areas or beneath major cities.

Night Court: Vampire group that oversees claimed territory. Headed by a single master vampire. Several Night Courts can exist in the same major city.

Norns: Immortals. Norse Fates.

OCDETF: Organized Crime Drug Enforcement Task Force. The OCDETF is a federal drug enforcement program. It is overseen by the attorney general and the Department of Justice. It mostly deals with disrupting major drug trafficking operations. The OCDETF is a task force that combines the resources of eleven US federal agencies as well as state and local law enforcement.

Odin: Immortal. Norse god of wisdom, healing, death, knowledge, battle, and the gallows, and is the titular king of the Aesir.

Persephone: Immortal. Greek goddess of the Underworld and springtime.

PCB: Preternatural Crimes Bureau. A PCB is usually found only in the police departments of major metropolitan areas in the United States. The PCB in New York City is headed up by a bureau chief. The five detective boroughs within the NYPD all field detectives specializing in preternatural crimes through the PCB. The PCB has jurisdiction throughout the five boroughs and its own detachment of cops that work in homicide, narcotics, major crimes, and CSU. The PCB is one of the least manned departments in the NYPD due to the type of cases it handles.

PIA: Preternatural Intelligence Agency. PIA is a national-level foreign intelligence organization overseen by the Secretary of Defense directly through the USDI. The PIA's intelligence operations extend beyond the zones of combat, and approximately half of its employees serve overseas at hundreds of locations and US Embassies in many countries. The agency specializes in collection and analysis of preternatural-source intelligence, both overt and clandestine, while also handling American military-diplomatic relations abroad. The agency has no law enforcement authority. (Equivalent to CIA)

Quetzalcoatl: Immortal. Aztec god of wind and wisdom. Can take the form of a feathered serpent.

Rajesh: Master vampire. Heads up the Queens Night Court.

Reed, Noah: Fire dragon. Currently hiding in human form as a three-star Army general who oversees the US Department of the Preternatural.

Santa Muerte: Immortal. *Nuestra Señora de la Santa Muerte* (English translation: Our Lady of Holy Death), commonly shortened and referred to as Santa Muerte. A personification of death associated with healing, protection, and safe passage to the afterlife.

SERE: Survival, Evasion, Resistance, and Escape. A military program that provides US military personnel, Department of Defense civilians, private military contractors, and other at-risk agents and personnel with training on how to evade the enemy, survive and resist the enemy if captured, and to escape.

Shields: Ward. Defensive magic used for protection on a large or small scale.

Skuld: Immortal. Goddess of fate and one of the Norns.

Spells: Offensive magic.

SOA: Supernatural Operations Agency. SOA is the domestic intelligence and security service of the United States that focuses on magical and preternatural crimes and terrorism. Employs human, preternatural, and magically affiliated people to field positions for domestic defense. (Equivalent to FBI)

Sorcerer/Sorceress: Second-highest rank of magic users and moderately more common than mages but are outnumbered by witches and wizards.

Soulbond: A binding of two or more souls to tie people together for magical needs. Illegal under the laws of all governments.

Taylor, Marek: Seer. CEO of PreterWorld, a social media platform geared toward the preternatural and supernatural community. His patrons are the Norns.

Tezcatlipoca: Immortal. Aztec god of obsidian, jaguars, war, strife, night sky, and the night winds.

Threshold: Ward. Applied to a hearth and home for protection to keep out negative magic, spirits, and demons.

Tloque Nahuaque: An epithet for Tezcatlipoca, which means "Lord of the Near and the Nigh."

Tremaine: Master vampire. Headed up the Manhattan Night Court. His maker was Lucien.

US Department of the Preternatural: Employs all manner of magically affiliated and preternatural people for military service. Active duty combat mages are seconded to the Army, Navy, Air Force, and Marines and are required to go through BTC and joint training.

Veil: The metaphysical barrier between Earth/mundane plane and other worlds/dimensions/planes, and versions of hell and heaven derived from myths.

Verðandi: Immortal. Goddess of fate and one of the Norns.

Walker, Estelle: God pack werewolf. Alpha of the New York City god pack.

Wards: Defensive magic.

Warlock: Most common rank of magic users. On par with witches.

Werecreatures: Humans who are infected with the werevirus. Can change form into various animalistic shapes. Werecreatures are either infected later on in life or are born with the disease.

Werevirus: An incurable disease that makes those who are infected change into monstrous beasts. Created by an ancient Roman mage, the werevirus was one of the first recorded instances of magically created biological warfare introduced into society. People are born with the werevirus or become infected through intercourse or blood. Two strains exist: a normal strain and a god strain. The god strain has stronger magical properties which can cause the infected to be susceptible to an immortal patron.

Witch: Most common rank of magic users. On par with warlocks.

Zeus: Immortal. Greek god of thunder and titular king of the Greek pantheon.

Zhang, Emma: Werewolf. Alpha of the Tempest pack.

AUTHOR'S NOTES

It takes a village for me to write a book.

Nora Sakavic is the best cheerleader a girl can have. She always believed in this series even when I didn't.

Leslie Copeland continues to be the best beta reader in the world. You see things I never do, and I'm grateful every time. I'm so happy we're friends.

Lily Morton is always there on the other side of the internet as a great alpha reader and even better friend.

Layla Reyne is my fellow suspense-writing twin. Her ability to help kill some darlings was greatly appreciated!

May Archer always volunteers for alpha reading duty, and I'm never disappointed by the help she provides.

Sheena J. Himes is always generous with her time, and her alpha reads for me are incredibly helpful.

Bear is forever and always on the other side of a text, and I'm so grateful to call her a friend.

Last but not least, to my readers. Thank you so much for enjoying the worlds I get to write about so that I can write more. You guys are amazing, and I wouldn't get to do this without you.

I took liberties with police work and federal agencies in this story. I don't work in either field, and I tried to blend both into the world I created as best as possible. Any mistakes belong to me.

I would be thrilled and grateful if you would consider reviewing *All Souls Near & Nigh* on Amazon or Goodreads. I appreciate all honest reviews, positive or negative. Reviews definitely help my books get seen, so thank you!

Cover design by AngstyG.
Professional Beta Reading by Leslie Copeland: lcopelandwrites@ gmail.com
Edited by One Love Editing
Proofing by Lori Parks: lp.nerdproblems@gmail.com

CONNECT WITH HAILEY

Keep up with my book news by signing up for my newsletter and get the free Soulbound prequel short story *Down A Twisted Path* and several free Metahuman Files short stories while you're at it.

Join the reader group on Facebook: Hailey's Hellions

Visit Hailey's website: www.HaileyTurner.com

Like Hailey's author page

OTHER WORKS BY HAILEY TURNER

M/M Science Fiction Military Romance:

Captain Jamie Callahan, son of a wealthy senator and socialite mother, is a survivor.

Staff Sergeant Kyle Brannigan, a Special Forces operative, is a man with secrets.

Alpha Team, the Metahuman Defense Force's top-ranked field team, is where the two collide and their lives will never be the same.

<u>Metahuman Files</u>

In the Wreckage

In the Ruins

In the Shadows

In The Blood

In The Requiem

In The Solace

<u>A Metahuman Files: Classified Novella</u>

Out of the Ashes

New Horizons

Fire In The Heart

M/M Urban Fantasy

<u>Soulbound</u>

A Ferry of Bones & Gold

All Souls Near & Nigh

A Crown of Iron & Silver

A Vigil in the Mourning

On the Wings of War

An Echo in the Sorrow

A Veiled & Hallowed Eve

<u>Soulbound Universe Standalones</u>

Resurrection Reprise

LGBTQ+ Epic steampunk-inspired fantasy:

Welcome to Maricol, where the land will kill you, kinship turns the gears of war, and burning the dead lest they come back to life is the only way to survive.

<u>Infernal War Saga</u>

The Prince's Poisoned Vow

The Emperor's Bone Palace

<u>Infernal War Saga Novella</u>

An Emporium of Hearts

Contemporary gay romance

Short stories previously published in the Heart2Heart Charity Anthologies.

<u>From the Heart: A Short Story Collection</u>

Audible

All of Hailey Turner's books are available in audiobooks. Visit Audible to discover your next favorite listen.

Hailey Turner Audiobooks

Thanks for reading!

www.ingramcontent.com/pod-product-compliance
Lightning Source LLC
Chambersburg PA
CBHW030114310726

48970CB00004B/1280